CW01080588

The Samurai Revival Trilogy (Vol. 3)

BITTER LEGACY

Rheagan Greene

Hamon Publishing

Author's note:

Although broadly accurate geographically, this story is a work of fiction. Any resemblance between people or events and real life is unintended and purely coincidental. Furthermore, use of the Japanese, German and Burmese languages, and historical references, have been simplified to facilitate reading. A glossary and maps, of Japan and Southeast Asia, are included at the back of the book.

ISBN 978-0-9573040-4-8

1st Edition (v. 1057)

Cover concept and design by Hamon Publishing (v.29)

Printed and bound in the UK by TJ International Ltd., Padstow

Hamon Publishing
Suite 55, 28 Old Brompton Road, London, SW7 3SS, UK
www.hamonpublishing.com

Dedication:

To my mother and brother, and in fond memory of my father.
Their support made life's worst bearable and its best
something to be shared with gratitude and pride.

Acknowledgements:

My sincere thanks to all those who have encouraged and helped
me to complete this book. Notably: Cathy, Garry, Kate, Maria
and especially Anna, Jo and my editor, Lynn Curtis.

Also, for sharing their knowledge and generous assistance:
Dr Mark Collins of The Priory, Narcotics Anonymous and
Simon King of Inside Japan Tours Ltd.

BITTER LEGACY

CHAPTER 1

17 May 2035

Calver Cats revival Thwarts Special Forces

The Calver Cats are back, and with appallingly familiar brutality! Barely ten years after international Security Forces assured us that the original gang had been wiped out, several major criminal organisations in the UK and Japan have ceded control to this reincarnation of the Cats. Why just these two countries? Nobody knows. However, what is clear is that with immense wealth being generated from the drugs and sex trades, this new version of the Calver Cats is bent on expansion, and the Special Forces seem powerless to stop it.

The name "Calver" is derived from the Japanese technique of gutting live fish. Many of those who opposed the gang, including several Peacekeepers, have suffered a similar fate. With the Special Forces being outmanoeuvred at every turn, rumours are rife of high-level moles within the peacekeeping authorities, but only yesterday in Tokyo this was denied vehemently by newly appointed Chief Inspector Yamanouchi...

Global Times

Calver Cats Continue Kidnapping

The Calver Cats gang has just claimed responsibility for yet another prominent abduction. Two days ago, here in Tokyo, Toshie Miyazaki, daughter and only child of Japan's internationally respected Minister for Homeland Security, was snatched outside a Peacekeeper training school.

Apparently, she was targeted specifically in revenge for Dr Miyazaki's actions some ten years ago which led to the execution of Hayato Fujiwara at the hands of a UK Peacekeeper.

These kidnappings started six months ago with the New York seizure *of Karen Weissman, daughter of Germany's representative to the United Nations for World Peace. No ransom has ever been requested and nothing was heard of her until yesterday when the Calver Cats released the shocking news that she had disowned her parents and voluntarily entered the sex trade...*

Japan News

CHAPTER 2

Tessa Pennington discarded her newspapers in disgust and settled back in her First Class seat. The Calver Cats situation was clearly continuing to deteriorate. But she still didn't want to be involved with confronting them; not again. Destroying the original gang had been more than enough for her. Yet here she was, about to begin the long overdue fight-back against its latest manifestation which had already threatened a violent end to her life. The strangest thing of all was that she had no idea why the Calver Cats were so intent on ensuring that it was she, and only she, who came after them.

She gazed vacantly through the aircraft window as the lights of London's new Estuary Airport disappeared into the distance, casting her mind back to the pivotal meeting she'd had with Colonel Potter, Head of UK Special Forces.

They had met in his office at the top of the imposing Art Deco-style headquarters building in Vauxhall on the south bank of the Thames. While they talked, the two of them had filled the pauses in their review of the latest Calver Cats atrocities with a gloomy scrutiny of the pleasure boats ferrying tourists along the river below; laughing and clicking away with cameras, they were blissfully unaware of the gravity of the topic being discussed so close at hand.

"...It's definitely a revival of the original Calver Cats," confirmed Potter. "Heaven only knows how or why; it's been ten years. But everything they do bears all the hallmarks of the Calver Cats we've regrettably come to know so well... They've even been leaving calling cards at the scenes of their crimes with the old Calver Cats logo on it."

"Actually, the logo's slightly different," reflected Tessa, glancing at the complex design displaying interlinking ribbons with a tiger's head at the centre. *(Reader: see back cover, lower left corner)*.

"It is similar, but the colours have changed and, although the ribbons are all black again, only two of the Cs are in the Fujiwara clan's vermilion now. What's more, the tiger's head is not black and distinct as it used to be, it's grey. Almost as though they don't have an Amafuji sword working on their behalf yet, but expect one soon. And we both know from whom they can get hold of one of those."

"Yes, but surely you're not the only person in the world with a sword manufactured by the Amafuji family? I know they stopped making weapons ages ago, but there must be others still in circulation."

"I doubt there are that many, but I agree there must be some. So maybe they're after one in particular. If that *is* mine, why on earth would they want it so badly?"

A much longer pause followed.

"I wish we knew what they're really after," continued Tessa. "It's got to be much grander than snatching a sword and perhaps settling some old scores. Don't forget, they targeted me repeatedly."

Potter nodded thoughtfully. Even with the subdued lighting he looked tired and stressed, his bald head glistening with beads of perspiration.

"How many attempts on your life have there been now?"

"Five in the last two months; they'd have got me last time if it hadn't been for my new Porsche."

"Don't remind me, I'm still trying to pacify the Chief of Police concerning that two hundred and eighty m.p.h. chase down the M40... Not to mention the damage their missiles caused! It was a miracle they missed you."

"Yes, it really was. Either they were extremely unlucky or... And then for them all to die like that. What madness drove them to wear suicide vests? Those haven't been used for more than twenty years."

There was another period of silence as they reflected on the brazen brutality of that attack, and how it had been carried out with callous disregard for the lives of the many innocent bystanders who had been unwittingly involved.

"Even so, are you really sure you want to do this?" queried Potter, fingering three wads of paper on the table as though they were covered in something he didn't want to touch. "I have a feeling they're trying to drive you to it."

"I agree, but do I have a choice? Does either of us? Ostensibly we have two new geographically disparate organisations, yet both are operating like the original gang. It's too much of a coincidence, they must be linked. The longer we leave them to fester the stronger they'll grow and the further they'll spread. At the moment, they're dictating the rules of the game. If we want to stop them, we need to find out who the bosses are and what they're really trying to achieve. Something big and nasty is brewing out there. Me walking into their trap may be the only way to find out what it is; and by accepting that Mission, I'll be authorised to deal with it."

Potter sighed in half-hearted assent.

"OK," he declared, failing to disguise his misgivings, "you know the drill. If you sign these papers you have *carte blanche* to do whatever needs to be done to close down the Calver Cats, again; whoever they are and wherever they operate worldwide excluding those few countries which still haven't signed the International Peacekeeper Treaty."

He pushed the papers over to Tessa; she perused them fleetingly. On the last page of each set was Potter's signature together with that of Oberst Müller, her UK and German guardians respectively. She took a deep breath and unscrewed the pen which used to belong to her best friend, Penny. It was her murder that had drawn Tessa into fighting the Calver Cats more than ten years ago. Although Penny was long-since dead, Tessa still used her pen to sign any Peacekeeper Mission she accepted. She signed with her Peacekeeper name, *Nariko*, as required in both English and Japanese, and added the date. She slid two copies back to Potter and kept one…

Tessa had always believed that wiping out the original Calver Cats gang would be enough. After all, it had been necessary for her to kill an awful lot of people to do it, and every single life she'd taken was torture to her. She hated violence, yet it seemed to follow her round like a shadow. There was no denying that the personal price had been high. However, very few people knew the whole truth, the number of fatalities involved, or that there had been three figures in charge of the Calver Cats at that time. She was still trying to accept that two of these had been her own brother and his wife, while the third had turned out to be a Japanese Peacekeeper friend of hers, called Hachiro. It transpired that he was secretly a member of the Fujiwara. This now notorious clan had turned to criminality following its disgrace after fighting against the Emperor during the struggle which had led to the

Meiji Restoration of the late-1860s. Indeed, only a handful of people knew that the origin of the Calver Cats gang could be traced back to the battle of Sekigahara in 1600 and a feud between two ancient Japanese clans, the Matsumoto and the Fujiwara.

However, the historical depth to the enmity did not make it any more palatable to Tessa. The struggle so far had cost the lives of far too many of her closest friends, several of whom had died in her arms. After the bloodshed had ceased ten years before, Tessa was desperate to retire from being a Peacekeeper and concentrate on bringing up Nyunt, her adopted Burmese daughter. But that was not to be.

During the final stages of the last gang's defeat, Nyunt had been kidnapped and forced to witness some dreadful violence. She was a young child at the time, and the memories had traumatised her. Tessa had done everything she could to help the girl recover from this, including several bouts of various therapies. But despite Nyunt's eventually saying she had learned to live with her past, she still wouldn't allow Tessa to relinquish her licence to use the sword which had saved both their lives.

Given all this history, it wasn't surprising that Tessa had been under pressure to consider accepting a new Peacekeeper Mission once the Calver Cats started their comeback. Initially, she had been determined to resist. But then Nyunt started flexing her wings, which generated all sorts of new problems for Tessa, and when these were exacerbated by the high level kidnappings of girls just like her daughter, what else could she do but to accept? Tessa hoped that this time it would be easier. But was that likely? Before, her extraordinary speed, strength and intuitive skill with a sword had helped her win the day. But she was ten years older now; and being a sword-wielding Peacekeeper with a licence to kill was not a career renowned for its longevity. She had already outlasted the odds.

But still Tessa wouldn't have accepted the Mission if it hadn't been for her worrying so much about Nyunt. The girl had originally been brought up in Burma by her father Htet, as her birth mother had been killed while she was very young. Htet was head of UK Special Forces in Burma and had been killed in front of Nyunt and Tessa by the Calver Cats, leaving the child orphaned. Tessa had arrived on the scene too late to save Htet; but before he died, he made her promise to look after his daughter. This she had done, and it was generally accepted she had done it very well.

After a bumpy start, Tessa and Nyunt had enjoyed some very happy years together. Having a child was the one thing in the world Tessa had never expected but always wanted. She couldn't bear children of her own due to an accident of birth, and not even the most advanced medicine of the day could enable someone such as her to conceive. Despite this, she had become a proud mother, albeit one who taught her daughter, and others, how to use a Samurai sword. Generally speaking, Nyunt had developed into a well-balanced, bright young woman although there were certain aspects to her character which Tessa found frustrating – not least that on occasion she could be very headstrong, making decisions quickly, perhaps out of pique, which she seemed reluctant to rescind even if she did subsequently regret them.

At first, Nyunt hadn't been interested in learning to use a Samurai sword, but then she changed her mind and Tessa had patiently tutored her. Although Nyunt didn't possess her mother's remarkable instinctive skill, she was certainly gifted with the weapon. Eventually, Tessa even procured a Kimi Amakuni sword for her.

These were accepted as the best Samurai swords in the world, a reputation earned over several centuries. Manufactured with supreme skill and artistry, not only were they beautiful, they were also imbued with remarkable qualities. When wielded by a competent fighter they were capable of shattering lesser blades, and they would ring when held by their true owner. Kimi Amakuni always regarded the sword she'd made for Tessa as the best she had ever produced. But she had been against making a sword for Nyunt because she was so young and headstrong. She only capitulated once Tessa had assured her that she would keep a watchful eye on the weapon.

On board the plane pensively sipping from her glass of water, Tessa replayed again the events which managed to transform her life so comprehensively from dream to disaster.

There was no denying that Nyunt still had some serious issues to deal with. But she was a young woman now, and determined to assert her independence. This in itself didn't trouble Tessa, who valued her own. So, whether Nyunt was immature or not, Tessa wanted to give her enough space to sort her problems out for herself. When she became interested in boys, Tessa had hoped for a breakthrough. Nyunt's first serious boyfriend had been Seiji in Japan, the eldest of three children brought up by the Hayasaka family. Asao Hayasaka, its head, was the long-time confident of Matsumoto, Tessa's Sensei. In fact, the Hayasaka family had been in service to the Matsumoto clan for many generations but were now more like close friends to them. They lived just outside the grounds of Matsumoto castle.

During Tessa's frequent visits there Nyunt and Seiji had often played together as children, so both Matsumoto and Tessa were delighted when they started dating – and were equally disappointed when the relationship fell apart. The details of the break-up were still clear in Tessa's mind...

The day had started normally enough. Tessa had spent the morning teaching at South Kensington Samurai while during the afternoon Nyunt had practised with Lee, Matsumoto's brother who ran SKS.

"Hello, darling," Tessa greeted her when Nyunt came home. "You look exhausted."

"Hi, Mum. How does he do it? He's ancient yet he still has me running round like a chicken with its head cut off."

"Well, he's had a long time to perfect his technique," replied Tessa with a wry smile.

"You always beat him."

"Yes, but I'm getting old too. I'm not as fast as I used to be."

"Yeah, yeah. You still move faster than the speed of light," retorted Nyunt.

"What time is Seiji picking you up?"

"Six-thirty. Oh, I need to get cleaned up."

Nyunt quickly put her sword away and rushed upstairs to have a shower. When she came back down she looked wonderful, dressed in a skin-tight red and gold Thai silk cocktail frock with a high neck. She had grown into the spitting image of the woman shown with her as a baby in one of the two treasured photographs which hung in her bedroom. They were the only reminders Nyunt had of her true parents. The pictures had been located and extracted by Curtis, a UK Special Forces operative based in Thailand, months after Tessa had escaped from Burma with Nyunt as a young child.

There was no mistaking the similarity she bore to the woman with the upright poise and fine-boned, striking face under long black hair. Also, Nyunt was strong and agile, and moved with captivating grace. But she had her father's eyes, as was demonstrated in the other photograph, which showed Htet standing alone, smiling into the camera. It was the same glint Tessa saw in Nyunt's deep brown eyes and her generous smile which often melted Tessa's resolve when they argued about anything. But it was a reminder too that the little girl Tessa had saved from a terrible future within Burma was now growing up.

"Darling, you look fantastic," acknowledged Tessa. "I'm sure Seiji will be like putty in your hands."

"You think I look all right?" queried Nyunt, doing a quick twirl.

"You look perfect," replied a smiling Tessa as the doorbell rang.

Nyunt opened the door to her boyfriend.

"Oh, wow!" exclaimed Seiji, prompting her to blush.

He gave her a gentle kiss on the cheek and came in, immediately bowing respectfully when he saw Tessa.

"*Konichiwa*, Nariko-san."

"*Konichiwa*," Tessa greeted him warmly.

Seiji, a recently appointed Peacekeeper like Nyunt, had developed into a fine young man. He was slightly less than six foot tall, lithe and phenomenally fit. He had a friendly weather-beaten face topped by black hair gathered into a neat ponytail at the back of his head. His brown eyes sparkled inquisitively and he had a disarming smile.

"My, what a fine pair of young Peacekeepers you are," observed Tessa affably. "But let's not stand on ceremony. I'm going to go to bed at ten, after which the place is yours. Have a good evening…"

However, it was only 9:30 when they returned and clearly all was not well.

"Why do you always have to be so damn stubborn?" demanded Nyunt as they came in.

Tessa looked up at them in surprise.

"It's not me who's being difficult," retorted Seiji, pointedly.

"Hello, Mum."

"Nariko."

"You're back early," noted Tessa tentatively.

"I got bored with him trying to boss me round," replied Nyunt indignantly.

"I only asked you to do me a favour."

"Yes, to ignore my heritage so I would fit in with your preconceived expectations!"

"That's not…"

"OK. Time out, guys," interrupted Tessa. "Sit down and stop practising verbal bokken blows."

In silence they did as ordered, Nyunt selecting the opposite sofa from Tessa and Seiji in the armchair.

"Now will somebody please tell me what the problem is? Guest first, I think, Seiji."

"I've been invited to a dinner at Tokyo University. It's a very important event and everyone who's anyone will be there. I wanted Nyunt to come with me…"

"You wanted!" she shrieked. "You mean I'm not even invited on my own account! How nice is that?"

"Nyunt darling, calm down. I'm sure he didn't mean it that way. Carry on, Seiji."

"No, I didn't. Anyway, it's a formal evening, very formal, so I asked Nyunt to go in a kimono. That's all."

"All right, darling," beckoned Tessa, nodding to her, "your turn."

"I'm Burmese, not Japanese. I want to go in Burmese national dress. What's wrong with that?" she replied, glaring at Tessa.

"Hey, I just happen to be here, don't try and put me on the spot! But technically, you're British; you just happened to have been born in Burma."

"So you want me to go in a nice, safe Caroline Charles evening dress?"

"Darling, you're doing it again," said Tessa, exasperated. "Honestly, you two, this is trivial. Are you really not able to sort it out on your own?" The stony silence which followed, prompted her to continue. "OK. Well, in case you're interested, I think you're both right and both wrong, and resolving issues such as this is what a relationship is all about. It's not the good times which define us, it is how we handle the bad ones. I'm going to bed now, but I really think it should be possible

18

for you to find a mutually acceptable comprise; probably safest if you leave it until tomorrow, though. So, I recommend you sleep on it and meet up again when you've both calmed down…"

They did follow Tessa's advice, but a compromise had not been forthcoming. Both Tessa and Matsumoto had tried hard to convince them that this was not important enough to fall out over, but their advice had only been perceived as ill-informed interference. The rhetoric escalated, positions hardened, and finally the young couple had parted, vowing never to speak to one another again.

In Tessa's eyes the situation was then exacerbated by Nyunt's starting to date a young man called Paul. He had a well-paid job in the City, working at the London headquarters of Beijing New York International Bank. He was tall, intelligent and handsome in an oriental way with straight black hair, dark skin and brown eyes. But apparently he had no knowledge of his true ethnic background as he had been brought up in America as an orphan.

Ostensibly he was everything Tessa should have wanted for Nyunt. However, for some reason she took an instant dislike to him. She wasn't sure why since he certainly didn't behave badly; quite the opposite, in fact. He was always well dressed, extremely courteous and very considerate towards Nyunt. Nevertheless, Tessa decided to use her contacts to have him checked out. She knew it wasn't a particularly pleasant thing for her to do but she was still a Peacekeeper and as such had a right to security and anonymity for herself and her family.

Fortunately, Potter hadn't needed much persuading. But his background checks didn't uncover anything other than what Paul had already told her. So, there was little more Tessa could do. She did share her misgivings with Nyunt, but not forcibly since she felt, and said, that her daughter was old enough to reach her own conclusions. Tessa just hoped the relationship would peter out and that would be the end of it.

But then, out of the blue, Nyunt announced she was going to Burma in an attempt to trace her relatives there. That seriously concerned Tessa. Nyunt's asylum in the United Kingdom had been resented by Burma which, despite some faltering moves towards democracy, continued to be run by a military Junta largely accepted as short-sighted, cruel and corrupt. Nevertheless, despite all that, Tessa would still have gone with her daughter had not Burma been the one country in the world where Nariko was definitely not welcome. Not only had Burma still not signed up to the International Peacekeeper Treaty, but many years earlier Tessa had been forced to assassinate General Soe Gyi there, the then second in command of the military Junta. She had gone to Kalaw in Burma intending only to kidnap or kill Bill Chalmers, a key member of the Calver Cats gang and close associate of her brother, Beauchamp. However, the General had interrupted her and in the struggle that followed she had killed him. The majority opinion was that the action was brave and justified, although as Tessa was a Peacekeeper with guaranteed anonymity, hardly anyone knew who had carried it out. But, technically both killings had been illegal, since Peacekeepers were only permitted to impose capital punishment in countries which had signed up to the Treaty. Furthermore, although Bill Chalmers, prior to escaping from custody in London, had been tried and officially sentenced to death, General Soe Gyi had never been brought before a court of law for his crimes.

Presumably Nyunt had expected Tessa to feel reassured that Paul was going as well, but it only made her more anxious. She tried everything she could to dissuade her daughter, but without success.

At first Nyunt sent frequent emails, saying where she was, what she was doing and whom she had met. But suddenly all communication ceased and the silence lasted for two weeks. Tessa was beside herself with worry and asked Potter if he could get Curtis in Thailand to mount some discreet enquiries. She had met Curtis several times, including the occasion he had flown a helicopter into Burma to rescue her and Nyunt after Htet was killed.

However, a few days after Tessa's request, Nyunt suddenly let herself into the London house. Tessa was overjoyed to see her, although also furious that her daughter had not been in touch. She doubted she would ever be able to forget the exchange that followed...

"Well, you could have let me know you were all right," she had complained, once she'd got over the shock of Nyunt's reappearance.

"How could I? You know what it's like out there – the Junta still makes it difficult to send emails and there's no mobile coverage. Besides, I had to have an emergency appendectomy. It was lucky Paul was with me. He bribed lots of people to get me admitted to the government hospital in Naypyidaw."

Tessa was horrified; she stared at her in disbelief.

"You allowed someone to cut you open in Burma?" she blurted. "Nyunt, you are *my* daughter, do you think they didn't know that?"

"The facility was perfectly clean and super-modern. They looked after me really well."

"You should have gone back to Bangkok! You must have an examination... I'll make you an appointment. In fact, I'll take you myself now."

"I don't want one. There's no need. I'm perfectly all right!"

"Please," Tessa implored her, "just let someone check you over. As a favour to me, if you like? An X-ray and a quick prod. It won't take long. Please darling?"

"No," insisted Nyunt, clearly determined. "Besides, we have more important things to discuss."

"Darling, there's nothing more important to me than your health and well-being. You know that."

"How about the death of my father?"

"What...? Why are you so keen to change the subject?"

"Because we're done as far as the other is concerned. So?"

"Nyunt, please... Your father died at the hill station near Kengtung where you lived for the first few years of your life."

"No, he didn't."

"Of course he did. We were both there. We saw what happened to him," replied Tessa, frustrated and confused.

"*We* were indeed there, but *my father* wasn't. Everyone wanted you to believe Htet was my father, and you fell for it, hook, line and sinker. We can discuss why in a moment, if you like. But General Soe Gyi was my real father and *you* murdered him in Kalaw! Didn't you?"

For a moment Tessa was dumbfounded, it was all utterly wrong.

"But that's nonsense! It can't be true. What makes you think Htet wasn't your father?"

"Paul and I traced some of my relatives in old Pagan and they told me how Htet murdered my mother and kidnapped me."

"Ridiculous... And what relatives? The Special Forces were never able to trace anyone related to you, let alone in Pagan, and you know I tried too."

"You obviously didn't try hard enough."

"Don't be silly. Why wouldn't I be interested in tracing your relatives?"

"Because you wanted to keep me for yourself, since you can't have children of your own."

By now Tessa's initial wonder at all these incredible revelations was turning to anger.

"How can you say such terrible things?"

"Because I believe it's the truth. I'm my own person now and free to do whatever I like. And I'm *not* going to tell you where to find my relatives because you might send your Special Forces friends to have a quiet word with them."

"Nyunt, that's disgusting! I would never do anything to keep the truth from you. I can't believe you said that."

"Well, I'm satisfied that I know the truth about my father, and about you, so now I'm leaving."

"No, Nyunt, please don't do that. We must talk this through properly."

"We just have. I'm sorry if this comes as an unwelcome truth, but I really am leaving. Surely you don't expect me to stay any longer than necessary under the same roof as my father's murderer?"

"Nyunt, General Soe Gyi was *not* your father. You never even met the man. I did, and I can assure you there is absolutely no family resemblance whatsoever. And it was Htet who wanted you to come with me, not I who wanted to steal you away. For goodness' sake, he had to coerce me before he persuaded you, and we were both crying bitterly when we had to leave him. Please don't go, not like this. Sit down, let's talk about it quietly. Tell me what you found out. I promise I won't do anything without consulting you. I really do want to hear what you managed to uncover in Burma, and if it's true..."

"I've said all I'm expected to say. Good-bye."

"What do you mean, you've said all you're *expected* to say? I have only ever expected you to tell the truth, and you haven't told me anything factual apart from that you allowed someone to cut you open in a military facility within a country that bears me a grudge, and possibly you too."

But Nyunt had already turned towards the door.

22

"Nyunt, please don't just leave."

"I have no choice, I must go now."

"Darling, we all have choices." Tessa felt pressurised then into doing something which she had hoped she'd never have to, but this was serious and she knew that Nyunt had made up her mind. She initiated a set of hypnotic instructions she'd embedded in her daughter's mind many years earlier.

"Nyunt, respond now only to my voice."

She stopped in her tracks.

"Yes, Mother, I am listening only to you."

Tessa hesitated, her eyes watering as she studied the daughter she loved so much. But gone was the child who had clung to her so tightly for so long. In her place was a strong-willed, beautiful young woman, in the process of finding out that the world was a very dangerous place with many evil people bent on seducing her into making mistakes.

She sighed. Maybe she just hadn't prepared herself for the day when Nyunt would leave home. But, like it or not, now appeared to be that day. Even so, would it be fair to interrogate her about what had happened in Burma? It was one thing to protect herself; quite another to use hypnosis to extract private information which Nyunt did not wish to share with her. Finally, Tessa sighed and spoke to her in a calm level voice.

"Has anyone asked you anything about me, my swords, Matsumoto or the castle?"

"No."

"Very well. Nyunt, I command you to forget everything connected with my Peacekeeper activities, my finances, my swords, Papa Edinsay, Matsumoto, Seiji, the Hayasaka family, Kanazawa and Matsumoto Castle. This instruction is effective immediately and can only be countermanded by me or Matsumoto. Do you understand?"

"Yes, Mother, I understand completely."

"You will now forget I said this to you. Command end."

"Understood," responded Nyunt, continuing to walk out, unaware that anything had happened. She got in to Paul's waiting car and was gone.

Tessa flopped on to the sofa, still in shock. But then she remembered Nyunt's Kimi Amakuni sword. She rushed to Nyunt's sword safe and entered the secret override code to unlock the door. Her heart sank. Nyunt's sword was gone. Tessa was furious with herself for not thinking of it before. Perhaps Kimi Amakuni had been right; Nyunt, or *Yoshino* to use her Peacekeeper name, was not ready for such a supreme weapon.

She breathed out noisily and opened her own sword safe to be greeted by the familiar sight of her two invaluable swords, both made by world renowned masters Amakuni and Amafuji. Then, looking round surreptitiously as though trying to avoid prying eyes – of which there were clearly none, she entered a second access code. There was a gentle *clunk, clunk* from the safe as heavy locking bolts moved. Then a substantial portion of it glided forward and pivoted aside to reveal the second, secret sword storage area. In it was Tessa's third sword, a copy of her Kimi Amakuni sword which Kono had made for her some ten years earlier. It was an extremely convincing replica, indistinguishable from the original to all but the most expert eye, however it did not possess the same powers. No one apart from Kono and Lee knew she had it, although she suspected Potter realised it existed after she had given it to him to examine in place of her real sword after the original Rippleside conflict.

One piece of good news was that that Nyunt's shoulder harness was still with Kono in east London, being adjusted. The shoulder harness was a unique device which Tessa had invented to allow a full-size Samurai sword to be drawn quickly over the shoulder. It had proved extremely effective and continued to provide her with a competitive advantage. So far no one had been able to replicate it and Tessa remained keen to protect its design. Nyunt's harness held only one sword whereas Tessa's held two.

Kono, who made both harnesses for Tessa, owned a workshop in east London where he maintained swords and supplied all sorts of weapons, spares and accessories that might be required by Peacekeepers. Officially he had retired, but his son now carried on the business under the watchful eye of his father.

Tessa's two best swords had vastly differing pedigrees with history extending back beyond the end of the brutal civil war which culminated in the restoration of Emperor Meiji in 1868. The Amakuni had made weapons for the ultimately victorious Satsuma-Chōshū Alliance, the core fighting element of which had been marshalled by the Matsumoto clan. However, the Amafuji made weapons for the losing side. It was led by the Fujiwara clan which had earned a reputation for callous cruelty throughout all the lands they controlled during the 250-year-long Edo period. In 1600 they had risen to power by changing sides during the battle of Sekigahara, virtually guaranteeing Tokugawa Ieyasu's victory and subsequently profiting by doing the bidding of the successive Shōguns. So they were willing to go to great lengths in order to maintain the status quo.

For this the Fujiwara and Amafuji clans were eventually disgraced. They lost all their wealth, and their landholdings were sequestered; those who survived purges against them had turned to a life of crime. It was the Fujiwara who masterminded and managed the infamous criminal gangs called the Yakusa, many of whom were armed by the Amafuji, whose swords were generally accepted to be almost as good as those forged by the Amakuni. However, for their loyalty to the Emperor, the Matsumoto and Amakuni clans had both been rewarded generously.

Because of the contrasting histories of the Amakuni and Amafuji families, it was unheard of for any one person to have an Amakuni and an Amafuji sword, not least since both were so rare. Tessa's Amafuji sword was one of the last pair ever made by the Amafuji clan, who had now died out. It had been bequeathed to her by Bryani, one of the original Calver Cats gang in London. Tessa had fought with and beaten her, but did not kill her as she wanted her to be interrogated by the UK Special Forces. However, one of the Calver Cats had shot Bryani to stop her talking and it was her dying wish that Tessa should take her sword.

For several days after Nyunt walked out, Tessa was not sure what to do. She hardly dared leave the house in case her daughter returned. But finally she was forced to accept this wasn't going to happen. She couldn't even talk to her either as her *cbc* remained switched off. Nevertheless, Tessa simply could not accept Nyunt's awful accusations. She resolved to go to Burma and unearth the truth for herself. The visit was going to be extremely dangerous, but Nyunt meant everything to her and it was possible that she was in serious trouble and either didn't know or simply couldn't do anything about it.

However, because of her deep-rooted suspicions concerning the whole affair, not to mention the danger she would be in while inside Burma, Tessa took great pains to plan her trip meticulously. Selling her two businesses many years ago had left her exceedingly rich, so her preparations included a wide variety of safety measures many of which were intricate and expensive. These included the changing of the alarm system and locking codes on her properties in London and Orkney, together with additional safeguards on her bank accounts. However, she also had Kono install a new sword safe in her house on Papa Edinsay, even driving up to Orkney herself to inspect his work. When she was finally satisfied that all the precautions she could possibly take were in place, she went to see Potter again.

She had told him of her plan to visit Burma. As she'd expected, he was vehemently opposed to her going. But he knew her well enough to accept that there was little he could do to stop her, so unenthusiastically he agreed to support her. Tessa finished the meeting by giving him a sealed envelope, to be opened only in certain circumstances.

It was three weeks to the day since Nyunt had walked out.

CHAPTER 3

At Tokyo's Narita Airport, Tessa passed quickly through Immigration and headed for the Skyliner Express to Ueno. She was already on edge and decided to take a particularly circuitous route to Kanazawa to make sure she wasn't being followed. After ten hours, she emerged from Kanazawa station and walked to the private limousine parking area. Almost immediately, a spotlessly clean old black saloon glided to a halt in front of her, its shiny chromium trim glinting in the bright station lights. As the passenger door swung open and the boot lid popped up, the uniformed chauffeur sprang out to take her bag.

They exchanged a brief bow of recognition and Tessa eased herself into the back of the car together with her sword case. They were soon passing Kenrouken Park, speeding towards the Higashi Chaya geisha district. At last Tessa felt she could relax; she knew the driver would be keeping a keen eye out for anything untoward. So she barely noticed the kimono clad geisha wearing geta welcoming businessmen to restaurants. She was too busy trying to decide how to explain her plan to Matsumoto. She knew he would be furious with her for even considering it.

The car drove out from between two rows of wooden lattice-fronted geisha houses, across a rickety wooden bridge and into dense forest. Then the engine started labouring as it climbed up a long steep hill on an unmade track. Trees closed in on both sides, compounding the darkness, only occasionally parting to offer a glimpse of the steep drop to the lights of Kanazawa far below. The car wound its way up the narrow track until suddenly it turned sharply right and struggled up an horrendous incline; the rear wheels spun and the car began to slide as it strained to reach the top. Then the slope eased and the car pushed its way through thick overhanging trees and along an overgrown track. Finally, it nudged through some high bushes and stopped in the middle of a flat, almost circular, area covered with black gravel and surrounded by a seemingly impenetrable forest. Tessa smiled. It was good to be back.

In front of the car loomed a large gatehouse framing a pair of substantial wooden doors; a high stone wall disappeared into the darkness in both directions. A single-storey wooden house stood to either side. As the chauffeur unloaded her bag, the door to the house on the right opened and a man came out, silhouetted against the light from within.

"*Konichiwa*, Hayasaka-san," said Tessa, smiling and bowing. "It is good to see you again."

"*Konichiwa*, Nariko-san. It has been far too long," rebuked Hayasaka wistfully as he bowed deeply in return. "But we are delighted you have returned at last. And I know Matsumoto can hardly wait, though don't tell him I said so."

Tessa blushed, but hoped Hayasaka hadn't noticed in the dim light. She doubted whether Matsumoto could possibly be more enthusiastic than she was.

"Well, that's nice," she replied playfully. "May I change here and leave a bag?"

"By all means. There is some green tea prepared too; perhaps we could talk before you leave? Seiji is not here."

"That would be good," Tessa agreed. "However, I don't want to be too long, I think it's going to rain."

Hayasaka nodded and beckoned her into his house as the limousine turned and left.

Tessa quickly freshened up and changed into a two-piece burgundy training tunic and trousers. Clutching her sword case, she joined Hayasaka and his wife Kaori in the lounge. They sat round the low table and drank their tea in contemplative silence...

"Our children seem to be wandering aimlessly," bemoaned Hayasaka, clearly frustrated. "What can we do to help them find each other again?"

"I regret to say, I have absolutely no idea," replied Tessa, equally exasperated. "I'm afraid I still don't understand why they're squabbling."

"It is only the impetuosity of youth," countered Kaori, generously, "it will pass with time."

"I suspect you're right," affirmed Tessa, "but I'm not too sure how much time *we* have, never mind them. The situation has become a lot more complicated..."

She explained that Nyunt had started dating Paul. How they had gone to Burma together and that Nyunt had returned only to accuse Tessa of murdering her father, before walking out with her Amakuni sword. Hayasaka and his wife were visibly shocked.

"That's dreadful," commiserated Kaori. "I can't believe Nyunt would say such things. It sounds so out of character."

"I agree. I don't know what's got into her. That's why I'm going to Burma."

"You... to Burma?" exclaimed Hayasaka, raising his voice in surprise. "You mustn't, it's far too dangerous. Supposing it's a trap?"

"It probably is. But what choice do I have? I haven't even had the courage to tell Kimi-san that I have been party to the loss of Nyunt's sword."

Silence engulfed the trio...

"I'd better be off," sighed Tessa. "Thank you for the tea. I'm sorry not to bring more positive news."

"That is not your fault," commiserated Hayasaka. "You shouldn't hold yourself responsible for any of it. We're not going to be able to sort it out to-day, but somehow we must try and get Seiji and Nyunt back together again."

"Indeed. But you know as well as I, we can clear the path but we cannot force them to follow it if their destiny lies elsewhere. We must be patient, and never lose hope." Tessa smiled, stood up and bowed. "I will be back in a day or two."

"Seiji should have returned by then," replied Hayasaka. "Perhaps you could have a word with him?"

"Of course, although I'm not too sure what to say..."

Finally Tessa was able to make out the massive lichen-covered rocks forming Matsumoto castle's impressively steep rampart. Smoothed on the outside to form a dizzyingly sheer slope, its grandeur was unmistakable even in the misty darkness. To announce her arrival, she thundered across the remaining planks of the drawbridge over the inner moat, reminding herself of how much she disapproved of the castle's poor state of repair. She jogged through the open main gates which, much to her irritation, had long since jammed open.

At the top, she crossed the honmaru bounded by its white-washed stone wall capped with a small tiled roof, passing under the enormous torii and down through the avenue of mature trees which had been trained to grow inwards to provide shade from the summer sun. At the end, where by all architectural precedent there should have been an enormous castle donjon, stood a traditional wooden Samurai house. Seeing it welcoming her, she couldn't stop herself from smiling with joy. At last she was home again.

The house had been beautifully built, with perfectly proportioned, multiple curved pitched roofs of grey glazed tiles. It was in relatively good condition, despite being two hundred and fifty years old. The fenced-off inner-courtyard beckoned the visitor on with a tantalising glimpse of the decoration within, while exuding an aura of dignity, sophistication and confidence.

Tessa paused at the foot of the five stone steps leading up to the covered gateway. Once more, she admired the intricate carving on the doors. She loved this place, which she was sure was one of the finest, if not the finest, traditionally built Samurai house in Japan.

The courtyard was crossed by a path of beautifully laid cream-coloured rectangular flagstones with two rows of smaller grey stones bordering them. It passed between six monolithic lanterns and several covered racks containing vicious throwing knives and shuriken. Matsumoto, after all, was a teacher of every sort of combat; it was how he and Tessa had first met.

A large burgundy-coloured banner was hanging across the front of the house. It had been gathered up in the middle to form an arch over the entrance, where wooden latticework doors had been slid aside to reveal the substantial audience hall within. Despite being slightly faded, the large white logos to either side of the doors were still clear, displaying the Matsumoto clan's coat of arms. They had owned this land and built the rampart more than four centuries before. The complex design was comprised of three Samurai swords facing upwards with their blades crossed near the centre, and a chrysanthemum flower to either side.

Only the Matsumoto and the Amakuni clans were permitted to incorporate the Imperial chrysanthemum within their family crest.

After the brutal civil war in Japan ended in 1868, the Emperor vowed that none of his successors would never be allowed to forget the debt of gratitude owed to these two clans. He not only showered the clans with wealth and landholdings, much of which had been confiscated from the Fujiwara, he also made them the sole members of the Chrysanthemum League, a gathering of elite fighters sworn to uphold the law and support the Imperial family. Individuals within the League were selected at the discretion of the Emperor alone, and bore on their wrist the tattoo of an imperial chrysanthemum. The only others so marked were the Chrysanthemum Guard, a select force responsible for the Emperor's personal security.

With her heart beating more quickly, Tessa was barely able to contain her excitement. She mounted the three shallow wooden stairs leading up to the verandah, flicked off her sandals and went in to the large room where a healthy fire crackled and flamed on the large stone hearth.

"Are you sure you're not getting slower in your old age?" Matsumoto greeted her from the kitchen.

"Positive," retorted Tessa, laughing. "Have you checked that antiquated stopwatch of yours recently?" She padded in to the kitchen where he was preparing a veritable sashimi feast. Nodding appreciatively, she draped her arms round his shoulders and kissed him on the nape of the neck. "I'll just go and change."

"Dinner will be ready in ten minutes."

"Oh, good," she said, moving her hands so she could massage his shoulder muscles, just as she knew he loved.

He smiled, put down his knife, cleaned his hands and turned to face her.

"I've missed you."

"And I've missed you too," she whispered, kissing him gently on the lips. "Back shortly, dinner looks lovely."

Matsumoto nodded.

"So do you," he added, as she walked away. She turned back and grinned.

They were soon sitting comfortably by the low lacquer table in the ceremonial lounge to the left of the main audience hall, dressed in exquisite silk hand-decorated yukata. The atmosphere was warm, familiar and relaxed; they talked long into the night, eating sashimi and drinking sake and green tea. It was well past midnight when they retired to the bedroom, curling up comfortably together on the large mattress.

When they woke, they slipped with contented ease into their established routine, starting the day with an impressively strenuous workout. They took pride in keeping in peak condition. After they had showered, they sat down to breakfast.

"So, Nariko-san, it seems we've spoken about everything except why you've come here in such a hurry?"

"True," replied Tessa, knowing she would not be able to put off her confession much longer. "What time will General Gyobu arrive?"

"Ten. Which also prompts me to ask why it is so important for him to be here?"

"We have serious business to discuss and I didn't want you to have to explain this." She turned her wrist towards him. Where there had once been a beautifully crafted chrysanthemum tattoo there was now nothing except a red patch of healing skin.

Matsumoto's eyes widened and his mouth fell open in surprise; he stared at her, speechless.

"Nariko-san, what possessed you to do that?" he blurted out. "It is a grave offense to deface a personal gift from the Emperor."

"I know," groaned Tessa. "But I felt I had no choice. I was worried that if I discussed things first I would be dissuaded from removing it, which might be even more dangerous. The risk of compromising the honour of the Chrysanthemum is too great..."

She spent more than half an hour recounting what had happened since Nyunt had started dating Paul, how she'd returned unannounced from Burma and had then walked out with her Amakuni sword.

As Matsumoto listened, his expression became transformed from one of dismay to extreme uneasiness. After Tessa finished speaking, he was silent for some time. She waited patiently, pouring them both some more green tea.

"Did you make her forget everything before she left?"

"Yes, and no one had questioned her about us. But I didn't ask her any more than that. I didn't feel it was right to interrogate her while she was under hypnosis."

"No, I agree, that would have been an intrusion; reasonable perhaps from our standpoint but not from hers... Hmm. Well, I understand your concern; but I'm still not convinced it merits such drastic action. The General will not be pleased."

"I'm sure that's an understatement, and I didn't want any of that anger to reflect on you."

With love in his eyes, Matsumoto looked at her reproachfully.

"Since when has anything we have done as individuals not been a part of what we do together? Anyway, Nariko-san, it would seem this meeting is now more apposite than either of us anticipated. Gyobu is under pressure to persuade me to accept a similar Mission against the Calver Cats."

Now it was Tessa's turn to be shocked.

"Why?"

"Well, perhaps he knows more than we do and feels that both of us might be needed to fix this."

"He might be right, but please, don't accept a Mission. At the moment I am fairly sure that only I am in their sights. The last thing I want is to be worrying about you too. They could use us against each other."

"They might do that anyway."

"Yes, but only *might*. I cannot believe they know everything about *us*, especially... Anyway, if I need help, I must know that you will be able to come to me."

"I will always come to help you, Nariko-san, you know that."

"Yes, I do. It's what I always used to say to Nyunt too."

"And I to Seiji. And despite everything those two headstrong and depressingly slowly maturing adolescents have done, we still mean it, don't we? Isn't that why we're really about to embark on this madness?"

"I suppose so," sighed Tessa, momentarily lost in sad reminiscences. "But if anything happens to me, I need to know you will take care of Nyunt."

"Isn't it about time they learned to look out for themselves – not least to admit when they have made a foolish mistake, and to apologise for it? Nariko-san, we are still in excellent fighting condition, but we are not as young as we used to be. Life has moved on. My first responsibility now is to you."

"Then please, please, don't accept this Mission from Gyobu. I promise I will contact you immediately if I need help. I confess I am already nervous for myself – I could not bear being anxious for you too. And we both know only too well what it means when a Samurai goes in to battle scared of the fight."

Matsumoto smiled, took her hand and fondled it while shaking his head slowly from side to side.

"Nariko-san, whoever is masterminding this has planned it meticulously. Just as they intended, we walk in darkness. I am sure you are right to be concerned and we do have to catch up. But we are pursuing a risky strategy by playing an ace so early. Let's listen to what the General has to say."

Just then, the sound of a helicopter approaching broke the peaceful scene. Ten minutes later, a strong, stocky figure strode towards the house; he looked authoritative, but also friendly.

General Gyobu was not tall at just over five feet, but anyone who underestimated his fighting skills because of that would swiftly pay a high price; he was a formidable swordsman. He was strong and athletic, with a suntanned complexion and black hair greased flat and tied at the back. Only the glint of an occasional white hair betrayed his age. He was dressed completely in black, with a gold chrysanthemum embroidered over his left breast.

With comfortable familiarity, he came up the steps and kicked off his shoes on the verandah. Tessa and Matsumoto stood and they all bowed deeply to each other. The General removed the fine Amakuni sword he was wearing.

"*Konichiwa*, Matsumoto-san, Nariko-san," he greeted them. "It is a pleasure as always to meet you both, but to what do I owe the pleasure of this pressing invitation?"

"It is a long and troubling story, Gyobu-san," replied Tessa, gesturing him to join them by the table. "Let me make some fresh tea, and then we can talk…"

Eventually, with fine porcelain cups of green tea before them; they all bowed and drank the first cup in three gulps. Tessa smiled at the General.

"Gyobu-san, you look tired. I am sorry that I am about to add to

34

your already heavy burden."

He laughed at this subtle prompting.

"I take it, Nariko-san, you would like the Chief of the Chrysanthemum Guard to begin our exchange? So be it.

"You are right, I am troubled, more so than I have been for a long time. Foremost in my mind is the kidnapping of Minister Miyazaki's daughter, Toshie. I believe her abduction is only the tip of the iceberg concerning what the Calver Cats are really plotting. But assuming this kidnapping is only the precursor, I still do not know to what.

"Anyway, since the Minister has been extremely supportive of the Emperor, and given the almost complete lack of progress being made by the Special Forces, I was asked to use the Chrysanthemum Guard's resources to investigate this awful situation. Regrettably, these days, we are only a small force, if hopefully the best, but our assets are spread thinly and the task is complicated by having to work surreptitiously."

He paused as Tessa poured him some more tea, graciously declining her offer of a plate of delicate red bean paste sweets.

"So you're acting independently from Japan's Special Forces?" she queried.

"Effectively, yes – and also our Police."

"Because the Chrysanthemum Guard and Chrysanthemum League clans are responsible for the Emperor's safety?" interjected Matsumoto.

"Precisely," continued Gyobu. "That has enabled our law-keeping forces to develop rather differently from in the UK. Whereas your Police and Special Forces operate at arm's-length, here in Japan the two organisations are headed by one Chief Inspector, facilitating a much closer working relationship. We prefer this, and certainly don't have any evidence to suggest the structure is counter-productive. However, even their collective efforts to establish the background to Toshie's abduction and her current whereabouts have been disappointing.

"So, the Chrysanthemum Guard has been pursuing its own *unofficial* investigation?" pressed Tessa.

"Yes. But the Chrysanthemum Guard, never mind the League, remains a clandestine organisation which few even know exists. So, although we have access to everything that the Police and Special Forces know, we are prevented from openly acknowledging that or sharing any new information we uncover. But even our efforts have only advanced the investigation slightly. We believe Toshie is probably being held somewhere in Southeast Asia. Burma is an obvious candidate. Following the collapse of their moves towards democracy, it remains a difficult country to penetrate and we know there are well-established links with the Calver Cats.

"I am not alone in being very worried for the poor girl's safety. We have heard nothing since she was snatched, not even a ransom demand."

"Is she a Peacekeeper?" asked Tessa.

"No. But she was a good student and had already been awarded a Restricted Carrying Licence. I met her several times; she was bright, focussed and determined." He looked at Tessa expectantly. "Now, I think I've said enough, Nariko-san."

Tessa smiled and took a deep breath.

"Gyobu-san, I presume you know that I have accepted a new Mission to stop the Calver Cats?" He nodded and glanced at Matsumoto, who smiled and shook his head from side to side. "Well, you were probably wondering what it was that provoked me into doing so…" Again, she described all that had happened with Nyunt.

"I am sorry to hear that your daughter may somehow have become entangled in this," commented the General, soberly.

"So am I, but your mentioning Burma has confirmed my suspicions that there is information to be found there. It is abundantly clear to me that Nyunt returned from her visit there a changed person. But why would anyone in that sad country go to the trouble of convincing my daughter that I killed her father? It's a very convoluted way to ensnare me. Furthermore, the Burmese Junta is too decrepit to come up with a plan of this complexity on its own and they lack the resources to implement it internationally. Furthermore, if I were to be captured, what would they do with a Peacekeeper? It would be major international embarrassment, irrespective of what they think of me as an individual and what I once did. China is already annoyed with them for still refusing to sign the Peacekeeper Treaty.

"No, whoever is behind all this, knew that using Nyunt would force me to act, and the only obvious course of action is for me to go to Burma myself and try to verify what, if anything, she discovered.

"Personally, I think Burma is simply a convenient location to hide the gestation of something far-reaching. I don't doubt the Calver Cats are involved, if not wholly responsible, but I can't understand why even they would go to such lengths to trap me. But it all fits. The attempts on my life in London, which were occurring with alarming regularity and peculiarly fine-tuned ineptitude, stopped immediately I accepted the new Mission. So, perhaps just as Nyunt is a lure for me, I am to be the lure for something even bigger. We will probably not be able to find out until I have been to Burma."

"That all makes perfect sense, Nariko-san," cautioned Matsumoto, looking extremely uncomfortable. "But it implies that while it will be easy for you to get into Burma, because that is precisely what they want, it will be considerably more difficult to get out. They are likely to do everything in their power to stop you."

With the atmosphere becoming palpably tense, they all took the opportunity to drink more tea. Gyobu looked particularly thoughtful.

"I agree with you both," he declared. "However, I cannot think of any other way by which we are likely to break the impasse. Time is running out for both the Weissman and Miyazaki girls. The recent spate of provocative newspaper articles is based on Calver Cats' communiqués and presumably has been calculated to deepen the Miyazakis' anguish... As if they could ever stop grieving over such a cruel loss. And now they have to contend with the possibility that Toshie, like the Weissman girl... It's stomach-churning stuff. Her death would almost have been preferable. We must find them both soon."

"So be it," continued Tessa. "I will go there as they intend and attempt to do two things: try to find proof that Htet was indeed Nyunt's father to remove this irrational doubt of hers, and see what it is the Calver Cats are planning. You know Curtis, Head of UK Special Forces in Southeast Asia?" Gyobu nodded. "He has organised in-country support for me, but naturally, I won't be able to take any swords. I suspect I'll be walking into a trap, but once it is sprung, I should at least be able to learn what is really going on and who is behind it all."

"Assuming you are able to escape and tell us," interrupted Matsumoto, deeply unhappy with the prospect.

Gyobu breathed in noisily.

"Nariko-san, I share Matsumoto's concerns. I too consider this to be a perilous course of action. However, can any of us think of a better plan...? What can I do to help?"

Tessa smiled.

"Well, if Potter contacts you requesting assistance, please supply it."

General Gyobu shrugged.

"I would try to do that anyway."

"Thank you. There is one other thing which I need to tell you, and which you may be able to help me with. Again, I have a suspicion it could be relevant, though I have no idea why.

"In London, I usually have my chrysanthemum tattoo covered by my watch. But once, I can't remember why, it was hidden only by the long sleeve of the blouse I was wearing. Although I am fairly sure it wasn't visible, Paul not only said he'd noticed it, but insisted on taking a closer look, ostensibly interested in the artistry. Of course, I didn't tell him what it meant, but..."

"That is strange. You think he might be involved?" quizzed the General.

"I'm probably too biased to express a balanced opinion," professed Tessa. "However, I wouldn't be surprised. But I have no proof whatsoever. Potter checked his background and didn't come up with anything."

"Hmm. So what do you propose to do?" asked the General.

"Well, actually, I've already done it. You see, I want to be prepared for all eventualities. So, I'm really sorry, Gyobu-san, but I felt I had no choice other than..." Tessa bared her wrist. General Gyobu's eyes widened in astonishment, but the only sound he made was a deep grunt of disapproval. Then he sighed.

"Nariko-san, I am sure you already know that discarding a personal gift from the Emperor could be interpreted as an insult. It is only he who can decide who bears the sign of the chrysanthemum, and, once marked, it is only on his authority that the mark may be removed. So far as I know, the only way he has ever done that has been rather permanent. According to the old laws... these are the laws made during the Edo period which still apply to the chrysanthemum forces, I should throw you into jail to await his pleasure."

"My most sincere apologies, Gyobu-san," intoned Tessa, bowing submissively. "But I am sure you understand that I intended no slight."

"Obviously, quite the opposite," interjected Matsumoto quickly. "After all, how could the Emperor, even if he in fact believed it prudent to have the mark removed, ever be seen to recommend such an action? It would be an admission of weakness. Clearly, by taking the initiative to disguise herself, Nariko has done nothing other than protect the Emperor's honour, and that of the Chrysanthemum."

Gyobu roared with laughter.

"Matsumoto-san, I wondered how long it would be before you sprang to Nariko's aid. But I know you both well enough not to be inclined to order the amputation of her wrist just yet." He looked sideways at Tessa with a wry smile. "After all, the last time that was done was at least a century ago."

"Oh, good, that's a relief," admitted Tessa.

"It should be, his head followed shortly afterwards," added Gyobu playfully. "I seem to remember it was an Amakuni. He used one of his own family's swords to settle a public brawl over a drinking bill. A most embarrassing affair."

"I can imagine," observed Tessa. "And I really am very sorry for my action. However, I remain convinced it is wise to take every precaution possible. Perhaps the mark's removal could be regarded as a pragmatic temporary measure, facilitating a dangerous plan, and minimising the risk to others if it goes awry?"

"Quite so," agreed the General. "Why don't you let me worry about appeasing the Emperor's disquiet, for now? I am obliged to report what you have done, but I am sure he will understand the rationale. Let us just hope that your plan enables you to gain information concerning the fate of Toshie Miyazaki... But then there is the matter of Yoshino's sword. Kimi-san will not be pleased to learn it is lost."

"I know. But technically, it isn't lost; Nyunt still has it. However, while I suspect that the loss of full control over the weapon irritates us all, and seriously embarrasses me, it is not the fundamental motivation for all this. Potter assures me Nyunt is continuing to use the sword to fulfil her Peacekeeper duties, although none of these has been against the Calver Cats. No, if she was simply being used in order to gain access to her Amakuni blade, that objective has been achieved by now and we would know to what end. There must be more to it.

My deepest concern is that Nyunt's ability for rational thought has somehow been hijacked. Why else would we ostensibly have her back amongst us? That may well become clear to me in Burma too."

"But supposing you are forced to fight your own daughter in order to recover the weapon?" probed the General.

Tessa paused and took a deep breath.

"I have considered that possibility," she replied, broken-hearted but determined. "If it comes to that, then so be it. I promised to keep a watchful eye on the weapon. It is now my responsibility to do whatever needs to be done in order to ensure either that it is not going to be used inappropriately or else to recover it."

"Very well," continued Gyobu, unconvinced. "However, I think I will suggest to Kimi-san that she should double the guard on her valley – just in case. Perhaps you should do the same, Matsumoto-san?"

"Hmm. I still wonder at the significance of the subtle alterations these new Calver Cats have made to their logo," mused Matsumoto. "That must mean something."

Gyobu nodded.

"I find Nariko's suggestion that they want her Amafuji sword quite appealing. Though why it has to be hers in particular, defeats me. Admittedly, Amafuji swords are far from plentiful, but anyone with enough money and power shouldn't have too much difficulty getting hold of one. So, when will you leave?"

"Tomorrow morning," replied Tessa. "I will spend a day in Bangkok and then fly to Rangoon."

"So soon?" exclaimed Matsumoto, surprised. "Couldn't you at least stay a few days longer?"

"I'd better not," she replied, desperately trying not to become emotional.

"All right then," said the General, ignoring the awkwardness between Tessa and Matsumoto. "I understand the situation and wish you well, Nariko-san.

"Hopefully, in Burma, you will find answers to our questions, and maybe even Toshie Miyazaki too…"

After the General had left, Matsumoto turned to Tessa.

"So, I suppose you want me to help you forget?"

She nodded, her eyes watering slightly under his reproachful gaze.

"Yes," she replied, nodding, "and to remember a few things differently. If something goes wrong, I mustn't be able to divulge anything important. Here is a list of what I think should be done. But perhaps we could decide together if there is something else which needs to be added." She studied his forlorn expression and linked her arm though his. "But let's go for a walk first…"

That evening they spent several hours planning Tessa's next moves and, at Matsumoto's suggestion, she contacted Curtis to tell him she now wanted to travel to Burma the same day she arrived in Bangkok. Then they ate a light dinner.

"Shall I help you prepare it?" asked Tessa tentatively. She knew it was time for her to eat some of the colourful, foul-tasting mixture of fish which would induce a trance-like state, making her susceptible to hypnotic suggestions; just as she, so many years ago, had done to Nyunt.

"No, it's all right, I will do it," he replied. "You stay here and enjoy the view. I think three double doses would be advisable, two tonight and one tomorrow morning."

Tessa nodded.

"Yes, we need to bury it all very deeply and cover it convincingly. But may I suggest you leave *us* until the final dose?"

Matsumoto replied with a nod and a melancholy smile.

A little while later, he returned carrying a small white porcelain plate with pieces of several different fishes arranged on it coiled into delicate swirls so that both sides were visible. The scaly skins were all brightly coloured, indicative of their poisonous nature. One was green with orange dots, another blue with yellow stripes, yet another black with patches of white. In the middle lay some gooey dark red fish organs and rolls of Fugu, all with dark green gelatinous seaweed liberally dribbled over. To Tessa, it always looked dreadful, smelled disgusting and tasted even worse; but she also understood the incredible power of this unique combination.

"We will prepare the way tonight, but complete the journey tomorrow at breakfast."

Tessa nodded, picked up her chopsticks and quickly ate everything on the plate. Then she sat back and tried to relax as a single tear rolled despondently down her cheek...

As the sun rose, Tessa and Matsumoto were already training hard together. Later, they convened in the audience hall to eat a substantial breakfast. Suddenly, Tessa glanced at her watch.

"Goodness," she remarked, "is that the time? I'd better be going."

Matsumoto nodded, stretched out his arm and opened his hand. As if in a daze, Tessa took the small piece of rice paper he offered and put it carefully in her purse. Reading it would be the final trigger for the hypnotic commands he had embedded, but already a thick fog had started to pervade her memories. They stood up.

"Seiji will travel with you to Narita," said Matsumoto. "Feel free to come back whenever you want, Nariko."

"Thank you, that's most kind," she replied. "I'd love to."

They bowed to each other and she turned and left, pausing only to pick up her double sword case. He watched broken-hearted, wishing she wouldn't leave, not again, not ever. The moment her back was turned, he could no longer hold back the tears that were forcing their way out. Unseen by any other, they trickled down his cheeks. He wasn't sure whether he should have allowed Tessa's dark premonitions to colour his outlook, but they had, and he was desperately fearful for her safety. She had come to mean everything to him, and he knew only too well that there were many in Burma, and elsewhere, who would delight in watching her die a slow and painful death. No matter how hard he tried, he could not contain the fear in his heart that he might never again see her alive.

Seiji was waiting for her at the castle gate; it had been several months since she had last met him. Tessa smiled, not only because she was always pleased to see him, but also because he was growing up to look so much like a younger version of his birth father, Matsumoto. It always amazed Tessa that, given such a strong family resemblance, people had not recognised Seiji's lineage; presumably that was due to Matsumoto's not being seen much in public. Indeed, not many knew that, a long time ago, he had been married. However, after only a year his wife had died giving birth to Seiji. So, for his son's own safety, Matsumoto had decided to keep his heredity a secret, which was why Seiji had been brought up by the Hayasaka as one of their own. This was common practice in Japan to help safeguard an important family's future generations.

Seiji bowed deeply as Tessa approached, and gestured to the waiting limousine. Their journey passed quickly and it took only three hours for them to reach Narita Airport. Tessa went to the check-in desk while continuing the conversation he had eventually started.

"…Seiji-san, I accept what you are saying is not unreasonable," she acknowledged tactfully. "I too feel it was wrong of Nyunt to be so inflexible. But we both know that you were being equally uncompromising, and two wrongs do not make a right. Now it seems that both of you are so entrenched in your respective positions, pride is preventing either of you from backing down, even for the sake of the other. You're staying apart, and are both unhappy. I'm sorry to be so frank, but I've already said all this to Nyunt," she added, smiling at his dejected expression and handing her ticket to the check-in clerk. "It seems to me that the real problem is that you're both too pig-headed to apologise."

Seiji grinned at her sheepishly as the clerk returned Tessa's ticket for her flight to Bangkok.

"Look," she asserted, "if you don't believe Nyunt is worth fighting for then so be it; find someone else. But even if she didn't realise it herself, perhaps Nyunt simply wanted to test whether you would fight for her. To see you bare your heart as women bare theirs and to see you prove she is important enough to make you give in to her when she needs to feel vindicated. If I am right, how do you think you fared in her test? Whether such a test is reasonable is another matter, but once the gauntlet has been thrown down, it stays there until someone picks it up. If, with hindsight, you feel you got it wrong, irrespective of her position, don't be shy of admitting it… and definitely don't give up. A mistake is only an opportunity to put something right later."

"But she has found someone else," moaned Seiji.

"Of course she has. How long did you expect her to wait for you? However, situations are rarely so far gone that they cannot ever be corrected. Think about it, do what your heart tells you to do… And now I have a plane to catch. Thank you for coming with me, it was good to talk. Take care, Seiji-san. I'm sure you'll do what's right."

"Thank you, Nariko-san," he replied, bowing deeply. "I respect your advice as always, and promise I will give it careful consideration."

"Seiji-san, just one last word from a person who took far too long to learn this lesson for herself; it really *is* sometimes far wiser to think with your heart than your head. You just need to rise to the challenge of divining what it is your heart really wants."

"*Sayonara*, Nariko-san," he said, smiling, backing away and bowing again.

Once on the plane, Tessa stowed her small carry-on bag and sword case, and settled in to her seat. Then, without thinking, she retrieved the rice paper note Matsumoto had given her and read it quietly to herself. It was as though he were there talking to her. Every word reverberated in her mind.

I command you to tread carefully and wisely, Nariko-san. May you find what you seek and return safely to remember all that you have forgotten. Your memory's darkness is now complete and will remain so until I illuminate it for you. Command end.

She ate the note and, not knowing quite why, smiled sadly to herself. She had already forgotten much of what she'd strived throughout her life to achieve. Locations, contacts, bank account numbers, passwords, email addresses, even relationships; they were all pushed deep down into her subconscious and comprehensively hidden.

"Good afternoon, Peacekeeper Nariko," the cabin steward greeted her. "I hope your trip to Japan was successful?"

"Er, yes, I think so," replied Tessa, taken by surprise and not sure how to answer, given she couldn't remember why she'd been there.

"Excellent. Then here is the lunch menu. I will be back in a few minutes to take your order."

CHAPTER 4

Outside Bangkok's Suvarnabhumi Airport Tessa found a blue-grey Range Rover waiting for her, standard UK Special Forces issue.

"Good afternoon, Nariko," greeted Curtis, putting her carry-on bag in the boot. He knew Tessa wouldn't allow herself to be parted from her sword case.

"I'm afraid the Oriental is full so I've booked you in to the Bangkok Orchid View. It only opened recently and is apparently very good."

Tessa nodded; she knew he was only announcing such information for the benefit of those who were presumably listening. She got in to the back seat, still holding her sword case; there was a large bundle on the floor covered with a black blanket matching the car's upholstery. When they were on the toll road heading into the city, Curtis checked his rear-view mirror and spoke into his radio.

"Delta to alpha and beta, are we being tailed?"

"Alpha here, sir, yes," came the quick response. "A very professional job, three plus vehicles."

"OK. You both know what to do. Delta out.

"Nariko," he continued, "don't make it too obvious, but say hello to your new self. She's hiding under that blanket."

"*Sawadee ka*," said Tessa, continuing to look ahead. "I do hope it's not too uncomfortable down there."

"Hi. Actually I'm British, but thanks anyway," replied a confident-sounding young woman. "Here's a replacement watch, some sunglasses and your rucksack…"

"I packed it myself," interjected Curtis. "It contains everything you wanted, including the new ticket for this afternoon instead of tomorrow, and a few extras you'll need in-country. There's a note about them, edible paper as usual. A decoy vehicle will be meeting us in town. Once I'm sure they've taken the bait, I'll drop you off near the market on Sukhumvit Road. Then you're on your own. Your new self will sit up and check in to the hotel in place of you."

Tessa nodded.

"Very comprehensive, as usual, Curtis. Thank you."

"You're welcome. But just for the record, I still don't think this is a good idea."

"I haven't found anyone who does," admitted Tessa, thinking that she could number herself amongst those ranks. "But nobody's come up with anything better, so it's what I've got to do. Keep your eyes and ears open, I've no idea when or where I'll eventually surface."

"We'll be on the look-out twenty-four seven. If you're lucky you might meet Potter when you come out. He'll be here in a few days for our annual review."

Tessa nodded.

"Well, let's hope I'm able to give you both some good news."

When they reached the outskirts of Bangkok, Curtis turned off the highway into the back streets. After weaving through them for some time, a Range Rover just like the one he was driving pulled out from a private garage to their right. Curtis quickly drove in. The door had just closed when several mopeds raced by. Once it was quiet again, Curtis opened the door and reversed out, going straight to a large bustling market where he stopped by a crowd of jostling passers-by.

"Good luck," he rasped.

"Thanks again. I'll be in touch," replied Tessa. "By the way, don't try to open the sword case, Potter had it booby trapped."

She grabbed her rucksack and disappeared into the throng.

Not long afterwards, satisfied she wasn't being followed, she approached a scruffy hotel not yet equipped with security cameras. It had served the same purpose for her many years before when she was going after Bill Chalmers. Surprisingly, it didn't seem to have changed much, it was just a little more rundown than last time – a not inconsiderable achievement given how dilapidated it had been then. So, like replaying an old cracked record, she booked in for one night using her German, as though having recently arrived from Frankfurt and simply wanting to sleep. She gave an assumed name and showed a false passport that Curtis had supplied, paid in advance and went upstairs.

In her room, she drew the curtains and carefully tipped the contents of her rucksack out on to the bed to survey what she'd got; essentially three false passports, a waterproof mobile phone, several bottles of hair dye and various sets of light clothes which could be packed tightly, including several extras in different sizes. She read the note Curtis had left, listing what she had in the bag and explaining why the other clothes were necessary. Then she ate it and set to work. She dyed her hair black and trimmed the fringe to make herself look more oriental. Then she applied some fake tan and inserted some brown contact lenses.

"Alarmingly familiar, if slightly older," she muttered, checking herself in the mirror.

Finally, satisfied she had transformed herself convincingly into a typical Japanese tourist, Tessa put on the Manga tee-shirt which would be part of the forthcoming recognition procedure and repacked her rucksack. Then she ruffled the bed to make it look as though it had been slept in, and quietly crept downstairs. Unseen, she left the hotel and took a taxi back to Suvarnabhumi Airport. Armed with the ticket stubs from bogus flights to Siem Reap and various other receipts from the area, she checked in to the Thai Air flight to Rangoon.

The plane departed punctually, arriving after ninety minutes at Mingaladon Airport. She walked across the tarmac to the Junta's ludicrously large, grandiose terminal building, taking small steps as Japanese women often do. She quickly passed through Immigration, relieved to feel as if nobody was paying undue attention to her. She strode out of the Arrivals Hall into the bright sunlight. It was late afternoon, still incredibly hot and oppressively humid. Her challenge now was to find her contact. A seething mass of drivers quickly surrounded her, noisily vying for her custom, but she soon heard what she wanted.

"Miss, my son likes Manga and I have Japanese car, please let me drive you."

Tessa turned to study the man addressing her. He looked to be unusually strongly built for a Burmese man, slightly taller than average and with a kindly face. He was dressed in a pale yellow short-sleeved shirt and a blue-and-red checked longyi; his clear brown eyes glinted challengingly in the sunlight. Tessa immediately liked his confidence.

"Leally?" she replied, mimicking poor Japanese English. "Toyota?"

"Nissan," he replied proudly. "Good condition too."

"Air-con?"

"Yes, and it works well too."

"OK. You dlive me Langoon, please."

He grinned broadly, showing a fine set of teeth stained red from chewing betel nut.

"Yes, Miss. Thank you, Miss. Let me take bag."

He led her to a battered old Nissan car. Tessa walked round it as though considering whether it was good enough for her.

"OK," she announced, "we go now."

The man nodded and held the back door open for her. She got in and took her bag from him.

Once they had left the airport, the driver addressed her.

"Where would you like me to take you, Miss?"

"Mrauk U."

"That's a long way over the mountains. Would you settle for Taunggyi?"

"How about Mogok?"

"Mandalay would be closer... So, my name's Khin," he continued. "Welcome to Myanmar."

"*Mingalabah*, Khin."

"I heard that you speak some Burmese. It sounds impeccable."

"Thank you. I had a good teacher. But, just for the record, I always call your country Burma. Only when a democratic government is in power will I start using a new name."

Khin roared with laughter.

"Curtis mentioned you were… independently minded. I am looking forward to working with you. How do you want to play this?"

"I'd prefer not to book in to a hotel tonight. Can we get one of your doubles to do that?"

"Sure, we'll go straight to the changeover point. Then what?"

"If you don't mind, I'd like to make a start north for Pagan. There's a place on the way I'd like to visit. With a bit of luck we'll be able to stay there tonight and… well, we'll see when we get there. If it comes to the crunch, I take it you don't mind if we overnight in the car?"

"I've slept in far worse," replied Khin, grinning. "Whatever we need to do to get the job done. Htet was like a father to me. He made sure

I was looked after when my parents were killed, and then trained me to become an agent. It's because of him that I am still alive so I am doubly motivated to help you. However, Pagan is going to be difficult. We've been monitoring an unusual military build-up there for weeks. Could it be that you're expected?"

"Highly likely," admitted Tessa, her worst fears having been confirmed remarkably quickly. "I've tried to confuse our foes by arriving a day early. How much has Curtis told you about what we're going to do?"

"Simply that you're here to find out where Nyunt was born and who her parents really were… and that you need to get in and out without being detected."

"That's a pretty good summary, but we think the Calver Cats might be up to no good here too. So if I could find out anything about that at the same time, it would be very useful. Have you heard anything about high profile hostages being held?"

"Ah. I did wonder whether there was something else. There has been some unusual activity at Hpa An prison recently. You know where that is?"

"The town, yes, not the prison."

"It's in the outskirts to the north-west; not big, but a fortress. Anyway, security has been heightened and some very smart helicopters have been seen landing inside. There have also been some foreign container trucks making deliveries, we suspect, of sophisticated electronic equipment of some kind."

"That sounds just the sort of thing we need to investigate, but we'll focus on Nyunt's background first."

"OK. However, from what I know of Htet, he will have made sure the details of any children he had remained secret."

"You mean he had more than one?" asked Tessa incredulously.

"I'm not sure, I don't think so but I can't be certain. Htet was a very clever man and would have done everything he could to protect his family, and especially any offspring. It is well known that he was particularly attached to Nyunt so I can't believe he would have lied about her being his daughter. But it wouldn't surprise me in the slightest to learn that she was not born in Old Pagan."

"I agree," sighed Tessa. "But someone has done a good job of making her believe Htet was not her father."

"So who does she think was?"

"General Soe Gyi."

"What!" blurted Khin, wide-eyed. "That paedophile sadist? He killed her mother!"

"Do we know that for sure?"

"Well, I haven't met anyone who was there, but I don't have any doubts about it… and in this country it pays to question everything."

"Well, I'm here because I need tangible proof. However, until I have evidence to the contrary, I'm going to continue to believe what Htet told me. He and I survived some very close shaves together. I owe him my life too so I'm not willing to give up on him in a hurry."

"Me neither," agreed Khin.

"I take it the decoys know it's dangerous?" continued Tessa.

"It's dangerous being born here and only gets worse as one grows older. Living is hazardous enough, especially if you're not on the army's payroll – and even if you are, you're still not completely safe."

"Hmm. When Nyunt was here, did your people follow her?" asked Tessa.

"Would you believe, we lost her at the airport? I think she was whisked away somehow. Anyway, we had a devil of a job finding her, but we know she spent some time in a hotel in New Pagan. Then we lost her again until she popped up in Kalaw. She stayed there for two days before flying back to Rangoon, leaving for Bangkok shortly after that."

"Do you happen to know whether there's a hospital in Naypyidaw?"

"Not a regular hospital, only a high security medical facility which the Generals use. Why do you ask?"

"Nyunt told me she had her appendix removed there."

Khin shook his head.

"I don't believe that for a moment."

"Neither do I," murmured Tessa.

It wasn't long before Khin turned into Dagon Township, on the western outskirts of Rangoon.

"Better duck down," suggested Khin as he negotiated the increasingly narrow streets. On her own initiative, Tessa picked up the roll of carpet from the other foot-well and started to unfurl it to cover herself. Khin nodded approvingly. He turned left, then right, then left again, constantly checking his rear-view mirror and scrutinising who was watching the car. Eventually he stopped by a wide bamboo panel. It quickly moved aside and he drove into a small courtyard. As the panel closed behind them Tessa sat up and looked round. They were parked next to a grey Mitsubishi saloon with a broad green strip along the side. Khin turned to her.

"No names, please. These are difficult times so it's standard procedure here."

Tessa nodded.

As Khin and she got out of the Nissan, a man and a woman approached.

"You have brought the extra clothes?" asked the woman.

"Yes," replied Tessa, reaching for her rucksack. "Here's a tee-shirt for now, and one for tomorrow and another for the day after. OK?"

The woman nodded.

"How's your spoken Japanese?" continued Tessa in Japanese.

"Good, like yours," she replied, also in Japanese. "I cleaned the house of a Japanese diplomat; his wife taught me."

"Excellent," affirmed Tessa, reverting to English. "I would like you to check in to a medium class hotel in Rangoon for the night. Then fly to Mandalay and make your way down to Pagan. Try and make sure that whoever is watching you, believes you are me."

"Understood," replied the woman, studying Tessa's haircut.

"But our enemies are expecting me to go to Pagan, so don't get caught and don't get hurt. If you think they've realised that you're not me, just melt into the background."

"OK," acknowledged the woman, turning to Khin. "I'll stay at the Maymyo Rangoon Hotel."

"Fine," he responded, as he swapped shirts with his colleague. "You take the Nissan. Have the other team leave for Mrauk U when you leave for Mandalay. But tell them to be careful. It's a long and lonely way up the Kaladan River from Sittwe. And come what may, they should trek back; it'll be slower but safer. As she said, be careful. And, whatever happens, do not let them take you."

"As always," replied the woman. "There's some food in the house, and two reasonable knives."

After the decoys had left, Tessa changed her tee-shirt and discarded her jeans in favour of a longyi. Then she applied some ground thanaka bark to her cheeks in an effort to make her face look more Burmese.

"Looks good," smiled Khin, gesturing towards the car. "Main road north?"

Tessa nodded and sat in the passenger seat of the Mitsubishi. For two hours they travelled in silence. Both of them were on edge and constantly checking what was going on around them, but no one seemed to be spying on them. Eventually, Tessa started to peer intently into the dusk, scouring the roads and tracks to her left.

"Did Htet ever mention to you a place he knew up here?" she asked.

"No," replied Khin, studying his rear-view mirror. "It will be dark soon; it would be good if we can get off the main road. We won't get much warning of any road-blocks."

"I know. I'm sure the place I'm looking for is around here somewhere. But I've only been once before, and that was ten years ago."

Suddenly they passed a dilapidated brick-built pagoda and she pointed to a rough track.

"There!" exclaimed Tessa jubilantly.

"I see it."

Khin slowed down, again checking his mirror before switching off the car's headlights and turning sharply on to the narrow track. The car quickly disappeared between tall sugar-cane plants. As the track deteriorated from rough to appalling, Khin slowed to a crawl, refusing to switch the headlamps on. Eventually, they stopped by a small guest house. If it hadn't been for the dull glow coming from one of the downstairs windows, Tessa would have thought the place was deserted. But after a while the door opened and an old woman peered out nervously. Tessa recognised her immediately and got out of the car. It was dark now and the only sound was of the wind rustling through the crops.

"*Mingalabah*," said Tessa, bowing respectfully while putting her hands together. "Do not be alarmed, we mean you no harm. I came here once before with a mutual friend. May we come in, please?"

The woman eyed Tessa suspiciously, but there seemed to be a glimmer of recognition in her faded eyes. She didn't smile, but gestured with her hand for them to enter.

Tessa went straight in. Khin stayed outside for a while, confirming they had not been followed before joining them.

Inside, Tessa stood facing the woman. The intervening years had not been kind to her. She looked wizened and tired. When her husband joined them, Tessa found he had fared even worse. He too was thin and walked bent over with a pronounced limp. A lifetime on a subsistence diet, tilling the land and maintaining the guest house in an effort to eke out a meagre living, had taken its toll.

"I am very sorry to disturb you both," said Tessa, "but we met before, many years ago. I came here for breakfast with Htet." The woman smiled, she did know who Tessa was.

"So, how can we help you?" replied her husband, not attempting to hide his irritation.

"Well, it's a long story. But it's to do with those photographs you were able to get to me. Er… would it be safe for us all if we stayed here tonight?"

The woman's husband was clearly about to say no when she interrupted.

"There isn't much, but you are welcome to share what we have."

"I have some food in the car, why don't we share that?" offered Khin. The husband nodded.

"I will open the barn," he added. "Move your car out of sight, and cover it with hay to mask its warmth…"

After they had finished a meal of chicken, rice and bananas, the atmosphere became more relaxed. They sat drinking tea round the old wooden table with a candle in the middle providing a dull uncertain light.

"So, why are you here?" asked the old woman.

Tessa smiled and reached in to her rucksack. She brought out a photograph of herself and Nyunt in front of the Houses of Parliament, which had been taken soon after they arrived together in London.

"It's about my adopted daughter, Nyunt," said Tessa, passing her the photograph. "She has grown into a fine young woman, but there's a problem. She came to Burma a few weeks ago, wanting to trace any surviving relatives she might have. I didn't want to her to come, but she wouldn't listen to me and came anyway. I think something happened to her while she was here because she returned to London convinced that Htet was not her real father. I've come to uncover the truth, once and for all."

There was a charged pause as the man and woman exchanged glances.

"So you are Nariko?" continued the woman.

"Yes."

"But doesn't Nyunt have the photograph we passed on to you for her?"

"Of course. It's still hanging on her bedroom wall."

The woman looked expectant and Tessa suddenly realised she was being tested.

"They both are," she added quickly. "The picture of Nyunt and her mother, and the other one with just Htet."

The woman nodded in confirmation that this was correct.

"Who does she think her father was?"

Tessa took a deep breath.

"General Soe Gyi."

The old man exploded, involuntarily blasting some tea out of his mouth.

"That murdering bastard!" he shouted. "Where did she get a stupid idea like that from?"

"I don't know," replied Tessa, her eyes beginning to water. "That's what I've come to find out."

"Did you really kill him?" the man asked.

"Who?" queried Tessa, embarrassed to admit that she had killed so many she wanted to make absolutely sure she knew whom he meant before she answered.

"Soe Gyi. Who else?"

"Oh, sorry. Yes, most definitely," admitted Tessa, having difficulty hiding a smile.

"So she thinks you killed her father?"

"She does indeed," replied Tessa, suddenly overcome with emotion. A lone tear escaped and trickled down her cheek. She wiped it away quickly. "I think Nyunt is being manipulated somehow, this is so out of character for her. She means so much to me, I had to do something."

"It is very dangerous for you in Burma."

"Yes, but if I can, I want to establish the truth. Do you know whether

Htet was definitely Nyunt's father, and if so where she was born?"

"I am sure he was her father," said the woman. "We knew him well. He often brought Nyunt here, but we never met his wife. As for where she was born…"

Suddenly the old man banged his fist on the table.

"No, woman!" he exclaimed. His wife put her hand on his arm and smiled. Tessa and Khin looked at each other, wondering what was going on. The old woman peered again at the picture of Tessa and Nyunt, happy together in London, and passed it to her husband.

"Do you have any more photographs of her?"

Tessa produced two more of Nyunt; one from Japan and one taken in Switzerland where they had gone for a skiing holiday. The old woman studied them, smiled, and handed them to her husband too.

"She has grown up well and looks happy… You have done Htet proud. Would you leave us for a few minutes, please?" she said. "We need to be alone."

Tessa nodded and she and Khin went for a walk outside.

"They know something," he said, "but they're not sure they should tell us."

"Yes," agreed Tessa. "Whatever it is, they've probably guarded the secret since Htet died, and now they're trying to work out whether to break their word to him and share it with us…"

Although Khin had already camouflaged the tracks his car had left leading to the guest house, he checked the car had cooled down and set about beating the ground again with some bamboo to help pass the time; Tessa soon joined in. But suddenly they heard helicopters approaching from a long way off.

"There's two of them," professed Khin, "moving very slowly."

"Perhaps they're searching for someone," suggested Tessa.

"In which case they'd be using infra-red detectors."

"Then we can't hide in the house or the barn," thought Tessa out loud. "The pagoda by the road… I saw an entrance."

As the door to the house opened, Tessa and Khin started sprinting off down the track towards the road. The door slammed shut behind them.

As the helicopters neared, Tessa was running flat out with Khin struggling to keep up. They reached the road and turned right. The pagoda was in sight now, but so were the helicopters – though they were still a fair way off. A menacing red glow was emanating from domes below both machines.

Finally Tessa reached the pagoda and shot in through the narrow gap in the brickwork. Covered in cobwebs, but safe inside, she put her hands up against the back wall panting. Khin joined her a few seconds later and fell to his knees, gasping for breath.

"They are searching. I've never seen that in such a peaceful area before. Maybe they know you were missed at the airport. So for the time being, they've lost you. Clearly someone with influence is keen to detain you."

Tessa nodded.

"I hope the guest house will be all right."

"I should think so; the spotters won't see anything unusual there. It is lucky we were outside and heard the helicopters early enough."

It was ten minutes before Tessa and Khin felt it was safe to venture out from their hiding place. They both relished being back in the fresh air; it had been hot, dusty and stuffy inside. They gingerly picked their way back to the guest house. It seemed the danger had passed for the time being.

Tessa knocked tentatively on the door. The old man opened it, appearing even more nervous than before. He looked round suspiciously and then beckoned them to hurry in. Tessa could sense from the atmosphere inside that the discussion which had taken place had been a heated one. She doubted whether the helicopters scanning the guest house had helped reduce their anxiety.

"Were they looking for you?" asked the old woman.

"Probably," replied Tessa. "I don't think they'll come back tonight."

"No, but they might tomorrow."

Tessa nodded.

"Now, we would like you to tell us something about Nyunt," demanded the woman.

"What would you like to know? We've lived together since she left Burma. That was after Htet was killed at his house in the hills near Kengtung."

"Can you tell us anything about her that someone else might not know?"

Tessa thought for a moment.

"She has a birthmark on her left thigh, high up at the back."

"What shape is it?"

"Er, it's sort of droplet-shaped," she replied, tracing an outline on the table with her finger, "with the narrow end facing upwards."

The woman smiled and nodded to her husband. He sighed, stood up and hobbled over to a dilapidated dresser. He opened one of the drawers and took out an old hunting knife. He used it to prise off some of the bamboo beading along the side and then poked the knife into a narrow slot, gently coaxing out the end of a thin cord. He pulled this until a folded photograph appeared. Then he replaced the beading and returned to the table with the picture. He sat down, apparently worn out by his exertions. After pausing for a moment to gather his breath, he passed the photograph to his wife. She looked at it, smiled, as though it had just brought back a wealth of happy memories, and pushed it across the table.

Tessa opened it and smoothed it out, holding it up towards the candle so she could see it more clearly.

It was a picture of five people: two couples and a young baby. The photo had been taken in front of what looked like a souvenir stall. Htet was shown with his arms round a beautiful young woman as she cradled a very small child. It was the same woman who was in the photograph which hung in Nyunt's bedroom in London. Next to them was another couple of about the same age. Everyone was smiling, but Htet was positively beaming, looking proud and loving.

"It's Nyunt!" exclaimed Tessa, overjoyed to be looking at a new picture of the daughter she loved so much.

"Yes," replied the woman, "she was just nine weeks old when it was taken. You can tell that her mother is holding her."

Tessa nodded, her smile broadening.

"And Htet looks on top of the world here. He died buying me time to escape with Nyunt… I knew she had to be his child."

For a while Tessa was silent, imagining what had been going through the minds of those in the photograph. They all seemed so happy and carefree, gathered together to celebrate the birth of a daughter. How things had changed.

"The photograph is dated on the back," continued the old woman.

Tessa turned it over; there was some writing in Burmese script. She handed the photograph to Khin.

"Sorry, I can't read this. What does it say?"

"*Twelfth of November 2013, Kyaiktiyo.*"

"Htet wrote in his passport that Nyunt was born on the sixth of February 2014," confirmed Tessa. "She's five months older than she believes."

"Htet was determined to keep her background a secret," added the old woman. "He was convinced it would be safer for her that way. I am not surprised he falsified her date of birth. Luckily, she was always small for her age."

"She put on a spurt when she reached her teens," noted Tessa. "He also wrote that she was born in Pagan."

"I am fairly sure that is not true, but I'm afraid he never told us where she was born. But I think his wife came from Hpa An, which is near Kyaiktiyo."

Tessa and Khin exchanged an uneasy glance.

"Do you know her name?"

"Yes, it was Thuza."

"*Kyay zu tin bar de,*" Tessa thanked her sincerely. "I have no idea who Nyunt has been talking to, but I'm sure she hasn't discovered any of this. Do you know where at Kyaiktiyo we might find the other people in the picture? They may know where Nyunt was born."

"Yes," replied the woman, "the thirteenth souvenir shop on the left when you come down the local path. You'll recognise it from this picture. I doubt it has changed much, nothing changes in Burma."

Tessa was stunned by how much she'd been able to find out.

"I take it you have never told this to anyone else?"

"No, and nor will we," sighed the old woman. "You may stay here tonight, but you must leave very early tomorrow morning. Your presence will be noticed. If you leave before dawn, you should avoid the army. You may take the picture with you. We have nothing else which could connect us to either Htet or Nyunt. You must make sure she learns the truth."

Tessa nodded.

"I promise. I swore an oath to Htet before he died that I would bring up Nyunt as my own. That I have done. However, now she has forgotten who her real mother and father were, and that is just not right. I do not intend to stop until she remembers them."

The old woman smiled, prompting Tessa to stand up and go over to her; she bent down and hugged her.

"Thank you again, for everything. I cannot thank you enough."

"You are welcome," she replied. "Our time in this world is nearly at an end. It is good that we have been able to do this for Htet before…" She smiled serenely at her husband.

Tessa looked at the old man who wore a resigned expression on his face. He simply nodded to them both.

Then he stood up and unfurled a rug for Khin to sleep on while the old woman pointed to another for Tessa, which was already spread out on the wooden floor. Tessa had noticed it previously because she recognised the design. She'd seen one just like it in Htet's house near Kengtung, over the trapdoor leading to his munitions dump…

Khin and Tessa both fell into an uneasy sleep. They rose at 3:30 a.m., had a quick cup of tea and some cold rice, and drove quietly away.

CHAPTER 5

Khin broke the silence half an hour later.

"From here we could go straight to Kyaiktiyo, but I think it would be better if went back to Rangoon first. There is always a military presence at Kyaiktiyo so we will need some good disguises, either as a tourist and guide, or maybe two locals."

"Passing me off as a local won't be easy. My spoken Burmese is good, but it's not up to scrutiny by an army officer and I can't read much Burmese script."

"And you don't have any identity papers. However, if you go up there as a tourist we'll be much easier to pick out."

"Maybe I should go up on my own as a local?" suggested Tessa.

"No." Khin smiled. "Htet would never forgive me if I let you do that; one way or another, we'll see this through together."

"Thank you," replied Tessa, feeling surprisingly relieved. "In which case, I think we need to do whatever we can, as quickly as we can. If we're lucky, maybe the bad guys won't realise what we're up to until after we've done it."

Khin nodded and the car's speed increased.

"We'll get you some ID in Rangoon. At such short notice it won't be perfect, but hopefully good enough to withstand a superficial inspection."

Tessa nodded, and returned to studying the photograph the old woman had given her. Suddenly she looked up and glanced over her shoulder.

"Do you have the feeling we're being watched?"

"Yes and no," replied Khin. "We're not being followed, but I suspect we are being chased. It's just that so far we've been able to stay one step ahead of them. But they seem to be throwing a lot of resources into finding us. I feel under more pressure here with you than I have been for a long time. Somebody is very determined. I doubt we'll be able to achieve both your goals before they find us. So I suggest we concentrate on Nyunt, and then get you out as quickly as possible."

"Fine. I don't want anyone to be hurt on my behalf. But if we're going back to Rangoon, we'd better get some more knives," said Tessa, checking the ones he had given her earlier.

Khin had been concentrating hard on the road in front and the traffic behind, but this exchange prompted him to slow down and glance back at her.

"Why do you think they're chasing us, and who are they?"

"Well, I suspect it's me they're after not least because there have been several incidents in London lately. But who they are, and why they want me, I have no idea. I've always felt that my problems with Nyunt were simply the bait to lure me into a very unpleasant trap, here. But it must be more than settling an old debt that is driving them. Somebody has thought long and hard about all this, and gone to great lengths to convince Nyunt of a complete pack of lies. Nobody would bother to do all that unless it was part of a much bigger, nastier game. More knives might not be enough to keep us from harm, but they could help buy us time..."

After another hour, they were once again in the little courtyard behind the bamboo panel. A different man and woman joined them from the adjoining wooden shack. Khin dispatched the man to get Tessa some identity papers and more knives. Then he sent the woman to buy food and water and some convincing Mon clothes for both him and Tessa. While they were gone Khin checked the car, filled it with petrol and put several extra cans in the boot.

The man returned first. He handed the identity papers to Khin for finishing and placed a scruffy brown paper bag on the table. He watched as Tessa unpacked it and studied the two knives.

"Those were very expensive," complained the man, "are you any good with them?" He cast a disbelieving sideways glance at Khin who pretended not to notice and continued working on Tessa's papers, scowling at the results of his labours.

Tessa smiled at the grumpy man.

"I've been told I'm not too bad," she replied lightly. She tossed one of the knives in the air, caught it by the tip of the blade and threw it at a bluebottle she'd noticed settling on a wooden upright a few yards away. "That one's not particularly well balanced, but it'll do the job."

The man raised his eyebrows, stood up and went over to the upright. He pulled out the knife and wiped the dead fly off it. Khin winked at him.

"These are the best I could find at short notice," the man said, more accommodatingly.

"And this is the best I can do at short notice," admitted Khin, passing Tessa a small piece of scruffy card. "Let's just hope we don't have to use either."

Some minutes later, the woman returned with provisions and the new clothes, so Tessa and Khin got changed. Then the woman helped Tessa practice strapping on an appropriately stuffed cushion to make it look as though she was heavily pregnant.

Tessa considered how to secrete her knives. There were numerous folds of material in her dress, making it very hot to wear but also providing numerous camouflage opportunities; the blades of two, she simply stuck through the material. Then she stuck one knife in each side of her padding. She found she could easily reach through the slits she had made for the other knives to reach the remaining two. For several minutes she practised drawing them to be sure she could get to them quickly if needed. Meanwhile, Khin and the other man started peeling the green stripes off the car. Underneath were bright double yellow ones. Matching designs were revealed on the bonnet, boot and roof of the car, making it look quite different. By then it was 9 a.m. and breakfast had been prepared.

"We'll eat this and go," ordered Khin. "If we're lucky we might be able to get there before nightfall."

Tessa nodded.

Suddenly the radio crackled into life. The woman went over to it and listened intently.

"What is it?" asked Khin, not stopping eating.

"There are reports of an explosion at an old guest house north of Rangoon. The army had approached it as part of a regular search, but before they could enter, it just exploded. Apparently it was a very sophisticated incendiary device. The two people inside and the building itself were completely destroyed. Seven soldiers were killed too, a number of others injured."

It was obvious which guest house the report was referring to; Tessa was horrified. Two innocents had just given their lives for her cause. She wondered how many more would be endangered before the truth was known. She glanced at Khin and for a moment saw shock and sadness in his eyes; then he carried on eating.

They were soon heading out of Rangoon towards Bago. Khin was driving as quickly as he dared without attracting suspicion. Neither of them said much, both nervously scanning the road ahead for army checkpoints. They didn't stop for lunch; simply halting for ten minutes in the countryside so that Khin could have a rest from driving. They both hastily ate a snack and drank some water, and then they were off again.

By the time they were rushing along the approach road to Kyaiktiyo the sun had started to wane. In the distance Tessa could see the Golden Rock, already brightly illuminated by the numerous floodlights that made the top of the hill resemble a garish bouquet of poorly arranged flowers.

She had visited this spiritual site many years before as a tourist. But, like so many of the previously significant locations in Burma, such as the plains of Pagan with its newly constructed gruesome watchtower, it was rapidly losing both character and meaning; not surprisingly, even UNESCO had been offended. Nevertheless, Tessa was still pleased to see it again.

Khin parked the car amidst the plethora of other local vehicles and they managed to hitch a lift in one of the last trucks up to the halfway stage, from where they had to walk. After nearly an hour, they were within sight of the top platform without ever having been stopped. There had been no army checkpoints and nobody paid any attention to the man with his ostensibly pregnant wife. It seemed whoever was chasing Tessa had not expected her to go to Kyaiktiyo.

When they reached the top Tessa insisted on having a quick look at the Golden Rock, perched precariously, almost miraculously, on the edge of a cliff overlooking the valley below. Leaning on the handrail, she admired the golden glow from the rock itself, set against the dark blue background of the sky and the final rays of the setting sun. From only a small distance away the rock looked as though it was on fire with a halo of insects circling the flames.

"I've always liked it up here," observed Tessa. "It's so beautiful, and everyone is intent only on having a good time with their loved ones."

Khin nodded.

"I remember as a child pushing the rock and feeling it wobble."

"I enjoyed doing that too," laughed Tessa. "Mind you, I did wonder what would happen if I managed to push it off."

"But women aren't permitted to approach the rock?"

"I know," she admitted, guiltily. "Sorry. I managed to get away with it at the time."

"So you've always been a forceful character, then," commented Khin with a wry smile… "Let's go. We need to get away from here as soon as we can."

Tessa nodded and they set off towards the other path down through the souvenir shops. It wasn't long before they were approaching the thirteenth. Tessa glanced at the photograph to make sure she had found the right shop. She also wanted to refresh her memory as to what the people looked like.

She stopped at the shop's doorway and peered in between the curtains while Khin stood behind her watching the people passing by.

"This is it," she confirmed under her breath, and went in.

They had already agreed that Khin would come in with her, but once she had made contact he would wait outside to keep a lookout.

The souvenir store was very small. There was a table full of knick-knacks near the middle, with lots more adorning all the walls. A woman was standing serving while a man sat in one of two nearby chairs.

"May my wife sit down, please?" asked Khin.

The woman smiled and gestured towards the empty chair, next to the man. Tessa sat down heavily and heaved a big sigh. Khin looked at her and she nodded, confirming what he already suspected. These were the two people in the photograph. He looked at the woman.

"I will wait outside so as not to crowd your shop."

The man had noticed Tessa arrive, but was already closing his eyes. The last customer soon left and Tessa was alone with the man and woman. She reached inside the folds of dress material and gripped the hilt of one of the knives.

"Would you like some water?" asked the woman pleasantly.

Tessa nodded gratefully. The woman filled a dirty glass from a bottle and told her husband to wake up and serve for a few minutes. Then she settled down on the adjoining chair.

"When is your child due?" she asked, passing the glass to her.

"It's complicated," replied Tessa. The woman's expression changed immediately. It was clear Tessa's English accent had made her suspicious.

"Please don't be alarmed," said Tessa quietly, "we are friends of Htet's and have travelled a long way to find you. We don't want to cause any trouble. Please let me explain." She placed the glass of water on the floor and produced the photographs of Nyunt she had shown to the old woman the night before. "This is Htet's daughter, Nyunt. I adopted her after Htet was killed near Kengtung. She is a young woman now. But there is a problem. She was in Burma a few months ago, trying to locate any of her relatives who might still be alive. She came back to me in London convinced that Htet was not her father. I am here to find out the truth. I have been given this photograph of you and Htet's family and was wondering whether you might be able to help me trace where Nyunt was born."

The atmosphere in the shop had become very tense. The woman flicked through the photographs and gestured to the man. He quickly peered outside, exchanged glances with Khin and returned to look at the pictures himself.

"Is this really London?" asked the woman.

"Yes," said Tessa, smiling. "Nyunt and I have been living happily there for many years. Htet was dying when he made me promise to take her with me from Kengtung. Ever since then I have been proud to have her as my daughter, and have done everything I can for her."

"Was it you who killed General Soe Gyi?"

Tessa was surprised to be asked the same direct question again. She hadn't liked the General and suspected her opinion was shared by many, but she hadn't expected so many people still to be harbouring ill feelings against him after so long.

"Yes."

The woman looked at her husband but he didn't say anything, he just continued studying the photographs. His wife sighed. For a long time nothing further was said. Tessa started to grow uncomfortable.

"I'm sorry. This must have come as a bit of a shock after so long. But I'm desperate to hear anything you might know. It's very important... but I can't stay long. We are all in danger while I am here."

The woman looked at her and seemed just about to speak when Khin came in.

"We don't have much time," he said urgently. "It's getting busy outside, and there are lots of soldiers although I don't think they're looking for us."

"Yes, sorry, Khin," acknowledged Tessa. "Just a couple more minutes, please."

"You are Khin?" asked the woman.

"Yes," he replied, peeping outside.

"You knew Htet?"

"Yes, very well. He became a father to me after my parents were killed. It's only because of him that I am alive today."

The woman smiled and nodded quickly to the man whom Tessa presumed was her husband. Khin decided he wasn't needed any more and went outside again. The man moved to the back of the shop and started sorting through what looked to Tessa like a selection of rather gaudy twizzle sticks with tassels. Finally, he found the one he was looking for and brought it over to his wife. She snapped it in two and pulled out a rolled-up photograph. Discarding the remnants of the stick, she unfurled the photo so she and Tessa could see it.

It showed Htet, Thuza and a baby Nyunt taken in front of a substantial ornate-looking doorway. On the wall hung a sign: Moulmein Women and Children's Hospital. On the back was a date.

"Eleventh of September 2013," said the woman, realising Tessa was struggling to read it. "Thuza was discharged the day after Nyunt was born."

Tessa's eyes started watering again.

"*Kyay zu tin bar de,*" she whispered as a tear rolled down her cheek.

"You may keep the picture, but you must leave now," said the woman standing.

"Would you like to have a photograph of Nyunt?" she asked Tessa, also getting up.

"Thank you, but we daren't. It's part of our past. You now hold all our futures in your hands. Good luck."

66

Tessa hugged the woman, nodded to the man, and went outside to find Khin.

He was standing with his back to the shop.

"Moulmein Women and Children's Hospital," she said triumphantly, "10th September 2013."

A momentary smile flashed across his face, but then his expression hardened.

"We must get down as fast as we can."

"Lead on," replied Tessa.

They turned left and headed down the hill at a ludicrously brisk pace for someone apparently pregnant, but no one seemed to notice. The narrow path was full of people coming up, but it was relatively easy to pick a way through the crowds by the light from the numerous souvenir shops, tea houses and food stalls. Tessa and Khin carried on as quickly as they dared. Soon they were on their own in the darkness as it seemed nobody else wanted to go down so early. Then they heard the sound of somebody running behind them.

"A woman," advised Tessa, listening carefully, "on her own, scared perhaps."

They were caught up by an attractive young Karen woman. Surprised to meet the two of them, she stopped short. They all studied each other. But then Tessa started chuckling noticing how Khin's demeanour had changed; he had already mentioned that he was single and without a girlfriend.

"Hello," said the woman, smiling at him, "do you mind if I walk down with you and your wife? I've been separated from my friends and…"

"It's no problem at all," replied Khin, quickly. "You are welcome to join us, but we're not married. I'm simply a close friend."

"Oh," said the woman, grinning at Tessa, "thank you. My name is Ohnmar."

Khin gave false names for both himself and Tessa, and they set off again. Soon Khin and the Ohnmar were happily walking side by side and talking together, Tessa was content to follow them.

Suddenly they rounded a bend and came to an abrupt halt. In front of them, seated in the middle of the path, were four young soldiers. All wore side-arms, though given the well documented ammunition shortage, Tessa doubted whether many, if any, of these were actually loaded.

The soldiers stood up and a sergeant went over to Khin.

"Papers!" he rasped.

Meanwhile, a corporal moved towards Ohnmar. He looked her up and down approvingly as she started nervously searching in her shoulder bag.

"We don't need your papers," he leered, glancing back at his colleagues. "We have other plans for you, Karen woman. I'll see yours, though," he added, glaring at Tessa. The other two soldiers, both privates, stood up.

The sergeant gave Khin's papers a cursory glance and returned them to him.

"Is that your wife?" he rasped, gesturing towards Tessa.

"Yes, sir," replied Khin obsequiously. Ohnmar looked surprised.

"What are you gawping?" asked the corporal.

"Nothing," replied Ohnmar.

The corporal nodded to the sergeant.

"OK. You and your fat wife can go," the sergeant ordered. "This one stays with us."

"Oh, she's a friend of ours, sir," interjected Khin, "we've known her for many years. We are looking after her. Can't she come with us, please?"

"No. Go away, before I change my mind."

"Don't worry, we're going to look after your friend real good," added the corporal, ogling Ohnmar.

"What do you mean, sir?" asked Khin, feigning innocence.

"We're the military, we don't need to explain ourselves to scum like you," retorted the sergeant. "Come to think of it, why the hell are you still here?"

"I'm sorry, sir, but we cannot leave without our friend. We are responsible for her."

The atmosphere was changing rapidly and Tessa readied herself as the two privates moved menacingly towards Ohnmar.

"Please let me go with my friends," she wailed, "I haven't done anything wrong. Why can't I leave with them?"

She started shaking, prompting Tessa to move alongside her.

"Move aside," ordered the corporal. But she simply nudged herself directly between him and Ohnmar and clutched her stomach.

"I think it's coming," she groaned in Burmese, trying to hide her accent.

"Then go while it's still alive," yelled the corporal, drawing his knife. "But she stays."

Tessa glanced at Khin, he clearly didn't want to leave Ohnmar alone with the soldiers.

"*Mahouq-pa*," hissed Tessa indignantly. "We will not abandon her. Not with you acting like a pack of horny schoolchildren."

The corporal's eyes widened with anger and he plunged his knife in to Tessa's generously padded stomach, just as she'd expected he would.

"Now that wasn't a very nice thing to do," she scorned.

With the corporal still gaping, she reached out for the hilt of his knife with her left hand and simultaneously punched him hard in the chest with her right, close to his heart. The blow completely stunned the man and forced him to take a step back, letting go of the knife. He started making pathetic wheezing noises as he desperately gasped for breath. While she watched the erratic pulsations in his neck, she withdrew his knife and flicked it at one of the privates. It struck him in the forehead and he collapsed dead. As Tessa continued to watch the corporal's carotid arteries, she could see that his heart was pounding furiously. She drew one of her own knives with her left hand while Khin grabbed the sergeant and spun him round in a neck-lock. Then she threw her knife at the remaining private. As the corporal stopped breathing in, Tessa punched him again, just below his Adam's apple. The blow made a horrible crunching sound and his eyes bulged outwards. As the sergeant's neck made a horrible snapping sound, Tessa's knife buried itself in the private's chest. A moment later, she punched the corporal a third time, forcing his diaphragm abruptly upwards into his chest cavity. It was too much for him and his heart stopped. Then there was silence.

Tessa spun round and put her hand over Ohnmar's mouth.

"Shh! No noise. You are safe now. OK?"

Ohnmar's heartbeat slowed. She looked Tessa in the eye, relaxed and nodded. Tessa smiled and looked at Khin.

"Well, that went well," she muttered sarcastically.

"Hmm. Ohnmar, here is some money," urged Khin. "Go back up and in to the first decent eating house you come to and buy yourself a good meal. Don't come down again until after daybreak or if you find your friends. In any event, only come down as part of a large group of people. If anyone asks anything, you weren't here, you saw nothing and spoke to no one. Understand?"

"Yes." She nodded and gratefully took the money. "Thank you."

"You're welcome. Now, be careful, and don't draw any attention to yourself."

"Will I see you again?"

"Only if you tell me where you live."

Ohnmar smiled.

"Hpa An…"

"Excuse me, guys," interjected Tessa, "don't you think…?"

"Ah, yes," said Khin, grinning as he snapped back to reality. "Ohnmar, go now and stay safe. I will find you."

She went over to him and momentarily grabbed his hands, then turned away and started walking quickly back up the hill.

Tessa removed her false stomach.

"Don't think we need this any more," she noted, "I'll toss it on the way down." Then she helped Khin roll the soldiers' bodies off the side of the road. Fortunately, there was a steep slope by the side of the path and the bodies rolled almost out of sight before lodging against some trees. Tessa cleaned her knife and helped Khin cover the tell-tale signs of conflict.

If we're lucky we've got twenty minutes before somebody notices they're gone," he said, worriedly.

"Then we'd better hurry," responded Tessa. "How long will it take us to get back to the car?"

"It's a long way."

"Race you," replied Tessa, and started off down the hill. Soon they were both running as fast as they could and Tessa threw her cushion away. Khin was trying hard to overtake her, but she refused to let him. Suddenly he fell, slithering to a less than graceful halt on some leaves. Tessa slowed and looked round. But he was already up again and sprinting after her, muttering Burmese expletives. Then it was Tessa's turn to fall. She tripped on a root and plunged forward dropping her bag. Khin looked worried, convinced she was about to break something. But Tessa simply dived down, did four quick handstands, recovered and carried on running. Khin couldn't believe what he'd seen. He picked up the bag and bounded after her.

Thirty minutes later they were both in the car, panting and covered in perspiration. They could see numerous flashlight beams dancing around the pitch black countryside and hear the sound of raised voices.

"Wow," gasped Khin, closing his door and starting the engine, "I didn't think it was possible to get down that fast... Not that I ever want to do it again."

He drove out on to the main road and headed south towards Moulmein.

"I think she liked you," commented Tessa, grinning.

"Did you really?" replied Khin. "She was very nice."

"Indeed. I hope she knows how to keep her mouth shut."

"Everyone in Burma knows that, otherwise someone kills them... Are all Peacekeepers like you?"

"What gave you the impression I might be a Peacekeeper?"

"Well, it has always been rumoured that it was a Peacekeeper acting out of their legal jurisdiction who killed Chalmers and Soe Gyi. Then, for example, there was the spitted bluebottle, you dispatching three soldiers quicker than I could one, the way you recovered from that fall. Your Japanese name... Need I go on?"

"Hmm. Peacekeepers are very secretive people. I don't know many others, so I can't really say if we're all similar. But it's a dangerous business and either one handles oneself well, or one dies."

"So how did you kill that first soldier?" asked Khin.

"It's called HICA: Harmonic Induced Cardiac Arrest. It's a difficult technique, utilising three carefully timed punches. It's not very pleasant to watch up close, but the nastier the person, the easier it seems."

"So was it easy killing Soe Gyi?"

"I regret to say, yes, extremely," sighed Tessa. "But I hadn't come to Burma to kill him; I only wanted Bill Chalmers. However, Soe Gyi jumped me from behind and nearly throttled me before I managed to turn the tables on him."

For nearly an hour after that they drove in silence.

"I would have thought they'd be setting up extra roadblocks by now," said Tessa eventually.

"Maybe. But there are a lot of freedom activists around here who could quite easily have been responsible for the soldiers' death. The army is probably searching for us in bigger places," replied Khin.

"With maternity units," added Tessa, prompting Khin to nod in agreement.

"I think we should head for Hpa An now. It's only forty minutes from Moulmein and we have a safe house there where we can change cars, eat and rest."

"Hpa An," laughed Tessa, "how convenient."

"Possibly, but it is pure coincidence," replied Khin, laughing. "There are some woods coming up. I'm going to stop and change the car's appearance a bit. Could you peel off the side stripes, please? I'll do the big films on the boot and the bonnet. There's a stripe on the roof too."

"Sure," she replied.

"Oh, and by the way, the choke on this car…"

"Is automatic," continued Tessa. "Htet told me about those."

When they stopped, they peeled off all the films, revealing black paintwork underneath, and Khin changed the number plates; he put some more petrol in the tank too.

"I think we're probably still just ahead of them," he commented as they set off again. "But it won't be long now…"

"I don't think this trail we're following is a set up."

"Neither do I. But four soldiers have died and yet the reaction does seem unusually restrained."

"Maybe it's not the usual people in charge?"

"Possibly," conceded Khin. "Perhaps whoever had lost us now feels they've found us again, and they are simply letting us carry on?"

"Could be," replied Tessa. "Maybe they also want to find what we're looking for. Or am I just being paranoid?"

"Who knows? Either way, I think we're running out of time."

"So where are Burmese birth certificates kept?"

"Assuming one was issued the original will be kept at the hospital concerned. There has been talk of archiving them centrally, in Naypyidaw, but nothing has been done so far. Knowing Htet, he will have made sure there was a birth certificate, but probably destroyed his copy when things got precarious."

"OK. But searching through lots of old files at a hospital isn't exactly going to be easy, is it?"

"No, but I have an idea, it might not be as difficult as we think. I'll know for sure when we get to Hpa An. But I think you should plan to exit as soon as we've tried to obtain the certificate. Either way, this is just getting too dangerous, for all of us."

"I agree," acknowledged Tessa.

It was after midnight when their car slipped quietly into the outskirts of Hpa An. Again, Khin switched off the headlamps so as not to attract attention and extinguished the sidelights too when he turned off the main road. It was difficult and slow driving in almost pitch darkness, but it seemed sensible given the absence of any other light source. Finally, the car pulled into a discreet private courtyard. They both listened to see if they could hear any movement around them. But there was none, apart from Khin's colleague who'd let them in. He offered to keep watch while Tessa and Khin slept for a few hours.

CHAPTER 6

The sun had already risen when Tessa woke. Khin was still sleeping so she had a look round. It seemed this facility was very similar to the one in Rangoon, just smaller. There was a square courtyard of beaten-down sandy soil surrounded on three sides by high bamboo fences, several panels of which looked as though they could be removed if required. On the fourth side was a two storey wooden house. It looked dilapidated from the outside, but from the inside it was easy to see it had been strongly built. The man who had been keeping watch since Tessa and Khin arrived was now busy spraying their car blue. It already looked completely different. There was also a young woman in the house; she saw Tessa and offered her some tea.

Tessa took it gratefully and went to get her map of Burma. It was then that she noticed that all the radio kit and various other items of Special Forces equipment were stored within a single large wooden crate, the door to which hung open. The crate itself was on the back of an old but sturdy-looking pickup truck, which was parked facing one of the outside walls of the house.

The woman started preparing a breakfast of fried chicken, vegetables and rice with fruit. As the inviting smell spread throughout the house, Khin woke up. The other man announced the car was finished and everyone sat down to eat.

"This is very good," said Tessa, acknowledging the woman who had cooked their meal. "Thank you."

She smiled back.

"What's the situation outside?" asked Khin.

"Not good," answered the man. "There are a lot of people searching for a British woman. It won't be long before they come here."

"Soldiers?"

"Some, but mainly Military Police."

Khin glanced uncomfortably at Tessa.

"They're the elite, better trained and better armed than the military.

We probably shouldn't have slept so long."

As soon as they had finished breakfast and cleaned the dishes, Khin had a long talk with the woman, who quickly put on a scarf and hurried out.

"I think we'd better prepare for a Code Alpha," said Khin to the man. He nodded and started packing valuable items in the crate. He also put a number of chickens in smaller crates, and left them near the pickup. Then he undid some of the strings holding the bamboo panels to the courtyard fence. For a while Khin helped him, but then re-joined Tessa as she studying her map.

"This feels bad," he whispered.

"I'm very sorry you're involved," admitted Tessa. "I'm sure I was the target all along. But I don't intend to let you or anyone else here die for me."

"Too late for that," he sighed.

"What do you mean?"

"The team we sent to Pagan; they're both dead. They were ambushed and triggered their car's self-destruct."

Tessa breathed out noisily and shook her head in disbelief.

"I'm so sorry."

"They were professionals doing their jobs. We will look after the families."

"Good. I wish I knew why this was happening. What about the other team?"

"I told them to abort. They're hiking back from Sittwe. It's a long way, so it will be at least a week before they reach Rangoon, but they should be safe enough now."

"I think the sooner we complete this, the better," stated Tessa. "I'm a magnet for trouble."

"I'm hoping to go to the hospital this afternoon," replied Khin. "We have a contact there."

He pointed on the map.

"Here *we* are, and here's Moulmein. It's not far and the road's good. But there are bound to be roadblocks. We'll just have to hope your papers will pass the inspections. Whether we're successful at the hospital or not, we need to get you out of Burma as quickly as possible. Myawaddy and Thailand are about ninety miles away. The road is good; it was metalled to facilitate fighting the Karen and the DKBA. However, it's very exposed and there are several army checkpoints as it crosses the mountains. We'll pick up some motorbikes in Moulmein, they'll attract less attention."

"You don't have to come with me."

"Yes, I do," Khin answered her with a smile. "Four good people have died trying to help us do this. The best we can offer them now is to make sure that they didn't die in vain. After that, it's up to you to finish it, as I know you will."

"Oh, I will. And thank you for everything. However, if we are fortunate enough to find Nyunt's birth certificate but I am … taken, then please try and get it to Curtis."

"Don't worry. I will..."

The woman rushed back in, breathless.

"It's got very bad out there. They're openly beating people, and not far away. But I've spoken with the cousin of my friend. She'll be waiting for you at ten to three, main entrance. She goes home at three p.m."

"Excellent," replied Khin. "Well done. That's …"

Suddenly, a buzzer sounded in the crate.

"Code Alpha!" yelled Khin. "Sixty seconds!"

Tessa gathered her map and shoved her belongings in the rucksack.

"Get in the pickup," ordered Khin.

There was frenzied activity in the house. Various items were tossed in to the crate and its door slammed shut. More went in to the back of the pickup, and the tailgate was closed as the woman leapt into the back. As Khin got in the driver's seat, the wall in front of them slid back, revealing a narrow track. The engine started and they were off. Tessa looked back just in time to see the panel closing in the rear view mirror. She also glimpsed the blue Mitsubishi speeding off in the opposite direction and the dull glow of a powerful incendiary device being ignited behind them.

"You must be very valuable," mused Khin.

"I don't know why," responded Tessa. "I can't believe this is purely to get back at me for killing General Soe Gyi."

"Oh, it's not that. His death is not important any more. This must be about something far more serious."

"Well, I wish I knew what it was..."

Once they were well away from Hpa An, Khin stopped the pickup so Tessa could fix her disguise. Once more she became his pregnant Mon wife and the woman helped her refresh the thanaka on her cheeks. Tessa removed her knives from the rucksack and hid them in her dress as before. When they set off again, they all travelled in the cab. Khin was driving, Tessa in the middle and the woman near the passenger window.

They had been forced to set off earlier than expected, so had ample time to avoid all but one of the checkpoints. However, although Tessa was on tenterhooks, it passed without issue. The back of the pickup had been given a cursory check and even less attention was paid to their identity papers. So they stopped for a quick lunch and bought some fruit and water.

The sun was beating down from directly overhead when they entered Moulmein but there was little apparent military activity According to the woman, everything seemed perfectly normal for the bustling rundown seaside town.

Khin drove into the backstreets and stopped outside a two storey house. They were greeted by a young man and all went in. Soon, two motorbikes had been organised and parked nearby. Tessa and Khin went to inspect them. They appeared to be in good condition and both started with one kick. On the back of each were two canvas bags with bottles of petrol in them.

"I want to tell you how to get to Myawaddy from here, in case we get separated," said Khin seriously. "Go down this road to the crossroads and turn right. Then take the third left and follow that road round until you come to another crossroads. Go straight over. The road heads north-east. After about five miles, there's a road off to the right, signposted 'Myawaddy' in Burmese. You'll be able to read that, won't you?" Tessa nodded. "OK. That road is barely more than a track but it's quiet, although you will have to pass through a couple of small villages. Try not to be noticed. Eventually you'll come to another T-junction, this time with the main highway. Unfortunately you have no choice but to use it. Turn right and after about an hour you'll be able to take cover in the hills. That hour is when you'll be most exposed, so try and travel at dusk; any later and you won't be able to see where you're going without lights, and they'll give your position away. Once in the hills there are a number of tracks off to the left which lead down to the Moei River; smugglers use them. They're not easy but I'm sure you'll manage. Once across the river, you're in Thailand, north of Mae Sot."

Tessa nodded and repeated the directions, then Khin gave her one of the keys. He pocketed the other and they started back to the house.

"Khin," said Tessa, putting a hand on his arm, "just for the record, we started this together and I'd like it to end that way."

He smiled.

"Me too; but best be prepared... At this time of year, the Moei River is not very wide, you should be able to wade across quite easily. However, much of the Burmese side of the river has been mined. If crossing near Myawaddy is not possible, then you should go further north, through Karen territory. It'll be a lot more complicated as it'll take several days longer and you'll need to stay out sight, from everyone. You should be able to get across the river near Mae Ramat or Tha Song Yang; it's wider there, but an easy swim."

"Hmm, that's a long way," observed Tessa.

"Yes, and dangerous. Let's hope it doesn't come to that."

They arrived back at the house and, after a quick cup of tea, Khin, Tessa and the woman got back in the pickup while the man closed up the house and disappeared into the backstreets.

"The hospital is about a mile, up there," said Khin, gesturing. "I'll show you a shortcut back to the bikes as we drive. We'll go into the hospital together, it'll look better." Then he addressed the woman who had come with them. "You stay with the pickup. As soon as we've left, move it to where I said. Wait for me there, but leave if you feel they're on to you." She nodded and Khin turned back to Tessa. "If things go badly and the two of us get split up, you make straight for the bikes." Now it was Tessa's turn to nod. Then she took one last loving look at the picture of Htet, Thuza and Nyunt outside the hospital and passed it to Khin, in case he needed it to show the nurse. He took it and smiled as he put it in his shoulder bag. "Do not be concerned, I will take good care of it for you and Htet."

As Khin drove, he gave Tessa copious instructions on how best to get quickly and discreetly to the motorbikes. Eventually, the pickup stopped some 150 yards from the hospital.

This proved to be a three-storey Victorian brick building with a domed tower over the stone entrance arch. It was reminiscent of the medical facilities built by the British in Rangoon and Mandalay, but much smaller and even more rundown than was shown in the photograph Tessa had been given. Any hint of former grandeur had long since faded; it looked scruffy and dilapidated. None of the windows had any glass left and Tessa didn't doubt there would be no air-conditioning, few lights and little in the way of sanitation.

However, ostensibly, everything about the place seemed calm although crowds of people were milling around, including numerous couples carrying babies, and pregnant women. For a couple of minutes they sat in silence assessing the scene. Then Khin checked his watch.

"Seems to be OK. We'd better go."

Tessa took a deep breath and they got out of the pickup. The woman slid over into the driver's seat and, as Khin and Tessa walked towards the hospital, the pickup drove past them.

"I didn't want to say earlier," said Khin, without looking at her, "but if they know why you have come to Burma, and they've worked out that we were at Kyaiktiyo, this facility is an obvious place to set a trap."

"I kind of assumed that," replied Tessa. "I have no choice but to go on, but you…"

"I owe it to Htet for what he did for me. Stay alert."

"Always," replied Tessa. "Thank you."

Khin led her to the main entrance and paused. They both looked round, exchanged glances and went inside. It was dark and extremely hot and it took a moment for their eyes to adjust. The foul stench was almost overpowering and Tessa grimaced at the thought of the quality of medical care the Junta was willing to provide for the majority of Burmese people.

The passage from the front entrance appeared to go all the way through the building; Tessa could see a bright opening some distance in front of her. To either side were doorways through which she peered. There were poorly equipped, unhygienic examination rooms, offices and overcrowded wards. These were large, with a few ancient beds and lots and lots of people – most were on mats, including many patients. It seemed the whole family would accompany anyone who was ill. Khin explained this was because the hospital couldn't provide much, let alone food, so that remained the family's responsibility.

He stopped at one of the offices and knocked on the battered door. A nurse quickly came out and spoke with him in hushed tones.

"There are some seats outside in the garden at the back," he whispered to Tessa. "Wait there for me. She's going to take me to the file room. I'll be as quick as I can."

There were so many people that Tessa didn't dare say anything lest her accent gave her away, so she simply nodded and waddled towards the light at the end of the corridor. She looked back once, but Khin had already gone.

When she stepped out into the sunlight, Tessa found herself in a large open grassed area. She blinked as her eyes adjusted back to the bright afternoon sun, and looked round. There were lots of people, mostly in groups of three or four seating cross-legged on colourful mats. Tessa worked out which backstreet they would need to take to get to the motorbikes. Then she went down the three stairs to the grass and sat on a nearby bench, planning how they would escape in a hurry. On the other side of the grassed area were some dense bushes which would provide good cover, but these were facing in the wrong direction from the route to the bikes.

Tessa waited and waited. As the minutes passed she became more and more uneasy. How would she know whether Khin had run into trouble? What should she do if she believed they were about to be discovered? She felt vulnerable and started fondling the hilts of her knives.

Suddenly, Khin emerged from the back of the building. He grinned at her and gleefully waved a piece of paper before stuffing it in his shoulder bag. Tessa was overjoyed and stood up, ready to leave.

But then came the sound of shouting and military boots running along the hospital corridor towards the back entrance. Khin rushed down the steps towards Tessa. One of the people seated on the grass stood up and drew a gun. In a flash, Tessa had drawn and thrown a knife. The man fired once, but didn't hit anything and fell back dead with her knife sticking out of his forehead. People started screaming and running in all directions. Then Tessa saw that another seated man had surreptitiously drawn a gun; he'd presumably stayed down so as not to attract attention. As she threw another knife, he fired. She saw blood spurt from a wound in Khin's side. Shortly afterwards the gunman keeled over dead, but Khin faltered and clutched his bleeding injury. He cast a pained glance at Tessa and, as their eyes met, she knew he wanted to split up. He staggered off towards the nearby bushes. She was sure he'd found Nyunt's birth certificate but knew the best thing she could do now was to draw the attention of the Military Police and give him the best chance she could of getting away. She looked round to check there was no one else suspicious-looking on the grassed area. There wasn't so she hastily discarded her frontal stuffing, drew her remaining knives and adjusted her position.

She was just about to recover one of the knives she'd already used when a major rushed out of the hospital on to the grass. He saw Khin and drew his gun, but Tessa threw her third knife. It struck the man in the temple and he collapsed. As Khin entered the bushes, he looked back and forced a weak smile; Tessa nodded and he disappeared. She was already retreating when two more soldiers emerged from the hospital, ordering everyone to stay where they were. Tessa threw her last knife, turned and ran. As one of the soldiers fell dead, the other spotted her and gave chase. When she entered a narrow backstreet, he fired at her. But then there was an angry shout from a long way off.

"Don't kill her, you fool! We need her alive."

Tessa carried on running. Although she was sure there were several following her, there was only one who was close. But she was out of knives, and if she stopped to deal with him by hand, the others would probably catch up.

She sprinted on through the backstreets as fast as she could, desperately searching for something to use as a throwing weapon. Suddenly she saw the man she'd met at the safe house. He was standing near the entrance to a side street. As she approached, she called out to him.

"Throw me your knife!"

He immediately tossed it to her, but as she caught it the soldier behind fired a single shot.

The bullet hit the man in the chest. He wasn't dead, but had been fatally wounded. Furious, Tessa spun round and threw the knife with all her might. It sank up to the hilt in the soldier's heart. She quickly looked at the man who had just been shot. He waved her away, but she ran over to him and tried to help him. Soon her hands were covered in blood, he didn't have long to live.

"Go," he beseeched her. "You can't do anything for me now, no one can. I will delay them…"

Tessa didn't want to leave him, but felt she had no choice. If she stayed, they would both be taken.

"I'm so sorry," she said. She ran back to get the soldier's gun and gave it to the man, before sprinting off towards the place where the bikes were parked. She did her best to wipe the man's blood off her hands on some washing she grabbed from a line she passed under. She heard the sound of shooting. But by the time she reached the bike, it seemed to have gone relatively quiet behind her. She was fairly sure she had lost her pursuers for the time being as the cacophony of sirens was a long way off. Tessa started the bike and sped up the road. As soon as she could, she stopped in a quiet side street and removed her Mon clothes; she was already wearing a pair of faded jeans and scruffy tee-shirt beneath. She stuffed all her other clothes in her rucksack as she didn't want to discard them too close to the town lest they were found and gave an indication of the direction in which she was travelling.

As she rode she wondered whether Khin had managed to get away. It wouldn't have been easy for him. He had been seriously injured and would need medical attention. She felt guilty that so many people were suffering because of her quest to prove she had not murdered Nyunt's father. She was sure she knew the truth now, however Khin had the evidence. She considered whether she should hand herself in on the off-chance that her capture would take the pressure off him. But she quickly concluded that Khin would either be well on the way to safety or already dead, in which case Nyunt's birth certificate would be lost for ever.

The road slowly zigzagged away from Moulmein. But finally Tessa found the turning to her right that Khin had mentioned and followed it alongside a river and on towards the range of mountains which she'd have to cross to get to Thailand. Eventually, she came to the T-junction with Route 85, the main road between Hpa An and Myawaddy. She paused to check that it looked safe. Much to her surprise, it seemed to be almost deserted. The only things moving were a remarkably ramshackle Chevrolet bus and a couple of motorbikes, one heading in each direction. Although it was nearly dusk, she felt it would be wise to keep moving and put as much distance between her and Moulmein as possible.

She turned right on to the metalled road and sped towards the mountains. She could see the road stretching away, flat at first but then climbing up through a densely wooded hill. She knew she was very exposed and had to stay alert all the time. It started to get dark but she was committed now, she couldn't afford to stop or switch on her lights. She must reach the cover of the trees before she could risk relaxing.

After forty minutes, Tessa started looking for somewhere to pull off the main road. She found a narrow, almost overgrown track and followed it through the dense forest to where it terminated in a small clearing. She parked her bike and listened. The countryside was completely quiet and very dark. She looked up and found that the sky was full of stars. Occasionally she could even see the sparkling pinpoint of a satellite passing overhead. As she leaned against a tree and ate some of the food from her rucksack, she realised it was going to be a far from comfortable night; there were insects everywhere. In an attempt to obtain a brief respite from their apparently voracious appetite for Caucasian blood, she decided to walk to the top of the hill; it took her twenty minutes.

From the brow in the moonlight, she could just make out the route of the road down the hill. It continued across a stream and up again. It looked to be a long way but she doubted there would be many such valleys before she reached Myawaddy. However, there were flashlights moving around where the road disappeared from view, it seemed there was a checkpoint which she would need to avoid. They were bound to be on the look-out for her, and just as she could see them from her vantage point, they could also scan the direction from which she was approaching. She hoped that in daylight she would be able to find one of the smugglers' routes, otherwise she was destined to walk the rest of the way to Myawaddy in darkness. She returned to her bike and hid all the clothes she no longer needed. Then, determined to get as much sleep as possible, she tried to settle down for the night.

CHAPTER 7

Tessa was woken by the noise of the dawn chorus. The air was crisp, but she wasn't unduly cold despite her clothes being damp. She ate a scanty breakfast as the warmth from the morning sun forced the swirls of mist to dissipate and evaporated the droplets of dew from the grass.

Suddenly she heard a truck struggling up the hill from the Myawaddy direction towards her location. She listened nervously. It took a long time to reach her, but sped up after reaching the brow and soon the sound of its engine grew less distinct as the vehicle drove on. It was followed by the sound of two motorbikes approaching from Hpa An. For a moment she worried they were going to come down the track she had used, but they passed where she was hiding and stopped. Tessa crept towards the road so she could watch them. The bikes were barely twenty yards away, both heavily laden. The two young riders were having an animated conversation, but she couldn't hear everything they were saying. From the snippets she could make out it seemed that the men had been looking for something and were now arguing about whether they should turn off the main road. But one thing she was sure she'd heard was that they were heading for Myawaddy.

Finally, they restarted their bikes and rode a short distance up the hill before turning off to the left and disappearing from view. She could hear the sound of their motorbike engines as they free-wheeled down an incline.

She ran back to her campsite, packed and manhandled her bike back up to the road. After checking this was clear, she pushed the bike up the highway until she came to the track the other bikers had used. It was similar to the one she had been on, but rutted from heavy use. She started her engine and set off after the two men. It wasn't long before her riding skills were being tested to the maximum. She hardly dared to use the front brake as the track snaked down so steeply; she frequently had to put both feet down to avoid falling off. However, she could still hear the engines of the other bikers some distance ahead. By now, they were no doubt aware that someone was following them.

The going remained difficult and it was late morning when Tessa finally reached a stream at the foot of the valley. A while back she had seen a bridge, but had long since lost sight of it in the trees. However, she doubted that it could be far away and, judging from the tyre tracks, the people blazing this trail before her had ridden to the right, so that was the way she turned. After a few minutes, she came to a place where the stream broadened out, making it easy to ford. Also, she could see from the still-wet muddy tyre tracks up the bank on the other side of the stream, that the bikers in front of her had simply ridden through. She followed their example and disappeared into the trees again. Soon, she was climbing up the other side of the valley and moving further away from the army check-point.

It was early afternoon and stifling hot when Tessa neared the top of the next ridge. Even though she could hear the bikers leading her were still moving, she decided to stop for a quick lunch in the shade. She was a long way from the army checkpoint now and had an excellent view of the countryside both behind and in front of her.

She was halfway through her paltry lunch when she heard the other bikers stop. She decided to wait until they started up again before moving off once more; she didn't want to catch them up. Itching to be on her way, it was nearly an hour before she heard her guides start again. She set off down the hill in pursuit. She soon came to a badly metalled road. It was in a very poor state of repair, but presumably had been constructed to facilitate military movements in the area. Tessa wasn't sure which way to go, but hadn't heard her scouts speed up as they surely would have if they had followed this road. So she checked all was clear and soon found a path similar to that she had been on. She took it and rode back into the dense forest.

She could see she had to climb another ridge now, but it was much lower than the one she'd just negotiated. She had already used all but one of her bottles of petrol and had less than three quarters of a tank of fuel left. If that wasn't enough, she'd have to walk the rest of the way. She pushed on and reached the brow of the hill as the light started to fail. She could see there was another valley to traverse, but it was neither as wide nor as high. She desperately hoped that she would be able to see Myawaddy from the other side of it.

She spotted the two motorbikes pushing on hard along the path as it wound its way down. Presumably the going was easier as they appeared to have speeded up. Tessa decided she would carry on until dusk and then find a safe place to spend the night. She hoped it wouldn't be necessary to spend too much more time in the open as she was running out of both food and water.

As the sun finally set, Tessa was pleased to find she was nearing the summit of the upcoming ridge. Keen to see what was on the other side, she carried on despite the going getting tougher. Just short of the top, she stopped her bike and walked the last few yards to look over. The two bikers in front of her were still moving, throwing up clouds of dust across the flat terrain. However, as she stretched her aching limbs, she felt positively euphoric and took a deep breath of exhausted satisfaction. To her right she saw a sprawling Burmese town, almost certainly Myawaddy, and nearby was a river: the River Moei, which marked the border between Burma and Thailand. In the quickly fading light it glistened like a not so unattainable silver snake.

Tessa decided to stop for the night and sat down, watching the numerous columns of smoke spiralling upwards into the sky as people started cooking their dinner. Eventually, the smoke thickened and merged with the deep blue heat haze. As the other bikers stopped, numerous electric lights were switched on across the river. These were noticeably lacking on the Burmese side. There was no doubt that she was looking into Thailand. Another few miles and she should be able to have a shower and a decent meal.

After a hasty breakfast, Tessa was impatient to get underway as soon as she could. However, she still didn't want to start before her scouts. So she decided to put her waiting time to good use by studying the countryside between her and the border. It seemed devoid of major roads and villages and she couldn't see any army checkpoints, but there was smoke rising from a few houses here and there. She waited until she heard the tell-tale sound of the other two engines and set off herself.

She was able to move down the hill quite quickly and was soon following the track across the plain towards where she knew the river lay. It seemed to go on for ever and Tessa quickened her pace; she was desperate to get out of Burma. Occasionally, she would have to slow down as she drove through a small cluster of wooden huts, but no one seemed the slightest bit interested in her. Ever conscious of her increased vulnerability as she neared the river, she pushed on as fast as she dared. Her bike's fuel gauge was well below a quarter now, but she wasn't worried. She was convinced she didn't have far to go and began to relax slightly, thinking about Khin and whether he had made it to safety. Then she started wondering again about why the Calver Cats wanted her so badly. Finally, she thought through what she could say to Nyunt...

Then she shot out from between the trees straight into a small clearing with several houses in it. She was extremely surprised and muttered some choice expletives, chiding herself for not having been more attentive. But she was committed, she had approached at breakneck speed and couldn't turn back; people had already looked up at her in surprise. She slowed down a little, partly out of respect and partly to give the impression that she was simply in a hurry.

Outside one of the huts were some women making rice noodles; sitting with them were three soldiers drinking tea. They seemed equally surprised to see Tessa and studied her suspiciously as she tried to hide the fact that she was watching them. They were two privates and a corporal. She hoped none of them had guns. The corporal stood up, apparently about to block Tessa's path. But then one of the women stopped working, said something to the man and offered him some more tea. He lost interest and Tessa drove past, quickly disappearing back into the woods. It took several minutes for her heart-rate to slow down again. She was very conscious of the fact she had no weapons and would have had no choice but to fight hand to hand, with the women as witnesses.

Not long afterwards she heaved a big sigh of relief as she arrived at the riverbank. The river itself wasn't particularly wide and, much to her delight as she'd never liked water, the dirty brown liquid didn't look particularly deep either. The bike-path she'd been following continued along the bank in both directions, but there was also a footpath leading straight down the steep incline towards the water.

She doubted it would be possible to take the bike across since even if should could get it down to the river, the bank on the other side was much steeper. She decided to abandon the vehicle since she didn't have much fuel and it was important that she got across quickly. If this wasn't the River Moei, she would have to make the last part of her journey on foot.

She rode the bike back into the trees and hid it in some dense bushes. Then she walked back to the riverbank and started down. Her slithering was interrupted by the sound of people approaching quickly from behind. They were booted feet, which Tessa presumed belonged to the soldiers she had just passed. She started bounding down the bank. As soon as she reached the river, she gritted her teeth and began wading through it. She was nearly halfway across when she tripped and fell head-first into the water, plunging completely beneath the surface. By the time she had stood up again, the soldiers were on the bank yelling at her to come back. They soon realised that she had absolutely no intention of either stopping or coming back, so one of them started down after her. Another drew a knife. Tessa slowly lumbered on towards the other bank while watching her pursuers over her shoulder. The soldier on the bank threw his knife at her.

Tessa had no choice but stop and turn as it was a truly excellent throw which would most definitely have proved lethal had she not reacted. She simply reached up and caught the knife by the blade. She flipped it over and gripped it by the tip. The soldier following her froze and the two on the bank went quiet. It seemed they knew she could quite easily kill any of them if she chose to.

However, it was one thing to kill someone who was in a position to kill her; it was quite another to kill someone who was simply following orders. These soldiers, none of whom looked to be out of their teens, were no real threat to her. She smiled and threw the knife back. It stuck harmlessly in a root jutting out from the riverbank beneath the man who had thrown it at her.

The soldiers did nothing more and Tessa was soon at the other side of the river. She staggered out of the water and started scrambling up the bank. But just as she hauled herself on to flat grass at the top she heard more troops coming. She ran forward heading for the cover of some nearby trees. As she dodged behind one, a gun fired and a bullet buried itself in the trunk she was leaning against. She didn't doubt that they would have followed her if they could, so it seemed likely she had made it to Thailand. She got her breath back and mused at how easy it had been for her to get out of Burma. The two bikers had acted as excellent guides and the small difficulty she had just experienced was nothing compared to what she'd been expecting. She had been lucky and was very grateful. She only hoped Khin had been equally fortunate.

She waited for several minutes, but there were no more shots and the sound of voices died down. When she carefully peered round the tree, it seemed all but two privates had left. Taking care to move quickly from covered position to covered position, she was soon far enough away from the river to feel safe. She sat down and drank the last of her water. She would have liked to have eaten something too but her remaining food had been soaked when she fell in the river. Her task now was to make her way to Mae Sot. She set off along what appeared to be the most frequently used path. It was midday and very hot, but the trees offered some shade until she came to a road. She still felt it likely that Mae Sot lay to her right, and carried on that way.

After another hour in the searing sun, she came to some houses and a small shop. She bought herself a small bunch of bananas, most of which she ate, and some more water. Then, following the directions she had been given, carried on walking. Finally, she found herself in Moei village. Not far away, she could see the ornate roof of a large monastery and heard the sound of a busy road. She took a deep breath and, after ten minutes more, was standing by the side of a dual carriageway. To her right was a large modern arch with "Freedom Bridge" on it in enormous letters. It clearly led from Thailand back across the river into Burma.

Tessa walked towards the bridge since she could see a number of shops and a rank of sǎwngthǎew there. Soon she was enjoying an excellent meal while admiring the river she had just forded. At first she had been the cause of considerable curiosity due to her bedraggled appearance and dirty, smelly clothes. But the primary concern in the restaurant was whether she could pay for her food, and she had plenty of money, even if it was still damp.

As soon as she had finished, she went across the road and bought some new clothes. Then she caught a săwngthăew into Mae Sot. That proved to be twenty-minute ride but Tessa was more than happy to relax on a bench in the back of the pickup together with the locals. It was a great relief no longer to feel hunted.

In Mae Sot, a typical lively border town, she soon found a place to stay and took a room at the Phannu Guest House; a quiet, clean family-run place set back from the road. Once in her room, the first priority was to spend a long time soaking herself under the glorious hot shower, after which she lay back on the bed and snoozed for an hour. When she woke, she put on her new clothes and went in search of the market. There, she purchased two good knives and walked to the restaurant she had been recommended to visit for dinner. It was early evening and the food at the Casa Mia proved excellent, enhanced by the friendly atmosphere. After another huge meal she relaxed, drinking tea, protected from the insects by several mosquito coils glowing nearby on the floor. Once more she wondered what had happened to Khin and Nyunt's birth certificate, assuming he really had found it. It was then that she discovered the picture of Nyunt which she had been given at the guest house north of Rangoon, had been seriously damaged when she fell in the river. She sighed, switched on the secure phone Curtis had given her and started thinking about what she should say to him. She'd have to own up to the fact that her incursion had pretty much been an unmitigated disaster. She had found out nothing of consequence about the Calver Cats' plans while many people had died helping in her search for Nyunt's relatives. While she was still deliberating, the phone rang.

"Hello," she said, tentatively. A metallic voice confirmed that the call was encrypted.

"Evening, Nariko," replied Curtis, "welcome back."

"Er... Hi, Curtis, how did you know I was back?" replied Tessa, sensing tension in his voice.

"It's a long story, I'll tell you when we meet. You're in Mae Sot?"

"Yes."

"OK. I'm already on my way, but it'll be early morning before we get there. I'll meet you at Canadian Dave's for breakfast; it's opposite the police compound in the centre of town, eastern corner. The coffee's really good. Seven-thirty all right?"

"Yes, of course, but…"

"Don't worry, I'll tell you everything tomorrow," interrupted Curtis, "I've got your sword case in the back, by the way."

Tessa was getting a bad feeling.

"Curtis, can't you tell me now what's going on?"

"There's no need, and I'm sure you'll be safe tonight. Get some sleep, I don't doubt you need it. Sorry, I've got a call from London coming through."

Tessa breathed out noisily.

"Hold on, have you heard anything from Khin?"

There was an awkward pause.

"Not a whisper. We know he was wounded in Moulmein, but we're not sure what happened after that. There is absolutely nothing you can do tonight, so just get some rest. I'll see you at Dave's."

The phone clicked and he was gone. Tessa was convinced something was wrong, and if the recent past was anything to go by, it was probably serious. But she trusted Curtis, and if he said there was nothing she could do, then there most likely wasn't. She might as well follow his advice, get some sleep and be fresh for whatever the morning would bring. She certainly was exhausted, and the prospect of a clean bed for the night was already beckoning her back to her room.

CHAPTER 8

Already apprehensive, Tessa arrived early at Canadian Dave's. The owner, unsurprisingly a Canadian expatriate called Dave, was a portly man with a ruddy complexion and thick black-framed glasses. He was busy arranging some tables on the pavement and greeted Tessa warmly. He gestured her to sit at one of the outside ones. She sat with her back to the restaurant, watching the people, tuk-tuks, pick-ups and spotlessly clean NGO SUVs passing by.

Then a smart if dusty Range Rover drove in to the police compound opposite. Standard UK Special Services issue, thought Tessa. One of the heavily tinted windows rolled down and she glimpsed four tough-looking men inside. Two more Range Rovers appeared. One passed by and parked at the other end of the road while the last stopped near to where Tessa was sitting. Curtis got out. He put on some dark sunglasses, appearing both tired and nervous.

"Hello," he greeted her. "I hope you slept well, I've been on the road all night."

"Morning," replied Tessa guardedly. "I slept like a log. But that was to be expected after two nights under the stars sharing my body with a trillion insects..."

Curtis handed her a menu.

"The usual?" asked Dave, barely glancing at him.

"Please," he replied. "But bring some coffee first."

"What's going on?" asked Tessa, not bothering to look at the menu.

Curtis sighed.

"Shit, tons of it. Choose your breakfast while I swallow some wake-up juice. Then we can swap war stories."

Tessa felt the pressure of something large and malevolent bearing down on her. She ordered some food and sat in silence. As soon as Curtis had emptied his first coffee he waved his mug at Dave to order a refill.

Tessa could contain herself no longer. She looked at Curtis, expectant and demanding.

"Hmm," he smiled, removing his glasses. "You first."

She described what had happened to her. How Khin had met her in Rangoon, how they'd dispatched decoys and overnighted at the guest house. She laid the crumpled remains of her photograph on the table. It made her want to weep just looking at it. She shook her head in despair, her expression reflecting the sadness and guilt she felt.

"It was a bloodbath," she acknowledged in exasperation. "They were after me within hours of my arrival, and were throwing everything they had at us. Even Khin said he hadn't experienced anything like it. I cannot believe how many people died just because I wanted to get hold of Nyunt's birth certificate, and all I have is that." She gestured towards the ruined photograph. "I suspect Khin found the certificate, but I know he was seriously wounded. I tried to cover his escape, but I've no idea whether he made it."

Curtis reached out for the photo as their breakfasts arrived.

"Let me take this. I'll see if our technical guys can do anything with it. Who knows? It may still be relevant."

Tessa nodded and started eating, while Curtis ordered yet another coffee.

"Trust me," he said, smiling at Tessa's surprise that he had tackled three large mugs of extremely strong coffee, "I need the caffeine."

They both ate in silence. When they'd finished, and Curtis's next coffee had arrived, he looked at her and took a deep breath.

"Remember I told you Potter was coming over for our annual review?" Tessa nodded. "Well, he arrived late yesterday afternoon. I sent a car to meet him. He doesn't like it if I go myself; says I should have more important things to do than act as his personal limo service. So, I sent Diedrick, she was your double in Bangkok. It's standard practice for the driver to stay in the locked vehicle while she finds whoever. When she and Potter came out, Nyunt suddenly appeared from another SUV and beckoned them over giving every impression of wanting to talk. They both went and were immediately surrounded. Diedrick managed to issue a *UAR* signal but was then stabbed in the thigh. Potter was shot with some sort of a dart and our Range Rover was covered with a metallised tarpaulin. According to Diedrick, Potter collapsed and was bundled into the people carrier

Nyunt had arrived in; she got back into it of her own volition. Then one of the guys gave Diedrick this note with instructions to give it to me."

He passed Tessa a blood-stained piece of paper.

"Is Diedrick OK?"

"She lost quite a lot of blood, but she's as tough as they come. She'll be fine."

Tessa nodded and unfolded the paper.

Good evening Mr Curtis,

What with all the bad news you're getting, you might be pleased to hear that Nariko has made it to Mae Sot. She's taken a room at the Phannu Guest House and is currently eating at the Casa Mia restaurant. But don't worry, she will be permitted to sleep safely tonight.

However, if you want your boss and the Peacekeeper back alive, tell Nariko she needs to be at the pagoda in Waley at 9 p.m. tomorrow. She should come alone, with her swords. If she is not there on time, or there are any tricks, the hostages will be killed.

Calver Cats

Tessa re-read the note.

"Where's Waley?" she asked quietly, expecting the worst.

"Just across the border inside Burma, about two hours south of here."

"What the hell do these bastards want from me?" she moaned.

"Beats me," replied Curtis. "But it includes your swords, and whatever else it is, it's big. Nobody goes to the trouble of kidnapping a Head of Special Forces lightly; there are bound to be serious repercussions. But whether we like it or not, we're still being tossed around in the storm like a wet leaf."

"Oh dear! Well, I suppose…."

No way!" exclaimed Curtis. "I've just lost my boss. I'm not going to lose a Peacekeeper too."

"What choice do we have? And they have my daughter too."

"Nyunt is no longer of concern to me. I understand you might not want to hear this, but I am not the only one who's questioning her loyalty. Maybe you should reprioritise and worry about yourself."

"Curtis, she's not herself. Someone has got at her... She was probably being forced to do what she did yesterday."

"Possibly, but I don't want you exchanging yourself for Potter. Neither does London, and I don't doubt that Potter wouldn't want it either."

"But if the Calver Cats wanted money or something, they'd have left the door open for negotiations. It's clear that I'm the only thing they'll settle for. Too many people have died for this, I'm not going to let Potter's name be added to the list."

"So you want to hand yourself over to the Calver Cats, in Burma? That's worse than suicide. Forget it, I won't let you go."

Tessa smiled.

"It's good of you to be concerned, I'm truly touched. But we both know you can't stop me. However, you have all today to come up with an alternative, and trust me, I sincerely hope you do. But if you don't, then I will try to free them both. Who knows? Maybe I'll be able to get away too. If not, I'm sure you and Potter will do everything possible to rescue me."

"They'll kill you."

"Only if I'm lucky... In Moulmein, one of the soldiers had a pretty clear shot at me but was ordered not to fire because they needed me alive. I suspect they've something far nastier planned for me, and it looks as though I'm about to find out what it is."

Curtis pensively drank some more of his coffee.

"Hmm. I wouldn't have expected you to say anything else, but I really don't think it's a good idea. Brave, but foolhardy... In fact, not even remotely sensible on any level."

"I agree. But presumably that's why you brought so much support with you," suggested Tessa with a wry smile. "Map?"

Curtis breathed out heavily, opened his bag and laid a large-scale map on the table.

"Waley is about forty minutes past Phop Phra. As I said, it's just over the border from Thailand. It's a dingy little place with a hundred plus long-term residents. There's quite a sizeable monastery though; one has to walk past it up the hill to get to the pagoda, which is here." He pointed to a black arrow-like symbol on the map. "Waley used to be a major crossing point for all sorts of black-market goods but then the Karen were daft enough to allow the SPDC, as it was then, to split them into two factions, the DKBA and the KNLA. After that it was easy for the SPDC to do a deal with the DKBA, convince them to kill the KNLA, and then double-cross them. As a result, Karen territory now covers only a fraction of what it used to, and Waley has declined with it. It's very run-down and as poor as most other villages in Burma. The land is heavily mined.

"There are three obvious river crossings," he continued, indicating locations on the map. "One with a Thai army post, here, one where you need to wade through the river, and another with a rickety old bridge. That's the most obvious one to use as the path from it leads directly through the village and up to the pagoda.

"I am still trying to locate Potter and get him out through other means, legitimate or otherwise. But if that fails and you're determined to go through with the exchange, then we'll need to leave here at six."

Tessa studied the map, sat back in her chair, and sighed.

"Wonderful. Seems straightforward enough."

Curtis finished his coffee and produced a thick, bluntly pointed metal cylinder from his bag.

"This thing pneumatically injects a tracking transponder. It's mandatory for all Special Forces field operatives. I have one, and so did Potter. Unfortunately, they are fairly easy to detect and remove; Potter's' was rendered inoperative less than twenty minutes after he was abducted. As you know, Peacekeepers don't have them, but if you're interested…?"

Tessa picked up the cylinder, studied it briefly and looked quizzically at him.

"Just place the sharp end where you want the sensor to be inserted and press the button. I would suggest one of your thighs…"

Before Curtis could say anything else, Tessa had placed the cylinder on her left leg and pressed the button; eliciting a loud *psssst!* She looked up at him with a shocked expression on her face. He burst out laughing.

"I was going to say," he added, "it stings like hell."

"Wow, I'll say! Anything else we need to do now?"

"Well, actually, yes, assuming you're up for it."

He took back the cylinder and loaded another metallic slug.

"You've just injected the transponder they'll find quickly. You could inject another where it will take longer."

"And where exactly do you have in mind?"

"Armpit, other side. But I warn you, it really does hurt; passes quickly though."

"Oh, wonderful," said Tessa, taking the injector from him. She pressed it up into her left armpit, pressed the button, and grunted. "Goodness gracious! I hope you don't want me to install any more of those things?"

"No. Two should suffice." He looked up at the Range Rover parked in the police compound. A man's hand came out of the window to wave at them. Then it held up two fingers. "Good, they're working. So, assuming the Calver Cats do take you tonight, we will be able to track you, hopefully for quite a while. That will enable us to focus our efforts on getting you back… So, what are you going to do for the rest of today?"

"Dunno. Write my Will?" replied Tessa, trying to lighten the atmosphere.

"Probably a good idea," replied Curtis quickly. "Do you need any help with that?"

"I was joking," retorted Tessa.

"Oh, I wasn't."

"Great. I'll be fine."

"OK. Well, I'm going to be busy getting clearances for my guys from the Tak Regional Police. But if you need me, give me a ring. Otherwise, I'll meet you here at four for an early dinner."

"See you later, then," said Tessa, standing.

"Do you want your gear?"

"No. I don't think anything horrible is going to happen to me before this evening."

CHAPTER 9

Tessa wiled away the day by wandering aimlessly. The time before a Mission action was always psychologically challenging. She hated the inevitability of violence during which she would usually be forced to kill in order to survive. Furthermore, on this occasion, she felt even her normal declining odds of returning intact were remarkably good compared to the likelihood that she would not make it back to Thailand. The Calver Cats had tried everything to capture her in Burma, and failed; they would surely not let her slip through their grasp this time. The best she could hope for was that she would be able to free Potter, and that he would manage to rescue her later, assuming she was still alive.

Also, there was Nyunt to consider. It was very worrying that the Special Forces were no longer sure which side she was on. Even Tessa had to admit that she couldn't understand much of what her daughter had done recently, but still she couldn't accept that a voluntary change of sides had taken place. There was something wrong with Nyunt. Maybe Tessa would find out what in Waley...

Eventually, she sat down again at Canadian Dave's. Curtis joined her. She was not surprised to find that, despite his best efforts, the situation hadn't changed. She would have to go through with the exchange.

It was 8:30 p.m. when the Range Rover stopped at the bottom of a stony track. Curtis glanced round from the front passenger seat as the two support vehicles stopped behind them. All three cars had switched off their lights as they'd left the metalled road a few minutes earlier. The track passed between two rows of ramshackle wooden houses and led down to the river marking the border between Thailand and Burma. The same river Tessa had negotiated further north to escape the Calver Cats.

"Hmm. That went disappointingly quickly," she remarked.

98

Curtis smiled apologetically and issued some orders to the occupants of the other two vehicles. Eight burly men got out and started scouring the area, soon confirming that the coast was clear.

Tessa took a deep breath and stepped out. In the moonlit night, all the houses she could see were unnaturally dark. She wasn't sure who had told the occupants to abandon their homes, but couldn't help concluding it was probably a wise precaution. If a conflict arose as a result of her trying to free Potter and Nyunt, it would be better if there were no innocent bystanders nearby.

She adjusted her knives, lifted out her double sword case and slung it onto her shoulder.

"Aren't you going to wear your swords?" asked Curtis in surprise.

"No. I don't understand why they want me, but they certainly want my swords too. This case is booby-trapped. If they get me, with a bit of luck they still won't get my swords. In fact, just between you, me and the gate post, there's only one inside anyway – call it insurance. Suffice to say, the case does have a quick release mechanism. I can get at the contents if I need to."

Curtis nodded and spoke to one of his team. They were all fighting men, incredibly fit, but not armed with anything other than truncheons and knives, as required by international law these days

Tessa looked at her watch, sighed, undid the strap and passed it to Curtis.

"You'd better hold on to this. If I don't come back, they could use it to prove I entered illegally."

He nodded and started conferring in hushed tones with his men. Tessa looked round. The settlement comprised a dozen or so wooden houses and a general store, all very run down. Where there were window shutters, they had been closed. There wasn't even a motorbike to be seen, just a rusting, rather odd-looking stretched three-wheeled tractor. It was as though an epidemic had passed through the village and all its residents had fled, or were lying dead in their houses. The only sound was of fast-flowing water which Tessa could tell was passing not far in front of where Curtis' Range Rover had stopped.

She adjusted her black track-suit and the wide belt through which her two knives passed. Curtis joined her.

"Our Ambassadors in Thailand and Burma are on stand-by, as is our representative to the United Nations for World Peace. There's not much more we can do now since we can't prove who took Potter or where he's being held. But if you do free him from Burma, an official complaint will be lodged immediately. With a bit of luck, we might even be able to convene an emergency UNWP meeting. If you are captured too, we'll do everything we can to get all three of you back."

"Thanks," noted Tessa tersely.

She walked forward to the last building and followed the path round to the left where she paused to assess the scene. She could see the river in the moonlight. It was about twenty feet wide with a rickety single-file bridge which started in front of her. The crude structure comprised two pairs of parallel tree trunks, one couple sloping up from the Thai side, the other from Burma. Across the tree trunks were some sparsely positioned roughly hewn planks, about three feet long. In the middle of the bridge, where the trunks had been forced together, there was a step more than a foot high and a rudimentary wooden archway to mark the border. To add rigidity, the bridge was secured to trees on both sides of the river.

Tessa scrutinised the crossing's primitive construction with a mixture of apprehension and disdain. It aptly marked the transition point between safety in Thailand and certain, as yet undefined, danger in Burma. Suddenly, there was a humming and spluttering sound in the distance. On a hill not far away lights illuminated a Burmese-style pagoda. The dull yellow glow developed into a brilliant white light, clearly illuminating the pagoda's gold-leaf covering. As she stared at this new feature in the otherwise barren darkness, a cold shiver ran down her spine. Curtis joined her.

"Nariko, this is madness. I really wish you wouldn't go."

"Trust me, I really don't want to. But the invitation seems clear enough."

"Supposing they won't release Potter or Nyunt?"

"Then I promise you, Curtis, an awful lot of them will die tonight."

"And even if they are freed, what about you? This is unlikely to be a Sydney Carton moment. The guillotine would probably be a mercy."

"Thanks for that, Curtis," replied Tessa with a wry smile. "But look at it from another perspective. You have children, don't you?"

"Yes, three."

"Congratulations. What wouldn't you be willing to do to save their lives? Besides, I promised Htet, whom I'm absolutely positive was Nyunt's father, that I would do as much for her as I possibly could. I'm not going to fail him."

"I understand all that," beseeched Curtis, "but Nyunt's grown up. She's a woman now and old enough to make her own choices. You've already given her much more than Htet could ever have dreamed possible. Maybe we don't know how or why, but she's got herself well and truly mixed up in this, and created one hell of a nightmare for you."

Tessa sighed, not absolutely sure he was wrong.

"Something or someone is making her behave this way. She is a good person, Curtis. She'll prove it to you one day."

"OK. But as I said, Potter would be dead against your doing this," he continued, in a last ditch attempt to persuade her not to go.

Tessa realised she was close to tears. She felt as if the whole world was bearing down on her and there was no escape from being crushed. There was little doubt that her future looked bleak, and she was afraid, very afraid. But she still had to try and rescue Potter and Nyunt.

"I'd better be off... I mustn't be late to meet my own destiny," she croaked, clearing her throat. "Thanks for everything, Curtis. I'll do my very best to get them back to you. Hoot once if you've got Nyunt and another twice for Potter. If I can come out too, I will. But if not, I would appreciate anything you can do to extract me."

"Don't worry," he replied firmly, "that I can absolutely guarantee." He took a deep breath. "Go over the bridge and follow the path through the bushes. Don't stray off it, we've detected minefields to both sides. When you come to a shallow stream, walk through. It's little more than a deep puddle and there are more mines around there too. Carry on into the village. When you come to the main street, cross straight over and continue up the hill. You'll be able to see the monastery on your right as you climb. The pagoda will be visible in front of you for most of the way. Good luck."

Tessa checked that the bank opposite was quiet, smiled resignedly at Curtis's worried expression, and mounted the bridge. She hesitated in front of the doorframe as if it marked the entrance to hell, but then she passed through back into Burma. She had no difficulty finding the path and soon arrived at the shallow stream; it was about two feet wide but only inches deep. She walked on, passed some wooden houses and stopped near the main street. A few of the houses had flickering candlelight visible, but not many. Most were completely dark and gave no indication as to whether anyone was inside or not, but she felt sure she was being watched. She carried on up the hill. A sprawling run-down monastery lay to her right in which she could see the dull glow from oil lanterns hanging from ceiling hooks. But otherwise there was nothing to suggest anyone was there. Meanwhile, the brightly illuminated pagoda grew larger.

Finally, she stopped short of the summit and studied the lie of the land. The pagoda was not large by Burmese standards, but, at some forty feet tall, was bigger than she'd expected. It had a white hexagonal concrete base, each face containing an alcove. The ones she could see contained vases of dead or dying flowers. The top two-thirds of the structure had been embellished with gold paint, not gold-leaf as she had supposed. Close to its pinnacle was a makeshift wooden frame to which some flickering light bulbs had been secured. The pagoda was located at one end of an elliptical flat area, covered with shorn grass. Although the pagoda was comprehensively floodlit, the ground around it only benefited from reflected light. So despite being sure that the path she had used would not be the only access, it was impossible for her to see where the others were. Furthermore, the sides of the hill were quite steep and would make for a difficult descent in the darkness. She heard some shuffling from the other side of the pagoda; and shrugging her shoulders edged her way forward to investigate.

She found Potter sitting on the ground, his hands tied behind him. His ankles were also bound. Nyunt was sitting near him, but her hands and legs appeared to be unsecured. Approaching silently from behind, Tessa was cutting Potter's hands free before he realised she was there.

"Keep quiet, both of you," whispered Tessa.

"Nariko," sighed Potter, "I do wish you hadn't come."

"Well, I can assure you this wasn't my first choice for tonight's entertainment."

Suddenly, there were several loud *twangs* as poles pivoted up from the undergrowth all around the top of the hill. On them were large spotlights which burst into life. Now the entire hilltop was bathed in brilliant white light and people started pouring onto the summit from all sides. Tessa was trapped and vastly outnumbered. She moved round to cut Potter's legs free. Then she looked at Nyunt.

"Hello, darling, I've missed you."

Nyunt looked back at her and there was a momentary glimmer of recognition in her eyes.

"Mother, I can't...," she started to say.

"Welcome, Nariko," sneered a man's voice. "Pleased to see you're punctual."

Tessa stood up; Potter and Nyunt followed her example. The three of them were surrounded by some forty men positioned strategically around the perimeter of the elliptical clearing. Their leader was standing about twelve feet in front of Tessa. Wearing scruffy jeans and a tee-shirt, he was sporting a sophisticated wireless headset and camera.

"And who might you be?" demanded Tessa.

"That's not important. Discard your weapons."

"I'm not going to do anything of the sort until these two are safely back in Thailand. That's the deal, isn't it?"

The man paused, apparently waiting for instructions.

"No negotiations, discard your weapons."

"I'm not negotiating. Have a word with that cowardly boss of yours who doesn't even dare show himself and tell him that he's going to have to let Potter and Nyunt go. Otherwise, you've got a very messy situation on your hands."

"You can't kill us all."

"Oh, don't be too sure about that, but one thing is certain, you won't be around to see," replied Tessa, relaxed and ready.

Again the man waited for instructions.

"OK, they can leave. But no funny business or you all die."

Tessa turned back to Potter.

"Time for you to go home. It takes about five minutes. Follow the path down the hill, past the monastery and straight across the main street. When you come to the shallow stream, walk straight through it. Don't stray, the land is mined to either side of the path. Once through the bushes you'll find a rickety old bridge with a doorframe on it. Go over and you'll be back in Thailand. Curtis is waiting. Nyunt, go with Potter."

"No, I… You mustn't…"

"You want to stay with me?" asked Tessa in surprise.

"Er… Always. Not here... It's just..."

"You're not making sense, dear."

"I don't think I can leave."

Tessa sighed.

"Nyunt, I would like you to go with Potter now, and that's final."

"No, I…"

Like lightning, Tessa punched her on the jaw; she collapsed like a rag doll. Potter caught her as she fell.

"Sorry, Potter, it looks as though you're going to have to carry her."

The man behind Tessa roared with laughter.

"Now we know how Peacekeepers resolve family disputes!"

Tessa ignored him.

"Good-bye, Potter."

"No, Nariko," he replied, lifting Nyunt over his shoulder, "this is not good-bye, only *au revoir*. Don't ever lose hope, I will find you."

"I sincerely hope so," replied Tessa, a slight tremor in her voice. "The path down starts over there."

She pointed to where he was to go, and some men moved aside to let him to pass. Potter calmly walked away and disappeared from view.

Scanning the disposition of the people around her, Tessa turned back to face their leader. There were a number of guns, several swords and a lot of knives. She would have difficulty defeating them all, but felt confident she could take out a lot of them. She considered whether she would prefer to die trying rather than be taken alive. However, she dare not start anything until she knew Potter and Nyunt had reached Curtis and safety. Otherwise all three of them might still be killed.

"So why's your boss too scared to come here himself?" she asked.

It was the man's turn to remain silent. She smiled, and started moving back towards the pagoda.

"Stay where you are!" he barked. Tessa ignored him and continued moving, sliding her sword case off her shoulder. She stood it on the ground in front of her, within easy reach.

Two people started closing in from behind; she looked round and saw that both had drawn guns.

Suddenly, there was a long blast from a car horn, then a pause, and two more.

"That, I presume, means your lot have arrived safely," conceded the man. "We've kept our part of the bargain, so now you keep yours. Discard your weapons, Peacekeeper Nariko."

Once more, Tessa weighed up her options. This was a battle she could not win; but should she fight it anyway, or hopefully live to fight another day?

"Discard them now!" barked the man. The men around her readied themselves.

Before they could react, Tessa drew both knives and tossed them over her shoulder high in the air. They stuck in the wood supporting the lights on the pagoda top. There was an abrupt flash, and the sound of splintering glass as some of the cables fell. Then the man sighed.

"I suppose that'll do. Now, take six paces towards me, away from the sword case."

Tessa took a deep breath. This was purgatory for her. It was also her last chance to try and take control. The case was still booby trapped; she could open it in such a way as to ensure it exploded. She would die, but so would a lot of the other people there.

"Six paces forward," repeated the man. It was only then that Tessa noticed a number of video cameras filming her every move.

"Who's watching?" she asked.

"Bugger me! Take six paces forward, I won't ask again," he demanded irritably.

Tessa made her decision and took five paces forward. She could hear her sword case being removed. She was defenceless now, except for her bare hands.

"OK, she's ready, Doktor," he advised.

A man in a white coat came into view from the side of the hill furthest from the pagoda. He was shorter than her, about five foot five tall, balding, with a sweaty sunburned face. He approached Tessa, looking her up and down, and smiled.

"How much do you weigh?" he asked in a strong German accent.

"*Schwäbisch?*" observed Tessa. "Fancy that. All the way from Baden-Württemberg; near Stuttgart, I think?"

For moment the Doktor looked taken-aback.

"I do not need to answer your questions."

"And I do not need to answer yours."

"As you wish. I will guess for now and weigh you later."

He raised a bottle of clear fluid and filled a syringe. Then he flicked it a couple of times and ejected a stream high into the air until the amount he wanted remained. Then he turned to Tessa.

"Just a little prick."

"We all have our problems, Herr Doktor. But trust me, yours are just beginning."

"Oh, I don't think so," he replied. Four enormous men approached. They weren't quite Sumo size, but close. Two grabbed her arms while the others held her legs. She was completely unable to move.

"Then you won't mind telling me your name, first."

The man smiled.

"Why not? I am supremely confident. Krollheim is my name."

"Then be afraid, Herr Doktor Krollheim," hissed Tessa, "I will come for you."

"No, you won't," he replied. "*Guts Nächtle*, Frau Doktor Pennington."

Tessa felt a sharp scratch as the needle entered her shoulder muscle. As he pressed the plunger, a loud rushing sound filled her ears. Then there was a bright flash and her vision became blurred and yet enhanced with swirling vibrant hues. The grass transformed into an iridescent orange, while the sky turned bright mauve. Tessa was worried she might have a rather daft grin on her face.

The Doktor pulled open the eyelids of her right eye, so he could study her pupil size. Then he smiled and gestured the men to release her. She stood stock-still, marvelling at the now pulsating colours of the scene before her. She could see men rushing around, but none of them seemed to be bothered about her.

Then someone came up to her and raised a meter of some sort. Tessa couldn't hear what he said, but thought it might have been "two".

Meanwhile, Tessa was trying to instruct herself to run away, but none of her muscles were interested in reacting and her thought processes were rapidly becoming catatonic. Suddenly her strength drained away and her legs started to buckle. She was grabbed by two men and was vaguely aware of being half marched, half dragged, down the hill. Then she was bundled in to a helicopter. As the engine began to turn, she lost consciousness.

Half a mile away, Potter and Curtis were feverishly weighing up the consequences of an illegal incursion into Burma. They had enough men, but were conscious that at least some of the land was mined.

"Bugger it, Curtis, green light! I'll handle the political flak. I'm not leaving her over there without a fight."

Curtis nodded and his men started over the bridge.

"Stop!" yelled the leader as he passed through the doorframe. "New mines activated." He had spotted myriad red laser beams now criss-crossing the path on the Burmese side.

Then the floodlights illuminating the pagoda went out and the sound of a helicopter engine starting up broke the relative silence.

"Damn! We're too late," groaned Potter. "But she won't be dead yet, they wanted her alive."

Muttering expletives, he climbed in to the passenger seat of Curtis's Range Rover. The woman who had been driving was busy strapping Nyunt into one of the seats.

"I'll tell you one thing, Curtis," said Potter picking up the telephone handset. "You're right about Nariko's right jab. I'd hate to be at the receiving end... Yes, Potter here, get me our Burma Ambassador, please, then our UNWP rep in New York. Oh, and after that, Oberst Müller in Berlin. Thanks."

"Müller is Nariko's other Guardian. I'm sure Germany will be keen to support us in lobbying for her release. By the way, have you got a transponder injector?"

"Yes, sir. Nariko gave herself two, we're tracking them now. It looks as though she's being taken to Hpa An."

"OK. While Nyunt's out, give her a transponder too, will you?" Curtis looked doubtful; people had to give their permission before such a device could legally be installed. "Look, everyone knows she's deeply entangled in this, but I believe that somehow, it's against her will. So, from now on, I want to know where she is. And don't tell her you installed it."

Curtis shrugged, went round to Nyunt in the back of the car and injected a locator upwards into her left armpit.

The phone rang and Potter started the first of several urgent calls. He was determined to do everything he could to get Tessa back, quickly and safely. He even started considering what it might be possible to do to ensure she could not be taken out of Burma.

CHAPTER 10

Slowly, Tessa became aware of consciousness returning. She didn't need to open her eyes to know she was in a very hot and humid place. Foremost in her mind, though, was the splitting headache she had which was being exacerbated by a very loud buzzing, like tinnitus from a jack-hammer. She even tried placing her hands over her ears hoping to reduce the discomfort, but it didn't. As she eased her eyes open, the bright light which flooded in was excruciatingly painful, so she slammed them shut again. Gradually, she became aware of a chinking noise close by; someone was drinking from a glass with ice in it.

"Oh, do hurry up," a man said. The voice sounded familiar but she couldn't hear clearly enough to place it. "I don't want to be sitting here all day, it'll be boiling soon."

Goaded on by this, she took her hands off her ears and used them to shade her eyes as she opened them. As her brain cleared she recognised who it was, and sighed. She took a deep breath and managed to sit up awkwardly.

"I thought you'd be up to your neck in this, Paul," she said with disdain.

"Really? Well, congratulations. Not that your sixth sense is going to help you now. Anyway, I believe you have the mother of all migraines?"

Tessa pivoted round on her mattress, shaking her head and breathing out noisily as if to confirm what he'd suggested. It was still unpleasantly bright, but she could see Paul sitting by a table barely six paces away. As usual he was immaculately dressed in a light blue short-sleeved shirt, cream slacks and polished brown leather brogue shoes. He was slightly tanned and grinning at her from behind reflective designer sunglasses.

"I presume you know that because you were instrumental in supplying it?" she accused testily, flexing her muscles to check she could move them all.

"Not personally," he replied, "but I take your point… Now, if you're trying to work out whether you can get to me fast enough, I'm afraid the answer is *no*. You see Rod, better known as Rhino Rod for obvious reasons, will most definitely stop you. In fact, I suspect he'd rather like you to try, but I really wouldn't recommend it. He's not known for his self-control."

Squinting, Tessa twisted round to survey the area. She was surprised to find she was still near the pagoda at Waley, but it looked as though it was mid-morning. Within easy striking distance stood a very strong-looking man in jeans and a red tee-shirt with a gold dragon motif on it; he was repeatedly clenching his fists together and leering at her.

"…The good news," continued Paul, "and there isn't much of that in your case, is that I have a glass of cold water and some paracetamol for you. Interested?"

"Is it only water and paracetamol?"

"How distrustful you are…"

In an instant, Tessa rolled off her bed and took two paces towards the man called Rod. Apparently, unperturbed, he didn't move a muscle. She reached out with her left hand to prevent him from backing away and punched him hard in the chest. Much to her surprise, he fell like a sack of potatoes. It had been a powerful punch but one that was designed to wind and stun, certainly nothing more for a man of Rod's stature.

But then, like a curtain of water falling away from before her eyes, Tessa's image of her environment changed completely and she could hardly believe what she was seeing. She was standing in a barred cage, which itself stood in the middle of what looked like a sandy prison compound. There were bedraggled prisoners watching her from all sides in complete silence. Paul burst into laughter.

"Peacekeeper kills ageing defenceless Buddhist monk in Burma, with her bare hands," he spluttered. "Now there's a memorable headline!"

Tessa looked down. At her feet lay a monk, dressed in dirty, torn, saffron-coloured robes. He was old, bruised from previous beatings, and emaciated; but most importantly of all, he was not breathing.

"Oh, no!" she groaned.

She kneeled down, rolled the monk onto his back and put his arms by his sides. Then she sat astride him and started pumping his chest to the rhythm of the Bee Gees song "*Stayin' Alive*", interspersing this with regular bouts of mouth-to-mouth resuscitation. Paul was beside himself with laughter. However, he stopped abruptly when the monk coughed and opened his eyes. Tessa rolled him into the recovery position and assured him he would be all right. Eventually, she reversed a respectful distance away, and, kneeling, put her hands together and bowed deeply to him.

"I am very sorry," she said apologetically. "Please forgive me. I would never knowingly strike anyone who was not intending violence against me, and I had to touch you to bring you back."

The man, clearly surprised to be alive, sat up and smiled at her.

"Do not be concerned," he replied in broken English. "It was clear you did not see *me*... and you hardly need my forgiveness for returning my life."

"*Kyay zu tin bar de*," said Tessa. Once more she put her hands together and bowed until her head touched the ground. But then she started to feel extremely nauseous. She sat up with a puzzled expression on her face.

"Oh, dear. Ready to puke, are we? There's a bowl under your gurney. I would strongly recommend you get to it quickly."

Tessa dived for the stainless-steel dish and began vomiting noisily. Paul started laughing again.

"I do just *love* being in control," he spluttered.

While she was being sick, Tessa heard some guards enter her enclosure and lead the monk away. Then she saw Paul pick up his *cbc*. She desperately strained to listen to what was being said. His call was answered with "*moshi-moshi*", the usual telephone greeting in Japan. However, her efforts to hear what was being said were interrupted by more bouts of painful retching.

"Hi, she's awake... Oh, yes, tell them it worked like a dream, she downed the old codger with a single punch... Yeah, but they got the hypnotic instruction wrong... They told her to kill him, and when he was dead, see where she really was. But they didn't say she couldn't revive the bugger. Took her a good five minutes, but she bloody did it... Yeah, I think it's funny too, but the camp commandant'll be pissed – he'll have to do his own dirty work now... Oh, half the prison saw it… Yeah, she's busy puking her guts out… Hah! Don't you worry, I intend to."

Finally, Tessa got shakily to her feet. Paul placed a white capsule and a glass of water on a horizontal support strengthening the prison bars. He backed away and gestured her to take it.

She walked over to the shelf and picked up both. She smelled the contents of the glass, held it up to the sun to study it and cautiously sampled it. Then she gulped down the rest and looked at Paul. He was picking up his gin and tonic, so she flicked the capsule neatly into his glass.

"Prefer your headache do you? Suit yourself," he mocked, downing the drink. "I confess, I partook of a tad too much wine last night thinking about all the fun we're going to have together, so the paracetamol is most welcome."

He returned to his chair under an umbrella and poured himself some water. Then he gestured imperiously for a young woman to remove the bowl Tessa had been using. Two armed soldiers stood by the door while a third unlocked it. Clearly nervous, the woman came in and took the dish. As she was hurrying back to the door Tessa spoke to her in Burmese.

"*Kyay zu tin bar de.* It is always the women who have to do the unpleasant work. I am sorry you must clear up for me."

The girl spun round, shocked.

"No problem," she said with a smile, bowing.

"You're such a fucking show-off," hissed Paul, interrupting the moment. "Shall I have her whipped for talking to you?"

"No, please don't."

"Since you said please, I won't… This time. Anyway, take a seat. We're going to have a chat."

"No, thanks, just release me."

"Don't be silly, you know that's not going to happen. Now, I presume you found that murderous little episode you just experienced convincing? On this occasion the illusion was only temporary, but later, well, that'll be another matter. I hope you're impressed? It's taken many years, significant resources and a lot of human guinea pigs to perfect this treatment. We wanted to give you a glimpse of what it'll be like living in the world we're sending you to. You see, consciousness represents only a tiny proportion of human brain activity. Control the rest and it's a trivial matter to alter someone's perceived environment and influence the way they make decisions and respond to different stimuli. Soon you won't even know that you're in an imaginary world, just as you didn't a couple of minutes ago. As we extinguish your conscious self and replace it with a new, more compliant version, you'll lose your self-awareness and become completely pliant. Look on the bright side, it's only the death of the self which awaits you now, not bodily death. Exciting stuff, isn't it?"

Tessa didn't say anything. She simply sucked in her breath and studied the cage. It was rectangular in shape and made from substantial steel bars, which also formed the roof over which some bamboo mats had been spread to provide shade. At one end was a rudimentary shower and chemical toilet; at the other was the door secured with a substantial padlock. The only other item of furniture was her bed. It resembled a hospital gurney, capable of having its height adjusted and headrest raised and lowered. On top of it was an integral thin mattress with a stained dark green leatherette cover. Ominously, a number of webbing restraints were dangling down from the frame.

"Paul, where are my clothes?"

"Oh, you don't have any. In fact, you don't have anything, any more. Out of the goodness of my heart, I lent you that tee-shirt," he replied, clearly enjoying the situation. "So be appreciative or I might just take it back."

"Come in and try," taunted Tessa.

"I will. Come in, that is. But rest assured, Nariko," he sneered, his tone hardening, "I won't ever *try* to do anything to you. I will do what I want, when I want. The sooner you accept that, the better it will be for you."

"I thought you were a creep from the outset, Paul. But I have to admit, I hadn't realised quite how warped you are."

Paul sighed.

"Maybe your first few doses have made you a little hard of hearing. I'll give you another brief heads up, but don't expect me to repeat this again. It is important that you understand and accept that your world has changed. I know this will be difficult for you, what with you being such a frigging control freak, but it is an indisputable fact. Just as you had absolutely no control of anything that happened to you after Waley, you have no control now and you won't ever again. What you eat, what you drink and what you wear are just a few of the more rudimentary examples." He started fiddling with a portable video player. "By definition this includes how you spend your time. Did you know, it's Sunday today?" he added, waving a Thai newspaper at her.

Tessa had assumed she'd woken up the day after she had been abducted. But if was Sunday, what had happened to Saturday?

"Oh, my word! Now, this is a really good bit," exclaimed Paul. "I'm not sure you'll approve, but indulge me for a moment and take a peek at this." He waved her away and placed the video player on the horizontal bar. She advanced quickly towards it, prompting him to step back hastily. She smiled and picked up the player, reversing back to her bed. Sitting down on the edge, she shaded the small screen with her hand so she could see more clearly. Her eyes widened. Incredulous and dismayed, she raised the device to eye-level. She was dumbstruck as she studied the moving images. All she could do was shake her head backwards and forwards in disbelief. It certainly looked like her and she really did appear to be having vigorous sex with a man she'd never set eyes on before.

"Paul, this is revolting. Am I here so you can fill me with drugs and force me to make cheap porn videos against my will?"

"I don't think it's so bad," he retorted, laughing, "and certainly not cheap in any sense of the word. You, of all people, are in no position to criticise me for enjoying watching. Look at yourself, the porn star is clearly having a ball. And you weren't doing it against your will, you even chose the man from a selection we offered you."

She went back to the bars near where he was sitting.

"Paul, if you think drugging someone so they do disgusting out-of-character things makes you look strong or clever, then you're very, very sick."

"Hmm, maybe," he gloated. "But if that is true, it's bloody good fun."

Tessa tossed the player towards him. It skidded across the top of his briefcase and neatly splashed in to his glass.

"Oh, bugger!" observed Paul. "Personally, I didn't think you'd make that shot, but it seems I've just lost my bet."

"I guarantee it's the first of many bets you're going to lose."

"I doubt it. But my point remains, you need to understand what you're dealing with. We knew what you were going to do before you'd even thought of it, and that applies to everything in your life from now on."

He opened his briefcase and took out another video player, the same as the one Tessa had just ruined, and switched it on.

"Oh, wow, you really should see this bit…" Tessa walked away, uninterested. "No? Well, I'm pleased to say that your remarkable sexual appetite, not to mention your incredible flexibility…, good lord, that's amazing…, combined with the knife-throwing prowess which you so amply demonstrated at Waley, helped boost your price beyond our wildest expectations."

"Price?" exclaimed Tessa, rounding on him indignantly.

"Yes, you've been sold – auctioned, to be precise. We've achieved an unbelievable six-month payback on you!" he boasted. "You are now the property of Sheikh Saif Al Rahal of Irabya – actually his name goes on for ages but that's the only part I can remember, or pronounce for that matter. Fortunately, everyone calls him Simitar for short; that's Scimitar without the 'c', by the way. Anyway, he seemed to quite get off at the sight of these videos; imagine what he'll be like when you're with him. I suppose that's why he wants you in good condition. Which not only means you're allowed to enjoy these luxurious quarters, but that your food will be healthy, and you'll be able to exercise too."

Tessa was appalled, and made no attempt to hide it.

"Hah! I can see you appreciate what we're doing for you. But don't worry, you'll love us soon enough, literally. Anyway, we've already received the down-payment, so all we've got to do now is to teach you how to behave, arrange delivery and collect the balance... It could have been worse. We were considering just harvesting your organs, but we soon established you're worth rather more intact, so we're going to leave the harvesting for the time being. A sort of escrow against performance to contract, if you will."

Tessa was aghast at his ghoulishness.

"Is this some kind of a sick joke, Paul?"

"Hardly. The Calver Cats run a business and you're an asset of ours, which we've sold for the highest price we could get. What's wrong with that? Admittedly in your case we do intend to maximise our own fun along the way, but that's only us showing our appreciation for everything you've done for us. Don't look so offended; it's nothing personal. And anyway, there's not a single thing you can do about it."

"So what exactly did you do to me after I was drugged at Waley?"

"Well, after you so generously gave yourself to us, the good Doktor injected a shot of something to calm you down while we flew you to Hpa An prison. There, you were stripped, your locator beacons were removed, and you were examined, very comprehensively. Well, by the Doktors at any rate. We all just had a look because we were curious. Our German experts used the next few hours to take the various samples and measurements they needed to develop your specialised treatment programme, after which they were able to inject you with something which accurately mimics the state you'll be in permanently once your therapy is complete. Then, freed from all social inhibitions, only the *real* you was left. You were offered, and readily accepted I might add, the chance to show us how sexually willing, responsive and … er … versatile you are. We just lit the blue touch paper and stood back, so to speak. True to form, our German friends were adamant they expected you to be..."

"Real me? Paul, don't talk rubbish! All your German misogynists did was to block my inhibitions and accentuate other responses in my brain. That's wasn't the real me, that was an automaton high on a concoction of puerile drugs."

"Whatever. Anyway, our German friends insisted they weren't in the slightest surprised by your – what shall we call it – performance. They said that as a uniquely successful Peacekeeper you were bound to be fit and supple, and, as a seasoned male to female transsexual who had benefited from the absolute best surgical procedures money could buy, they were anticipating a good sexual response."

"What?"

"Oh, come on, you know what I'm talking about. There's no point in trying to hide anything from us now."

Tessa looked at him, momentarily puzzled. She was also annoyed. Her hackles always began to rise when people talked about what they classified as abnormalities in an insensitive, sensational and prejudiced manner.

"I'm not boring you, am I?" he asked, not bothering to wait for a reply. "They pointed out that genetic women are built for having children and as such have all sorts of emotional and biological overheads. Furthermore, they are female by default, whereas the likes of you have made a conscious decision to turn into the woman you are today. A good post-op Male to Female transsexual like you is basically built for sex without being cluttered by all those pesky overheads… You know, periods, stuff like that. So they expected you to be able to do it more frequently while experiencing, and frequently giving, more pleasure than a genetic female. We had rather pooh-poohed the idea, but once we saw you in action…"

"Paul, your naïve, perverted weirdness is boring me now," interrupted Tessa. "Am I to endure your wittering for much longer?"

"For as long as I please, actually. And I'll go easy on you now since it is your first day, but interrupt me in future and you'll be punished." He opened his briefcase again, took out an air pistol and a box of chemical darts, and grinned at her. "Now where was I? Oh, yes. After *playtime* came the auction, and as a result of Waley and your enthusiastic, highly proficient and extremely gymnastic performance, I am pleased to say that your surprisingly pretty body fetched a near-astronomical price. It would have been more if you hadn't had that damn Chrysanthemum tattoo so comprehensively removed, but *c'est la vie*. Once the dust had settled on all that, you were flown here, Rangoon's Insein prison to be precise. I can assure you that Potter and Co. have absolutely no idea where you are. Yes, they tracked you to Hpa An, but they've lost you now, and you'll only surface again when we tell you to…" Tessa had heard about Insein prison, a large facility used primarily for the repression of Burmese political dissidents. It had been notorious for decades due to its harsh insanitary conditions and human rights abuses. "…So, as I said before, your past belongs to you only while we allow it to. But your future already belongs to us; what you do, what you think, who you love and who you kill."

"Paul, you're spouting the biggest load of specious drivel I've ever heard. What's more, everything you're doing is illegal and a crime against human rights. It's illegal when some misguided political or religious extremist does it, and it's illegal when a twisted pervert like you does it. You will be judged for this one day, and, rest assured, when you are, I will be there to watch.

"Fine words, Peacekeeper, but somewhat hollow in the circumstances, don't you think?"

"Not at all. And to prove my point, and I'm really sorry to ruin the momentum of your rather comical and misinformed diatribe, you are wrong about me. You see, although it's got nothing to do with you, I am not, and never have been, a transsexual. So go stuff that in your pipe and smoke it!"

For a moment, Paul was silent.

"Yes, you are."

"Paul, despite your self-professed omniscience, you clearly don't know squat."

"Hmm. Well, that is interesting, so… Never mind, I'll ask you again later."

"The answer will still be the same. I do hope you haven't tried to sell me under false pretences. You might upset your client, which could be very bad for business."

"Yeah, yeah. You just don't understand how insignificant you and your opinions are now," continued Paul. "We started planning your future years ago. You'd be shocked who's involved…"

"Tell me. If you're so confident, you've nothing to lose."

"Hah! Getting Nyunt to Burma was one of the final phases, and didn't that just work like a dream? Naturally, you were so distracted by all those attempts on your life, you didn't notice what was happening around you…"

"But supposing I had died?"

"Oh, we considered that. But if only half your reputation was justified, that was unlikely; besides, the guys doing the attacking weren't trying that hard. We filmed the lot, showed them in your auction too."

"What have you done to Nyunt?"

"Not the full nine yards, yet. If you behave yourself we won't, but we've postponed that decision for now." He made a point of looking at his watch. "Sorry, I'll have to leave you to it shortly, but…"

"Hurrah!"

"Oh, I'm not quite finished yet. Do you like the design on your hand?" Tessa had in fact noticed the intricate henna design on her right hand. It was quite beautiful, but since she hadn't asked for it she

118

wasn't in the slightest inclined to make a point of admiring it.

"Doing things to people without asking their permission, is not acceptable, Paul."

"Oh, dear. You really are going to have a tough time here. Shame, but so be it. Anyway, the lady artist tasked with authenticating the auctioned goods wanted to practise on your skin to check she could do it right. Apparently she hadn't used that type of ink before. It's a sort of high-intensity henna. It lasts for a couple of months, but will be replaced before then with a real tattoo by the Sheikh's own people."

"Practise?"

" Oh, my goodness, I'm sorry, you haven't seen the real one yet, have you? Look at your crotch, Peacekeeper. Boy! I'm so loving this."

Paul watched with considerable amusement as Tessa lifted her tee-shirt and looked down. There was a tattoo over her crotch. Even upside-down it was clearly a regal-looking Arabic coat of arms, a crown cupped by two scimitars. She was incensed.

"I think it's rather fetching," crowed Paul. "As I'm sure you've worked out, it's your new owner's. Well, he will be your owner just as soon as your treatment is complete and we've received the balance."

"You really are a very nasty piece of work, aren't you, Paul?"

"Trust me, you ain't seen nothing yet. Right," he said, looking at his watch again, "we both have a busy day ahead of us, so I'll leave you to ponder your hopelessness, while I go and have my meeting in a nice air-conditioned office. But don't worry, I'll be back around lunch time." He stood up and re-packed his briefcase, preparing to leave. "Oh, by the way, you forgot to thank me for organising those two guys to lead you safely out of Burma. You'd pissed off the army so much by killing all those soldiers they were intent upon giving you a good beating before handing you over. We were worried they might damage you so we facilitated your escape. Oh, and that friend of yours in Moulmein, the one who got shot? He's dead."

"You always knew Htet was Nyunt's father, didn't you?"

"Well, I kind of assumed it," said Paul, grinning. "However, that's no concern of yours now. For the rest of her life, Nyunt will despise you for having killed General Soe Gyi, who she'll continue to believe was her biological father. Be seeing you."

Tessa watched him walk towards a door at the end of the large triangular compound. As far as she knew, no one had ever escaped from Insein prison; she didn't feel confident that she would be the first. There were numerous guards and her cage, positioned as it was in the middle of the compound, could be seen from all sides. Nevertheless, she walked to the door and inspected the padlock. She doubted she could pick it, especially without being seen.

"Oh, you won't be able to break that," Paul shouted back to her, "and even if you did, you'd never make it out of the compound."

Laughing, he disappeared from view.

Regrettably, Tessa was inclined to agree. Furthermore, she wasn't sure her chances afterward would be good, being chased through the northern suburbs of Rangoon with hardly any clothes on.

She prowled round her cage like an angry tiger; disconsolately scrutinising its construction. It had been built sturdily and there was no clear opportunity for escape, although the welds securing the door hinges looked a trifle suspect. When she found a mirror, she looked at her eyes. The pupils were still dilated. She returned to her bed, which she now noticed had two side panels which could be swung up as arm rests. Both had two sets of retaining straps. Lower down there was even a set of stirrups to hold her legs up and apart. She concluded it was more like an operating table than a gurney and, as such, found it surprisingly intimidating. However, she wanted to lie down, and it was the only alternative to the dirt floor. She tried to relax and consider her situation, quickly concluding that no matter from what perspective she viewed it, she was in serious trouble. She was reminded of the definition of fear she used when teaching at SKS...

"Fear is an unpleasant emotional state comprising psychological and psychophysiological responses to perceived threats consciously interpreted as real danger. This could include: separation from support in a threatening environment, unfamiliarity and sensory impairment. Fear results in increased tension, diminished self-assurance and possibly panic, prompting increased alertness, concentration on the source, fight-or-flight responses and symptoms such as cardiovascular excitation, superficial vasoconstriction and dilation of the pupils...

"Hmm," she mused wryly, "seem to have most of that at the moment, and I suspect it'll only get worse...

"Potter, I could do with a little help here."

CHAPTER 11

After a while, Tessa heard some more prisoners being allowed into the compound. She sat up and looked round. There were more than a hundred bedraggled, undernourished men circulating around her cage, at a discreet distance. Some limped while others had nasty cuts, sores and bruises. Clearly the main topic of conversation was her, but she couldn't make out what they were saying as soldiers prevented them from approaching. Tessa decided to give herself a bit of a work-out and started doing various stretches, push-ups, abdominal crunches. As she was running on the spot, she kept muttering, "Never let them wear you down."

Despite the intense heat, the other prisoners started exercising with her and soon most of them were mimicking her routine. Even some of the guards looked as though they were surreptitiously trying to join in. But they soon stopped when Tessa started shouting rhythmic lines for them to repeat.

"We work out so we stay fit!"

"Burma will one day be free!"

Then the soldiers waved their guns at the prisoners to stop them from joining in.

However, while Tessa was furiously pumping her own weight from a high horizontal support which ran round her cage, one of the inmates shouted out to her.

"You Nariko?" he asked in broken English.

Tessa barely slowed what she was doing.

"Yes," she panted.

New rumblings circulated around the prisoners.

"You Peacekeeper kill Bill Chalmers and General Soe Gyi?"

"Yes."

"But illegal for Peacekeeper kill in Burma."

Tessa stopped exercising and wiped her brow. Then she carried on in Burmese.

"Only because the oppressive military Junta here has refused to sign the International Peacekeeper Treaty. Bill Chalmers had been tried in a court of law and sentenced to death in England. So, according to international law, he was a legitimate Peacekeeper target virtually everywhere else in the world. Hiding here was not acceptable. Chalmers was my only target; it was not my intention to kill General Soe Gyi. But he attacked me while I was escaping and we fought, one on one. He lost."

There was silence. Even the guards seemed to be thinking about this. Tessa began exercising again.

"It is OK. We are pleased you killed them. They were evil men," came the response. "You speak good Burmese. Where did you learn?"

She smiled.

"My daughter taught me."

More mutterings circulated.

"You saved Htet's daughter?"

Tessa stopped exercising.

"You are well informed. I adopted her. We have been living happily together in London."

"So why are you here?"

"They kidnapped her," replied Tessa. "I sacrificed myself so that she might be free."

The soldiers round her cage started looking uncomfortable. Then a different voice yelled out.

"Stop talking to her! If any of you talk with her you'll get an extra beating," announced an army captain who had just walked into the compound. He was brandishing a long wooden staff, similar to a bokken. As he walked towards Tessa, he started randomly hitting prisoners he passed.

"Stop that!" yelled Tessa.

Unfortunately, this only seemed to make the captain keener to strike people.

"Everyone can see you're a mindless bully," continued Tessa. "Why don't you come over here and try that on me? Or are you too much of a coward?"

This certainly got the captain's attention and he approached Tessa's cage.

"If I were allowed to, whore, I would give you a beating you'd never forget."

"Why don't you try?" she replied generously. "But weak men like you don't have the courage, do you?"

He was standing barely three feet away from her now. She glared at him.

"Cowardly bully!" she yelled in Burmese at the top of her voice. "Cowardly bully! Cowardly bully!" She kept on taunting him. Then some of the prisoners joined in and it wasn't long before the chorus was reverberating around the compound.

This racket attracted the camp commandant's attention. He stormed into the compound and fired several shots in the air to quieten everyone. Then he ordered all the prisoners to be returned to their cells. He wagged his finger at Tessa.

"It would be in your interests to behave, whore," he yelled. "I'm not a patient man!"

Tessa shrugged.

"I'll deal with you later," hissed the captain, turning and walking away.

"Any time, cowardly bully," scoffed Tessa, returning to her bed.

She was just beginning to drift off to sleep when she heard a group of soldiers approaching. It seemed her lunch was arriving, although the thought crossed her mind that maybe it was coming now precisely because she was drifting off to sleep. After all, sleep deprivation was a very effective form of torture, exacerbating any impression of vulnerability and psychologically dislocating a subject. She wondered whether she would be forced to listen to loud noise for extended periods too.

There were three soldiers, followed by the girl who had previously been to clear up. She was carrying a grey plastic tray this time. On it was a bottle of water and a plate with a domed cover over it. The lead soldier arrived and gestured Tessa to move back from the door. She complied, interested to learn their routine and put them at ease. With guns raised, the padlock was unlocked and the door opened. The tray was placed on the end of Tessa's bed and everyone left.

Under the dome she found an excellent chicken curry with rice, and there were some small bananas too. She stared at the food indecisively. She had heard that prisoners in Burma were not provided with much in the way of sustenance. As in the hospitals, food had to be brought to them by family members or friends. But to make this more difficult, the Junta frequently relocated prisoners far away from where they lived. Should Tessa eat the food or see if she could get it to the other prisoners? Finally she decided that she had to maintain her strength so she threw the bananas to other captives and started eating the curry. It proved to be extremely tasty until she found a blue tablet buried in a piece of chicken breast. She discarded the tablet with disdain and carried on eating, but was far more cautious about what she put in her mouth.

When she'd finished, she tried to assess her options. Obviously, she needed to escape, but it wouldn't be easy. There were always at least four soldiers in the compound watching her cage. It would certainly be futile to try and escape during the day; she would have to leave under cover of darkness. She doubted she could pick the padlock but thought she might be able to snap either it or the door hinges. However, breaking out like that without making a noise would be almost impossible, and she wouldn't know where to go afterwards since she had no idea how the prison was laid out. Frustrated by her inability to formulate a viable plan, she lay down on her trolley bed. She desperately needed to stave off the depression which was threatening to engulf her. It was late afternoon, incredibly hot and she was covered in perspiration. Once more she was just dropping off to sleep when her heart sank at the sound of approaching footsteps.

"You just can't keep out of trouble, can you?" called Paul. "I told you what would happen if you did anything stupid."

Tessa took a deep breath and pivoted off the bed, just in time to see Paul pull the trigger on the air pistol he'd been brandishing earlier. A dart struck her in the right thigh. She quickly plucked it out and for a moment thought nothing was going to happen. But then her arm and leg muscles started twitching until they contracted and seized solid. She toppled back and found herself propped awkwardly against the bed, with all of her muscles frozen solid.

"Super stuff, isn't it?" mocked Paul, unlocking the padlock to her cage. "You can move your head a little, breathe and talk, but nothing else. The muscle seizure only lasts a few minutes, but then they'll relax completely for several hours. I've only given you a little dose for now. I simply wanted to show you what happens when you don't do as you're told. Now, since you and the captain seem to be getting on so well, I thought I'd give you a little personal time together."

Tessa grimaced as she watched the soldier walk slowly and purposefully into her cage, his face set in an extraordinarily broad grin. She could see that many of the prisoners were watching as he approached.

"Any time, eh?" he sneered. "Well, I can take a whore like you whenever I want. But I choose now."

Tessa could think of lots of things she wanted to say, but given her inability to move, decided discretion would be wiser. Instead she concentrated on trying to get her mind to a different place. It proved remarkably difficult and her muscles started to go limp.

"Hold her down, kneeling for me," ordered Paul.

The captain enthusiastically complied, gripping Tessa under both armpits and moving her down and round to face Paul.

"You must be obedient. If you don't behave this will prove to have been a joyous party compared to what will happen. Now, do you promise?"

"Of course not, Paul. You don't really…"

Tessa couldn't finish speaking because Paul had slapped her across the face.

"So this is how you treat women, is it?" she hissed.

He hit her again, on the other cheek. Her face was smarting.

"Promise me you'll behave."

"Paul, you've attacked a Peacekeeper. Your life is forfeit and I'm going to take it!"

"Stand her up," ordered Paul. "You stubborn fool," he continued, and punched her hard in the stomach.

Tessa gasped for breath.

"Enjoy that did you."

"No, Paul."

"Then beg for mercy."

Tessa looked down and sighed.

"Paul…"

"Start with *please*."

"Please, Paul…" He grinned expectantly. "Go away and play with yourself."

He took a deep breath.

"Suit yourself. Put her on the bed and cut off her tee-shirt."

Tessa clamped her jaws together as the captain manoeuvred her body onto the gurney. Then he drew his knife and waved it in front of Tessa's eyes before lifting up her tee-shirt at the bottom. In one quick fluid movement he ran the knife up to the neck, after which he slit both sleeves and unwrapped her like a much-desired Christmas present. She was completely naked and unable to move. Leering, the captain looked round at Paul.

"Oh, all right, you can have a feel if you like, but nothing more."

As the man started groping her body, Tessa could feel the heat of his breath and the foul smell of his garlic-ridden breath; his forehead was speckled with drops of perspiration. She could also see from his carotid arteries that his heart-rate had increased. However, his excitement was far outweighed by her outrage and revulsion as his rough, callused hands moved across her with puerile excitement.

"You enjoy yourself too?" he boasted.

"Cowardly bully," she hissed. "I bet you can't get women any other way."

"Keep calm," interrupted Paul, aiming his comment at the captain.

He shrugged and licked his finger, then he ran it down from between Tessa's breasts towards her genitals. But Paul's hand stopped him.

"That's not for you," he said. "You've had your fun, leave us now."

The man shrugged, turned and left.

"You really must behave," Paul instructed Tessa. "I said you'd be punished, and this is me being nice because it's your first day. But any more of your games and, I assure you, it will be far worse."

"You're a perverted sadist," hissed Tessa. "You will face justice for this."

He sighed.

"I was going to offer you the blue pill again. It would have taken the edge off today's procedure, but you've blown that now."

He reached under her mattress to swing up one of the supports. He locked it in position perpendicular to the gurney and pulled her arm onto it so he could strap it down with the webbing restraints. He repeated this process with her other arm and then her legs. She was now spread-eagled with her legs some eighteen inches apart. But he didn't tighten the straps. She would be able to release herself when she could move.

"You do 'alf look undignified," jeered Paul. Then she heard him walk away.

Tessa wasn't sure how long she lay there before her muscles finally began to regain power. She tugged her arms free and awkwardly sat up. She was surprised by how vulnerable she felt being completely naked. The captain even brought a couple of his colleagues over to letch at her. Ignoring her own humiliation, she approached the bars close to him.

"You're a childish cowardly bully," she said loudly. "You and your friends should grow up!"

Then she lay back down on the bed.

Half an hour later, the girl was brought to Tessa's cage again. This time she had a tray with some fruit, water and a pot of hot black tea. She seemed embarrassed at finding Tessa naked, but didn't say anything. Tessa refused to move from her bed and so the tray was left just inside the door.

She ate the fruit and drank the tea, but was surprised to find another blue tablet on the tray in a small paper cone; clearly it was important to Paul. She crushed it using her plastic spoon, the only cutlery she'd been given, and sprinkled the powder on the ground.

CHAPTER 12

As dusk fell, Tessa was back on her bed with her torso covered by her ruined tee-shirt. She could hear the other prisoners moving around, but there was a palpable atmosphere of unrest in the prison. She hoped it wasn't anything to do with her predicament; she preferred to think it might be the prelude to an earthquake which would swallow her up, preferably taking Paul and the captain at the same time. Then she heard the door into the compound open and recognised Paul's footsteps approaching.

"Evening, Nariko," he called. "Did you have a nice afternoon? I did. It's lovely at the Strand, isn't it? So clean, cool and civilised. And what a fantastic afternoon tea they serve..."

Tessa didn't budge, she simply turned her head to peer at him; he was carrying a briefcase.

"...I know it's only your first day, but I'm still very disappointed that you've made so little progress. So, on the off-chance that you're getting stupid ideas about trying to escape, I thought we'd better have another talk, to make sure you've got the message."

"Oh, I've got the message, Paul," retorted Tessa. "The message about how bitter, twisted, perverted, ignorant and screwed up you are. That is what you expected me to divine, isn't it?"

She knew these words were hardly likely to ease her situation, but doubted whether anything she did would alter his plans for her, so she might as well stick to her principles.

"That rather proves my point, doesn't it?"

Tessa pivoted round and stood up, trying not to appear embarrassed at being naked in front of her tormentor. He grinned, opened the briefcase and loaded a dart in the air pistol.

"Very brave with that in your hand and bars between us, aren't you?"

"Would you prefer to be restrained by the captain first?"

"Oh, yes, please. But like you, he's too much of a coward to come in here on his own unless I'm doped up to the eyeballs."

Paul looked irritated by that, they both knew he'd made a mistake and let her win a point. He raised the pistol and aimed it at her.

"Why don't you give me a syringe so I can inject myself?"

"Hah! You would too, wouldn't you? But that wouldn't be good for my image, and, more importantly, you still wouldn't get the message." He started raising his voice until everyone in the compound could hear him. "When we tell you to do something, you will do it!"

"Losing your temper, Paul?" jeered Tessa. "Why are you bullies always so weak and puerile?"

"Lie down on the bed and you'll get this in the thigh," he hissed. "Any more lip and I guarantee it'll hurt more."

Tessa knew she couldn't avoid the darts for ever; sooner or later, he would get her.

"Why don't we just have a little chat," suggested Tessa, "like adults?"

"You'll talk when I tell you to. *Five, four, three...*"

"Hold on a second," said Tessa.

But then there was a loud *phut!* as another dart stuck her in the thigh. She just had time to twist back onto the bed before her muscles again started twitching, then contracting, and finally seizing solid. In the background she could hear the chinking of a glass.

"I would offer you a T&T with ice and lime, which, obviously, I know is your favourite; but I doubt you'd be able to hold it. Cheers!" laughed Paul. "I'll be over when you're cooked."

Tessa declined to respond and simply waited for the partial relief of her muscles going limp. However, the sound of some mosquito nets being rolled down her cage and the padlock being unlocked indicated that something different was about to happen. A single bright light bulb above her was switched on and a soldier placed a small table and chair at the foot of her gurney. Paul came to her side. Tessa rolled her head round and watched him place his briefcase and glass on the table. Then he reached under her mattress to swing up the arm and leg supports again. He locked them all in position and, with her once more spread-eagled, strapped her down tightly this time; even after the toxins had been metabolised, she wouldn't be able to move.

"What was it you said to me in London once? You don't have to like your boss, only respect him. I suppose that's true, but in certain circumstances fear can be a good substitute for respect, can't it? Now,

I don't think I'm going to make you respect me for my intellect, although maybe you should, but, Peacekeeper Nariko..." he leaned over her to look into her eyes, "...I can sure as hell make you scared of me. You see, I don't think you will become obedient purely as a result of my threats. You're too arrogant, stubborn and egoistic for that. So, I'm going to demonstrate just a small selection of the things we can do to you if you don't follow instructions. The sooner you learn to do as you're told, without question, the sooner your life will get easier."

He started fiddling with the contents of his briefcase.

"This is not just about the Calver Cats, is it, Paul?" she asked seriously. "Why are you really doing this?"

"All sorts of reasons," he replied, pausing to savour the moment. "But the fact that you killed my mother, my father and my step-father certainly has something to do with it."

Tessa opened her eyes wide in surprise. He simply looked away and started unwrapping things.

"What do you mean?" asked Tessa. "When? Who were they?"

"Caprice Caille, Ryota Fujiwara and Beauchamp Caille."

Tessa was dumbstruck.

"You mean you're Adam?" she asked incredulously. "My nephew?"

He nodded and began filling a syringe with thick yellow liquid.

"Wow! You've definitely got my attention now. Before you do whatever you're going to do, tell me how my brother came to be your step-father, if that's the way round you meant it?"

Paul hesitated for a moment, but then replaced the plastic cover he had just removed from the syringe's needle.

"I suppose you might as well know. My mother was Caprice and my genetic father was Ryota Fujiwara. She married your brother just after I had been conceived. Beauchamp knew about it and agreed to raise me as his own. He was a good man."

Tessa wasn't sure she concurred, but decided to let the comment go.

"So why weren't you more Japanese-looking?"

"I was. That's why I was sent to the US where I was surgically altered to make me appear more European. Nobody got a clear view of the real me until my face had recovered and my skin was bleached. They told everyone I had alopecia and shaved my hair to hide the fact that it was black. As soon as I could, I moved permanently to the US, had my face changed back to how it was meant to look and let my hair grow."

"And Beauchamp knew all this?"

"He most certainly did. He and Ryota were great friends, and my being out of harm's way kept the Fujiwara line safe."

"Hmm. But technically you're not truly a Fujiwara."

"I am! Just as much as…" He stopped talking abruptly.

"As much as who, Paul?"

He ignored her question.

"I passed the most difficult test when I started dating Nyunt and you didn't recognise me. Can you imagine what a buzz that was? However, we all have to learn to accept things we're not comfortable with. You're about to, and I already have; I'm only second-in-line to the Fujiwara empire."

"Oh, I see. Well, that must be a terrible disappointment; who's first?"

"No more questions."

"OK. But you should know that I was not the one who killed Beauchamp, your mother did that. I just wounded him."

"You're lying!"

"Don't be daft, Paul. Consider the state I'm in and ask yourself why I would lie?"

"You killed my mother too."

Tessa breathed out noisily.

"No, I didn't kill her either. Someone else killed her… honestly, Paul, that is the truth."

"You killed my birth father too, didn't you?"

"Yes, I did do that, but not the others. Ryota challenged me to a one on one duel and he lost. It was a fair fight; there is no dishonour in that, for either of us."

Paul considered what she'd said, then returned to his preparations. Meanwhile, Tessa tried not to think about what he might be about to do to her.

"And you killed Bryani," he added suddenly.

"I don't know where you're getting all your information, Paul, but it's a terribly inaccurate source," replied Tessa, exasperated. "I did not kill Bryani. She was shot by one of the Calver Cats. We fought and I slashed her sword arm. But I wanted her alive so she could tell us who was running the original Calver Cats. One of her own guys shot her. I don't do guns, you must know that?"

"And you killed Hachiro."

"Good grief! Yes, I did. But, like your father, it was during a fair duel. Why do Hachiro's and Bryani's death matter to you, unless…?"

"Who said they did? Although Hachiro was my uncle… The point remains you messed up my life, big time, so now I'm returning the favour."

"Paul, look at me. If you're interested in the truth then let's get this sorted. It's always important we know the truth. After that…"

"Shut up! I've heard enough."

He strapped a pulse monitor around her arm and studied the read-out for a moment. Then he swabbed the top surface of her left hand; she could feel the chill of the alcohol evaporating. He picked up her hand, and making sure he inflicted as much pain as possible, inserted an IV cannula into a vein. Her heart started to beat more quickly as he taped it in position.

"Ah, excellent, I see we're making progress," boasted Paul, glancing at her pulse count.

"Whatever I've done, Paul, I did it while acting within the law."

"Bullshit! What about Uncle Bill and General Soe Gyi?"

"Bill Chalmers wasn't a *real* uncle, was he? Anyway, both of them had broken the law, and were trying to kill me; like everyone else you mentioned."

"But you didn't bother to consider the consequences your actions would have on my life, did you?"

"Nobody suggested I needed to. I've never knowingly tried to hurt you in any way. I didn't even know where you were, for goodness' sake." She was irritated to hear that there was a distinct nervous tremor in her voice. "You hadn't been in touch for years."

"It wouldn't have made any difference if I had, would it? You haven't been in touch with Belinda or Carlisle, have you?"

"Yes, I have, Paul. I'm surprised you don't know that. I've done my best to help both your sister and your brother. But perhaps you should take the actions of your step-father into account, and all the demons I was battling with."

"We'll get to that soon enough. Did my step-dad really molest you?"

"Yes."

"I don't believe you."

"Oh, for goodness' sake, Paul. Everything I've said is true! Bill Chalmers and General Soe Gyi both had reputations for child molestation, maybe that's why they all got on so well together."

Paul was silent for a moment.

"The point remains, you've damaged my family more than enough to deserve to have yours wrecked. Look at all the people you've killed. Don't you accept that you deserve to pay penance for that?"

Tessa wasn't sure how to answer this; she did feel guilty about having killed so many.

"I wouldn't put it that way. I have always abhorred violence, and still do. But, unwittingly, I was sucked into a battle against the Calver Cats that refuses to go away. Maybe one day I will be judged for all that I've had to do, but you have no such authority. If my life is forfeit, it is not for you to take or manipulate it. Only the law can do that."

"The law's an ass."

"Perhaps, but that doesn't mean you have the right to operate outside it."

"You should have taken the blue pill, I was being charitable. I think we'll make a start, shall we?"

He picked up her wrist and inserted the syringe in the IV cannula.

"Will you promise to obey me in future without question?"

"No, Paul," she sighed. "You know I'll never do that."

"Oh, yes, you will."

Tessa braced herself. As a Peacekeeper pain had often been a companion of hers. However, none of her training or combat experience had prepared her for this. As soon as he started depressing the plunger, a deep stinging sensation coursed through Tessa's veins. It was as though a swarm of angry bees was being released inside her. Involuntarily, she took a sharp deep breath and moaned. Then she clamped her mouth shut, determined not to yell out. Despite having no apparent muscular control, she found herself writhing in agony and clenching her fists. She wasn't sure how long the pain lasted, but she was suddenly aware of Paul giving her another injection. The aching eased and she began to relax again, now covered in perspiration and panting.

"...Our German friends use highly refined chemicals to achieve their ends," he was saying. "Me, I prefer more natural compounds. That was a mixture of snake and frog venoms. The antidote is extremely effective so I can control the duration of the treatment quite finely." He leaned over to peer into her eyes. "Ah, back again, jolly good. The art is not to let the subject quite pass out..." He prepared another syringe. "Right, that was what I call, level one. Let's up the ante a bit and try level two, shall we?" He inserted the syringe in her IV cannula. "Do you promise to obey me without question?"

"No, you little shit!" roared Tessa.

This time, she couldn't stop herself from crying out. The pain was more pervasive than anything she had ever had to endure before. Her whole body convulsed, every muscle was agony, even her heart hurt. Although her eyes were clouded with tears, she could see Paul watching her carefully. Just when unconsciousness threatened to relieve her, he gave her the antidote. As the toxins and her pain dissipated, he looked at his watch.

"That's very impressive; no one's managed that long before. This might take a little longer than I thought. What fun! Mind you, I might need more gin."

It seemed to Tessa that it took her ages to recover. But she was still able to watch him pour another drink and add some ice to it. He took a swig and peered at her dispassionately.

"Well, what shall we do now?" He stood up and seemed to be thinking as he studied her body. "As you know I enjoyed the films of you in Hpa An, but unfortunately I was not there to try you myself. It was..." Paul hesitated and despite her discomfort, Tessa was suddenly on tenterhooks listening, "somebody else who had you first; in private too, the lucky sod. Anyway, he said you're very, how shall I put it, *comfortable*. I think it's high time I checked whether I agree with him. You don't mind, do you?"

"Yes, Paul, I do mind," rasped Tessa.

"Shame," he clambered on top of her and undid his trouser belt. Tessa was livid, but he simply roared with laughter.

"Get off me!" she snarled.

"I'll do what I want with you, when I want," he replied. "Learn that now or I'll continue."

"Get off me! You perverted bastard!"

He slapped her.

"No!" he hissed, moving his face so it was only a few inches away from hers. Then he moved his hand down.

"Get off me now!" she yelled.

He brought his hand back and slapped her again, really hard this time on the other side of her face.

"Do what I say or else."

"Never!"

"Murdering whore, do what I say!" he demanded.

"I am not a whore and I only kill those who are trying to kill me," she retaliated. "Taking advantage of a woman when she's drugged and defenceless doesn't make her a whore, it makes you a pathetic wimp. When I mess with you, Paul, you'll be fully sentient!"

He slapped her again. Her face was stinging terribly now; she was sure she had red marks all over it.

"You still seem to have difficulty learning that it's I who'll be doing the messing, and you'll mess with whoever I want, when I want, whore!"

He bent down and pulled her eyelids open to study her pupils.

"Will you promise to obey me without question, whore?" he yelled into her face.

"*Mahouq pa!*" she screamed defiantly.

Without getting off her he quickly leaned over and picked up a syringe which Tessa hadn't noticed him priming. Before she could even think about preparing herself, he emptied the syringe into the cannula.

Immediately her muscles tensed and her chest heaved. She was vaguely aware of and repulsed by what he was doing with his right hand. But then the pain came. It was severe beyond belief, penetrating every sinew of her body with the sensation of molten lava coursing through her veins. Her brain seemed as though it was about to explode. She had no choice but to cry out in agony. Her body convulsed and tears streamed down her face. She could no longer see or hear anything as stars exploded in front of her eyes. She had no idea how long this went on, but was sure she made a lot of noise…

Finally, he gave her the antidote and she became aware of him standing over her once again, smiling with enjoyment.

Meanwhile she continued to moan, panting and rolling her head backwards and forwards as her body quivered from the effects of the poison. Paul took a long swig of his drink. Then he made a point of ensuring she watched him loading another syringe, of pink fluid this time. He leaned over to study her pupils and glance at the pulse meter and, then as Tessa gritted her teeth, he emptied the syringe into the cannula. He peered at his watch and sat back to drink some more gin.

Tessa was surprised not to be experiencing a new pain. If anything she just felt cool, as though snow was falling all over her body. She knew something must be happening to her, but had no idea what. It was a few minutes before he spoke again.

"Why doesn't your sword ring?"

"It does ring," she gasped. Then she realised she actually wanted to tell him more. "All Amakuni swords ring."

"My man, Tony, couldn't make it ring."

Tessa decided she wouldn't answer this. However, she found words were gathering in her mind like a volcano. Finally, she simply couldn't stop them from erupting.

"Of course not, it will only ring for me."

"I take it you've worked out that the last stuff I gave you was truth serum. Don't bother to try and resist, the truth'll come out eventually… But after you'd opened the case for us in Hpa An, it wouldn't ring for you either?"

Tessa was momentarily furious at the thought that she had held her beloved sword and not done anything with it. But then she couldn't prevent herself from speaking.

"You must have drugged me too much. I have to be healthy and in control for it to ring."

"Hmm. That's interesting, we never knew that…"

"So where's your Amafuji sword."

"I don't know."

"…Hmm. Why didn't you being it with you to Waley."

"Insurance. I wasn't going to give you what you obviously wanted."

"I see… OK. Let's move on. We know there's a man in your life, and it's not that old codger in SKS. So, who is it?"

Tessa was desperate to answer, but clamped her jaws together.

"Come on, I can see you want to tell me. Spit it out."

Tessa was concentrating so hard on staying silent she started going red in the face. Paul smirked and took another swig of his gin.

"This should be good," he mused.

Tessa was fit to explode; finally she couldn't contain herself any longer.

"David," she yelled at the top of her voice. "David Kensington," she shrieked, starting to sob. I hope you burn in hell, Paul."

"Oh! How boring, only that dead toff. We thought there was another. But I daresay with your past, it's not so easy. Which is a fine segue to another old favourite, isn't it?"

But Tessa was barely listening; she was back with David, her first true love, remembering the special times they'd shared and then how he'd died in her arms in Orkney. Tears of sorrow rolled down her face.

"How touching," sneered Paul, using a damp cloth to wipe her face. "You're a transsexual, aren't you?"

Once more there was silence while Tessa tried desperately to fight answering.

"No, I am not, you sadistic bastard," she eventually answered, her voice charged with emotion.

"Hmm, my goodness. Well, well, well. So what was wrong with you?"

"Nothing was wrong with me. I was just unusual, that's all."

"Unusual in what way?" pressed Paul.

Tessa started breathing deeply, panting with the effort needed not to talk.

"None of your fucking business!" she yelled.

Paul shrugged and rattled the ice cubes in his glass. He was standing over her now.

"Take your time, I can wait," he chimed.

Tessa was bright crimson, with her jaws clamped shut, fingers digging in to the palms of her hands. Suddenly Paul hit her across the face again. This had precisely the effect he wanted; the momentary stinging sensation broke her concentration.

"Hermaphrodite!" she cried.

"Wow! Bloody hell!" exclaimed Paul, clearly pleased with himself. "Fancy that. Wonder why I wasn't ever told. Mind you, it does explain why Uncle Beauchamp always called you a freak."

"People whose bodies are different aren't freaks, Paul, they're just different."

"Whatever. So, was Penny a mix-and-match too?"

Tessa was exhausted. For the time being, she didn't have the energy to fight.

"Yes," she sighed.

"Amazing," observed Paul. "Here's another good one. I know you're a woman, now, but are you bisexual or homosexual, and if so, which way?

"Bisexual," replied Tessa.

"So, you've never slept with another woman?"

She took a deep breath and held it, grinding her teeth.

"Oh, this looks very promising," mused Paul, taking another swig from his gin.

Finally, Tessa could contain herself no longer.

"Not really," she gasped, clearly upset.

"Not really? What the hell does that mean?" he probed.

"Damn you, Paul! Penny and I were both hermaphrodites; what do you think it means, you moron? We supported each other through hell." Tessa was overwhelmed with emotion and started sobbing again. "We freely gave and received everything from each other, and then your blasted relatives murdered her! They deserved what they got, Paul, just as you deserve what you'll get!"

For a moment the heartfelt sincerity of this outburst shocked even him into silence.

"You loved her?" he asked, quietly.

"Not in the perverted carnal sense you presumably mean. But in every other way, yes... You bastard," she moaned, "you cruel unfeeling bastard. Why are tormenting me like this?"

He took a deep breath.

"Hmm. Moving on," he continued. "I think you'll agree now you're not going to escape tonight. In fact, you're never going to escape from us." He loaded yet another syringe. Tessa gulped. She wasn't going to give in, but she also wasn't sure how much more of this she could take. She began to wonder whether death might be a preferable option. "Listen to me, whore. Promise to do what I say and I'll stop. Otherwise, we're just going to have to carry on like this. What's it to be?"

She thought for a moment.

"Paul, you say I can't lie at the moment?" He nodded confidently. Tessa grinned, and then started laughing, soon she was roaring with laughter. For the first time that evening, tears were streaming down her face from something other than pain. "In that case," she snorted, "you really must be a stupid, weak, sadistic perverted bastard with no charisma. Fancy that, I was right all along!" It seemed she had struck a nerve. His expression changed to one of abject fury. "I will never comply with the likes of you and your disgusting deviant illegal pursuits," she cried.

He hit her across the face again.

"You're as bad as the captain. I bet you can only get a woman if you anaesthetise her first."

He hit her again. Both of them were red in the face now, but she still couldn't stop laughing.

"What a sad case you are, Paul," she scorned. "Change your ways or you'll come to a sticky end."

"Not only is no one interested in your opinions, nobody wants to hear them." He quickly emptied another syringe into her, so fast that it hurt as the fluid entered her vein. She clenched her jaws together, but already an icy coldness had started to spread throughout her body, except for her head which felt as though it had burst into flames. "I would wish you sweet dreams, but you're not going to sleep and your dreams will be anything but sweet."

Tessa heard a rumbling sound and her body began to shake. Gradually the volume of the noise in her head increased. Paul leaned over and held her eyelids open again. It seemed to be getting brighter and darker to Tessa in synchrony with the pounding of her heart. Then she saw a bright flash and her vision clouded over. She started moaning and saw him laughing at her. She began to feel pain again, but it was transient, first in one part of her body, then another, then there was a brief period where she couldn't feel anything. All she could see was bright psychedelic lights, moving like the Aurora Borealis in front of her eyes, and still the rumbling went on. Soon she was in agony and started hallucinating: life-like horrific scenes in which she was witnessing appalling acts of barbarism. Occasionally, she noticed

Paul studying her, coldly, analytically.

Then he studied his watch and leaned over so he could whisper in her ear.

"It's midnight, and this is going to fix the first set of markers," he boasted. "There's no coming back for you now, whore." He injected something else; it didn't contribute much towards the pain, but made her head feel as though it had turned to boiling mud with hot gas bubbling up and exploding. This procedure happened again at 12:30 a.m. and 1 a.m., at which point Paul picked up his phone. Tessa was writhing, barely sure what was real and what was imaginary. Nevertheless, she still tried her utmost to listen to what he was saying.

"It's done, all the markers are set… Yeah, I'm having to move the schedule up, it's all happening tomorrow… No, air's definitely out. Damn Potter… Already done, they'll be here tomorrow. Yep. I'm going to grab some sleep. I'll be in touch."

Sometime later, Paul released her and had some soldiers lay her on the floor. Then she was left alone in the gruesome, dream-world into which she had descended. She rolled around the floor of her cage, moaning from the mental and physical torture…

CHAPTER 13

It was already light when reality finally extinguished Tessa's nightmares. She was covered in perspiration, lying naked on the dirt floor of her cage. Her brain was aching terribly and at first she couldn't remember where she was.

Once a semblance of rationality had returned, she found there were red marks on her wrists where the restraining straps had bitten in. Also, the cannula was still taped to her wrist. She ripped it out in disgust, ignoring the discomfort.

"Silly whore," droned Paul. She hadn't even noticed he was there. "Not only had I not given you permission, but now I'll have to insert another one… You remember where the bowl is, don't you?"

Tessa was aware of prisoners moving around the compound. Then she vomited repeatedly, eventually dragging herself awkwardly to her feet, using the gurney to help pull her up. There was a bottle of water on it, which she drank quickly.

"I have to admit, it is immensely pleasurable dominating you."

"Morning, Paul. I'm so pleased you're here."

"Careful, sarcasm counts as disobedience."

"Well, unfortunately, just because it's a nice day doesn't mean you're not still a sadistic inadequate bastard. Remember that bit?"

"Tsk, tsk," chuckled Paul.

The girl Tessa had seen before came to take away the bowl. The expression of pity on her face suggested to Tessa that she looked every bit as bad as she felt.

"You'll feel rough for about an hour, so I'll come back after lunchtime for another chat. Do what you're told and I'll go easy on you. Anything else and last night will seem like a holiday."

"Give me my clothes."

"Say please."

Tessa breathed out noisily and lay back on the bed.

"You will never beat me down, Paul."

"I already have, you just don't know it," he boasted, throwing a tee-shirt at her. "That's me being charitable again. You owe me."

Tessa agreed with him on that, but was too exhausted to respond; she simply spread the tee-shirt over her torso and tried to rest.

She was just drifting off to sleep when some food arrived. It looked good and she was ravenous. However, with it was a small paper cup with two white tablets in it. She tried to make it look as though she'd taken them, but in reality, threw them away. Slowly, she began to feel better. Her head was still throbbing, but the discomfort was more manageable. She started exercising gently and replaying in her mind what Paul had said. What markers were set? If he was going to subject her to some sort of radiotherapy to burn away parts of her brain, she couldn't possibly fight that. And what did it mean if, thanks to Potter, air was no longer an option?

By late morning she was feeling almost normal. But suddenly the prisoners who had been milling around outside her cage were herded back to their cells. An uneasy hush descended on the compound and the captain, holding his staff in one hand, dragged a woman out to where everyone could watch him giving her a merciless beating. The woman's hands were tied behind her so there was nothing she could do to defend herself?

"This is how we treat whores," he boasted.

She cried out with every blow. The only noise was of the staff hitting home and the woman sobbing and pleading for mercy. He was clearly enjoying this shameless brutality.

Tessa was furious and would have liked to intervene, but was convinced that any such attempt would only result in the severity of the beating being increased. Ultimately, with the woman close to death, she was dragged away, whimpering.

After an uneasy pause a monk in saffron robes, also with his hands tied behind him, was dragged into the compound by two young soldiers. Tessa recognised him immediately as the man she had mistakenly punched but then revived. The captain began hitting him. The sickening *thwack* of the staff blows reverberated around the courtyard. Nevertheless, the monk remained composed and silent throughout.

"What crime has he committed?" demanded Tessa in Burmese.

"He's an NLD dissident," barked the captain. "He masterminded the second saffron uprising and prefers a painful death to answering my questions."

"Sounds to me like he's a brave and principled man," responded Tessa. "But a cowardly bully like you wouldn't understand anything like that, would you?"

Although this elicited a smile from the monk, the captain simply beat him harder.

Suddenly, three soldiers approached Tessa's cage. One was carrying a glass of water and another paper cup.

"Medicine... you must take," ordered the soldier in English. He gestured her away from the door. As she reversed back, Tessa flexed her muscles. She wasn't in top condition, but neither were her potential opponents. She sensed her time had come to make a stand.

"Cowardly bully!" she yelled at the captain. "Cowardly bully! Cowardly bully!..."

It wasn't long before the whole compound had joined in with her taunting. The captain glared at her angrily and the three soldiers looked nervous. By the time they had unlocked the padlock on the door, they weren't concentrating any more. Tessa dived down and completed two quick handstands. On the third, she brought her feet round and kicked the bars of the door. The impact was so violent that the door shot open, scattering the soldiers. Tessa continued her handstands, stopping only when she was between the captain and the monk.

She smiled at the soldier; he seemed unsure what to do.

"*Mingalabah*, cowardly bully!" she jeered. "You said you could take me any time. I choose now. Or are you too scared of being humiliated by a woman in front of all these witnesses?" She indicated the prison cells all around.

The two soldiers who'd brought the monk approached, but the captain ordered them to wait.

"You asked for it, whore," he sneered.

He gripped the staff anew and aimed a downward blow at Tessa. But she deftly darted to one side and avoided it.

"Hah!" she mocked. "Is that the best a cowardly bully like you can do?"

Furious, the captain raised the staff again and began a fast sweeping horizontal blow. This time, Tessa didn't move. Instead, at the last moment, she reached out with both hands. The staff hit them with a loud *crack*. She clamped her grip shut and immediately did a quick aerial somersault backwards, wrenching the staff from the captain's grasp. Then she launched it straight at one of the two soldiers standing on her left. It struck him in the centre of the forehead, knocking him out. As the staff bounced back, Tessa renewed her grip on it. She moved swiftly to her right and used the staff to prod the other soldier in the stomach. As he doubled up, she thwacked him over the head. He staggered forward and collapsed unconscious. A new expectant hush filled the compound. Tessa smiled at the captain.

"It's just you and me now," she goaded. "What's more, it seems you're not just a cowardly bully, you're incompetent too. This is a good staff, but you clearly don't know how to use it, do you?"

Tessa started whirling it round. First, just in her hands, then round her waist, over one shoulder and then the other. When she stopped, she brought the staff down vertically by her side. A tumult of applause broke out in the compound. Tessa took a bow.

Then she saw the prison commandant enter the compound, Paul was with him. Both of them looked livid. Paul clearly wanted to intervene, but the commandant held him back.

"No," he insisted, "it's about time that whore was punished for all the soldiers she killed. Now she'll get the beating she deserves. Don't worry, she won't be very damaged."

"I'm not worried about her, you fool, I'm worried about *him*," replied Paul, pointing at the captain.

"Hah!" laughed the commandant. "Now you will see that she is nothing."

Tessa whirled the staff again, took a quick step towards the captain and prodded him in the stomach. As he doubled up in pain, she brought the staff vertical again.

"Oh, dear, does that hurt?" she laughed. "Promise to do what I say and I'll stop, otherwise we'll just have to carry on. What's it to be?"

"Nariko, drop the fucking staff!" yelled Paul.

"Anything you say, Mr Sadist Pervert," she said, and thwacked the captain hard on his left bicep. Then she whirled it round and gave him another blow on the right thigh. She moved so fast the captain couldn't evade her blows. By now the prisoners were in hysterics. Then the commandant drew his gun and fired two shots in the air; the watchers fell quiet.

"Kill her!" shouted the commandant to the captain, who was rubbing his bruises.

"Fucking hell, no!" yelled Paul. "Do not bloody kill her!"

"What's the matter, Paul, worried about your investment? Perhaps you should order me to protect myself?" mocked Tessa.

"You get back in the cage," he yelled.

"I said, kill the bitch!" yelled the commandant. "Do it now!"

Tessa fondled the staff, testing its strength; finally widening her grip. Then she raised her knee and brought the staff down abruptly. The impact snapped it like a dry twig. She discarded the parts, and Paul appeared to relax slightly...

"Come on cowardly bully," she hissed, provocatively at the captain, "show us what you're really made of."

She turned her back on him and walked towards the monk. The quiet as everyone held their breath spoke volumes. Meanwhile, Tessa was listening to the captain drawing his knife. Just as he threw it, she spun round, catching it neatly in her right hand.

"Thank you. Just what I needed," she said. "I thought a cowardly bully like you would attack when my back was turned." She used it to cut the plastic ties binding the monk's wrists.

"I doubt either of us is going to come out of this very well," she said to him. "But at least the captain is being taught a lesson."

"I prepared myself to die today. I suspect it is my time. But, although I do not approve of violence, I confess I find this very entertaining."

Tessa fondled the knife in her hand. She could kill herself in an instant, and it wouldn't hurt much.

"You mustn't do that," beseeched the monk, reading her thoughts.

"It's quite an attractive option," she mused.

"I understand why you might think that, but life was given to you as a gift. Together with it came responsibilities and all the obstacles your destiny places in front of you. Your life is not yours to take. Death is never an attractive option and only arrives at the appointed time. I don't believe yours is now. However, if it is the captain's destiny to die here today, it will give many people hope. And, the news will spread quickly."

Tessa smiled, put her hands together and bowed.

"May you go in peace."

"Oh, don't worry, I will... Do not lose hope, Nariko. You have many friends here, more than you know."

She smiled and walked back towards the captain fondling the knife.

"Oh, bloody hell," screamed Paul, again trying to push forward, but the commandant refused to let him pass. So he put his briefcase on the ground and opened it, starting to load a dart in his air pistol as fast as his shaking hands could manage.

"I call for a free and democratic Burma!" yelled Tessa at the top of her voice. Then she threw the knife at the Junta's flag on top of the nearby flagpole. The knife pinned the flag to the wood, causing it to tear noisily as it flapped in the breeze. The compound erupted into ecstatic cries of approval.

Paul finished just as the captain drew his gun. But Tessa was already doing handstands; she finished directly in front of him. As he pulled the trigger, she thrust his arm aside. He fired harmlessly into the air. Then she punched him hard in the chest. Winded and stunned, he moved two paces back, wheezing pathetically as he desperately tried to refill his lungs. Tessa followed him, and, carefully watching the irregular pulsing of the arteries in his neck, prised the pistol from his grip. In a moment she had emptied the magazine safely into the ground, the plumes of dust testament to the waste of expensive, difficult-to-obtain ammunition. She tossed the gun aside and, with her left hand on the captain's shoulder to keep him still, punched him again, just below his Adam's apple. The blow made a horrible scrunching sound as his soft palate was forced backwards, blocking the windpipe and preventing his lungs from emptying. A moment later, she punched him one more time, a strong upward blow deep into the diaphragm. For a second he stood perfectly still, arms twitching by his sides; then his knees gave way and he crumpled to the ground, dead.

"Oh, fuck!" exclaimed Paul. "Nariko, revive him."

"Why should I do that, Mr Sadist Pervert? He's about to join the majority of your family. It won't be long before you're there too. Won't that be a fun reunion?"

"Revive him!" he screamed desperately. "It's in your best interests."

"Paul, I don't believe you'll do anything which is in my best interests. He's got ten seconds, then it's too late. You know how to do it, you revive him."

In fact, Tessa knew that her final punch had ruptured the captain's heart. There was no coming back for him. Histrionically, she started counting down from ten, but no one moved. Finally, she turned and bowed respectfully to the monk and began walking back to her cage. The prison compound erupted to the chant of "Nariko, Nariko, Nariko…" She could see Paul hurrying towards her brandishing his pistol. The commandant was running to the fallen captain. Tessa sat on her bed; she knew what was about to happen.

"You stupid fucking idiot!" yelled Paul, over the continuing chanting from the compound. "What is it with you? Why can't you just do as you're told?"

"I'm a Peacekeeper, and that man was a cruel and cowardly bully – ring any bells? I was just doing my job."

"So you think it was a good idea to kill the commandant's son?"

Tessa exploded into laughter.

"Whoops! How on earth are you going to stop him having me killed?"

"Nariko, you should know by now that there are worse things than death."

He fired the air pistol and Tessa lay back on her bed as her muscles contracted. He came over, cut off her tee-shirt and moved out the arm and leg supports. Then he strapped her down tightly, even fastening an additional strap just below her breasts.

"So, what aberrant torture will it be this time?"

"You'll find out soon enough. And you'll regret not having taken the tablets."

A shot rang out from the compound and the chanting stopped.

Tessa sighed.

"What did you expect?" commented Paul, clumsily fitting a fresh cannula.

"One day he'll pay dearly for his crimes, as will you."

"Possibly, but you won't be there to witness it." He prepared a syringe, injected her and packed his briefcase. "That was a strong muscle relaxant, it will make sure you don't start any more trouble."

He left and she started to doze off...

Tessa was woken by the jab of a knife point being poked between her breasts. She opened her eyes to find the prison commandant standing over her. He trailed the blade down her torso, across her navel and on. She could hear the metallic rasping across her skin and feel the sharpness of its tip. She wasn't sure whether it was drawing blood or not.

"You murdering whore."

"I only kill murderers and I am not a whore. I didn't choose to be trussed up like this."

"You murdered my son."

"He had ample opportunity to kill me. He used a staff, a knife and a gun while I had nothing. That doesn't make me a murderer. I am simply an International Peacekeeper doing my job. It is you who just murdered a defenceless monk. That must be enough bad karma for many generations."

He brought his knife directly over her right eye, barely a centimetre above the pupil.

Suddenly, Paul grabbed his hand and pulled it away.

"If you so much as touch her again, I will personally have you, and every one of your family, cut into little pieces and fed to pigs," he hissed. "And if anyone else touches her, I will hold you responsible. Get out!"

"She must be punished," rasped the commandant.

"She will be, but not by you."

"I'll give you your four days, but if she is not out of here by then, I..."

The commandant spat at Tessa and stomped away.

"Hmm, I don't think he likes you, Paul," mused Tessa.

"He hates you far more," replied Paul, mopping away the commandant's spittle. He opened his briefcase and filled a syringe. "To think I even gave you a second chance to take the tablets. I shouldn't have bothered, should I?" He had barely started injecting her when her eyes closed. She woke to find the mosquito nets down and some nervous soldiers spraying insecticide throughout her cage. Then two large standard lights were set up by her gurney. Still groggy, she drifted off again...

Suddenly, a metallic clanking close by prompted Tessa to open her eyes. A Burmese man in a white coat was standing over her. She managed to raise her head a little and saw that there was a nurse with him, dragging a trolley of medical equipment.

The man glanced around and bent over Tessa, holding the eyelids to her left eye open to examine the pupil.

"Blink your other eye if you can communicate?" he intoned.

Tessa frowned, wondering what was going on. Then she blinked.

"Good. We must be careful not to be seen talking, so just listen," he whispered, busily removing some equipment from vacuum packs. "I am a doctor. I am to implant a location transponder in your liver. However, I will insert a harmless biodegradable pellet there – it will be gone in a year. However, they will check that I have implanted a transponder, so I intend to embed one inside your mouth. To remove it, all you will need to do is grab it and pull hard." He looked away as though checking that all his equipment was ready.

"May I have some water, please?" asked Tessa. The doctor nodded to the nurse who helped her drink some from a bottle with a tube.

"Thank you," mumbled Tessa. "Why…?"

"There are many people grateful that Soe Gyi is dead," he continued, looking at the nurse. "Careful, the corporal is watching us." Suddenly he spoke more loudly. "You say there is something wrong in your mouth."

"Yes," replied Tessa, "could you look at it, please?"

"I am not a dentist, but I will see."

The doctor held her mouth open and moved her head round to get some light in it.

"Ah," he exclaimed. "I think you have bitten your cheek. A couple of stiches will sort that… No, there is something in it."

Tessa watched as the doctor reached in to her mouth with a scalpel. Then she felt him cut and tasted the blood in her mouth from the incision. Although the discomfort was considerable, she stayed completely silent and he jubilantly produced a slither of chicken bone from her mouth. Then he reached back in again and started suturing the cut he had just made. But Tessa could feel that where there had been nothing, there was now something small and hard. She marvelled at his dexterity.

"There. That should solve your problem. Eat on the right for a couple of days."

"Thank you," replied Tessa.

He prodded beneath her rib-cage several times, marked her and swabbed the area with some acrid disinfectant. After a while, he started talking again although ostensibly studying his equipment.

"Soon you are going to be injected with a concoction of drugs, mainly rohypnol and heroin, but there are a number of other components too. The rohypnol will make you forgetful and compliant, and also more susceptible to hypnotism. Apparently, the treatment programme will take fourteen days. So you must escape before then, or you may not remember to try. If there is more work to be done on you, I will try to be the surgeon, but they may not let me attend you twice. While you are being drugged, you must keep your brain active. Establish a routine. Count the days, sing songs, do arithmetic, recite poems…, anything cognitive like that will help you resist the drugs." Tessa already knew of such techniques, but remained silent. "And whenever possible, exercise. Keep up your strength. It will help your mind stay fit too."

He started speaking more loudly again.

"Now, I will insert the locator into your liver. It is a thick needle and must be inserted a long way; I am not permitted to use any anaesthetic. So prepare yourself…"

Tessa felt a sharp scratch just below her rib cage quickly followed by an intense stabbing pain advancing into her. She could feel her eyes bulging and moaned aloud. The doctor removed the tube's centre and used it to push something into her liver. Again she winced.

"Withdrawing now."

He disinfected the wound again and applied a single butterfly stich to close it while the nurse dabbed Tessa's face with a damp cloth. As the doctor drew close to apply an adhesive plaster over his handiwork, he started whispering.

"I am going to leave you a sharpened nail which I am sure you will be able to put to good use, even if only to make marks so you don't lose track of time. I will drop it on the floor and press it into the dirt between the two front legs of the bed. You can recover it later. I am sorry for your discomfort and indignity. Good luck."

"*Kyay zu tin bar de*," said Tessa quietly.

"Corporal," shouted the doctor. "I am finished here."

Despite the stinging of her new wounds, Tessa tried to console herself with the thought that it had not been too bad. She wanted to sleep, but found it was difficult with such bright lights still beaming down on her; she had a nasty feeling that the fact they had not been removed was significant.

She wasn't sure how long it was before she was roused by the sound of more metallic clinking, but it must have been several hours as it was already dusk. She discovered another Burmese man in a white coat, and a nurse, setting up surgical instruments again. The man started prodding her abdomen. It seemed he was about to do something else to her, but this was not the surgeon who had operated before.

"Who are you?" asked Tessa.

"He assures me he's a surgeon," answered Paul, entering her field of view. He checked her pupils. "Wide awake, good. Thanks to your bloody-mindedness, I've had to bring our schedule forward. That means our German friends can't be here themselves, so this man is going to do the honours." He held up a sealed bag with a thin rounded box in it. "Do you know what this is?"

"An internal insulin pump?" replied Tessa, desperately hoping she was wrong.

"Clever. However, this one's full of drugs designed to make your character more suitable to your future life. Enough to last about six months. Although I won't bore you with all the details, I know you're inquisitive so here's a brief summary. The drugs include some powerful ecstasy derivatives, nasty stuff to get high on. Amongst other things, they'll make you more emphatic and reduce your susceptibility to negative social signals. Hurrah! You'll be obedient. Plus there's some heroin based stuff which does a few more exciting things, not least making an addict of you. And, my personal favourite, there are some compounds to increase post-orgasmic bliss. Sadly, you will suffer permanent brain damage, but you won't notice. Indeed, if the drugs are given in large enough doses, they're lethal. But when activated by one of these…" he held up a grey box with a black button on it "…you will receive a precise predetermined dose. The pump is about to be implanted just outside your abdominal cavity. Those pills I provided were the anaesthetic, so don't blame me if you don't enjoy this. I'm off now to the Strand as I can't stand the sight of blood and I could murder a glass of cold beer. Be seeing you…"

"Paul, surely you're not serious?" remonstrated Tessa. "That's cruel even by your debauched standards." He shrugged and walked away. "I hope you choke on your dinner," she called after him.

"In your dreams," he laughed.

With growing trepidation Tessa watched the doctor complete his preparations. She just had time to mutter, "Oh, boy," before the nurse gave her a rubber gag to bite on. Initially she refused, but the surgeon made it clear he would force it into her mouth if she didn't take it voluntarily. Tessa bit down on it and lay back, her breathing growing faster and deeper.

Eventually, the man glanced into her eyes. Tessa thought that maybe a faint wisp of a smile had crossed his face, but couldn't interpret what it meant. Then he swabbed her abdomen with what smelled like iodine.

She couldn't help watching as he unpacked a scalpel. The sight of it made her squirm. Her body was desperate to move away, but was strapped down so tightly she wouldn't have been able to move even if she'd had full muscle control. Her heart started thumping. She ordered herself to relax, to breathe slowly and to force her mind somewhere more pleasant.

But then she felt him put two fingers down on her and push apart slightly. Already her eyes were watering. Suddenly she felt a sharp burning sensation where he began cutting which quickly transformed into searing pain. It was so intense she had considerable difficulty in not crying out. She moaned and bit harder on the gag as tears started pooling in her eyes. The nurse dried them; she didn't seem to be enjoying watching.

Despite the relaxing effect of the drugs Paul had given her, all Tessa's muscles tensed. She clenched her fists and screwed up her feet. The pain seemed to go on forever. Then she felt the surgeon groping inside her, as though tugging at something, and groaned loudly. She heard him ask for the pump, the nurse handed it to him and he started pushing it in. Tessa gasped and her body twitched. The doctor muttered something to the nurse and started to withdraw the pump.

Tessa refused to cry out, but was almost screaming with her mouth closed. At one point she unintentionally spat out the mouth gag, but the nurse quickly reinserted it. The surgeon asked for the scalpel back. Tessa's distress reached new heights as she wondered whether he had both hands inside her now. But then she felt the pump being pushed in again. She winced violently at one point and heard a number of distinct metallic *clicks*. It felt as though an electric shock was coursing through her. The agony was excruciating beyond belief, but still the procedure went on and on. She doggedly clung to consciousness, but knew she was losing the battle. Finally the surgeon seemed satisfied with what he had done. He withdrew his fingers, swabbed up some blood and sewed her up. The wound was disinfected and a tissue regenerator was passed over the wound several times before it was dressed. The small incision over her liver was similarly treated to accelerate its healing. Then she was given an injection of something.

On the edge of consciousness, she was past caring. Tears mixed with droplets of perspiration rolled down her ashen face; her body was trembling and racked with pain. But without a word the doctor simply cleared up and, after the nurse had removed the gag and dabbed her face, they left.

Tessa wasn't sure how long she lay there moaning and panting, but eventually she could hold on no longer and passed out. When she came round her body had relaxed again. She was still in agony and her abdomen was throbbing dreadfully. She wasn't sure how long she stayed alone in such discomfort, but soon realised something was wrong. Her heart rate had decreased and there was a persistent humming in her ears; her blood pressure was dropping and her breathing had become shallow. She was dying, and wasn't sure she wouldn't welcome the release…

"That's wiped the cocky grin off you face hasn't it?" said Paul suddenly.

"Freedom beckons," mumbled Tessa weakly.

He looked at her for a moment, and then felt her pulse.

"Christ almighty!" exclaimed Paul.

"I hope so," sighed Tessa, and closed her eyes.

In a moment the straps holding her down had all been removed. Paul dabbed her face with a damp cloth and spread a blanket over her.

Then he ran out. Tessa hoped that it would all be over soon...

Suddenly, someone was feeling her forehead. She opened her eyes to find the surgeon who had fitted the pump examining her.

"She's in shock," he rasped, speaking fluent English, "why didn't you summon me earlier? She is close to death."

"If she dies, so do you."

"It's not my fault she's dying. You were the one who stopped me from using the anaesthetic the Germans sent with the equipment. I'm not being held responsible for your..."

"Fucking save her, or, so help me God, I'll shoot you here and now," yelled Paul, his voice tense with anger and fear.

The surgeon breathed out noisily and opened his bag.

"I see she's had another cannula installed recently, what else has she been given?" he demanded... "Well?"

"Curare, and a variety of scorpion, snake and frog toxins."

"What? You fool! Why didn't you tell me earlier? Do the Germans know? That was not part of their programme, she should never have had the surgery today... I'll give her something to ease the pain and boost her metabolism but she is very weak. I shall follow the Germans' instructions to the letter now. We should move her, immediately."

"No way. She's staying here."

The doctor look irritated. But Paul was clearly adamant.

"Then get me a chair, some clean towels and hot water. I will stay with her tonight."

Tessa drifted in and out of consciousness. But the pain began to ease and she started to feel a little better. Although still very weak, she realised her life was no longer at risk. Feeling slightly disappointed, she opened her eyes. It was dawn and the surgeon was watching her. He dabbed her face.

"Nariko, do not be concerned," he said in a low voice. "You were never in danger of dying. I induced your symptoms to mimic the effects of shock. I thought it might enable us to free you, but it did not. I am sorry I had to inflect such pain on you, but I had no choice. My family..."

"I understand," acknowledged Tessa feebly.

"You will be moved in three days. A joint British and German motion is going before the UNWP demanding your release. It will receive unanimous support. The Junta intend to swear you are not in Burma. So, you only have two full days to recuperate. It is not enough, but…"

"Why are you telling me this?"

"In Burma, if you help my friends, then I will help you," he replied. "You do not stand alone, Nariko. There are many of us risking our lives for you." Tessa started to drift off again. He smiled. "Difficult times lie ahead. But although your body may indeed be imprisoned, your spirit need not be." By now she was struggling to keep her eyes open. The doctor smiled. "There is more to tell you, but later will do. Sleep now."

CHAPTER 14

It was mid-morning when Tessa woke up. She was still racked with pain and kept her eyes closed. She became aware of a cool breeze wafting over her, and a humming sound; an air conditioning unit had been brought in. Then Paul started a telephone conversation and, resisting the temptation to sink back into oblivion, she did her best to eavesdrop.

"*Moshi-moshi*… Yeah, she'll be OK. She's still out cold… Well, it wasn't my fault maybe the Germans… Yeah, all thanks to that bastard Potter… Oh, they've both arrived. But the bloody crane dropped the prison unit. Apparently, it regularly drops things but the stupid buggers neglected to tell me that in advance… No, I don't think there was any malice behind it… Oh, yes, the service container is fine, thank goodness… Yes, I'm transferring the gear I can from the damaged one into another… Oh, it should be fine; I've found some excellent Burmese welders… Really, he wants to visit her here? That's not exactly convenient… If he must… Yep, I'll be in touch."

Tessa waited and then moaned softly before easing her eyes open. Paul came over to her, looked at his watch, and injected her with something.

"What was that, sadistic pervert?"

"Good morning to you too," he replied testily. "Morphine… Do you fancy something to eat?…" She raised her eyebrows to check she'd heard him correctly. "Don't worry, I still couldn't care a fuck about you, I just want to build up your strength."

"How thoughtful," murmured Tessa sarcastically. "Scrambled eggs, boiled rice, bananas and water."

Paul nodded and left; she heard the padlock being fastened behind him.

Tessa dozed until he returned with the Burmese girl who been cleaning her cage. She looked frightened but bowed respectfully to Tessa, prompting Paul to breathe out noisily.

"This is Mya, she'll stay with you for a while," he announced. "If you need anything, ask her."

The girl nervously unfolded a small table by Tessa's bed and placed a covered plate on it together with a bottle of water.

"I want some clothes, Paul."

"There's a fresh tee-shirt over there."

"I said clothes, not a tee-shirt."

"Don't push your luck. Enjoy your breakfast," he retorted and walked out, locking the cage door as he left.

"*Mingalabah*, Mya," said Tessa, forcing a smile. "Would you pass me the tee-shirt, please?"

She got it and spread it over Tessa.

"Thank you... Is something the matter, Mya?"

"No," she replied with a tremor in her voice, looking round.

"Are you scared?"

She nodded.

"Of what?"

"Him, here. The soldiers threatened my family, and..."

"...of me?"

"Maybe a little. Did you really kill the captain with your bare hands?"

"Yes, but you have no reason to be afraid of me."

"But if you do something wrong, he will punish me."

"Quite possibly, he's that sort of a person. But I'm in no condition to do anything at the moment, so let's worry about that later."

She helped Tessa sit up and put the tee-shirt on. It was very painful and Tessa was completely exhausted, but Mya supported her while she ate the food, although Tessa insisted that she had the banana. Then a soldier came to the cage and pushed a rolled mat through the bars. Mya laid it out and kneeled down on it while Tessa dozed.

When she next woke, Tessa inspected the dressing over her wound. Gritting her teeth, she prised it up; the incision had certainly been sutured very neatly and, thanks to the action of the tissue regenerator, was healing well. She felt around the wound; it was extremely tender and there was definitely something hard inside her. She considered removing it, but suspected that would probably only result in its being reinserted. However, even that might serve to exacerbate Paul's problems since he was obviously under time pressure. But there was no denying her situation had taken a serious turn for the worse. Paul no longer needed to approach in order to drug her, and the drugs were clearly not going to do her any good. How long would she be able to resist them? Furthermore, if she was going to be moved soon, she needed to recover that nail and secrete it somewhere, preferably without Mya seeing.

The effects of the morphine began to wear off, but despite her increasing discomfort Tessa's appetite started to recover. She and Mya chatted and had a late lunch together, soon becoming friends.

Mid-afternoon, a nurse arrived with the tissue regenerator and a fresh dressing. She insisted Tessa lay back while the machine was run over her wounds several times. This was always a most unpleasant process as the procedure stung dreadfully. Tessa was familiar with such devices, having had many wounds similarly treated in the past. When used correctly, they were very effective at accelerating the healing process and shouldn't leave scars. However, the nurse was so rude to Mya that Tessa took a dislike to her. So, despite the nurse's protestations, Tessa measured her own temperature and then broke the thermometer without telling the nurse what the reading was. Then she snatched the fresh dressings and insisted that Mya could reapply them far more competently. Mya smiled as the nurse stomped away. Tessa stayed on the bed most of the day, occasionally staggering round her cage with Mya's assistance to get some exercise. Eventually, Paul came back. He looked harassed and dirty; Tessa couldn't help laughing, even though it hurt.

"Oh dear, what on earth have you been doing to wipe the cocky grin off your face?" she asked.

"Bugger off. Just take these, they'll help you sleep."

"Bugger off yourself, you perverted sadist."

"You want me to hurt her?" he snarled looking at Mya.

"No."

"Then take the damn pills."

"No. And if you even upset her, I'll tear the pump out."

Paul glared at her, but Tessa could see he believed her.

"Oh, suit your fucking self then."

He threw the pills on the ground and left.

"Sweet dreams, sadist pervert," shouted Tessa...

Tessa woke soon after dawn feeling considerably better. She was still very sore, but when the now jumpy nurse arrived to apply the tissue regenerator again, they could both see that the wounds were healing extremely well.

Mya fetched some breakfast, and, after a short rest, Tessa started walking round the cage to promote her circulation. When Mya wasn't looking, she checked with her foot that she could find the nail quickly, and that it remained hidden. Then, as her strength returned, she swore an oath. She would never let them wear her down and wouldn't allow them to take control of her mind. She would continue to resist, and not only escape, but also make sure that all those responsible for this brutal treatment being meted out to her, and others, faced justice. Even though she knew none of it would be easy, she had overcome insurmountable obstacles before and would do so again. This new resolve made her feel much more positive about whatever her future might bring.

Lying on her bed, she started planning how she would keep her mind focussed. She practised humming tunes, trying to imprint some of her favourites: Enya, Ani Choying Drolma, Yusuf, Allegri, Gilbert & Sullivan and Puccini. Then she started working through multiplication tables and remembering favourite stories and characters, from Molly Moon to Sherlock Holmes. Late morning, Mya left to go and collect lunch. However, she was gone too long and Tessa began to grow suspicious.

Suddenly, shouting broke out from opposite sides of the prison. Tessa looked round to see what was happening. Then she heard the tell-tale *phut!* of a chemical dart being fired, and the stinging sensation of it hitting her thigh.

"Damn!" she exclaimed, quickly plucking it out. Then she collapsed on the bed as her muscles started twitching. They tensed and finally seized solid, causing considerable pain in her abdomen. Tessa waited for the relief of her muscles relaxing. It was not long before she heard the padlock being unlocked and recognised Paul's footsteps, but there were two others with him.

"Didn't see that one coming did you, Peacekeeper?" mocked Paul.

"Hello, sadist pervert," hissed Tessa. "I was wondering when you would dare show your face again."

"Nice to see you too, whore," he sneered. Standing by her side, he folded a handkerchief and laid it over her eyes.

"I hope that's clean, Paul," said Tessa.

He chuckled and pulled her tee-shirt up over her breasts. Someone else approached her bed and yanked the dressing off roughly to inspect her abdomen. After a little prodding and kneading, a new dressing was applied.

"As you see," assured Paul, "your goods are in excellent order and preparations for the conditioning programme are progressing completely according to schedule."

Someone else approached her bed. Tessa was enveloped in a cloud of strong musky male perfume. By now her muscles were completely relaxed, but, gathering all her strength, she abruptly shook her head. The handkerchief slid off and she found herself looking into the eyes of a tanned Arab dressed in a well-tailored dark blue blazer and off-white slacks. On his jacket was a crest just like her henna tattoo.

"Ah, hello," said Tessa, as the man hurriedly stepped away. "I've been wanting to meet you. Come closer. Surely my buyer should not be shy." The man looked nervous and unsure what to do. Tessa studied what she could see of him with disdain. He was quite tall and somewhat overweight, with a bushy black moustache and small beard on his suntanned face. He was wearing expensive gold-framed glasses. But Tessa couldn't see his hair since it was covered by a red-and-white-checked keffiyeh, secured by two thick black cords near the crown of his head.

"You can approach her," said a confident voice with a German accent. "She cannot move her arms or legs, and will not remember what happens here."

"*Guten tag*, Herr Doktor Krollheim," droned Tessa, "how nice to meet you again. I presume you're here because Paul confessed he nearly killed me?"

Paul and the Doktor looked at each other coyly.

"Gentlemen," chided Tessa. "Surely you haven't been misleading your client? Especially one that's paying you so generously."

The Arab rounded angrily on Paul.

"What is she talking about?"

"Nothing. She's just trying to unsettle you," retorted Paul quickly.

"Then tell me what happened?" he demanded.

Tessa quickly butted in.

"That inexperienced idiot tortured me with snake venom and then had the Doktor's little toy inserted without anaesthetic. The shock damaged me, almost killed me in fact. If that doesn't make me spoilt goods, the pervert also stuck his finger..."

"Shut up," hissed Paul.

"I am a Peacekeeper, I tell the truth. Sir, you shouldn't do business with these people," warned Tessa. "They will double-cross you as soon as it suits them..."

"Quiet, or I'll have the Doktor silence you," interrupted Paul.

"So, who are you?" asked Tessa, meeting the Arab's gaze.

He moved back to her side; but Tessa could see the Doktor hurriedly preparing a syringe.

"I am Sheikh Saif Iqbal Mubdallah Ikraam Tayeb Al Rahal of Irabya. My friends call me *Simitar*. If you like, you can call me that too. What shall I call you?"

"*Habibi*." The sheikh's smile softened at the friendly informality of her Arabic greeting, while an expression of trepidation crossed Paul's. "You shall call me your worst nightmare. You will rue the day you ever set eyes on me. I will wreak devastation and dishonour upon you and your family. Your dynasty's fall from grace will be complete for time immemorial." The Sheikh took a step back, visibly shaken. However, the Doktor calmly swabbed her arm. "Be afraid, Sheikh" continued Tessa as she felt the needle slide in, "and you too, Doktor. I will find you all..."

"*Cháus, Liebling*," the Doktor broke in, sneeringly.

There was a sound like rushing water in Tessa's ears and her world turned hazy and echoic. She suspected he had just given her more of the drug which had been used at Waley, but maybe not such a large dose. She tried to concentrate on listening to the sometimes agitated conversation around her.

"...We are ready," exclaimed the Doktor, clearly frustrated. "We have all the necessary data." He placed a hand on Tessa's forehead and pushed it round to the left. Then he shoved her head backwards and thrust a hypodermic up her nose. Through misty eyes she could see the glistening needle in front of her and did her best to recoil as the doctor moved it further up her nasal cavity. She even felt the point sink in slightly at the back of her nose. "All I need do is inject this directly into her brain and she becomes an automaton. Yes, there will be some frontal lobe damage, but nothing too fundamental; the markers will do the rest."

"Fine, let's do it," endorsed the Sheikh. "I am purchasing her and I don't care what state she's in. I only need her to be alive and sufficiently sentient to be responsive to my demands."

"No," insisted Paul, "that is not our deal, and you both know it. This is the final test for your long-term procedure, Doktor. I shouldn't need to remind you the two previous applications were far from successful; your credibility is at stake here. We have invested too much in her not to see the adjustment treatment completed. The pump is installed now, and we need your procedure to deliver a complete and permanent alteration to her mental state. There will be no shortcuts, and that's final."

Tessa was relieved to see the needle being withdrawn from her nose, but she could sense the reluctance with which it had been done. Then the dressing on her wound was yanked off again. She felt something cold and metallic against her skin. Suddenly there was an intense shooting pain in her abdomen; it was so sharp her whole body twitched.

"You see, the pump works perfectly," boasted the Doktor. "She cannot escape now and I guarantee she will be fully adapted in two weeks."

"All right," the Sheikh acquiesced. "So how do you intend to move her? You said there'd been a change of plans."

"Nothing of consequence. Transportation and pick-up will be as I advised three days ago. The prison container was damaged during off-loading, but we're modifying another. Everything's fine, you have no cause for concern. She leaves tomorrow..."

Eventually, laughing, the three of them left.

Laugh all you like, thought Tessa, but somehow I will get every one of you. Nevertheless, she knew the odds were stacked against her. So far, apart from her brief interlude with the captain, everything had gone according to Paul's plan, and there really had been absolutely

162

nothing she could do about it.

She lay back and waited for muscle co-ordination to return. It didn't take long and she rolled clumsily off the table. Pretending still to be incapacitated, she crawled around in search of the nail. It proved to be a fine implement, a short pencil-chisel rather than a nail. One end was rounded while the other was flat like a screwdriver and very sharp. Both ends looked as though they had been flame-hardened and ground. She carefully hid it anew and returned to her bed.

Not long afterwards, Mya returned with some food...

It was only just light when the nurse arrived to inspect the wound on Tessa's abdomen. As bad tempered as ever, she treated it again with the tissue regenerator and gave Tessa two dressings; one to apply immediately and another for after she'd showered. As she was leaving, she also told Mya to collect the breakfasts straight away.

While she was alone, Tessa slid off her bed and discreetly recovered her chisel. The options for hiding it were not plentiful. Furthermore, if Paul followed his usual modus operandi, she would be drugged while being moved. If she hid it in her vagina, definitely not her preferred location, it would be discovered if she was raped. She shuddered at the thought. That only left one place.

Tessa sat on her bed with the chisel under her thigh while she ate her breakfast. She was half-way through when she saw Paul approaching. He stopped outside the cage.

"You're leaving in two hours. Get cleaned up."

"Lovely, where are we going, darling?"

"To your new owner, whore," replied Paul.

"How nice. Perhaps I could have some suitcases for all my gear?"

"Ha, ha, ha!"

"Paul, for the record, I will never consciously do what you or your friends ask, and I am not a whore. What your drugs allow you to make people do, doesn't change who they really are."

"Hmm, do I detect a note of desperation creeping in to your final insults?" he boasted. "Trust me, drugs can change who a person really is. Ready or not, you're leaving in two hours."

Tessa finished her breakfast and secreted the chisel in her hand. But she was finding it increasingly difficult to hide the chisel.

"Shall I hold it for you?" whispered Mya. "You can trust me."

"You mustn't let anyone see," insisted Tessa, "or ever say anything about it. I don't want you to get into trouble."

"I understand."

Tessa went to the shower area and exchanged the chisel for the soap. Mya sat by and smiled while Tessa washed, applying the spare dressing before putting her tee-shirt on.

"I think you should go to toilet," suggested Mya, surreptitiously fondling the chisel. "I will help you. I have hidden things there too. You will need to push it up a long way or it will drop out. It hurts..."

Tessa followed her advice and then, with Mya shielding her from view, pushed the chisel as far as she could up her rectum. She winced as she stood up, but the chisel did not drop out.

"Thank you for all your help," said Tessa.

"That's OK. What he is doing to you is not right."

"What the Junta is doing to the people of Burma is also not right. Maybe one day we will both be free from our tormentors."

"I hope so," replied Mya.

Tessa gave her a hug.

"How sweet," shouted Paul from across the compound. "I daresay those lesbian tendencies of yours will come in handy for the Sheikh. Let's go. You can walk or be carried. What's it to be?"

Tessa looked round. There were four soldiers with him, all armed, but she felt sure she could handle them. This might be her chance, but she needed to get out first.

"Oh, I suppose we might as well walk," she sighed.

Paul unlocked the cage and gestured her to follow him.

But once she was in the open, the other prisoners started chanting and soon the whole compound was reverberating to the chant of "Nariko, Nariko, Nariko..." The volume was deafening, and quite intimidating. Even the commandant firing shots into the air failed to stem their exuberance. Tessa was amazed, and touched, but wondered whether this was ruining her chances of escape. Nevertheless, she put her hands together and bowed in respectful farewell. But Paul was clearly rattled. He turned round and glared at her.

"OK. I've had enough of this." He produced the grey box with a black button on it. "Let's make a start on that much-needed character adjustment, shall we?"

A wave of apprehension swept through Tessa, but then he pressed the button and she felt the pump vibrating inside her. A deep throbbing sound filled her ears, her vision blurred and it seemed as though fireworks were going off inside her head. She dropped to her knees with an absent expression on her face. Mya screamed and burst into tears, but was quickly pushed away by the guards. Tessa couldn't hear the shouting anymore. She saw Paul laughing and wondered whether she should join in, but felt unsure about everything. In fact, devoid of emotion, she didn't have a care in the world. Her eyelids felt as though they'd been weighted and she lost the ability to think. She was vaguely aware of passing a pickup full of heavily armed soldiers staring at her. But then she was shoved into the back of an SUV, and everything went dark.

CHAPTER 15

When Tessa came round, she had a horrendous headache. Her brain felt as though it was boiling, with bubbles of gas forming, coalescing and exploding on both sides of her skull. It was extraordinarily painful and she only just managed to stifle the urge to groan. Nevertheless, she kept quiet with her eyes firmly shut not wanting to indicate that she had come round until she had marshalled her thoughts. Slowly her discomfort eased and she became aware of voices in the distance. Then she remembered what had happened while leaving Insein. Where was she now? She knew she was lying on something hard, and there was a lot of remote clanging. As her grogginess dispersed, the conversation became clearer; she recognised Paul's voice.

"OK. Listen carefully. Under that grille is Nariko, the most dangerous Peacekeeper you are ever likely to come across. Give her a half a chance when she's conscious and she'll kill you, all of you. But if you follow my instructions, not only will you survive the next eleven days, you'll have some fun and get rich too. Now, while you're sailing, Markus here is the boss. Don't ever forget that. Always do whatever he says, without question. Don't think, don't argue, just do it. Understood?... Good.

"During the voyage, Nariko will be undergoing a drug programme which will alter her character; she'll become obedient and weak-willed. Basically she'll do whatever she's told. The complete procedure takes fourteen days, slightly longer than your journey, but by the time you arrive she won't know the difference between her new dream world and reality."

A man with a Geordie accent butted in.

"How long'll she be dangerous?"

"Seven or eight days. Now, while you're underway, her days will be broken into two twelve-hour cycles, always *precisely* as shown on this wall schedule. There will no time-zone changes for you while you're travelling. The black marks indicate when she's to receive her drugs. But only Markus is allowed to do that. He'll use the grey box to dose her at nine in the morning and nine at night. She'll have been conscious for about two hours beforehand but will pass out soon after she's been dosed. She'll wake up after about an hour and be completely obedient for the next two hours or so. During that time she's allowed out of her enclosure, but she has to spend the first hour exercising to make sure she retains her muscle tone. Just tell her to work out, she'll know what she needs to do. After she's got cleaned up, you can do what you like with her. It's part of her conditioning. However, don't *ever* get rough with her. She's not to be damaged in any way. A single bruise and you'll all be in serious trouble. Whatever happens, make sure she's locked back under the grille by noon or midnight. She'll be tired and ready to go back to sleep by then anyway, and trust me, you'll be exhausted. And don't stay with her while she's under the grille, including when she's sleeping. The silence and isolation will make her more appreciative when she does have company. And don't ever let her out of her compartment into here…"

"Yeah, but what 'appens if she gets the wrong dose?" asked the Geordie.

"She won't. However, if the button is held down for more than twenty seconds it empties the pump, which'll kill her…"

By now Tessa was sure the conversation was taking place in a different room, so she eased her eyes open. It looked as though she was lying in a small shallow enclosure within a corrugated metal container, at right angles to the main axis and near the end, which was to her right. The floor and sides of her enclosure were made from sheet steel and above her was a grille of thick round bars. Her horizontal prison was some six feet square and about twenty inches deep, leaving a few inches between her and the grille. The floor was bisected by a low steel wall. Where she was lying was just steel, sloping away from the lengthways divider. On her left, where the floor met the wall, were three long narrow slots. They looked like drainage holes. In the section to her right was a mattress and shallow pillow. Through the grille, she could see some exercise equipment, a shower area and a toilet. On the wall to her left was a door, slightly ajar.

"…back to the schedule," continued Paul. "The yellow bars show her meal times while the numbers in them denote her menu, green shows her exercise times and red when she's to sleep undisturbed. Markus will be watching to make sure you both stick to what it says. The schedule also shows who is with her when she's not under the grille. Markus always has her in the evening, because he's responsible for monitoring her.

"When feeding her, only give her the quantities shown; Markus will check her plate before you take it in. She'll be fully awake for breakfast and dinner, so make sure you only feed her as I showed you, through the chute. You'll be eating the same food. Leroy, you do all the cooking and keep the kitchen in order, and Jack, you're to keep everything else tip-top and spotless. You've got all the food provisions you'll need in these freezers – no alcohol and no smoking. Water, power, air-con, et cetera will all be supplied from the service container which will be below you; it also has a large gas cylinder to supply power. Markus will connect it all after you're craned on board…"

Suddenly, a new and rather unpleasant ache reminded Tessa of the chisel she'd been given. It was her only weapon and she needed to hide it somewhere safe. She felt through the central drainage slot to her left and found some blobs of weld. She smiled. Not only did they give her somewhere safe and out of sight to lodge the chisel, but they also suggested the weld quality might not be good. She carefully reached up her rectum to recover the chisel and soon found out why it was so uncomfortable and hadn't fallen out. The sharp end had embedded itself and proved difficult and painful to extract. Finally, she got it out and lodged it through the slot. Then she tried to wipe the blood off her fingers.

"…While you're at sea," Paul went on, "there'll be a complete communications black-out to make sure you can't be tracked. So if you have calls to make, do it after we're done here and then give your phones to Markus. The Special Forces are doing all they can to find your cargo, so make sure you don't attract any attention. Don't, for example, open the container doors. Now, you'll be loading soon. Any questions?"

"Supposing she croaks on us?" asked the Geordie.

"Markus will make sure she doesn't. The drugs will trash her mind, but we know they work and we know they don't kill. So, if she dies, it's your fault; and if she dies, you die."

"But the German bitch snuffed it," interjected another man with a strong Caribbean accent.

"Yea, and the Nip," added the Geordie. "We don't want any trouble if this one dies and we ain't dun' nuffin'."

"They died because people like you got careless. The Japanese girl was not locked up when she should have been while she was being treated in Irabya. She tried to escape and when she was cornered went out of her way to make sure she got herself shot. As for the German, she only died because she was travelling in the limo with her new owner when he was hit in Shanghai. So, stick to the schedule and everything'll be fine. But whatever you do, don't underestimate her. She might look cute, but I've seen her kill tougher guys than you with her bare hands. Unfortunately, since this is a replacement container, not everything works, including the cameras and satellite communications. But don't let her know that."

"So, what about our money?" interjected the Caribbean man.

"Once the container has been unloaded at your destination and Markus tells us you did your jobs well, you'll both be paid in full.

"Now, she'll be coming round soon. I'm going to have a word with her first then I'll introduce you. So you've got ten minutes to do whatever you need to do before the doors are closed."

Tessa heard Paul approaching and screwed her eyes shut, trying to mimic how she felt when she'd first come round. She moaned, blinked and immediately tried to sit up. There was a loud *thump* as her head hit the bars on the grille.

"Ouch, I bet that hurt," mocked Paul.

Tessa rubbed her forehead and looked round, trying to give the impression she was having difficulty working out where she was. She stared at Paul.

"How come I always feel sick when I see you?"

"Comedian to the last. But two weeks and we'll have fixed that."

"So where am I now?"

"You're in a shipping container about to depart on an eleven-day cruise."

"Lovely. Hope it's silver service. I do have standards, you know?"

"Ha, ha! You really are determined to put on a good show, aren't you? But I bet deep down you're feeling bloody helpless, which of

169

course you are. But don't worry, you'll soon forget everything about your past and will happily accept you're someone else's property, a commodity to be used and sold as desired. Your one purpose in life will be to satisfy the needs of others."

"Paul, when I find you…"

"Shit, you're stubborn! Maybe you're just in denial. Have you the mother of all headaches? Brain feel hot, effervescing? Well, that shows the drugs are working. The symptoms will diminish as the treatment progresses and the required cells are cooked into oblivion. You see, our German experts have carefully tailored a drug treatment programme to neutralise or enhance targeted parts of your brain while leaving the rest largely untouched. Those venoms I gave you weren't just for my personal enjoyment, although I have to admit that was considerable. In fact, you were aware of only a small amount of what I did to you that night. The toxins helped me evoke responses to enable other compounds to fix markers in various parts of your brain. These attract the chemicals you're being given now, reacting with them to either kill cells or increase their sensitivity. The areas primarily affected will be your amygdala and hippocampus, both deep within the cerebral cortex. As I indicated earlier, your fear response and scepticism will be significantly decreased, while your enjoyment of sensual experiences, such as sex, will be heightened. Meanwhile, the damage to your hippocampus will be a bit like that resulting from Alzheimer's Disease, leading to memory loss, disorientation, the inability to form or retain new memories, and so on.

"By the end of the treatment, I'm afraid there won't be much of the old you left. Formative elements to your past will either have been obliterated or appropriately reprioritised; you will become submissive and compliant. Personally, I can hardly wait. You'll be desperate to please and will do everything asked of you, absolutely everything. You'll drift aimlessly through the remainder of your life, at the beck and call of whomever we choose. You won't even notice when death approaches as we'll choose when and how that happens… I note you're beginning to look worried; I don't blame you. But it's definitely going to happen and there's nothing you can do about it. Every day you're cruising, I will be basking in the knowledge that I was instrumental in melting your brain."

"Paul, you are a deeply disturbed person," observed Tessa. "You should get help."

"Yeah, yeah. In addition to the drug therapy, the next days will serve to break you in. A bit like a horse, but in your case it's about conditioning the subconscious as the drugs do their work. By the time we meet again, you'll be raring to become Simitar's latest concubine, although I suspect that's a bit of euphemism for the role he really has in mind for you. But look on the bright side. We're going to keep you in tip-top condition so after a few months, when all the fuss has died down, you'll kill him and escape, only too pleased to do whatever *we* ask of you."

"I hope the Sheikh read the small print; but I did warn him... So, what exactly will I be doing for you?"

"Oh, nothing much, just assassinate the Emperor of Japan. If you miss him, we'll get Nyunt to do it. Better you though don't you think? Either way, we'll then organise the destruction of the Chrysanthemum League, starting with Matsumoto Castle and the Amakuni Valley. By the end of your little cruise, you'll be eager to tell us everything we need to know to help with the plan. You'll even give all your treasured possessions to us. Yes, you did bury everything very deeply, impressively so, in fact. But we'll soon be able to access the lot: your bank accounts, other Peacekeepers, where your Amafuji sword is. Everything you possess will be ours."

"Why are the Chrysanthemum League and my Amafuji sword of such importance to you and your boss?"

"That's no concern of yours... Besides, I don't have a boss, we're partners."

Tessa laughed.

"Don't be daft, you know that's not true. He's the boss and you're a lackey. A senior lackey perhaps, but a lackey nonetheless."

Paul gritted his teeth; he was angry.

"You've a nasty mind and a nasty tongue. Thanks for making it so easy to destroy both. We'll be doing the world a service."

"You know he'll dump you when he's done, just like you expect to dump the Sheikh?"

"Nice try for a desperate last fling."

"It's the truth. You see, I've met lots of your kind, and you're just not up to it. The moment you've served your purpose, he'll get rid of you... Anyway, I don't think you have confidence in this drugs nonsense or you wouldn't still be too scared to tell me who your *partner* is."

Paul paused pensively. Tessa smiled sweetly to goad him on.

"Come on, prove me wrong, *joint boss*. He's put *you* in my sights, return the favour. Surely you're not still too scared to tell me who he is?"

He chuckled.

"You are good... Anyway, after you've done everything we planned, you will go from being an esteemed member of the Chrysanthemum Guard to the most infamous Peacekeeper ever to have walked this earth. Meanwhile, the Fujiwara will be ready to fill the vacuum. Maybe we'll have you publicly executed. A fitting end to the pathetic existence of a freak, don't you think? Would you like me to write your epitaph?"

Tessa didn't rise to the bait. She knew their intentions now, and they were more monstrous than she would ever have believed possible. But she still needed to find out who Paul was working with.

"I see you're impressed."

"I'm impressed by your madness which is matched only by your gullibility. All this is really about you writing your own epitaph. Your boss is clearly much cleverer than you are. I accept he has planned this well, but I won't be the fall guy, that place is reserved for you. He's not going to share anything with you. Tell me who it is and I might be able to help you."

Paul smiled, shook his head, bent over and spat in her face.

"You are nothing now, whore!" he sneered, as Tessa wiped her cheek. "Don't think this is some sort of experiment which may or may not work. My mother started developing this programme years ago and we've perfected it; the science is fool-proof, and... Oh, but time marches on. I want to introduce you to the guys who'll be tending to your every need..."

In response to his call, Tessa heard three men enter. They walked into her field of vision; all looked hard and uncaring.

"This is Leroy," announced Paul. "Leroy, this is Nariko."

Tessa scowled at the enormous Rastafarian. Wearing lime-green shorts and an orange and red tee-shirt, he looked lustful, arrogant and strong. His jet-black hair was long and tied in tightly woven plaits, coloured at the ends; even his six-inch beard ended in a similar braid. He had huge patches of sweat under his arms and on his chest, and to say that he stank was a considerable understatement. Tessa thought he was revolting.

"Look, she just a-glarin' at me," he jeered. "I reck'n she already gone mad for me."

"Highly likely," laughed Paul. "Come on, Jack, your turn, don't be shy. I'm sure you won't be later."

Leroy moved over for Jack. He was Caucasian, slightly overweight but still well-built. His rectangular, sunburnt face was topped with crew-cut ginger hair. He wore a brightly coloured blue tee-shirt with parakeets on it and cropped jeans which had frayed where they had been clumsily shortened; from these two very hairy legs protruded. He too was sweating but seemed to smell less than Leroy. His arms were covered in tattoos, featuring a large eagle on the right and a dragon belching flames on the left. Tessa didn't like him in the slightest either, but with his green eyes and shaped facial stubble, he cut a marginally less repugnant figure.

"Hello, pet. Me name's Jack, I'm frum Newcastle."

"You sound it," retorted Tessa dismissively, surprised by how much every syllable of their strong accents seemed to grate. She put it down to them being her prison guards since their accents alone were not in the slightest objectionable.

"Dun't you fret, pet, I'll make sure you git a good time."

"They fancy themselves as studs," added Paul. "Out of the ten pictures we showed you, you said you liked them the least." He laughed, clearly enjoying the situation. Tessa simply sighed as a third man appeared. "Markus here is a nurse who's been trained by our German friends. He'll be in charge of making sure your brain melts by the required amount every day. But it's a long trip, so I daresay he'll have a go with you every now and again too. After all, there's not much else to do."

Markus looked less physically imposing than the other two, and much more intelligent. He was not quite six foot tall, also Caucasian, with neatly styled short bleached hair and a narrow chin strip beard. His face was completely white, even his cheeks seemed to be devoid of colour. With his calculating grey eyes, he radiated an air of coldness that convinced Tessa he was capable of considerable cruelty.

None of them looked as though they would do anything other than carry out their orders. It was becoming more and more apparent to Tessa that Potter was likely to be her only hope of rescue.

"The walls are soundproofed," continued Paul, "and the lights automatically simulate day and night. The date clock is there so you'll know when you're beginning to forget…" Tessa simply stared in disgust at the trio of men leering at her. "Don't look at them like that. You need them to be nice to you. Well, gentle at least. But regardless of what you might feel now, you'll soon believe they've always been your best friends. Although the Stockholm Syndrome certainly holds true in many cases, the drug therapy will accelerate it considerably for you. And, since you'll be deprived of all other sensory stimuli except when one of these three comes to talk to you, you'll be desperate for their company, no matter what they ask you to do."

"One day, Paul, I will settle this debt you've run up with me," hissed Tessa.

"Oh, please! Do you really think your threats scare me? You'll never be in a position to do me any harm; you won't even remember you wanted to."

"You're wrong, Paul. If you truly believed that, you'd tell me who your boss is. But you're still scared it won't work, aren't you?"

"Actually, I'm almost inclined to throw you some morsels to chew on. But I don't think I'll give you the satisfaction of knowing who it was that first raped you. Boy, I wish I'd been there."

"Paul, rape is a heinous cowardly crime. Furthermore, as a Peacekeeper, I guarantee that anyone who has abused me will pay with their life. That includes you, your boss, and you three."

Paul roared with laughter.

"Crap! Now, I'd like you to return that thing I lent you." Tessa sighed; she had become very attached to her tee-shirt. "Yes, I want it back. There'll be a clean one waiting to make sure you're smart when you disembark. Now, take it off."

Markus raised his eyebrows and crossed his arms, clearly keen to enjoy the show.

"Only weak people and perverts are voyeurs, Paul."

"You think? I suppose it'll feel degrading at first, being naked in front of these *hungry* animals. But you needn't be embarrassed; you haven't got anything I haven't already seen. These lads will be interested now, but the novelty will soon wear off."

"I tell you what," replied Tessa, smiling, "if you want it, why don't you come down here and take it? Or are you still too frightened to get close to me?"

"Look, you can either give it to me now or I'll press the button again." He held up the grey box. "Then in a few minutes you'll be desperate to give it to me."

"Paul, if necessary, I will come back from the dead to sort you. Now, just press the button if it makes you feel big and important, but the truth is really that you're just a pathetic sadistic pervert."

Paul squatted down, just out of reach.

"Sounds to me as though you're scared, Nariko-san."

A shiver ran down Tessa's spine. Whenever she'd been in a tight situation before, she'd always felt sure she would be able to find a way out. But this time she couldn't see one. She was scared; petrified in fact.

"Yes, Paul. Congratulations. In that you have succeeded."

"At last," he exclaimed, moving closer to gloat. "I knew we'd get through to you in the end. What a shame it's too late."

Tessa tried to look indecisive.

"What would it be worth if I told you where to find my Amafuji sword?"

In truth, she had no idea where it was, but he clearly didn't know that.

"I'll make it easier for you," replied Paul, moving even closer.

Suddenly, Tessa's right arm shot through the bars and grabbed his tee-shirt. She yanked it down and he fell clumsily headfirst onto the grille, dropping the box. Tessa's left arm shot round his neck and clamped him down. Their faces were inches apart now.

"I am scared, Paul, scared of what I'll do when I catch up with you," she hissed. She looked up at Leroy and Jack. "If you guys move a muscle, I'll snap his neck. You see, Paul, without your toys, your lies and your hired muscle, you are nothing. Look at them. It took less than a second for them to respect me more than you."

"You can't escape," he gasped, "let go of me."

"If I'd intended to escape, I'd already be out and you'd all be dead. But I could still kill you, Paul. Maybe I should savour your last agonising breath. Are you scared, Paul? You should be."

"If you kill me, there'll be no one to prevent Nyunt suffering the same fate as you."

"You'll need to do better than that to save your life. You've already proved you don't care about Nyunt and not even the Sheikh can trust what you say. In fact, why should these guys trust you? You're double-crossing everyone else. Are they really that stupid?" Markus surreptitiously started drawing the air pistol which Paul had been using in Insein. "Markus," snapped Tessa authoritatively, "if you so much as move another millimetre, I'll take out his eyes." She raised her right hand, placed two fingers against Paul's eyeballs and started pressing. He moaned as the pressure increased until they both turned bloodshot. Markus froze. "Now, Paul, I'm sick of having to listen to your pathetic diatribes, so press the goddamn' button and let me have some peace and quiet."

"I'll press it when I'm ready," he hissed.

"You will do what I tell you," hissed Tessa, and punched him hard on the nose. There was an unpleasant scrunch as it broke and blood started gushing out. But she simply grabbed his nose and wiggled it hard, prompting more cracking noises. "Oh, dear, nasty compound fracture that, and two lovely black eyes, what a shame. Now, press the button or I'll pluck your eyeballs out. *Five, four, three...*"

Paul desperately groped around until he found the box and manoeuvred it to his right hand. Then he pressed the button. As Tessa felt the pump whir, she released her grip on him and laughed at his shocked expression. He stood up and held a handkerchief to his bleeding nose.

"You fucking bitch," he whined.

"Better than being a pathetic pervert like you," replied Tessa, and closed her eyes.

CHAPTER 16

Tessa woke up on the mattress looking at the bars a few inches above her. She had another splitting headache. If Paul was right, these would reduce in severity as the treatment progressed; she felt strangely encouraged to note that one day had certainly not made any difference.

It was dark, except for the red glow from two emergency lights. She looked at the calendar clock and found it was 2 a.m. on 7th April; day one of her eleven-day cruise. She would presumably arrive on 17th April, somewhere. However, it was much earlier in the morning than Paul's schedule had predicted; maybe she'd forced him to dose her early. She smiled remembering the shocked expression on his bloody face after she'd finished with him. But then she realised she was naked and felt down to her crotch. It was wet and slimy.

"Ugh! You bastards," she moaned, shaking her head.

Suddenly, she felt completely alone, defenceless and vulnerable; her eyes watered and tears started trickling down her face. She started to sob quietly. As her spirits plummeted through misery and despair; she seriously considered slitting her wrist with the chisel. Despite everything she had achieved before this, her confidence had deserted her. Would Potter be able to find and rescue her before any permanent damage was done?

She was driven to praying for strength in her hour of need. Although she had never been an advocate of organised, corporate religion as she called it, that was too intolerant and self-centred for her liking, she had always believed that there must be something more to life than simply a transient existence. Yet it was difficult to see how a Peacekeeper who had killed so many would be eligible for assistance. Nevertheless, it was worth a try. Her desperate, heart-felt mutterings broke the empty stillness which threatened to drown her in despondency.

Finally, she insisted she get a grip on herself. After all, she hadn't even tried to escape yet. She needed to use her time productively, not feeling sorry for herself. First, she had to study her prison. Only with a thorough understanding of its construction, and potential weaknesses, could she decide how best to proceed.

The mattress lay on a horizontal solid steel floor and the three walls around it were also of sheet steel, except for a locked flap to her right. The food chute Paul had mentioned, thought Tessa. All the bars above her were set in a single rigid frame, which was hinged by the edge on her right. She found she could just reach the hinges through the bars. There were two and both pins were welded in place; there was no way she could remove them.

She moved off the mattress to continue her investigation within the half of her enclosure that sloped down to the drainage slots. She found the other edge of the grille frame was retained by a single padlock. She rammed her hand up through the grille. The padlock was substantial and she doubted she could pick it. However, the entire locking bracket through which the padlock looped was secured to the upper false floor by only two bolts, neither of which was welded; although she couldn't twist them.

She scrutinised the long wall to her left with the three drainage slots, one of which was directly in line with the padlock. If she could get her hand through the central slot, she might be able to reach up underneath the locking mechanism.

All the slots were about two inches high and some ten inches long. She found it was possible to squeeze her hand into the slot but the edges of the metal were quite sharp and she certainly couldn't stretch up high enough even to touch the bolts.

However, the floor and walls appeared to have been made from the same relatively thin steel. The sheets had been hammered over along the edge of the false floor, on which the grille rested, to form the walls. But clearly the construction had been hurried. The builders had taken short-cuts and made vertical cuts in the long wall to simplify forming the draining slots. These cuts, which spanned the full height of the wall, had subsequently been welded closed. So the central drainage slot lay at the base of two such cuts. These had been tacked crudely together with four welds; half were not much more than a single blob, the others slightly longer. All were uneven and pock-marked, potentially indicative of more flawed welds. Perhaps the Burmese welders had been trying to help her. If she could use her chisel to break these eight welds, maybe she would be able to push the central section of the wall back far enough to reach through to the underside of the bolts securing the padlock mechanism. Maybe then she could remove the locking nuts and push open the grille.

She reached into the slot for her chisel. More than four inches long and a quarter of an inch in diameter, it looked like a fine tool, and was just what she needed.

Determined to try and boost her morale, she selected the weakest-looking of the welds she had to break. It was on the left, just above the drainage slot.

She drove the point of the chisel into the join and pushed. She was amazed the chisel went in at all, but whoever had cut the metal had used shears sufficiently coarse to leave a little gap between where the edges came together. She was convinced now somebody had intended to assist her. Satisfied she could push the chisel in no more, she levered it gently backwards and forwards. She wanted to generate a fatigue crack in the weld, but not to distort the join so much as to make it easy for her guards to see what she was doing.

However, weak weld or not, it was hard work and her hand was soon aching. Nevertheless, the sheets were flexing. She stopped for a rest and listened for movement elsewhere in the container; everything was quiet. She resumed, yanking the chisel from side to side with all her strength. Suddenly she saw a crack appear. However, her hand was sweating so much she had difficulty gripping the chisel. She took a deep breath and wiped her hand on her thigh. She pressed on and watched with glee as the crack spread along the weld. When she thought it was about to break, she withdrew the chisel and satisfied herself that there was no visible damage to the sheets. Then she turned her attention to the next weld up.

Eventually, a tiny crack appeared in that one too. It spread more quickly this time and Tessa's heart started racing; she might actually be able to do this. Suddenly, there was an abrupt *ping* and the weld broke. She quickly removed her chisel and hid it again, in case the noise had attracted someone's attention.

She put her ear to the floor and listened. She could hear the rhythmic vibration of a ship's engines; clearly they were at sea. But she couldn't hear anything else.

She looked at the clock. It was nearly 6 a.m. Her guards would no doubt be starting to prepare her breakfast soon. She stood no chance of breaking all the welds before then, so she double-checked that her handiwork could not be seen, and returned to her mattress.

It was then that she realised that being at sea introduced a further layer of complexity to her predicament. If she escaped, where would she go? She might have to overcome the entire ship's crew before gaining her freedom, and all before someone pressed the button on a transmitter to her pump, as there might be several on board. She decided to leave worrying about that until later. For the time being she had to stay focussed on escaping and taking control of the container. So she also needed to understand her guards' routine in order to know when she could safely work on the welds.

She inspected her right hand; it was red and grooved where she had been holding the chisel. It wasn't serious, but she didn't want her guards to see any marks on her. They might ask how she got them while she was drugged. She decided what she would need to help her, and how she could ask for it. A box of tissues perhaps; she could wrap some round the chisel as a rudimentary handle to prevent her being so marked when she used the chisel in future.

Then the lights went on in her compartment and she sensed movement elsewhere within the container. She couldn't hear voices but she could feel the thumping of people moving around on the metal floor. At 7:30 a.m. precisely, the door to her compartment opened and Jack came in.

"Hello, pet. How are we today?"

"Awful," replied Tessa. "Did Paul leave some paracetamol?"

"I'll ask Markus if you're allowed anything, pet."

He walked round the bottom end of the grille. He was clearly keen to get a better view. Tessa grimaced, this was nauseating.

"I got yer breakfast 'ere, pet. Eat it up, it's good grub, I just had mine."

He placed the tray near the top of the chute. Tessa watched with interest as he unlocked and opened the lid. Then he lowered the tray down onto a shelf level with her mattress and locked the chute lid down again. Finally, he undid another padlock, which Tessa hadn't seen, and rotated a vertical circular sheet which eventually revealed a window through which she could access the tray.

She reached over and slid the tray out. Her breakfast looked very good. Muesli with semi-skimmed UHT milk, scrambled egg, smoked salmon, rice and fruit, a small pot of green tea and a cup. The food had already been cut into pieces so the cutlery provided comprised only a fork and a spoon. However, she was surprised to find that both were metal.

"I could do with some water down here, Jack. Any chance of a bottle?"

"I'll ask Markus that too, pet."

As Tessa ate her breakfast, Jack walked back round her. Tessa tried not to notice his leering, but the prospect of what would happen after she had been given another dose of drugs did not bear thinking about. Eventually, he came back.

"No paracetamol, pet. But I've some water for you."

"Thank you, Jack."

"You're welcome, pet."

"There's something else. I know one or more of you guys screwed me last night because my fanny's sticky. That's not very nice for me and probably not for you either. If you're going to carry on doing that, I need some tissues."

"I'll try, pet. But that's a lot of asks."

Tessa shrugged and returned her attention to eating her breakfast, which wasn't particularly straightforward while lying down.

At 8:30 a.m., Jack came to take her breakfast tray away and used the chute to pass down a box of tissues. She thanked him obsequiously, and congratulated herself on two small victories.

At 9 a.m. Markus came in. He stood at the bottom of her grille brandishing the grey box. Tessa didn't see any sexual element in his scrutiny, there was just cruel academic interest which she found significantly more offensive.

"It's time is it?" she asked. "Nine a.m. and nine p.m., I suppose?"

He nodded and pressed the button. She closed her eyes…

Tessa awoke just before 2:30 p.m., once more to a dreadful headache, but feeling oddly heartened. Not only was she consistently waking up earlier than Paul had predicted, but her headaches weren't easing;

she felt they might even be lasting longer. Maybe the drugs therapy wasn't as fool-proof as they thought. Encouraged, she started working on the remaining welds, but progress was very slow because she was so nervous of attracting attention. Working while her guards were moving around was much more risky since if she made any noise they would quickly be able to come in and discover what she was doing.

As the last vestiges of her headache subsided, she decided her escape plan needed to include time spent on making sure she retained her mental faculties. Although it would be frustrating not working on the welds during the afternoons, she needed to be patient; rather a slow success than a fast failure. She remembered what the first Burmese doctor had told her: use the chisel to keep track of the days, recite arithmetic tables, sing songs and think of books. She resolved to devote her afternoons to monitoring her journey and keeping her brain active, while she'd use the nights for breaking out.

Then she felt her crotch. It was wet and slimy again, she had been violated once more. She used some tissues to dry herself and tried not to dwell on what had been done to her. At least she had no memories of it happening, but her hatred for her three guards was growing exponentially. When the time came, and she was beginning to feel it would, she intended to show them as much mercy and compassion as they were showing her.

She recovered the chisel and moved down to the bottom of her compartment. There was a small ledge beneath the grille where the false floor joined the wall. Only someone lying in the compartment could easily see under it, so that was where she decided to scratch her marks. She started on the left with: Dep 7/4 - 1. Then she moved over to the right and added ETA 17/4 - 11. After hiding the chisel again, she began exercising her brain: humming songs, reciting the plots of books, and finally calculating prime numbers and working through multiplication tables. She was still battling with her twenty-nine times table when her dinner was served. At 9 p.m., Markus came in again with the grey box.

For four days, Tessa's life followed the same routine. She was always fed and dosed at nine and always seemed to wake up several hours before her guards expected; making her grateful that she'd never needed much sleep. However, her headaches weren't becoming less severe, they were definitely worsening. Nevertheless, she carried on cracking the welds with relentless determination. Some were strong, others were weak; but she was unwavering in her resolve to break at least one every night.

When she woke on the morning of 12th April, her sixth day, she had only one more weld to break before she could try accessing the underside of the padlock mechanism. It took her over an hour, but finally it gave way and she was able to push the sheet above the drainage slot inwards. That was not the best direction for her to reach through as it obstructed her access, but it meant the sheet could be clicked back in position more easily; making it difficult for her guards to see she had moved it.

She relaxed for a while to recover from her not inconsiderable exertions and began to wonder how she would react when drugged if asked whether she was trying to escape. It would be a disaster if she told them of her scheme. But she thought it unlikely that they would expect her to be plotting an escape from what they presumably felt was a highly secure prison and a debilitating drugs therapy. Also, maybe she simply wouldn't remember.

She gathered herself, took a deep breath and reached her hand up under the sheet. She had to adjust her position several times before she was finally able to touch the bottom of the two securing bolts. She grinned euphorically, neither had been welded. All she needed to do was to loosen and remove the nuts and the whole mechanism would simply lift away from the floor with the grille. But it was getting close to her mealtime, so she decided to return the sheet to its original position and make sure there were no tell-tale marks from her handiwork. Eventually, she lay back on her mattress and waited for her breakfast.

She started considering how to loosen the nuts. It wasn't going to be easy with only a chisel…

On the next day, the first thing she noticed was that she had bright red marks round both her wrists. It seemed she had been restrained during the previous night's session. She wondered why, but her anger and frustration at not knowing only served to exacerbate her usual thumping headache. Instead of bothering her for twenty minutes, they were lasting for nearly an hour now. But although Paul's drugs were not affecting her the way he had predicted, they were having an impact. She couldn't remember as many songs now and could barely manage multiplication tables up to nineteen.

She pushed the plate back and placed some tissues along the edge of it to stop its sharp edge from cutting into her skin. Then she thrust her arm through the gap and started attacking the nut closest to the vertical wall as it was the easiest to jam the chisel against. But the point kept slipping. So she carefully scratched a little groove in the side of the nut to give it purchase. Then she altered her position, and pushed with all her might, again and again, frequently re-gripping the chisel. It nearly slipped out of her hand once which worried her greatly. Not only would it make a horrendous clatter if it hit the steel floor, but she might lose it altogether. She laboured for thirty minutes. The chisel continually slipped, painfully banging her fingers. But suddenly the nut moved. She quickly repositioned the edge of the chisel on the next flat of the nut and pushed it some more. It moved freely now. She retrieved the chisel and used her fingers to twist off the nut completely. She pulled it out. It wasn't even self-locking. For once she was extremely grateful to engineers who, for whatever reason, had not done their job well. She wondered whether they were friends of the Burmese doctor and had purposely produced weak welds and failed to use the proper nuts and bolts.

"Nearly there, *pet!*" she whispered as she screwed the nut back. "One down, one to go." Spurred on by her faster than expected success she threw caution and her daily schedule to the wind, and started attacking the second nut. She was dismayed to find that it seemed to have been secured far more tightly than the first. Furthermore, no matter what she did, she just could not get a good purchase on it with the chisel. She tried again and again, and was soon sweating with the effort and frustration of struggling to move it. But it would not budge. She paused to consider the situation. What she really needed was a spanner.

She groped round on the floor through the drainage hole on the off-chance she would find something she could use. She did find a fragment of steel which had presumably been discarded during her prison's construction, but nothing else. Eventually, she lay back deflated. Had she really been thwarted within sight of her goal?

Then she had an idea. Could she make a spanner out of a fork? But how could she get to keep the fork they provided with her food? Maybe there was a way… She smiled, rubbing her sore wrists; she would have to trust in her acting ability. She reached back to find the piece of scrap steel and hid it just though the top drainage slot. Then she hid her chisel behind the bottom slot for a change and bent the central plate back to its normal position.

CHAPTER 17

At 7:30 a.m., Jack came in with her tray and noticed Tessa massaging her wrists.

"Morning, pet. Them's frum the handcuffs. No real damage. Markus examined you."

"Why was I restrained, Jack? Isn't fucking me enough?"

"You asked for 'em, pet. I heard you m'self." Tessa looked at him, dumbfounded. "Honest, pet," he assured her, "I'm not telling porkies. You're quite different when yer're high."

Tessa gulped.

"What do I say?"

"Not much really. We start by letting you exercise for an hour and then shower. Then we tell you how beautiful you look. I suppose you must really like that 'cause after... well, you're pretty much begging for it."

"Surely not?"

"Yeah. It's difficult for us to keep up. You're quite something, pet."

"Don't I talk about my past?"

"No, and it's more than our lives are worth to ask. So, every session's a new 'un as far as we're concerned."

Tessa breathed out noisily. Although part of her was disgusted beyond description, she was also pleased that they were probably not asking her whether she was trying to escape.

"Eat up now, pet. Got to keep your strength up; it's my turn today."

For a moment, Tessa contemplated what she would do with the three of them when it was her turn, but then she returned to watching Jack open the chute. She pulled the tray out and inspected her food. It looked and smelled good, but she knew she wasn't going to be eating any of it. She glared up at him.

"I don't want this."

"You've got to eat it, pet. There's nothing else for you."

"Jack, what part of '*I don't want this*' didn't you understand? I don't

186

bloody want it!"

He appeared nonplussed, unsure what to do. Tessa slid the tray nosily over on to the metal section of her enclosure.

"Leroy's cooked it special for you, pet. It's good, I'm going to get mine now."

"Well, you can have this lot too. Get me something else."

"I don't think you're allowed anything else, pet. I'll ask Markus."

He left her alone in the enclosure and went to consult the others. Meanwhile, she carefully adjusted the positions of the plate, fork and spoon. Then she readied herself for the show. Markus came in with Jack.

"What..." started the nurse, but Tessa immediately interrupted.

"I'm not eating this crap, get me something else. All you lot do is fuck me and feed me. I've had e-*bloody*-nough!"

She grabbed the tray and shoved it vehemently towards the top drain slot. The plate came to an abrupt halt in the corner as it jammed against the slot, prompting some of the food, together with both fork and spoon, to slide obligingly through the hole.

"Shanky whore's tossed my cooking!" exclaimed Leroy from the doorway.

Markus looked ready to explode.

"You'll eat what you're given," he ordered Tessa.

"But..., but..., I don't want to. I'm so fed up and... and... I'm scared. I don't understand, what's happening to me."

Markus kneeled down by the grille, well within reach, though Tessa didn't move a muscle.

"Don't worry, Nariko, everything's going to be fine. We're going to look after you," he said, soothingly.

"You'll take care of me?"

"Yes, we will. There's no need to be scared, we're your friends. We're here to help you."

Tessa tried to look contrite and worked as hard as she could at producing some tears. She didn't succeed, but seemed to have got close enough to persuade Markus.

"I... I'm sorry about the food," she snivelled. "You cooked it beautifully, Leroy. I... I'll clear it up." She changed position, moved the plate, scraped up some of the food which had spilled, and thrust her arm through the drainage slot. She soon produced a handful of food which she deposited histrionically on the plate. Then came the spoon, followed by some more food.

Markus watched with considerable satisfaction. It seemed she had persuaded him that the drug therapy was working; he winked at the others. Meanwhile, Tessa was trying to give the impression she was desperately reaching round for the fork. In fact, she'd already found it and carefully pushed it as far as she could towards the central drainage slot.

"I can't find it!" she screamed in panic.

"What, pet?" asked Jack.

"The fork… I can't find your fork!" she shrieked, pretending to be on the verge of tears again. She rammed her arm further into the drainage slot and twisted it round knowing full well what would happen. As blood oozed from the cut made by the sharp metal, she picked up the small piece of sheet steel.

"I can feel it," she cried jubilantly, but then tossed the piece of steel far into the corner of the drainage section, well away from her. The fragment rattled against the side several feet away from the slot. She looked up at Markus, her expression doleful and scared. "I'm very sorry, Markus. It slipped. I've lost the fork. I'll do whatever you want, please don't punish me."

Before he could say anything, Jack interrupted.

"Christ, boss! She's fucking bleeding. We need to fix her up. Shit! You know what he said about her being damaged."

Markus looked at Tessa's arm; blood was trickling down it.

"Am I in trouble?" she whimpered.

"No, you're not in trouble," he said, his tone and stance softening. "Everything is fine, don't worry about the fork. Just carefully pull your hand out and let me have a look."

Soon, Tessa's new wound, a two-inch cut along the side of her arm, had been disinfected and dressed through the bars. She had cleaned up the mess she'd made, and Jack had brought in another breakfast tray. It was the same as before, but this time she ate it all without objection. Then she waited to be dosed again…

When she woke up, she went first to mark the day and date. She looked at the clock. It seemed to be early on 15th April, but the last date she had scratched was 13th. What had happened to the 14th April? She swallowed hard. Surely she hadn't forgotten to mark it? She knew that on the 13th she had stolen the fork at breakfast-time. She looked at her arm. The dressing was different. How had she managed to lose a day? What had Markus done to her? Had they discovered her escape plan?

In a panic she moved over to the bottom drainage slot and quickly reached in; the chisel was still there. She breathed a sigh of relief and carefully released the central flap and bent it back. Then she stuck her arm in and up towards the top drainage slot. She started feeling round for the fork, but couldn't find it. She pulled out her arm and peered in, but it was too dark to see anything. She took a deep breath and pushed her arm back in, searching methodically this time from one side to the other, then moving her arm further in. She had her arm pushed in almost up to her shoulder when she finally touched the fork handle. With one final stretch, she nipped it between two fingers and dragged it out; extremely pleased with herself. It seemed her plan was intact. Perhaps Markus had simply anaesthetised her between doses. Whatever had happened, there was no point in her worrying about it now; her first priority was escape and she was rapidly running out of time. However, she scratched *Escape or die!* under her date marks as a reminder, in case she lost focus. Then she studied the fork and planned how she would convert it into a spanner of the right size. There would be no second attempt; her adjustments would have to work first time. She concluded she would need to end up with the nut being a tight fit between the middle two prongs, with the outer two wrapped round them to add rigidity.

She removed the nut she had already loosened to act as a die. Then she used the chisel to bend away the two outer prongs of the fork. She soon realised that re-fashioning her fork's purpose in life would be considerably harder than she had imagined. She thrust the nut between the middle two prongs of the fork. It didn't go very far as the prongs were extremely rigid, so she widened the gap with the chisel first and then pushed the nut back in using the chisel as a ram. Still not satisfied, she pushed the nut, held in position with the chisel, and fork horizontally along the floor into the low metal wall dividing her enclosure. Soon, the middle prongs were completely splayed out with the nut jammed between them, as close to the handle of the fork as she could get it.

Then she repositioned herself and, keeping the nut in place with her finger, used the chisel to bend the two central prongs as tightly around the nut as she could manage, completing the process by shoving the bent fork in the corner of her enclosure. This was all incredibly difficult. Several times the nut slipped and on one occasion she stabbed her finger with one the prongs. Her hands were red and aching, but she persevered resolutely. Eventually, the central prongs were curved convincingly back round the nut at almost ninety degrees to the fork handle. Then, to make sure the nut was gripped firmly enough, Tessa started trying to curl the outer prongs round the ends of the inner prongs. This proved unbelievably hard and she began to worry that her attempts at this might reduce the effectiveness of the inner prongs. Eventually, she was forced to give up. She hadn't achieved all she'd hoped, but she had managed to give the central prongs a modicum of additional stability. She lay back and admired her handiwork.

Although the end result of her labours was decidedly crude, it certainly resembled a spanner and seemed to work well on the nut she had. But the manufacturing process had taken much longer than she'd expected; not only because it had been so problematical, but also because her brain was working frustratingly slowly. After relaxing for a moment she felt some vibrations along the floor suggesting movement elsewhere in the container. She checked the time; her breakfast would be arriving soon. She hurriedly cleared everything away, returned the nut and the steel plate to their normal positions and moved back on to the mattress. She would have to postpone trying the spanner until tomorrow.

On 16th April, her tenth day, Tessa woke just after 2 a.m. Her headaches were quite disconcerting now, and for some time she had difficulty even focusing her eyes. Eventually her vision cleared, but she was worried that her brain was being damaged, although perhaps not as much as Paul was expecting. However, she would have to work on regardless if she wanted to escape. She was desperate to try her spanner, and it wasn't long before she was carefully pressing it up on to the tight nut. Finally it engaged. But the moment she tried pulling the handle of the fork round, it completely lost grip. It seemed that since she had not been able to lock the two outer prongs tightly around the central ones, they were flexing, allowing the nut to slip.

Tessa tried to check that she was twisting the nut the right way, only to find that it took her mind depressingly long to work out which way was clockwise and which anti-clockwise. In the end, she used the other nut as a guide. Then she returned to the tight nut and had another go. Again the spanner spun round. She removed it and tried to think of a way she might be able to intertwine the outer prongs more effectively. But after all the difficulty she'd had, she wasn't sure she could improve it.

She was growing frustrated and close to tears; it was again looking as though success might elude her. She lay back and relaxed, concentrating only on her breathing, refusing to be disheartened. She needed to focus her mind and think. Then she caught sight of some scratching on the wall, *Escape or die!* it said. She definitely didn't want to die here, so she had to escape. Somehow she'd have to make the spanner work. Maybe she could jam the nut in position by also forcing the edge of the chisel between the prongs? But to do that, she'd need both hands.

She tried various positions and finally managed to get both arms round through the gap. It was a considerable strain, but eventually she manoeuvred the spanner up on to the nut and thrust the sharp end of the chisel through the prongs as well. Then, carefully, she pulled the fork handle round. Again the spanner slipped, but she knew the chisel had moved out of position. Sweating and trembling with the effort, she tried again and gingerly pulled the spanner round. It moved round relatively easily and again she concluded the spanner had slipped.

"Concentrate," she insisted. "Never give up."

She repositioned her tools and tried again. The spanner moved even more freely this time. What was going wrong now? Her eyes started watering and she pulled the spanner out to inspect it. It looked just the same. She took a deep breath and reached up to the nut and tried twisting it round with her fingers. It turned easily. She couldn't believe it; she was stunned.

"Thank you, thank you, thank you," she mumbled joyously.

She removed the nut completely and pressed both bolts upwards. They both moved! She had done it, she could get out. However, it was too close to breakfast-time to do anything now. She was not prepared. Her escape would have to wait until evening. She returned everything in her enclosure to their normal positions and lay on her mattress developing a plan.

CHAPTER 18

Tessa awoke to the realisation that she was clean and dressed in a frilly lime green tee-shirt; it felt strange to be clothed after so long being naked. She was surprised and immediately checked the time and date. It was the afternoon of 17th April and, most important of all, there were no rhythmic vibrations from the ship's engines. She had missed another day, and the ship had presumably arrived at its destination. Also, for the first time ever, the door to her part of the container was slightly ajar. Clearly there was no time for self-pity, she needed to work fast. She decided she'd just have time to undo the padlock nuts before her food arrived. She moved off the mattress and prepared to bend the plate back. But then she heard a commotion further up the container. There was a lot of loud clanking followed by a new voice saying, "…*hypnotist.*"

Tessa recoiled in horror, remembering what the doctor in Burma had told her. The drugs she was being given would make her more susceptible to being hypnotised. Bordering on panic, she considered ways in which she could give herself a permanent reminder of what might be about to happen. Not wanting to get the chisel out she started using a fingernail, which had been allowed to grow quite long, to scratch into her left thigh – high up where it would be covered by the long tee-shirt. She made deep vertical marks, a long and a short one, and then joined them with a horizontal cut. The pain was excruciating and she was soon bleeding, but she managed to produce a quite nasty wound which resembled the letter *h* from below. But then she began to worry that she might not remember why she'd made the mark. So she decided to work on it some more. She was still doing this when the door to her compartment opened and a stranger entered. She pulled her tee-shirt down and looked round at the newcomer. The man appeared to be Arabic, six feet tall and about fifty years old. He was wearing a dark grey suit, purple shirt and a rather garish green silk tie, with a single large red spiral on it. He had curly black hair with a white tuft near the front, a mottled complexion and piercing brown eyes. As he peered down at her and smiled, Tessa was sure he fancied himself. He seemed to be studying her with a mixture of arrogance and chauvinistic contempt; she took an instant dislike to him.

He kneeled down near her and opened a brown attaché case; she felt sure he'd noticed her bloody finger. But he simply lifted out an mp3 player and set it up near her head on a stand which housed some loudspeakers. He glanced back at and told those watching to leave him alone and to close the door. Then he produced a tatty old wooden metronome, which he slowly and decisively wound up. He seemed to be savouring these preparations. Tessa was becoming progressively more and more anxious. Then he smiled at her and started the metronome. She soon found it was impossible to stop herself from listening to its regular *tick-tock, tick-tock…*

Tessa opened her eyes to find an Arabic man standing by the grille watching her.

"Thank you," he purred, apparently rather pleased with himself. "It's been a pleasure."

"Likewise," she replied, "goodbye."

But then she wondered why on earth she had been so polite to this stranger. He nodded, picked up his attaché case and tapped on the door.

As he disappeared from view, Tessa became conscious of her leg hurting. She speculated as to what had been done to her now. When she looked down she found that a crude *y* shape had been carved in her thigh; it was a very fresh wound. She couldn't understand what purpose it could possibly serve. But otherwise, she felt strangely good; on top of the world, in fact. Whatever that man had said or done, it had certainly helped. She was quite sure she could singlehandedly defeat an army. Then she heard voices and realised that the compartment door had been left ajar again. She listened to the conversation.

"All done," boasted the Arab. "A very interesting woman… remarkable life. She was much more resistant than I had been led to believe she'd be, but she'll answer any question now. I tested her with some private stuff and her bank account details, and she responded without hesitation, including her passwords. All the barriers are definitely down. But I need to have a word with Paul about something I found."

Tessa was aghast. What the hell had he done? What drugs had he used in order to extract so much information from her?

"Do you now?" replied Markus, "no wonder you took so long. Anyway, we're behind schedule; she was due to be dosed a while ago."

"Oh, you should leave her alone for at least an hour and let everything sink in properly."

"What was it that you found which was so surprising?" asked Markus casually.

"I'm sorry, I really don't feel able to tell you. It's for Paul's ears only."

"Can't he ask his own questions?" continued Markus.

"Yes, anything he wants. However, I think what I found could be of great significance."

"OK, fine," said Markus reluctantly. "We'll feed her now and dose her later. But Paul's arrival in Tunis has been delayed by a day, so he can't join us yet. However, I have your payment here."

"Excellent, thank you," replied the man enthusiastically. "I can meet Paul anytime it's convenient for him."

"Sure. But just let me check one thing with you?" asked Markus. "Did he say you could ask about her bank accounts and things?" Tessa detected a distinctly menacing tone in the way Markus spoke and the Arab hesitated before answering.

"Well, no, but she was resisting so I thought…"

Tessa heard a *phut!* It seemed that Paul's air pistol had just been fired, a supposition supported by the muffled sound of a body falling.

"Jack, tie the stupid asshole to that chair," ordered Markus. "He wasn't being paid to think, or to ask her anything. Who knows what other information he extracted? Shit, Paul'll be livid. Bind him loosely. I don't want there to be any marks, and tape his mouth. He'll be high for several hours. We'll make it look as though he died of a drugs overdose and dump him in the sea. Leroy, cook the whore's dinner."

"So much for doing business with Paul," muttered Tessa as she heard the clanking of cooking utensils. But she'd have to postpone worrying about what the Arabic man had done to her until another time.

Aware that she needed to work quietly as well as quickly, Tessa pushed the metal flap back and removed both nuts, which were only finger-tight. She pulled her arm out, allowing the steel plate to spring loosely back in position, and secreted the chisel under her thigh. Then she gingerly jiggled the grille; it appeared to be free. Her plan was to get out silently and surprise whoever came in with her food. But just as she braced herself to ease the grille open, she heard Leroy approaching. He pulled open the door to her prison compartment and came in carrying her tray. Tessa was still lying in the left-hand side of her enclosure. She didn't say a word, and neither did he. He simply walked round and placed the food near the top of the chute. She noticed that he was armed now with a large hunting knife. Tessa revised her plan, checked his position and took a deep breath. She tensed up against the grille. It would have to be fast and furious, but she felt supremely confident. Leroy focussed on unlocking the food chute.

With all her strength, she pushed up on the grille. Nothing happened. She tried using her legs while waggling the grille backwards and forwards with her hands. The metalwork rattled unenthusiastically, and refused to budge. Tessa was both surprised and distraught. She was sure the bolts were free and had expected them simply to pop out. But it seemed they'd jammed. Not surprisingly, the noise attracted Leroy's attention.

"Yuz a smart girl, yuz knows you ain't goin nowhere," he drawled. "Ain't no future for yuz 'cept whoring, so quiet down and eat yuz food. I cooked it jus' like y'asked. Smells good, dunnit?

Tessa had to admit it did smell good, very good in fact, and she seriously pondered postponing her escape so she could eat first. But then she caught sight of the scratched markings *Escape or die!*

Idiot! she thought, shocked by her own stupidity. She snapped backed to reality – if she failed to escape now, she'd probably never get another chance. She nodded and smiled at her guard. Leroy turned away again. She hastily shoved the central steel plate back and thrust her arm underneath. Then she reached up and put a finger under each bolt and pushed hard. They resisted, so she jiggled them at the same time as gently shaking the grille. Suddenly, both bolts shot high in the air. She yanked back her arm and grabbed the grille with both hands. Her time had come.

The bolts both landed with a loud *c-clang* and Leroy spun round in surprise. But she was already pushing the bars with all her might. The heavy grille swung round incredibly fast and the outer edge caught him square across his chest, with the padlock digging in. It clearly hurt, and he was forced violently back against the wall. Shocked and off-balance, he stayed pinned there attempting to find a grip on the grille. But Tessa had already picked up the chisel and sprung to her feet. She grasped the top of the grille and hoisted herself up, her weight forcing Leroy back against the wall. Her face was inches away from his now, his arms still struggling to gain purchase on the bars. But Tessa descended on him like one possessed. Before he could protect himself, she thrust the chisel in his left eye and deep into his brain. He groaned and slumped back, his limbs already beginning to tremble uncontrollably. Tessa was so incensed she considered doing more, but knew he had already been fatally injured. So she simply reached down and drew the sheathed knife by his side.

"Now who's screwed, Leroy?" she sneered.

She heard someone by the door and, still clinging to the grille, swung round to find Jack staring at her. For a fraction of a second he froze, stunned by the unexpected gory scene; but Tessa didn't hesitate. She flicked the knife at him and bounded across the compartment following its trajectory. He collapsed on the door threshold with only the hilt of the knife protruding from his chest, the blade embedded in his heart.

"Bye, *pet*," mocked Tessa, yanking the knife from his twitching body. She forced herself on; the nurse still had to be silenced. She burst into what appeared to be the container's control room.

Markus spun round. He had just finished loading the air pistol. He aimed it at her and fired *phut!* But Tessa was high on a mixture of adrenaline and furious determination, goaded on by weeks of enduring mental and physical torture at the hands of these people. To her, everything was happening in slow motion. She watched the dart glide gracefully towards her and nonchalantly raised the knife. She angled the blade so that the dart hit it and ricocheted harmlessly into the wall.

"I warned you, Markus," she hissed. "But thanks for the fork, sucker!"

For a moment, he wondered whether there was any way he could escape with his life. He saw the small grey dosing box on a table some distance away. Tessa followed his eye line, the Arab's closed attaché case was next to the box. But then Markus lurched towards a large red button beside a computer screen. Tessa immediately threw the knife. However, as the blade crunched through his temple, Markus's dying body pressed the button.

Then there was silence. Tessa stepped back against the wall and braced herself for the pump to start whirring. She hoped she would just receive a single dose and would come round before anyone discovered her. But she felt nothing. Surprised and puzzled, she gathered her wits and glanced round.

The Arab was tied to a chair with a zoned out expression on his face. He had a piece of tape over his mouth.

"You poor bastard," she scoffed, "that'll teach you. I wonder what you did to me."

However, she was sure it wasn't over yet. Markus may not have dosed her, but he'd certainly done something. Perhaps he'd issued an alarm, but hadn't Paul said the container's communication systems weren't working?

In any event, she needed to get moving. She reached into her mouth, gripped the tracking transponder and pulled. But it didn't come away. So she stabbed around it with her fingernails and pulled harder. This time the flap of skin gave way. She withdrew the device and threw it back in her prison compartment. As she was spitting out some blood, her gaze fell on Markus's computer screen - *Auto-destruct in 10, 9.*

"Oh, shit!" exclaimed Tessa.

She ran to the double metal doors at the end of the container. There were two large wheels with big red arrows pointing clockwise, ending in the word *"Locked"*. She yanked them anti-clockwise. Cranks retracted pairs of bolts at the top and bottom of each door, and she pushed them open. Her eyes widened in amazement. *7...6...* Although it was dusk, it was clear she was in a shipping container high up over the bow of a docked ship. Her container appeared to be near the middle of the row. More importantly, it was a very long way down to the water on her left and there was essentially only quayside to her right. She certainly couldn't climb down quickly enough to escape and she seriously doubted whether she could leap sufficiently far to avoid landing on the deck.

"Hmm! Die on the deck or cook in the container? Not here," she concluded, and reversed back as far as she could. *4…3…* She sprinted for the doorway. As she reached it, she grabbed the locking wheel on the left and launched herself out. The door swung open, pivoting her round. When she thought she had flown out suitably far, she let go and looked down; she wasn't going to make it to the water. Then, from behind, came an enormous *whoomph!* The container had exploded and she immediately found herself caught up in the hot blast. As it boosted her seawards, she realised she might just make it after all. She straightened herself up moments before shooting past the edge of the deck, barely a foot away. It was still a long way down to the sea, but she used the time to straighten herself out and take a deep breath. Then she slid, feet first, into the murky harbour water.

Back in London, in the Special Forces headquarters, Potter was still working when Flood rushed into his office.

"Sir! One of the ships we're tracking just had a container blow up," he gasped. "The… er… *Thanh Điệp Nguyên…*, or something. It's registered in Hái Phòng and operates out of Đà Nẵng – where we know the Calver Cats have had an operation for a long time. It left Rangoon three days late, citing loading delays. That was the day Nariko was moved from Insein prison."

"Yes!" exclaimed Potter, banging his fists on the desk. "Where is it?"

"Docked late this morning in La Goulette, Tunisia."

"How did it get there so quickly?"

"It's a very fast ship. And it missed scheduled stops in Mumbai and Muscat."

"That sounds promising. Who did we send to Tunis?"

"Johnson, sir," replied Flood. "She took her husband."

"Put her on alert and see what pictures you can get."

"Already done, sir. I sent an encrypted SMS myself and she's already confirmed receipt. But there's too much cloud cover for any satellite images."

"Tunis Police?"

"They're saying it's a local matter, and not an uncommon occurrence. They're going to investigate it and let us have a copy of their report."

"Great," grumbled Potter. "Mind you, it might be better if we can handle it discreetly ourselves. Keep me posted. Get our whole North African monitoring team back to the office – and nobody leaves until we know what we're dealing with."

"Very good, sir. But even if it is Nariko, she might have died in the explosion."

"Possibly. But we're going to work on the assumption she's alive and needs help, until we have evidence to the contrary."

"Works for me, sir," replied Flood, grinning. He turned and left.

"Come on, Nariko," encouraged Potter as if trying to egg her on through the ether. "I bet you're not dead. Just let us know where you are."

CHAPTER 19

Tessa travelled a long way down in the cold dark water. When she was finally able to start back up her lungs were already bursting. She had to drive herself hard to reach the surface where the ship's bow was silhouetted against a rippling orange light. Ever since her brother had tried to drown her she'd hated being underwater, and this time was no exception. There was a lot of debris falling around her. She even saw one of Jack's tattooed arms, but felt no remorse at his passing. She knew some shrapnel had hit her too, but didn't think her injuries were serious.

Finally she emerged, gasping for air. She swam to the ship's bulbous nose and, obscured from view by the vessel's enormous bow, clung on while she recovered. She could hear people running around on the quayside above; but it was already quite dark so hopefully no one had witnessed her escape. However, she needed to distance herself from the ship; not only to make sure she wasn't recaptured, but also in case someone activated her drugs pump. But it was a long way up to the quayside and she needed to get there unseen.

Then she noticed the ship's berth ended not far away and that the dock appeared to turn back on itself. She decided to swim round and see whether she could find a way up that was out of sight of her container ship. She took a deep breath and, swimming underwater as much as she could, moved away unnoticed. When she reached the corner, she went round and stopped to peer back at her ship. She could see gantry cranes scurrying around like enormous four-legged tarantulas, frantically unloading containers. It seemed she had been in a row of seven on top of a stack of five. However, her container had been completely destroyed, as had the one beneath it. The adjoining containers had all sustained serious damage too and the fire from the explosion was still burning fiercely. She could hear sirens in the distance, but for the time being at least the ship's crew seemed totally preoccupied with preventing more containers from being damaged.

The berth she had just entered proved to be empty. In the distance, she spotted two iron handrails set vertically in the concrete wall leading up between some large black mooring fenders. She swam nearer and found that the rails were either side of a column of cut-outs designed to serve as steps. She listened for activity nearby and, satisfied there wasn't any, started climbing.

By the time Tessa reached the top she was exhausted. She cautiously scanned the quayside. Several fire engines had parked near the container ship, but nobody seemed to be even remotely interested in what was happening in her direction. There was a warehouse not far away, so she clambered on to the quayside and ran over to it, slumping down in the shadows panting. She removed her tee-shirt and wrung it out. She didn't want to leave a trail of water someone could track. But then she looked back at the path she had traced across the quayside. Although she thought she'd run in a straight line, the watery footprints weaved from side to side.

"That's not good," she mumbled, realising she was shivering. The water had not been particularly warm, but not that cold, and despite its being early evening the air temperature was high. She hoped she'd warm up soon. But as she studied her nearest footprint beginning to evaporate, she had the overwhelming impression that with it all her strength would also fade away. She felt appalling, weak and tired with a splitting headache, and all her muscles were aching. She simply wanted to go to sleep. Her vision blurred and her eyelids became incredibly heavy. Maybe it would be all right to close her eyes for few seconds? Her head drooped forward and she blacked out…

She snapped awake, crumpled on the ground. It took a while for her to remember where she was. But then reality flooded back. She needed to get away, not least since she already seemed to be suffering from withdrawal symptoms. She wasn't sure how long she had been unconscious but her footprints had all disappeared. There was no more time to lose; she had to force herself on. *Escape or die* was her new motto, and distancing herself from this place had to be her priority; a challenge complicated by her not knowing where she was. She took a deep breath and looked round again. Across the dock, she could see some white domed buildings.

"Middle East? Or… Oh, hell! Am I already in Irabya?"

She tried to get up but couldn't, she was too weak. So she started crawling along the side of the warehouse, hoping she would find some strength along the way. However, it wasn't long before her knees started hurting. She stopped and marvelled at her idiocy. She was unlikely to be able to escape the Calver Cats on all fours! *"Get up!"* she urged. *"Walk away with pride and live to win another day."* With her teeth clamped together, she forced herself to her feet using the handle of a locked door to hoist herself up. For a while she leant against the building, recharging her muscles. Then, taking care to stay in the shadows, she started moving away. Two warehouses on, she heard the sound of a fork-lift truck and headed towards it. She peered round the corner of the building and found an articulated container truck being loaded. This could be her ticket to freedom; she simply needed to hitch a clandestine ride.

With her back against the front of the warehouse, she sidled forwards, eventually stopping near the loading bay entrance. The truck was parked with about half the container inside the building; the cab was empty. Bending down, she spotted two pairs of shoes some distance inside the warehouse. Presumably, they belonged to the men supervising the loading.

In her present state, secreting herself in the cab was not an option. So she would somehow have to find a place either on the roof of the container or under the trailer. She opted for under the trailer as she doubted she had the strength to climb up to the top. As she heard the forklift travelling deeper into the warehouse, Tessa moved forward and ducked down.

The trailer chassis had been manufactured from two deep C-section steel beams and, slightly closer to where the men were standing, a large toolbox was suspended on each side. She moved between them and found two short opposing lengths of the same C-section beam had been incorporated within the structure as crossbars to provide rigidity. Together these formed a square in which Tessa felt sure she could lodge herself and remain unseen. She only hoped the loading was nearing completion and the truck would leave soon. It would be quite a strain keeping herself wedged in position and she wasn't sure how long her strength, or consciousness, would last. Nevertheless, she lifted herself up and quietly manoeuvred her body into as comfortable a position as possible. Unfortunately, there were a number of large bolt-heads which conspired to make her life a misery no matter how she adjusted herself. But a few bruises seemed a small price to pay.

Fifteen minutes later, she was thankful to hear the container doors being closed. Then, after what felt to Tessa like an inordinately long exchange of goodbyes, the driver got in the cab and started the engine. But after the truck had travelled only a short distance, it stopped. She lowered her head to see what was happening and caught a glimpse of some harbour gates. She waited nervously as papers were scrutinised and two men walked round the vehicle; but neither looked underneath. Finally, the truck started moving again and Tessa heaved a sigh of relief. She peered out again just in time to see a sign. *Welcome to La Goulette*, it read.

Probably not Irabya, she mused. Maybe French-speaking North Africa?

But then her deliberations were rudely interrupted by the pain she felt as the truck started bouncing violently along the pot-holed road. Tessa was soon so weak and uncomfortable that it was taking all of her strength and concentration to stay lodged in the truck chassis. While she was worrying that it might not be possible for her to hang on for much longer, the truck entered a lighted area and stopped. Tessa peered out to find it was queuing at traffic lights; it seemed she was in a town. The truck moved off, only to stop once more after barely two minutes. With her reserves of energy rapidly dwindling, Tessa lowered her head; the truck was waiting for some more traffic lights. It was clearly a populated area and she couldn't hold on for much longer. She'd have to risk trying to get away. She attempted to ease herself down gently, but ended up falling clumsily on to the road. She gathered her senses, mouthed an expletive, and rolled out from under the truck, stopping abruptly as she bumped into the side of a high kerb. Then the truck started moving round a corner to the right. She looked back in horror to see the rear wheels heading straight towards her. Then, with a loud screeching noise, they mounted the kerb a few feet away. Tessa flattened herself against the tarmac and the tyre treads missed her by millimetres.

"Phew," she muttered, shaking her head. "What a day!"

She waited for a moment to see if the truck driver had seen her and stopped, but he hadn't. So she struggled to her feet and studied her surroundings. Then a car approached. Although it was clear that the driver was shocked by her dishevelled appearance, he simply gave her a wide berth.

She was in the centre of a sizeable bustling town. Nearby were some stalls where some shoppers were openly staring at her. At first she thought it was due to her unconventional arrival. But then she glanced down at herself. She was covered in oil stains from the truck chassis and was wearing only a frilly tee-shirt. She gulped at the enormity of the challenge still facing her. Not far away, she noticed a large brightly illuminated hotel called the Grand Tunis.

"Ah-hah! So, I'm in Tunis. And that looks like a very fine hotel," she exclaimed, wondering how the reception staff would cope with her predicament.

Re-energised, she stepped out confidently, crossed the road and marched into the foyer. Then she caught a glimpse of herself in a mirror. She was gobsmacked and sorely tempted to stop and gawp at herself. She wasn't wearing a frilly tee-shirt, it was a shortie nightie; the sort one would expect to find in a sex shop. Furthermore, in addition to her oily unconventional clothing, her hair was matted together with blobs of grease and her face was dirty and drawn. She looked absolutely dreadful and completely out of place in a brightly lit, marble-floored hotel reception area. She carried on towards the check-in desk, trying to ignore the staff's astonished expressions. Fortunately, the extravagantly furnished foyer was largely devoid of people, or witnesses as she preferred to consider them.

"Good evening," said Tessa pleasantly. "Sorry about my unusual attire, but it's been a difficult day. I would like a room, please. Perhaps we could do the paperwork after I've had a wash and bought some new clothes?"

The man behind the desk gulped and asked her to wait a moment while he rang for the manager. Meanwhile the woman receptionist with him pushed a bowl of sweets towards Tessa and gave her a glass of water.

"Thank you," said Tessa, smiling. She gulped down the water and ate several chocolates. She noticed that her hands were shaking.

The manager appeared and looked Tessa up and down.

"*You* would like a room?" he asked incredulously.

"Yes, that's right, as quickly as you can, please. I daresay you like me standing in your foyer like this as little as I like being here."

"Have you any identification… your passport, a credit card?" he asked, convinced she was trying to wrangle a free room for the night.

"Trust me, if I'd managed to arrive with my luggage, I wouldn't look like this. However, I appreciate your dilemma. If I could telephone a friend in London, you will receive whatever assurances you need that my bills will be paid in full."

"I'm very sorry… er… madam, but we can't permit just anyone who wanders in off the street to make an international telephone call at the hotel's expense."

Tessa took a deep breath to help her keep calm. She felt like hitting the man, but simply smiled.

"I understand. But on this occasion it is more important than you could possibly imagine. I must make that call. Please!"

"Perhaps I should call the Police?" suggested the manager.

Suddenly the woman receptionist interrupted, adjusting her headscarf.

"Sir, I will pay for her call."

The manager looked at the receptionist disapprovingly.

"Please, sir. If I looked as bad as she does, I would want someone to help me. I will use our pay phone."

The manager shrugged and she walked round to Tessa.

"This way," she said, smiling.

"Thank you," acknowledged Tessa. "I will not forget your kindness."

Tessa thought hard, it was quite a struggle to remember the number, but finally she dialled something and hoped.

"Potter," barked the man at the other end of the line.

"Hello Potter. I…"

"Yes!" he cried jubilantly. "Nariko! Brilliant, I knew it was you. Tunis?"

"Er… yes. I need you to tell the hotel manager here that I'm good for my bills."

But Potter was clearly overjoyed to hear from her and started reeling off questions…

"Potter!" interrupted Tessa, surprised by the volume of her voice and the tension in it. "Listen to me, please! I'm in the lobby of the Grand Tunis Hotel. I'm a hell of a mess and I need you to talk to the manager, now!"

"Oh... yes, just a moment. Susan!" he yelled to his PA, "contact Johnson. Reception at the Grand Tunis. Now! OK, Nariko, pass me over."

The receptionist brought the manager over, and Tessa handed him the phone. The man's demeanour changed visibly as pomposity melted into obsequiousness. He returned the phone to Tessa.

"Our sincere apologies, madam. A room will be prepared for your use immediately."

Tessa nodded and lifted the receiver to her ear.

"Nariko," continued Potter, "we've been monitoring all routes out of Rangoon since you disappeared. Gwen Johnson is already in Tunis. She'll be with you in minutes. Use the name... Susan, false ID, please... Use the name *Carol Beavis* to sign in."

"All right. Please tell her to be quick."

Exhausted, she put the phone down.

"Thank you again," said Tessa to the receptionist. "How much did the call cost?"

"Oh, not much. Don't worry, it was worth it to see the expression on the manager's face."

Tessa smiled at her, and they went back to the front desk. There was frenetic activity now as the manager had one of their best suites prepared. A pristine white towelling gown appeared and the receptionist helped Tessa put it on. But all this was happening too slowly for her; she was wilting and was sure it wouldn't be long before she fainted. Suddenly, someone was standing beside her.

"Hello, Carol, remember me?"

Tessa turned and found a smart-looking woman of similar build to herself with auburn hair. She recognised her from meetings she'd had with Potter. She nodded and smiled, noting the shock and concern in the other woman's eyes.

"God! You look as though you've been through hell and back," whispered Johnson.

"Several times," sighed Tessa, "and... I'm about to pass out."

"Michael, she's feeling faint. Help her, please," said Johnson. "Don't worry, Carol, we'll take care of you. My husband's a doctor."

A strong arm looped around her shoulders and started to take her weight. Johnson completed the hotel formalities and she and her husband helped Tessa up to the suite. She flopped onto the sofa and Michael started examining her while Johnson brought some water. Although physically and emotionally drained, Tessa couldn't allow herself to rest, not yet.

"Not important," she gasped, impatiently brushing his hand away.

"What have they been giving you?"

"Not sure. Something with heroin and rohypnol, twice-daily."

She raised her right hand, now with a noticeable tremor.

"When was your last injection?"

"9 a.m., I think. But it wasn't an injection; it was from the pump implanted here…" She raised her nightie, oblivious to the fact that she was wearing nothing underneath. Michael didn't bat an eyelid and simply kneeled down to inspect her abdomen, but his wife looked on dumbstruck.

"Good grief," he observed, shocked and disgusted. He pressed around the now completely healed incision. "I think it's in as deep as they could get it without opening the abdominal cavity."

"They can activate it remotely and deliver a lethal dose," said Tessa, beginning to panic. "It's got to come out now! You're a doctor, use that." She nodded towards a knife on a bowl of fruit.

He hesitated. Tessa grabbed his arm.

"Look, it's coming out now. Either you do it or I will. It went in without any anaesthetic; it might as well come out the same way"

Michael's face started to go red.

"Nariko, I'm going to need my arm back uncrushed if you want me to operate on you."

They both looked at her hand tightly clamped round his arm.

"Oh, sorry" replied Tessa, releasing him. "I…"

"Don't worry, I understand," he smiled, rubbing his new bruises. "Look, I'll do it for you, but my own way. I'm going to get my bag."

"No time," wailed Tessa. "They might activate it any moment. Use alcohol from the mini-bar for disinfectant and sticky tape to close the wound. You can beautify it some other time; I may only have minutes. Do it now, please!" Her eyes started watering. "Don't think about it, just…"

"No, Nariko. My bag's close by. I'll fetch it while you get scrubbed up. Gwen, give her a hot shower and make sure you scrub around here." Tessa looked dismayed. "Don't worry," he intoned. "Our hotel is right next door. I'll be back in two minutes. It'll be worth it. I've got some stuff that will help me, and perhaps stave off your withdrawal symptoms too."

Tessa was too weak to object. She breathed out heavily and slumped back in the sofa.

"Please be quick," she implored.

He nodded and headed for the door.

"Darling," called Gwen, "bring my briefcase with you, please."

After he'd gone, Tessa couldn't stop herself from thinking back to what had happened to her in the shipping container; it wasn't long before tears were running down her face. The stress of the last few weeks was already beginning to come out. Johnson sat down and put an arm around her.

"Don't worry. You're safe now. We will not leave you."

Tessa sobbed for a while, but then tried to pull herself together.

"They'll assume I tried to escape, but they won't know whether I'm alive or not. They'll be looking for me… for anyone who booked in to a hotel tonight."

"I know. I'd already worked that out. I'll take care of it."

"No one else must know I'm free! Tell Potter. Nyunt is in terrible danger and it will get worse for her if they know I'm alive…"

"OK. But come with me now," said Johnson gently, "let's get you cleaned up. Michael won't be long. He's a very good doctor, he'll sort you out."

"Surgeon?"

"GP actually, but this won't faze him."

No sooner had Tessa come out of the shower than Michael returned carrying two bags. He handed one to Gwen and opened the other. He took out various drugs and a plastic case containing medical equipment.

"It's not a full kit, but it'll be a lot better than using a fruit knife." He took several small bottles out of his bag, together with some dressings and a hermetically sealed scalpel. Then he held up a small bubble pack and pressed out a single white tablet. "This is diazepam,... valium. It's not ideal and won't stop all your withdrawal symptoms, but it should help to ease them. Take one and tell me how you feel." He handed her the tablet and a glass of water and started preparing for the operation. Tessa took it and waited.

"Gwen," ordered Michael, "fold a bath towel in two and spread it on the bed for her." After a couple of minutes, Tessa was still feeling awful, so he gave her another tablet. "Take the minimum you can get away with, please. I've only got six." Tessa nodded. "Now lie on the towel."

"I think I feel a bit better," said Tessa, as her shaking lessened.

"Good, now take two more. It will zone you out and help with the pain I'm about to inflict. I'll be able to work faster if I know you're not experiencing too much discomfort."

Tessa didn't care any more. She took the pills and lay back on the bed.

"OK. Gwen, fill the basin with very hot water and put a capful of this disinfectant in it. Bring a face towel soaked with drinking water for Nariko to bite on and another treated with disinfectant... And leave the basin full for me. Better bring all the other towels too."

Tessa was feeling groggy by this time and everything grew hazy. She wasn't even aware of Michael leaving her to go and scrub his hands. But she partially resurfaced in time to feel him swab around where the pump had been inserted with concentrated disinfectant. The pungent clinical aroma filled her nostrils.

"Ready?" he asked. Tessa nodded and, as she bit down on the face towel, he unwrapped the scalpel. "I'll be as quick as I can, but this is still going to hurt like hell..."

After twenty minutes, the pump was out. Tessa was as white as the sheets she was lying on, but relieved beyond belief. Michael inspected the pump.

"Beautiful piece of work," he noted. "But... Hmm ... That's odd."

"What?" whispered Tessa.

"Well, the dosage wheel had been sealed with a blob of wax to ensure it delivered a maximum dose each time, but it looks as though someone has broken the seal and cranked it down. It's only been giving you half what was intended."

"Wow! I don't think I could have stood more," she admitted. "It must have been the surgeon in Rangoon; he probably did it while he was implanting the thing. I hope I can thank him one day. Thank you for removing it."

"You're welcome. Have some more water. I've stitched the wound but I won't dress it until it's stopped weeping. I don't have a tissue regenerator with me so it will be very sore for a while. Try and get some sleep now. We'll be next door if you need us."

Tessa nodded, and he and Gwen cleaned up before lowering the lights.

Unable to sleep and beginning to believe she might actually have defied the odds and managed to escape, Tessa surveyed the room. It was attractively decorated with a terracotta-tiled floor on which several richly patterned hand-woven rugs had been laid, together with dark orange walls and red curtains. Ornate wooden cupboards stood in green-painted alcoves to either side of the door. The ceiling had Moorish designs carved deep in the plaster and there were wooden friezes on the walls in Arabic designs. A stark but wonderful contrast to the quarters of her last few weeks, she thought. Then she drifted into sleep.

Gwen came to check on her soon afterwards, and reported back to her husband. While he carefully finished dressing Tessa's wound, she phoned Potter to give him an update. The call lasted a long time as they planned what to do. Michael joined his wife just as she put the phone down.

"I hope you're not expecting to get any sleep tonight," she said, kissing him. "We've got more work to do."

After explaining, she went down to reception while Michael gathered up everything they had used to operate on Tessa. Gwen returned ten minutes later.

"That receptionist is brilliant," she said, handing him two new key cards. "We've got both these rooms for tonight. However, the second one isn't registered on the computer yet. She'll do that tomorrow. She's taking all the security cameras off-line and wiping the past half-day. You and Nariko need to move to the other room as quickly as possible. We'll exchange all the clean towels from there with the ones here and make it look as though only I've been using this room."

As Gwen started gathering things together and cleaning up, Michael woke Tessa.

"Nariko," he said gently.

Immediately her eyes were wide open.

"Oh, hello, you're new here aren't you, what can I do for you?" she asked provocatively.

"I beg your pardon?" he replied, astounded.

"Oh, shy too, how sweet. How can I please you? I'll do *anything* you like."

He looked at her dilated pupils; it seemed the valium had returned her to a totally submissive state.

"Oh, boy… Well, I'd like you to remain completely calm and relaxed, and help me move to another room. Would that be all right?"

"Are you sure that's all you want," replied Tessa, sounding disappointed.

"Absolutely. Just don't exert yourself and break those new stitches of yours."

"OK," she chirped.

"Right, good. I'll help you get up, and then come with me, please."

Like an automaton, Tessa obediently got up and followed him into the sitting room. Gwen looked up in surprise at his shocked expression.

"Zoned out and totally submissive," he sighed, gesturing at Tessa. "That's a dreadful thing to do to anyone."

"God, I hope there isn't any permanent damage," murmured Gwen.

It wasn't long before everything had been exchanged between the two rooms and Gwen had been back down to reception to check that the security tapes had been wiped. When she returned to the new room, she set about cutting her hair to match Tessa's and dying it blonde. Just as she finished, Potter phoned to give her some more information and she confirmed everything was going according to plan. She put the receiver down, stood up and hugged Michael.

"I've got to go to the other room now. If anyone comes looking for Nariko, that's where they'll start. I'll come back here at breakfast-time. If anything happens in the meantime, you must *not* try to help me; get Nariko to safety. Don't look so worried, darling, I'll be fine. If for any reason I don't come back, use my *cbc* to call Potter. He'll tell you what to do."

Michael sighed and pulled his wife closer.

"Gwen, I know you too well to argue. And I know you enjoy this stuff and can take care of yourself. But please, please, don't do anything foolish."

She kissed him.

"I won't, darling, I promise. I'll see you for breakfast. Now, don't worry, just take good care of her."

Reluctant to let go, Michael finally released her. Gwen discarded most of her clothes and went out wearing only a bikini and a flimsy green nightdress.

Back in the original room, she checked everything was in order. Then she stripped, rinsed out her bikini, climbed in the bed where Tessa had lain, and tried to get some sleep.

At 2:30 a.m., the phone rang. Gwen was awake instantly but she still let it ring for a while.

"Hello," she said, recognising the receptionist's voice. "…But it's the middle of the night. Who are they? What do you mean, they won't say?… OK, OK. Give me a minute."

Gwen grabbed a towelling robe and went down to reception. She found the receptionist, looking very scared, in the company of three people. Two were tough-looking men while the other was a scruffy, strongly built woman of Arabic appearance.

"Hello," said Gwen, smiling encouragingly at the receptionist. "What can I do for you?"

She nodded towards the group of three.

"Who are you?" asked Gwen, eyeing them with disdain. "And what do you want with me at this hour?"

"Shut up," grunted the larger of the two men. He took out a photograph and compared it with one of Tessa before passing it to the woman. "Where were you before you came here?"

"It's none of your business," retorted Gwen tersely.

"Want to watch this woman die?" he said, drawing a knife and gesturing towards the receptionist.

"Don't be silly, of course not!"

"Then answer my question."

"I was on a cruise ship going round the Mediterranean," retorted Gwen crisply.

"So why aren't you on it now?"

"Because I jumped off."

"Why the fuck would you do that?"

"Because my husband's an alcoholic. I'd warned him that I'd leave if he got drunk again. I'm hoping this'll teach him a lesson. Fortunately, the ship had only just left and I'm a very good swimmer."

The woman handed the photograph back to the man.

"They're sort of similar, but I'm not sure..."

"What are you talking about?" asked Gwen.

"Speak when you're spoken too, bitch," retorted the woman.

Gwen looked offended, shrugged and turned to go back to the lift.

"Where the fuck do you think you're going?" demanded the first man.

"To my room. I don't see why I should stand around here being insulted by the likes of you."

"You leave when I say you can," hissed the man.

"Give me your room key," demanded the woman, as the man waved a knife at her.

Looking as irritated as she could, Gwen gave her the key card. The woman handed it to the second man.

"Check the room," she ordered. "But be careful, she might be up there. She's dangerous and they want her alive if possible. Only kill her if you have to."

He nodded, drew an air pistol and went up in the lift.

"What cruise ship were you on?" asked the first man.

"The Borealis," replied Gwen.

"It was here yesterday," confirmed the woman to the other man. "I'll contact the port agent and check her story."

She made a phone call, came back and nodded.

"Fits."

"OK. Check her crotch, just to be sure," he added.

"No way!" exclaimed Gwen, stepping back.

"You can be dead or alive for this," the man taunted with relish. "You choose."

"Oh, for goodness sake," replied Gwen. "Look, there's a Ladies

Room over there."

The woman nodded and together they went to the powder room.

There, much to Gwen's amusement, although she tried to feign disgust, the woman looked to see whether there was a scar on her abdomen and a tattoo over her crotch. Satisfied there wasn't, they returned to reception.

"It's not her."

"The room's clean," advised the second man as he came out of the lift.

The first man turned to the receptionist.

"You're sure this was the woman who checked in?"

"Yes," exclaimed the receptionist with an expression bordering on panic. "I watched her sign the register myself."

"Bugger!" the man exclaimed. "That was our best lead."

"Press the button anyway," advised the woman. He produced a small grey box with a black button and pressed it while she timed how long he had held it down.

"OK. That'll do," she announced. "Should we leave them? They've seen us."

"Are you going to say anything about this?" asked the man in a threatening tone, brandishing his knife again.

"Er, definitely not," replied Gwen quickly.

"Leave 'em," he droned, turning away. "The security cameras are down anyway."

The gang of three left and Gwen watched their car drive off.

She heaved a sigh of relief and went over to the receptionist who was shaking.

"Well done," said Gwen, reassuringly, "we'll be fine now. Let's calm our nerves with a mug of hot chocolate and maybe a shot of something stronger..."

Eventually, Gwen went back to bed. But she only lay awake, convinced she couldn't even begin to imagine the dreadful things Tessa had been forced to endure.

CHAPTER 20

At 7 a.m., Gwen felt she could return to the other room. She knocked quietly on the door. Michael opened it immediately and they embraced, relieved. He had been so worried that he too had hardly slept. She explained what had happened.

"…It was close a call. That receptionist held together incredibly well. She deserves a medal."

"Closer than you think," asserted Michael, pointing to the covered glass containing Tessa's recently removed pump. In it was a pool of light blue liquid. "It was activated about 3 a.m. I think its tank emptied. I don't doubt the dose would have killed her…"

They ordered a substantial breakfast and settled down to eat it together.

Meanwhile, Tessa had woken up. She felt strangely distant and once again had a splitting headache; she was also sweating profusely. She tried to focus on the room whose decoration she'd thought so attractive the night before. But all she found were bland off-white walls, a dark blue carpet and beech cabinets. The décor was modern European, luxurious, but definitely not where she had gone to sleep.

"Damn!" she exclaimed, checking her abdomen. There was a fresh dressing over a new wound. Had her pump just been removed, or what? Maybe she'd only dreamed about getting away. Paul had suggested she wouldn't be able to tell the difference between her fantasy world and reality. Perhaps she was with her new owner and had somehow woken up unexpectedly, like Toshie. She looked round, beginning to panic. Everything was moving in and out of focus. But she noticed a bowl of fruit on the dresser with a knife in it. Better safe than sorry, she thought. She eased herself out of bed and went to pick up the knife.

She heard some voices in the adjoining room, but they sounded so distorted that she couldn't make out what they were saying. *Escape or die!* she reminded herself. If she hadn't got away before, she would now. She walked silently to the bedroom door which was slightly ajar. She could see the back of a woman's head; the blonde hairstyle bore a striking resemblance to her own. Facing her was a man. He seemed vaguely familiar. Wasn't he the one who had led her from her bed last night, presumably to enjoy her services? Tessa's head was spinning but she tried to concentrate. She needed to act.

"Good morning," greeted Michael as she opened the door. "How did you sleep?"

As Gwen turned round, Tessa raised the knife.

"Nariko, no!" she exclaimed. "It's me, Gwen Johnson. You're safe."

Suddenly not sure what she was doing, Tessa hesitated.

"Nariko," asked Michael gently, "you still want to please me, don't you?"

She froze. There was a battle raging in her mind.

"Yes," she whimpered, her shoulders drooping, "of course I do."

"Good," he continued gently. "Drop the knife and come over here. We're all going to have some breakfast together."

At first, Tessa couldn't decide what to do, but the plates of food on the table looked very inviting and she was hungry. She dropped the knife.

"Where would you like me to sit?"

"Over here, please," ordered Michael. Gwen swallowed and went to pick up the knife.

First, Michael had Tessa take another valium tablet and then they ate breakfast. Afterwards, Tessa fell asleep on the sofa while Gwen phoned Potter once more.

When Tessa woke up, she was herself again this time, remembering them immediately but with no recollection of changing rooms or the incident with the fruit knife.

"We're being met as you wanted," assured Gwen.

"As I wanted?" queried Tessa.

"Yes, don't you remember? Before you left London you gave Potter a sealed envelope with instructions on what to do if you needed help."

"Oh, that was clever," said Tessa, shrugging. "Can I do anything?"

"No, just rest and conserve your energy," replied Gwen. She and Michael had already agreed that they weren't sure Tessa was stable enough to do anything important. So as they prepared for their departure, she lay on the sofa and watched television. She kept listening to news programmes as she hadn't heard what had been happening in the world for a long time. Michael had just left to do some errands when Tessa sat up abruptly and increased the volume. Gwen sat down with her, curious to learn what was of such interest.

"...fortune smiles brightly on our proud and free country as to-day we honour the visit of reclusive Sheikh Saif Iqbal Mubdallah Ikraam Tayeb Al Rahal of Irabya. His Royal Highness has left the comfort of his luxurious fortress in Al Kharadis to consummate personally a business deal which rumour has it has run into difficulty.

"Some Western nations regard the Sheikh as a controversial figure and both the UK and Germany have issued arrest warrants relating to a variety of trafficking and sex-related crimes.

"However, the Sheikh nonchalantly shrugs these accusations aside, dismissing them as scurrilous politically motivated Western attempts to discredit him and his country.

"And here he is now..."

The picture switched to the scene of a suntanned, portly man coming down the steps beside a smart executive jet and on to a red carpet. The cameras zoomed in for a close-up of him shaking hands with various officials, giving Gwen and Tessa a clear view of his face. He was wearing a white thawb topped with a keffiyeh secured by two thick gold cords. His robe was embroidered around the edges, but what caught Tessa's attention was the ornate crest on the left breast of it. It was the same as the tattoo on her crotch.

"I'll say your fucking business has run into difficulty," she hissed, threateningly. "I promised you we'd meet again, Sheikh."

Gwen looked at her in surprise.

"Sorry," said Tessa. "I wasn't swearing, it's just that his business appears to be primarily about sexual exploitation."

Gwen nodded; it wasn't that which had surprised her. It was the fact that Tessa had implied she intended to take action against the Sheikh outside of her Peacekeeper remit, as it was widely known that Irabya had no intention of signing the International Peacekeeper Treaty.

"My kidnappers will still be in town," insisted Tessa. "We must be careful."

"I know, we're leaving soon," acknowledged Gwen.

"OK boss. All done," confirmed Michael, closing the door behind him and grinning at his wife. "The SUV's in the hotel's underground car park. I've put all of our stuff in it from the other hotel, but I haven't checked out. I left one suitcase and told them we'd be back in a couple of days. Here's a tracksuit for Nariko, and a pair of black burqas complete with eye-slit niqabs."

"Good job, darling," smiled Gwen, kissing him on the cheek. "We'll make an agent of you yet."

"No, thanks. Nariko, how are you feeling?"

"Weird, weak, headaches, hot flushes... vulnerable."

"Well, take this then." He handed her the last of the valium tablets. "Hopefully, we'll be well away from here before you start to feel really bad again."

Tessa took the tablet and changed into the tracksuit. Then she and Gwen inserted brown-coloured contact lenses and dressed in their burqas and face masks.

"OK, let's go," instructed Gwen.

Pretending to be their chauffeur, wearing a dark suit and reflective sunglasses, Michael led them down to the car. He held the doors open as they got in the back. With its heavily tinted windows, no one could see who was inside. Gwen took out her *cbc*.

"OK, up the ramp and turn right. We want to take the P3 highway south towards El Fahs."

The SUV pulled into the blazing sun and headed out of Tunis. Tessa was only vaguely aware of their surroundings as they drove away from the hotel. Her brain struggled to take in the exotic shapes whisking by: mosques with brightly topped prayer towers, souks with colourful fruit and spice stalls, a plethora of cafes with men smoking hookahs outside. In her mind they all merged into an indistinct blur. But even she noted that, encouragingly, no one seemed to be taking the slightest notice of their car.

They were soon speeding down a wide, almost-empty highway. After an hour, they turned onto a much smaller, even quieter road on which they continued south-east into the sun for another hour and a half. The route Gwen selected was somewhat more circuitous than necessary as she wanted to make sure they were not being followed. Also, she didn't want to arrive too early.

Eventually, she announced that they would need to make one last left turn, and that their destination wasn't much further now. Tessa looked up inquisitively, experiencing a rare interlude of lucidity. She found there was barren desert as far as she could see to her right and high sand dunes to the left; the sky was deep blue with a bright sun beating down from it. As they approached a gap between two dunes, Gwen leaned forward.

"I think it's here," she said, pointing to a rough track marked by a row of concrete posts, almost submerged by drifting sand. "Now you can give full vent to your Dakar Rally ambitions."

Michael grinned and enthusiastically turned off the road.

"As soon as we're out of sight, I'll lower the tyre pressures," he said as they passed between the dunes. They stopped shortly afterwards, and Tessa simply gazed aimlessly out across the desolate sand-scape.

Then they set off again, only slowing down some twenty minutes later as they half-slid down a sizeable sand dune towards a deserted landing strip. There were some tumble-weeds blowing across it together with numerous sand spirals, looking like ghosts seeking somewhere to take refuge. In the distance were some derelict buildings, but not a single human being was to be seen.

"We need to check the place out," insisted Gwen. "Drive along the runway, and go round the buildings at the end. But be ready to put your foot down if there's any trouble."

Michael nodded nervously. This was not the sort of thing he was used to, or enjoyed, doing. However, after ten minutes, Gwen was satisfied.

"OK, darling, well done," she said discarding her niqab. "Park over there and I'll send the all clear. Then I suggest we have lunch. I'm not sure how long we'll have to wait."

Tessa got out of the car and, with Michael's help, removed both her niqab and burqa. But she was beginning to feel distant again and stood supporting herself awkwardly against the SUV with a vacant expression on her face. Michael looked her over but felt there wasn't much else he could do now, so he got out the food and offered some bottles of water round.

Gwen remained on high alert throughout, continually scanning the surrounding desert dunes and buildings for anything suspicious. She also insisted that Michael stay in the driver's seat, ready to start the engine at a moment's notice. Eventually, Tessa clambered into the car again and curled up in a foetal position across the back seat. But Gwen refused to sit; instead she paced around, frequently lifting her binoculars to scour the horizon.

Suddenly, the whistling of the wind was interrupted by the purring of powerful jet engines; a plane was approaching from the south, out of the sun. Gwen had Michael start the car's engine. She closed Tessa's door and strained to identify the aircraft. However, it was trying to remain obscure, so she couldn't see it properly until it swooped close overhead. It was a sleek triple-engined executive jet. Gwen smiled with relief and put her binoculars away. The plane circled the airdrome several times before landing and taxiing over to them.

Tessa opened her eyes, eased herself out of the car, and rose shakily to her feet. She felt dazed and wilted in the stifling heat and had to hold on to the car to prevent herself from falling; she had started shaking again too. She stared vacuously at the aircraft shimmering in the heat. It was completely black except for a large gold chrysanthemum motif which glistened in the sunlight. The steps unfurled and two heavily armed Ninja warriors ran down, a woman and a man. Gwen went towards them but they simply bowed and ran on to take up defensive positions some distance from the plane. Then two distinguished-looking men appeared by the plane door. One was dressed in black with a gold chrysanthemum embroidered on the chest of his collarless jacket. He calmly surveyed the area. The other was wearing a burgundy-coloured tunic armed with a sword. He glanced round urgently, and, on seeing Tessa, rushed down the stairs.

Tessa's heart started beating more quickly and she staggered forward. She didn't know who he was, but was sure he was a friend who had come to help her. He stopped in front of her. She stared at him, her ashen face covered with droplets of perspiration, eyes sunken in darkened sockets.

"Nariko-san, I am Matsumoto. Listen now to my voice only. I command you to remember who I am to you. Command end."

Tessa tried to say something, but all that came out was a pitiful choked whimper, then her legs weakened and she started to collapse. Matsumoto leaped forward and caught her, scooping her up in his arms as though she weighed nothing.

"*Anata*," she wailed. "I am so sorry. They have done terrible things to me."

She started sobbing uncontrollably.

"*Omae*," whispered Matsumoto, gently brushing her hair away from her eyes. "We are together again. That is all that matters. I am so pleased to have you back. I will take you home now and look after you."

"Thank you," she mumbled, and passed out.

Matsumoto turned to Michael.

"Thank you for helping my wife to find her way back to me."

"Oh, you're welcome. She's quite a woman," replied Michael.

"Indeed she is," acknowledged Matsumoto, smiling with a mixture of sadness and pride.

Gwen and Gyobu looked on in surprise.

"Your wife?" exclaimed Gwen. "I never knew Nariko…"

"Neither did I," blurted Gyobu, clearly astonished.

"I apologise, Gyobu-san, we felt it would be better if nobody knew," answered Matsumoto, glancing momentarily at his friend. "But, yes, Agent Johnson, Nariko and I married many years ago. However, the needs of our respective children made it difficult for us to be together, so we decided it would be prudent to keep our union secret. Now I think our children are old enough to start solving their own problems. Nariko and I always hoped to finish our lives together. Since you have made that a possibility once more, I thought I would share this information with you. I am most grateful to you and your husband. Thank you for being so efficient, Agent Johnson. You are a credit to your organisation. Good-bye."

He bowed and carried Tessa on to the plane.

"Agent Johnson, I am General Gyobu. Potter has told me what you did. Well done, and my thanks also for all your help. We are indeed indebted to you both. Be careful when you return to Tunis, there are many Calver Cats still searching."

"Have you a doctor with you?" asked Michael.

"We have indeed," replied the General, and called back to the plane. A man and a woman dressed in white joined them. The woman acted as interpreter while Michael described how he had treated Tessa. Then he gave them the glass containing the drugs pump.

Gwen and Michael stayed to watch the black jet take off. Then they drove straight to Tunis airport and caught the first flight for London.

The executive jet had been airborne for two hours when Tessa regained consciousness. She looked down at her hand to see an IV cannula had been inserted. Her heart started racing as she watched an injection being prepared.

"Go on," she hissed, "do your worst, Paul, you won't break me. The pain, the visions, the noises – I can take it all." She started to raise her voice. "You will never beat me down!"

Matsumoto rushed to her side.

"Nariko-san, this nurse is a friend. She is going to help you."

She reached up, trying to touch his face.

"*Anata*, is it you? Are you really here?"

"Yes, Nariko-san." He took hold of her hand and bent down to kiss her forehead. "It is really me. I will stay with you. Do not worry yourself any more."

He nodded to the nurse and seconds later, as the drugs took effect, Tessa's head rolled to one side and she drifted into unconsciousness.

Matsumoto returned to his meeting. The General remained placid and composed. The doctor was clearly under pressure, but adamant in his preliminary diagnosis.

"I regret there is little scope for uncertainty," he continued. "The drugs Nariko was being given constitute a sophisticated and powerful concoction. They are highly innovative, with a remarkable degree of persistence. Indeed, the concentration in her blood is still elevated to a surprising degree. I have no reason to suspect they are anything other than extremely effective. It is incredible that she managed to escape at all.

"We were told she was forced to endure eleven days of, apparently, a fourteen day programme. I accept the dosage levels were possibly somewhat lower than intended, but there is still a high probability of permanent brain damage. Although we currently do not understand precisely how the drugs work, it is clear that they were being targeted on specific centres within the brain; doubtless with the use of markers administered earlier. I would imagine these were installed while she was being forced to experience the emotions the drugs were intended to adjust or suppress. Perhaps anger, pain, hatred and fear for subsequent desensitisation and… er… others for enhancement. That would explain her strongly adverse reaction to the IV which we just witnessed. With a series of scans of her brain, together with a more comprehensive analysis of the chemicals being used, we will be able to quantify the damage that has been done and the resultant impairment. But in the dire circumstances in which we find ourselves, where we cannot rule out substantial irreversible injury, and possibly deep-rooted programming, I do not believe we have any other viable alternative which will safeguard everything that is at stake."

The General breathed out noisily, glancing at Matsumoto who'd put his head in his hands.

"I am sorry," added the doctor, "but I'm afraid you must prepare yourself for the worst. It is quite possible that the Peacekeeper Nariko you knew is gone for ever. She may require permanent institutionalisation, for her own safety and that of those around her."

Matsumoto's face was ashen. He should never have let her go to Burma he told himself with guilt.

"Very well, I agree," he resolved, broken-hearted but finally acquiescing to the doctor's demands. "We will take Nariko to the Cognitive Neuroscience Unit in Tokyo. But, whatever happens, her escape must remain a secret. If she is unable to finish this, then I most certainly will."

CHAPTER 21

Tessa opened her eyes. Above her was the intricately carved ceiling of the audience hall in the Samurai house, to her left lay the glowing embers of what had been a substantial fire. Lying to her right was Matsumoto. He too was staring up at the ceiling, apparently unaware that she was awake. She reached across the tatami mat and gripped his hand to check that he was real. He smiled at her.

"*Ohayou gozaimasu, omae.* How do you feel?" She rolled over to him and they embraced.

"Not very well, *anata.* I am weak and my head feels ready to explode."

"And all that will get much worse before it gets better. But we have a couple of hours of peace. Shall we watch the dawn together?"

"Yes, I would like that. But why will it get worse?"

He took a deep breath.

"Because you must be weaned off the drugs to which you have become addicted."

She sighed sadly. But he simply smiled, stood and helped her up. After washing, she took her place on the verandah and waited patiently; revelling in viewing the majestic panorama she loved so much. Matsumoto joined her and they sat in silence with a small table between them. On it stood a black lacquerware tray with a pot of green tea and two fine porcelain cups. The sun was starting to nudge its way above the horizon.

"What have they done to me?" asked Tessa, her tone betraying her despondency.

"Well, the drugs they were giving you were a clever combination and definitely could have caused permanent brain damage. They were being targeted by markers which will persist for several months yet as it was deemed too dangerous to attempt to negate them, but eventually they will disappear without further intervention. This means that the rehabilitation plan devised for you by our experts will address only those drugs designed to ensure your dependency, submissiveness and interaction with the markers… However, while the markers are present you will remain highly susceptible should the drugs be injected again. This will not be easy, Nariko-san, but we will get through it together."

"How long will it take?"

"We don't know precisely. Rohypnol was a major component of what you were being given. It is both physically and psychologically addictive. Its withdrawal symptoms involve anxiety, muscle pain, headaches, hallucinations and seizures, and peak some three to five days after last use. But you were also given a number of other drugs, including several heroin derivatives. We anticipate the most difficult phase will be in about five to eight days from now. I have everything we need. Neither of us will leave here until this is over, and there will be no visitors."

"It's not going to be much fun, is it?"

Matsumoto shrugged.

"Life usually isn't."

Tessa drank some tea and settled back in her chair, keen to savour the scene of the sun rising over the distant mountains. The dark blue sky lightened as a turquoise corona crept tentatively up from the horizon, soon to be blasted away by a slither of bright orange light.

"You will need to take two pills in the morning and two at night," Matsumoto informed her. "Each dose has been precisely calibrated to wean you off your dependency. You will experience much mental and physical discomfort, which must be endured if you want to get better. You do you want to get better, don't you, Nariko-san?"

Tessa turned away from the yellowing radiance; already there were beads of perspiration on her forehead and her hands had started to tremble. She looked into his eyes and smiled.

"Yes, *anata*, I want to get better very much indeed. I have debts to settle, and things I hold precious to recover."

Matsumoto nodded.

"You'd better let me have my two pills."

"You've already had them. That's why you felt all right when you woke up."

She breathed out noisily and pondered as to where he would have stashed the other tablets…

It wasn't long before Tessa was a complete mess; soaked in sweat, crying and shaking. Her state continued to worsen throughout the day. Nevertheless, Matsumoto remained calm, talking to her reassuringly and hugging her whenever she would permit it.

She got some relief that evening when, as if by magic, he produced two pills for her. She swallowed them hungrily and they alleviated many of her symptoms. That allowed her to eat and sleep a little. But at dawn, it started all over again, soon becoming far worse. She quickly descended into the depths of withdrawal.

As the days passed, Tessa's periods of lucidity decreased in frequency and duration. She was experiencing intense pain, her headaches were agony and her emotions oscillated between extremes with alarming alacrity. As she became agitated and abusive, her personal hygiene lapsed and she began sleeping in obscure places within the castle grounds, despite the nights being cold and wet.

By the fifth day, she was in a dreadful state, dishevelled, dirty and stinking of urine. But she refused to wash or change. The level of invective she directed against Matsumoto was cruel in the extreme and, for the first time, she threatened violence in an attempt to extract more drugs from him. However, he had hidden the tablets well and removed all the weapons he could from the castle.

As Tessa's condition deteriorated, Matsumoto became increasingly vigilant about only having one knife out at a time while preparing food, and always watching it carefully.

On the sixth day at lunchtime he was busy cutting fish for sashimi. He hadn't seen Tessa since she had disappeared across the honmaru after breakfast. Suddenly there was a loud *crash* from the back of the Samurai house. Matsumoto rushed to Tessa's study, fearing that she might have harmed herself; the bookcase had been tipped over, but the room was empty. When he returned to the kitchen, she was waiting for him, brandishing the knife.

He smiled.

"Hello, Nariko-san. Let me have the knife, please. I need to finish our lunch."

"Give me the pills first!" she yelled.

"I'm sorry, I can't do that."

227

"Why are you always so cruel to me? I must have more!"

"You will get your next pills this evening, not before."

"No, now!" she shrieked. "Or..."

"Or what, Nariko-san?" he asked, calmly.

"Or I'll kill you," she replied, raising the knife.

Matsumoto knew only too well how good she was with a knife, and the short distance separating them meant not even he would have time to react.

"If you kill me, Nariko-san, you will not get any more pills. I am the only person who knows where they are and nobody else will come here to help you."

"Then get them for me!" she screamed, shaking violently.

"No, I love you too much for that."

"Please! I will do it."

"*Omae*, let me have the knife, it's time we ate."

Tessa glared at him.

"I hate you!" she shouted.

Then, like lightning, she threw the knife. So fast was her throw, Matsumoto didn't even have time to flinch. The blade whistled past his ear and struck the wooden wall behind him. He heaved a sigh of relief.

"Thank you, for missing."

"Don't flatter yourself," she hissed, turning away, "I didn't fucking miss."

Matsumoto raised his eyebrows and removed the knife from the wall. On the end was a large bluebottle. He smiled, locked the knife away and went to try and console his wife. But she had run away and he didn't see her again until it was time for her next pills.

Tessa's days had settled into a distinctly unpleasant routine. She would appear bedraggled for breakfast and dinner, greedily snatch away her tablets, and wander off, swearing and accusing Matsumoto of obscene crimes. He gave up trying to keep track of her as she never failed to return for her pills; always in a marginally more dishevelled state than the last time.

Frequently, Tessa would begin a tirade of insults by emptying the contents of several cupboards over the floor. This was always in a desperate attempt to locate more drugs, despite having done it to no avail many times before. Then she would rant and rave abusively, eventually ending up in a sobbing inconsolable heap on the floor. She regularly threatened him, and would persistently leave muddy tracks across the pristine tatami mats. She tried using sexual blandishments too, but not even that had any effect on him.

She became so distressed she could barely sleep, so he stayed up with her until she pushed him away and ran off into the darkness. But whenever he could, he urged her on with encouraging words. He could see she was making progress. Although the tablets always looked the same, each pair was slightly less potent than the ones before.

Finally, Tessa started to calm down. She was less abusive and began experiencing brief periods of relative lucidity. Slowly, these lengthened. She even washed herself.

She woke on the eleventh day to find herself sitting astride the long plank at the end of the garden, some 100 feet over the castle moat. Early in her training Matsumoto had insisted she jump off the plank and swim round the castle in an effort to overcome her fear of drowning.

"Whoah!" she exclaimed. "This is one hell of a place to wake up."

Despite being wet and shivering from the cold, she took a deep breath and rejoiced at being able to admire the view. Everything looked and smelt very different; more acute, more colourful, more full of life. Indeed, apart from her splitting headache and the fact that she was weak, frozen and exhausted, she felt relatively normal.

She forced herself up, opened the door and walked back to the Samurai house. Without making a sound, she entered the master bedroom. Matsumoto was sleeping soundly. She sat down cross-legged and watched him in silence. He was resting peacefully and she smiled, remembering how much she loved him. Eventually, his eyes opened. He was shocked to find she had managed to approach without his hearing and wondered what she was going to do.

"*Ohayou gozaimasu, anata*," she whispered.

"*Ohayou, omae*," he replied. "How are you feeling today?"

"Tired and cold."

"Then rest with me a while and I will help you get warm."

They snuggled together and in his close embrace, she soon fell fast asleep. Matsumoto watched her, lovingly stroking her hair. Then he kissed her on the forehead and closed his eyes…

They slept until mid-morning. He woke first, followed a few minutes later by Tessa.

She looked at him and smiled. They kissed. But then she started crying.

"Shhh, Nariko-san. Everything is going to be all right now."

"Is it? They forced me through hell, and I've done the same to you."

"Oh, it wasn't that bad… Well, maybe once or twice when I feared for my life! But we have been Peacekeepers for many years and, yet again, we have thwarted our foe's best attempts to destroy us. I believe, Nariko-san, the tables have just turned in our favour."

"But they pummelled my very soul into the ground."

"Then we shall nurture it tenderly and help you to grow proud and strong once more. Maybe we should start with some breakfast? I will go and prepare it."

"Thank you. I will wash first."

After a surprisingly relaxed breakfast, Matsumoto again produced two pills. Tessa scowled and toyed with them disapprovingly.

"No, thank you," she said finally, pushing them away. "I would prefer to manage without."

He smiled.

"Then we both deserve to be congratulated," he observed, grinning. "You are ahead of schedule. The doctors insisted you would need longer, but I said they didn't know you like I do. It is up to you now whether you take them or not. But if you do, I am assured they will simply let you down gently and diminish your cravings, which will continue for a while."

Tessa thought for a moment.

"In that case, I will take them so that I can start training. I need to get fit again; I have work to do."

"Then I shall train with you, for I suspect we both have work to do."

That evening after dinner, while they were sitting round a roaring fire, Tessa started shivering.

"Are you cold?" queried Matsumoto.

"What they did to me has left an inner coldness which not even this fire can warm."

"I understand, but it is distressing for me to see your heart so hardened. You must not be embittered by what they did. No doubt many before have suffered a similar or worse fate. It is for them you should now seek justice."

"But we only fight with our wits and our swords. They use much darker, more evil weapons."

"Indeed, but we will still achieve an honourable victory in the end."

He produced another two tablets.

"Have you heard anything about Nyunt," asked Tessa, frowning at the tablets.

"Apparently she rarely leaves her flat in Chelsea. She has accepted a Mission to stop the Calver Cats, but has done little to meet her obligations. Potter described the results she was achieving as 'uncharacteristically lacklustre'. However, he is not pursuing the matter. Suffice to say, not a word has been said to her about your survival. Instead the search for you has ostensibly been continuing. Hopefully, our enemies will conclude that you died while trying to escape."

Tessa nodded.

"I really don't think I want to take any more of this poison. Paul said it would damage my brain, and if it has I certainly don't want to risk exacerbating the situation. Who knows what he has done to my darling daughter?"

"Nariko-san, these drugs are very different from the ones you were taking. They will help you, not harm you. Also, you should know that your brain is not impaired. The doses you were receiving had been reduced sufficiently to ensure there was no lasting effect. You owe much to that surgeon in Burma. He did more than save your life."

"How do you know about him?"

"After we came back from Tunisia, you spent several days being examined at the Cognitive Neuroscience Unit in Tokyo University. You were anaesthetised most of the time, but on occasion you were woken. Although you were not aware of where you were or what was happening, you told us everything." Tessa cringed inwardly. Sensing this, Matsumoto smiled reassuringly. "After having analysed the drugs which were being administered, the doctors recommended that your brain be scanned. As a result of many tests and consultations with numerous experts, the unanimous conclusion was that you have suffered no significant damage. Perhaps as much as would be experienced by a person who had drunk an awful lot more alcohol than they should, every day for eleven consecutive days, nothing more." He nudged the pills towards her. "You will be fine."

She took a deep breath and pulled the blanket tighter around her.

"No, I will not take them. I will do this on my own now."

He looked at her quizzically. She chuckled and smiled at him.

"All I need now is a warm heart to warm my soul."

CHAPTER 22

For several days Tessa trained relentlessly with Matsumoto. They laboured hard, delighting in each other's company. Far from distancing them, the trials of the last few weeks had brought them closer together. Finally satisfied they had returned to their normal supreme fitness, they agreed it was time to have a meeting with General Gyobu.

The following morning, Tessa had just finished changing into a smart kimono when she heard the sound of a helicopter approaching. It landed in front of the castle and the General was soon striding up to the Samurai house.

"*Ohayou gozaimasu*, Nariko-san," he said warmly, bowing to her. "You look rather better than when we last met."

She smiled and bowed back. Then, leaving the General and Matsumoto to talk alone for a while, she went to make some green tea. By the time she returned, they were waiting in silence. She placed the tray on the table and poured their drinks, sensing tenseness in the atmosphere between them.

"So, Nariko-san," stated the General, "you wish to return to the fray."

"There are a number of issues I wish to address."

"I daresay. How are your physical wounds healing?"

"Very well, thank you. There were only two of significance; on my abdomen, where the pump was inserted, and the *y*-shape on my thigh. But whoever carried out the plastic surgery to minimise the scarring has done an excellent job on both. They're barely visible, and that disgusting tattoo is completely gone."

"Good. I will pass on your praise... That mark on your thigh, do you remember how you came by it?"

He placed a picture of it on the table in front of her. Tessa stared at it for several seconds. She had no memory of how she'd come by it and was even tempted to ask whether it really had been on her.

"I'm sorry, I have absolutely no idea."

"You were asked about it in Tokyo and said it was self-inflicted to remind you of something, but you couldn't tell us what."

"Really?" She looked questioningly at Matsumoto who shifted uneasily, but said nothing.

"So, you still don't remember?" pressed the General.

"No, I can't think why I would have done that to myself," Tessa admitted. "But it must have been something pretty bad if I was willing to self-harm. A *y* is a strange letter to choose."

"Well. It resembles a *y* from above, but if one turns it round, it looks more like a hastily carved *h*, and that is how others would see it."

General Gyobu reached over to the photograph of the scar and rotated it through 180 degrees.

"I still don't see what it could mean," responded Tessa, puzzled. "Do you have a theory?"

Matsumoto took a deep breath.

"Yes, I'm afraid we do," confirmed the General. "What do you know about hypnotism?"

"Not a thing. I don't think I've ever heard the word before." She looked round to find concerned faces staring back at her. Her brow furrowed in frustration. "How come I don't know what that is? I'm sure I should know. What is…? For goodness' sake, I can't even say it."

"Hypnosis," prompted the General. "It's an altered state of consciousness through which deeper parts of the mind can be accessed and manipulated. It is induced by focussing the mind's complete attention on something innocuous, perhaps against the subject's will. Once hypnotised, the subject unwittingly becomes susceptible to suggestions from others, enabling their judgement to be modified and boundaries of acceptability to be moved. This makes possible involuntary memory changes and real-time alteration of the subject's perceptions, which can regulate their response to external stimuli and what they believe is being experienced. Also, pre-programmed hypnotic instructions may subsequently be triggered through the use of various verbal or other stimuli."

"You mean, empowering someone to control me without my knowledge?"

"In an extreme case, yes."

Suddenly, Tessa felt vulnerable again.

"I find it remarkable that a person with degrees from some of the most prestigious universities in the world cannot remember the meaning of a word I know to be in common usage."

"It seems that someone hypnotised you and, amongst other things, instructed you to forget about being hypnotised and even the meaning of the word itself. Perhaps they did this as a result of seeing that mark. However, it is also possible that they embedded other instructions."

As the gravity of what he'd said sunk in, Tessa took a deep breath. She stood up and walked to the honmaru perimeter wall, peering through one of the arrow slots. In dejected solitude, she watched the birds circling distant paddy fields. Matsumoto joined her.

"Don't worry. We can beat this too."

"I suppose so. But when did it happen, and what did they instruct me to do? How many of our secrets do they now know?"

"Perhaps none. Before you left, you insisted I take harsh measures to ensure you forgot everything which might be of interest to others. So I made sure that all sensitive information was buried extremely deeply. Hypnotism alone would not have been enough. They would have needed the drug therapy too, and that was not complete. Furthermore, the DNA of those who died in the container has been analysed; one of them was an accomplished hypnotist. He probably took whatever secrets he did manage to extract with him to his grave."

"But he could have recorded what I told him, or transmitted it?"

"There were no unusual communications from the ship at any time. Potter was doing everything he could to find you, including monitoring all transmissions from ships carrying containers originating from Rangoon. It was no accident that Agent Johnson was in Tunis to help in your escape. As for a recording, there might have been one, but the fire and explosion were so intense it is unlikely anything survived. Personally, I doubt you were expected to say anything of consequence to the hypnotist. His task would have been to pave the way for others to interrogate you, and we know that Paul's arrival was delayed. He never saw you after you left Rangoon."

Tessa nodded, still incensed. He led her back to the table.

"I do believe there is someone who can help us," continued Gyobu, ignoring Tessa's watery eyes.

"Wonderful," she observed sarcastically. "How soon can you get them here?"

"Actually, she's waiting in the helicopter, wearing a blindfold for security reasons. I daresay she'd quite like to be released. Shall I have her brought up?"

Tessa clamped her jaws together as tears started trickling down her cheeks. Matsumoto moved over to her, and she leaned on him as he put a comforting arm around her.

"That's not very Japanese," she snivelled.

He smiled.

"This is no time to stand on ceremony."

"Good, because it's very nice," purred Tessa. "When will this all end?"

"Nariko-san, they wanted to break your spirit, and used everything their twisted minds could come up with. But when I tried to do the same thing on your first visit here, I couldn't. Although Paul may have come close to breaking you, I don't for a moment believe he did. Your physical scars have already disappeared. Now we will investigate whether there are mental scars which also require attention, and if there are, we will heal them too."

"He may have programmed me to kill you."

"We accepted that was a possibility, but if he had, I doubt I'd still be alive. I don't think he even considered that you might escape – let alone that we were married. No, this will be something more basic and disgusting, probably just another way of him exerting control over you."

"And maybe the buyer's too," added Tessa.

"Quite possibly."

"General," started Tessa, sitting up decisively and drying her eyes, "you'd better bring our visitor up."

He nodded and eventually returned leading a blindfolded woman. She was in her fifties, just over five foot tall and a trifle plump, but impeccably dressed in a cream trouser suit, brown blouse and heels. After her blindfold had been removed she straightened her hair and smiled at everyone, clearly very pleased to be able to see once more. She had a kind face, short greying hair and dark brown eyes that glistened in the sunlight. She bowed deeply. Then she glimpsed the view across the Samurai house's courtyard and over the white perimeter wall to the mountains in the distance.

"Wow, it's beautiful here!" she exclaimed in admiration. "Where are we?"

"Professor Kawashima, we didn't bring you all this way blindfolded to tell you our location on arrival," responded the General gently, putting down her large black flight bag. But then he continued in a more official tone. "As I said before, you must never say anything whatsoever about this consultation, to anyone."

"My sincere apologies, I quite understand," she responded contritely. "But it would be difficult not to react at all when confronted with such a wonderful vista. Anyway, if I can help, I will."

The General nodded and introduced Matsumoto and then Tessa. But she simply looked down; she found the Professor's eyes unfathomable and felt extremely uncomfortable in her company. She had seen a look like that before, and something deep down warned her not to continue. The Professor looked back at her strangely and Matsumoto and the General watched in surprise as Tessa started backing away.

"I'm sorry, I can't do this," she exclaimed, beginning to panic.

"Nariko-san, Professor Kawashima isn't going to hurt you," implored Matsumoto, following her.

"You talk to her if you want," said Tessa, moving further away. "But I won't... I'm not allowed to."

"Not allowed? By whom, Nariko-san?" he pressed, gently taking her arm.

"That's none of your business," she exclaimed, shaking herself free. "I won't do it!"

"That's fine. Don't worry," he said. "Just stay here on the verandah. Our special guest has travelled a long way, we must at least make her welcome for a short while."

Grudgingly, Tessa sat down, unawares that Professor Kawashima had already opened her flight bag. She took out a variety of devices: a heavy brass pendulum, a motorised black spiral painted on a white disc, and an old wooden metronome.

As Matsumoto returned, she smiled up at him.

"I think I'm beginning to understand the problem. However, I don't need to know anything more just now. Let me see if I can get her attention. After that we should be able to discuss the matter further at leisure." She pointed towards her paraphernalia. "With your permission?"

He nodded.

She took off her jacket, slipped the brass pendulum into her handbag and picked up the spiral disc and metronome. Then she looked round and saw the low black table with four silk-covered zabuton.

"Perhaps she might be persuaded to join us for tea?" the Professor asked, one eyebrow raised quizzically.

"I will go and make some," replied Matsumoto, clearly disturbed. "But if I had to guess which of those would fascinate her most, it would definitely be the metronome."

"Then we should start with that," replied the Professor, and made sure it was wound up.

When Matsumoto returned carrying a tray with tea, four cups and some Japanese treats, Professor Kawashima joined him at the table.

"If I may, I would like to sit here, please, with the General opposite me. Perhaps you would sit next to me with her opposite you?"

Matsumoto looked her in the eye.

"Professor, her name is Nariko. She is my wife and the lady of all you see."

"My sincere apologies," replied the Professor, bowing deeply. "Please understand, I meant no disrespect. However, even now I can see that Nariko has been deeply affected. Maybe I can help, but it will take time. However, we are confronted with one of the most difficult challenges, how to hypnotise her... Nariko... against her perceived will. I suspect whoever hypnotised her before has instructed her to resist being hypnotised again unless a code-word or other trigger is first issued. Without hearing that, she may be programmed to react adversely... a booby-trap, if you will. I daresay Nariko's heightened stress levels are due to her struggling against that programming, which is good. Ideally, we could do with her being distracted for a moment."

Matsumoto nodded and gestured them to sit down at the table. He watched while the Professor placed the metronome out of sight, and then went back to Tessa. He sat down with to her and for a while they watched the mountains in silence. She was trembling.

"*Omae*," he said, tenderly. "I have made tea for our guests. But you are the lady of the house; it is your duty to serve it. If you do not do so, it will be an insult, not only to our guests, but also to me. Please, will you join us?"

Tessa looked at him with tears rolling down her cheeks. He was shocked by the sheer terror he saw in her eyes.

"Why am I so scared?"

"I have no idea. But there is no reason to be afraid. I will always be with you, and will make sure you are not harmed. Please, come with me and serve the tea."

He stood and beckoned her to accept his hand. Reluctantly, she wiped her face and went with him, almost having to be dragged the last few steps.

Matsumoto sat down in silence. Tessa was visibly quaking, glaring at the teapot as though willing it to move on its own so she could beat a hasty retreat. Finally she picked it up gripping the handle with such force that her knuckle went white. She walked to the other end of the table and kneeled down to fill the Professor's cup, shaking so much that she could barely get the tea in the cup. She glowered at the spout of the teapot, as though it was to blame, determined not to look at anyone. Not a word was said. The only sounds came from birds, insects and the wind rustling in the trees. Then she filled the General's cup. He thanked her profusely, but she simply gave a quick bow and went to Matsumoto. She filled his cup and he extended his hand towards her. Tessa looked up at him, and in that moment of profound tenderness the Professor placed the metronome on the table and started it. For Tessa, all the sounds of the world disappeared, to be replaced solely by the relentless *tick-tock, tick-tock*. She didn't even hear the dull thud of the teapot landing on the table as her grip relaxed.

When Tessa next surfaced, she was lying in the middle of the audience hall. It was early evening. Not far away Matsumoto was sitting, looking pale and distressed. Opposite him was Professor Kawashima, who appeared to be very tired. The two of them were talking quietly. Tessa sat up.

"What am I doing here?" she asked.

Matsumoto smiled and beckoned her to join them.

"You have been asleep."

"Really? I remember being rude to everyone at the table," she noted with a wry smile. "But it was as though I was watching my own life through a veil. It was bizarre and suddenly all I could hear was this incredibly loud ticking sound, and…"

"What else do you remember from today?" probed the Professor.

Tessa looked at her and smiled; the previous enmity was gone.

"Not much. I remember the General visited, and you came with him, Professor Kawashima. But as soon as you'd been introduced, every fibre in my body told me that I should run away. But I couldn't leave here, not yet…"

"You don't feel like running away now?"

"No, I just feel a little distant, as though I've been removed from reality."

"Then we have made a good start," said the Professor, glancing at Matsumoto.

"Excellent," he declared, standing. "I think some sustenance is required; none of us has eaten since breakfast. I daresay we would all feel better with some food inside us."

"Where is the General?" asked Tessa, looking around.

"He left shortly after you… fell asleep," replied Matsumoto. "He will return when we have finished."

"Finished what?"

"Let's have our dinner first, then we can talk. Please show the Professor to the guest room. She has kindly agreed to stay with us for a couple of days. I will prepare our meal."

After they had all eaten and Tessa had cleared away, they gathered round the fire in the audience hall. Tessa looked expectant. Matsumoto nodded to the Professor.

"Do you know what hypnotism is, Nariko-san?" she began.

"Yes, of course I do. Why?"

"I hypnotised you earlier."

"Why did you do that?" she asked, glancing angrily at Matsumoto.

"Because, Nariko-san," he responded, smiling calmingly, "when you were on the ship in Tunis, you were hypnotised against your will. We now know that the Arabic man who you noticed tied to the chair when you escaped was the one who did this to you. He implanted a number of instructions and altered your interpretation of reality in certain areas. However, he died in that container, and we do not believe he had an opportunity to report on what he'd found, or what he was able to do. Given time, Professor Kawashima hopes she can repair the damage.

"Tell me more," insisted Tessa anxiously. "Tell me everything."

Matsumoto smiled.

"After that man had hypnotised you, he sent you into a very deep trance, a process facilitated by the intensive drug therapy to which you had been subjected. First, some walls were built in an attempt to ensure that only people with intimate knowledge of your programming would be able to hypnotise you in future. Secondly, you were carefully and systematically removed from your previous life experiences in order to justify future actions which suited the purposes of those who instigated the procedure. For example, close bonds were transformed into uneasy acquaintanceships and responsibility for pivotal experiences became blurred. This has influenced your conscience in such a way as to make reasonable to you actions which previously would have been unacceptable. Finally, a number of hypnotic commands were buried deep in your subconscious, which would make you respond to the wishes of certain people.

"Today, the Professor believes she managed to strip away the barriers to hypnotism which not only made you forget the meaning of the word, but also motivated you to distance yourself from her. Tomorrow, you will need to be hypnotised again so your memories can be reassembled correctly; only then will it be possible to remove the embedded instructions."

Tessa listened disconsolately.

"So did the man find out that we were married?"

"Yes." Matsumoto smiled. "But it seems he was unprepared for that revelation and did nothing about it. Perhaps he wanted to consult others first, but you subsequently prevented him from doing so."

"And what about the castle, did I tell him where to find us?"

"No," replied Matsumoto, purposefully. "You weren't even asked. Either they didn't know you knew, hadn't got round to asking, or they know already."

"I'm sorry," interjected the Professor, "this probably all sounds a little strange to you. That's because your memories no longer fit with your life. Put another way, your mind has been jumbled up and no longer corresponds with the reality supported by your past."

"I have got that, thank you," retorted Tessa, a trifle impatiently. "So, how do you propose to convince me that this is real and not fantasy? That I am not, in fact, simply being programmed some more."

"We're not going to try," interjected Matsumoto. "At this time, we doubt there is any way we could prove categorically to you what is real and what is not. Which is why I have insisted that you are told everything; you must make your own decision concerning on-going therapy. I would simply suggest you trust your heart and not your head."

"Before you were hypnotised," the Professor carried on, "the evil people who did this to you were unaware that you and Matsumoto are married. Since their initial programming was carried out with the aid of a recording… you remember the mp3 player?" Tessa nodded, "…it seems likely that significant parts of your programming were either inappropriate or ambiguous. The hypnotist may have realised there was a problem, but did not know how he should amend the programming. It is that element of equivocality which hopefully will allow you to reach the correct decision."

There was a long silence as Tessa weighed up what they'd said. She was desperately searching for something she could anchor her thoughts to as an indisputable indicator of actual, rather than adjusted, reality.

"Hmm, tricky," she mumbled eventually. "So, you're telling me that I have no way of knowing whether anything any of us says or does is real or not? Indeed, I may not be here at all, and you may not be who you say you are?"

The Professor took a deep breath.

"That is correct."

"Actually, I disagree, Nariko-san. I believe that what you and I have between us transcends anyone's evil intentions and programming. And I can prove it," stated Matsumoto. "It seems likely the Calver Cats are intent upon destroying the Chrysanthemum League. It is natural for them to have wanted you to kill me. But you didn't, even though you had ample opportunity. And when your programming told you to run away from the Professor, again you did not. Instead, when I insisted you serve the tea, you came, despite not wanting to. You must reach your own conclusions, but I believe you know that I am real, and this place is real, and therefore that while I am with you, no one will be permitted to harm you."

Tessa wanted to believe him, but wasn't sure.

"So what happens now?"

He smiled.

"We all get some sleep. Tomorrow, you must decide what happens next, because that is all that I will allow to happen."

The Professor shifted uneasily.

"In that case, I'll think about it then," said Tessa, standing. She bowed to the Professor, smiled and walked into the darkness.

Matsumoto watched her go with a forlorn expression on his face, but made no attempt to follow her; instead he led the Professor to her room. Then he returned to the audience hall and sat by the fire, waiting in case Tessa decided to return. She didn't. So, after two hours, he went to find her.

It was not long before they were sitting in silence, side by side on a stone bench at the end of the honmaru far from the Samurai house. The view over the valley with the lights of one of the villages twinkling in the distance, was exquisite.

"Beautiful, isn't it?" said Matsumoto, eventually.

"One hell of a fantasy if it's not real," Tessa acknowledged.

"True, but that's not enough, is it?"

She shook her head.

"As I see it," he continued, "you must choose between three courses of action." Tessa smiled, she was curious to hear whether his three options matched hers. "First, you could conclude, for whatever reason, that both the Professor and I are simply figments of your imagination. In which case, perhaps the best course of action would be for you to kill us both, and escape… somewhere. But that would be risky, because you might be mistaken. In which case you would in fact have destroyed what you treasure most and realised the dreams of the evil ones who hypnotised you. Second, you might decide that it is not possible for you to discern, with any degree of certainty, what is real and what is not. So maybe the best thing would be to kill yourself – a little hard on you, if you were wrong, and a big disappointment for me. Nevertheless, perhaps the safest option for everyone else in such a difficult situation. The third option would be the least painful for all of us, and that would simply be to trust *me* and permit the hypnosis to proceed."

Tessa smiled.

"So aren't you lucky?"

"Why, because I know you have no weapons? Then perhaps I should give you what Potter sent."

He placed a wooden box on the bench between them; inside were her *cbc*, its charger, some keys and an unusual-looking grey knife. Tessa surveyed the items with relish. She picked up the knife, caressing it with glee and submerging her psyche in its deadly familiarity.

"It truly is a magnificent weapon," observed Matsumoto as she closed the box and put the knife on the lid, "the finest sintered blade I have ever seen."

"Major General Sinclair, or rather Isamu-san, lent it to me when I went to Burma after Bill Chalmers. I never quite got round to returning it. I bet Potter had to force himself to part with it again… So what makes you so sure I won't grab it and kill you?"

"Well, Nariko-san, there is always the possibility that I might reach it before you. But even if I did, I would hesitate to kill the one I love. However, if you believed I was an imposter, you wouldn't hold back."

"Hmm, it's still very tricky."

"Indeed, it is. I don't envy you."

He watched her pick up the knife and toy with it.

"But I suppose there is always the slow and comfortable ruminative option," suggested Matsumoto with a wry smile. "We could just postpone worrying about it until tomorrow, and simply go to bed."

He stood up and offered her his hand. She grinned and, arm in arm, they walked back to the Samurai house.

CHAPTER 23

It was still early when the three of them assembled for breakfast. Not much was said apart from a cordial exchange of greetings. Independently, Tessa and Matsumoto had both decided they wouldn't initiate any discussion of how they would spend the day. That didn't leave many alternatives for breaking the ice. Finally, Professor Kawashima could contain herself no longer.

"I've been wondering about the pole out there," she ventured tentatively, "it seems to have a little disc..."

Tessa produced the sintered knife and quickly threw it. There was an abrupt *click* as it stuck the tiny circular disc and sank in to the hilt.

"Ah. Clever trick that."

"No trick, Professor," replied Tessa in a subtly menacing tone. "Would you like me to do it again?"

"No, that won't be necessary." She changed position uncomfortably, apprehensive Tessa had reached a conclusion supporting violence against her. "Hmm... Maybe it would be better if I left. It's not a problem. I'll go and pack my bags. Would you ask the General to collect me, please?"

"Stay where you are," growled Tessa... "Why should I trust you?"

The Professor sat down heavily, her heart in her mouth. She looked to Matsumoto for support.

"Sounds like a reasonable question to me," he replied, shrugging.

"Why shouldn't you trust me?" blurted out the Professor. "I was brought here specifically to..."

Tessa sighed, shaking her head.

"Professor, you'll need to do a lot better than that. I don't expect answers which are simply platitudes or more questions. Such responses are not in your best interests."

"S-Sorry," stammered the professor. "I'm not used to being in this sort of situation. Er... I am Professor Ayako Kawashima. I live and work in Tokyo where I have a Chair at the University's Cognitive Neuroscience

Unit. I have focussed on studying the neural mechanisms of human cognition with a view to ascertaining the critical aspects of human behaviour in terms of psychophysics. I have established a reputation as a hypnotherapist who specialises in administering anaesthesia and healing…"

The Professor continued talking for ten minutes, unaware that Tessa was mentally checking everything against the Internet searches she had carried out during the night.

"Who were the co-authors of the paper you published in March 2018?" she demanded.

The Professor was visibly taken-aback by the detailed question but nevertheless answered without hesitation. Tessa made several other specific inquiries, receiving equally confident responses.

"So, is it easy to hypnotise someone?" inquired Tessa.

"Fairly. Assuming they are a willing subject or have a predisposition towards hypnotic suggestion."

"Could you teach me how to do it?"

"Quite possibly, if we had time."

Tessa smiled.

"Ah, I understand," perceived the Professor. "So, who do you want to hypnotise?"

"You," replied Tessa lightly. The Professor swallowed nervously.

"But you might not know whether I was truly hypnotised or just acting."

"Indeed. So I thought if I practised first, I would be much better equipped to distinguish fact from fiction."

Matsumoto roared with laughter.

"Very clever," he acknowledged, proudly. "I hadn't thought of that. I'm up for it. Sounds like an excellent plan to me."

Totally bewildered by the unexpected course of the discussion, the Professor shrugged and nodded reluctantly.

"Very well. I can teach you how to use either my pendulum or the disc, but not the metronome as you are still programmed to react to that."

She looked at Tessa as if asking for permission to leave the table.

"Now, *that* was a good answer," noted Tessa, placing the Professor's locked metronome on the table. "I removed it from your bag while

246

you were sleeping."

"I didn't hear you."

"You wouldn't, Professor... If I was eventually to allow you to continue treating me, is there any risk that you might cause any further damage?"

"I think it highly unlikely. Reprioritising your formative memories is likely to be a stressful process for you as you will need to revisit the events your mind regards as key, but it is not particularly dangerous."

Tessa nodded.

"You will stay with me?" she asked, looking at Matsumoto.

"Always, Nariko-san."

"Then let's get on with it, shall we?" said Tessa, surprising the Professor by nudging the metronome a little way towards her, but still leaving it beyond reach.

"Er... I will need my treatment plan. I believe it is important we adhere to a well-defined plan with such potentially complex therapeutic procedures, so I developed one yesterday afternoon on the off-chance that we would need it." She started to stand up, but then sat down again abruptly. "So that's why you were interested in my March 2018 paper. May I refer to my treatment plan, please?"

Tessa smiled and produced it from under the table.

"I did warn you, Professor," laughed Matsumoto.

"Indeed you did," she responded. "Perhaps we should all relax for a few minutes first. I would most certainly benefit from that."

It was nearly an hour later when they reconvened round the table in the smaller ceremonial lounge. The metronome was directly in front of Tessa. The Professor sat to her right while Matsumoto was to her left. From her position between them, Tessa watched the Professor's hand move slowly and purposefully towards the metronome...

Suddenly, Tessa was in a large room. It was pitch-dark except for the middle which was illuminated with a bright, clinically white light. She was standing beside a hospital gurney on which lay a body, covered with a clean sheet. Major General Sinclair was opposite her, he took hold of the sheet and started pulling it down. The body revealed was that of her dear friend Penny, disfigured almost beyond recognition. Tessa wailed in despair. "No," she screamed. "This cannot be! Why?"

But as quickly as the scene had appeared a dense swirling mist formed, only to dissipate as another landscape formed. She was training at Matsumoto castle for the very first time, on her knees in the mud, her sword was gone... Then she was in Pennysview, her cottage in Orkney, kneeling over the dead body of first true love, David, Lord Kensington of Graemeshall. Tears were pouring down her cheeks. She felt inconsolable, heartbroken, no longer sure whether she wanted to live or die as the merciless destructive onslaught against the cottage continued...

Next she was at the Beng Mealea temple ruins in Cambodia in the midst of the battle of all battles. Fighting to survive, she was killing all those who threatened her. She hovered over the carnage she had caused; the sights, the sounds, the smells; the families and futures she had destroyed – the guilt of her own actions weighed heavy on her soul... Now she was in Burma, face to face with Bill Chalmers, watching his eyes bulge as she punched him for a third time... Then General Soe Gyi was staring at her aghast as his eyes glazed over and life deserted him.

Again the fogs of time swirled and Htet had just been shot by Burmese mercenaries. He knew he was dying but was determined to ensure Tessa would take Nyunt to be her daughter. She experienced again the challenges and emotional roller-coaster of the early months of their time together, but also how that had been transformed into one of the most joyous phases of her life. However, soon she was reliving the disappointment of Nyunt's relationship with Seiji falling apart, and her own instant distrust of her daughter's new boyfriend, Paul. The deep foreboding when Nyunt had insisted on visiting Burma... Now Tessa was back within Insein prison being subjected to horrendous torture and degrading treatment. The adulation she received when she killed the captain. The pain she felt when the monk was executed. The terror of being held captive on the container ship; drugged, alone, abused, and her desperate attempts to maintain her sanity and escape...

It was early evening, when the Professor ended the session. Tessa blinked as she emerged, exhausted, from her trance. The Professor looked ashen and, to her surprise, she found that Matsumoto had been weeping. She felt her own cheeks. They also were wet, and there were marks where her tears had stained her kimono. She sighed.

"Welcome to my life," she muttered.

"*Omae*, I never..."

She reached out and put her hand on his.

"It's all in the past and, in reality, cannot be changed. I wouldn't want it to be anyway. It has made me what I am today, and at least now I can remember it all. I am not ashamed – just a little tired, and hungry. Let's eat and get some sleep. I know we have more to do tomorrow."

Tessa remembered having breakfast with Matsumoto, and seeing the metronome on the table once more, but not much else. It was late afternoon when she realised she had re-joined the world. She sincerely hoped it was the real world, but of that she still remained slightly unsure. Professor Kawashima smiled.

"I suspect we have progressed as far as we can, for now," she announced as Matsumoto served some green tea and snacks. "So, Nariko-san, your past is now structured correctly and we know that, while you were hypnotised in the container, five sets of instructions were embedded. Each has its own trigger which, when used, would send you into a trance, allowing other commands to be initiated. One was from the hypnotist. I am not sure he was meant to install this since its characteristics are markedly different from the others, but maybe he felt its existence would safeguard his own interests. It seems he used only his voice as the trigger. You were wise not to release him, but since he perished during the destruction of the container I do not believe his programming is relevant now.

"The second set was for the buyer's use. It is likely that these commands were installed according to his local requirements, so the code word, or words, are likely to be in Irabyan. However, although embedded, these instructions were never activated, and, interestingly were also subordinated to the master controls – perhaps as security pending payment of the outstanding balance."

"More likely to make sure others could control me regardless of what he said," interjected Tessa.

"Possibly. The third set of commands appears to be the most simplistic and almost general purpose in nature, as though a number of people were meant to be able to use them.

"The final two sets are the master controls. We know one was for

Paul – having seen so much of him, you were able to help us confirm that much. However, we don't know much about the final set.

"We do know that these final three sets of instructions incorporate specific noises within their triggers. The sounds could be anything; a small hand-bell, the buzzing from a watch, or a tune from a *cbc*. There might be voice components as well…"

Tessa had listened intently so far but, unable to hold back any longer, she interrupted irritably.

"But have you been able to remove them?"

"No, none," admitted the Professor.

"So we've hardly achieved anything? The use of any of these last three triggers will hypnotise me instantly."

"I had hoped for more," acknowledged the Professor apologetically. "Unfortunately it is not possible for you to describe the triggers accurately enough for me to eliminate them, which suggests the sounds are user-specific." Tessa looked frustrated, and clearly Matsumoto was disappointed too. "However, we do at least understand the extent of the problem and, if it were feasible to bring Paul in for questioning, I could ask him, under hypnosis if necessary, about all the triggers and who his accomplices are. Also, to give you some protection, I can teach you how to recognise and resist hypnotic attacks, regardless of who they are issued by. These will not be fool-proof, but are better than nothing; although you will need to be trained."

"Hmm," pondered Tessa, exasperated. "Well, bringing Paul in would blow our cover… That's certainly tempting from a personal standpoint, but we would probably lose the advantage we've fought so hard to gain." Matsumoto nodded, but said nothing. "So, what about the metronome?" demanded Tessa. "A couple of *tick-tocks* and I'm anybody's."

"Oh, that's not so problematic. Your heightened sensitivity to that is a residual effect of their drug regime. That is already decreasing and you should be back to normal in a month or so. In the meantime, it is not practical as a weapon as it needs to be used in a quiet environment to ensure you're not distracted…"

The next day, they all met again for breakfast. Once more the metronome stood in the centre of the table; encouragingly, Tessa realised that she wasn't afraid of it any more. However, with it was the brass pendulum.

"That is my preferred device," the Professor commented as Tessa picked it up. "Nariko-san, I have a life which is very different from all this, and a family whom I love dearly. If it became known that I had helped here, it could be dangerous for you as well as me and my family. I do not wish to take this knowledge away with me. I *will* teach you how to hypnotise me. Not only will that give you a better understanding of hypnotism, it will also enable you to instruct me to forget everything I have experienced here. You should lock this instruction with a code word of your choosing. It will be safer for us all that way.

"However, I suggest we install your defences first. That will probably keep us busy for the morning. After lunch, I will show you how to use my pendulum. It shouldn't be difficult for you to hypnotise me as I do not intend to resist."

Tessa nodded and watched the Professor take out her treatment programme, on which she had scribbled a number of additions. Then she reached out towards the metronome…

It was mid-morning when Tessa knowingly opened her eyes again. Matsumoto smiled at her.

"That was a good session," noted the Professor, already looking tired. "Now, the instant anyone attempts to activate their commands, you will, for a split second, see an image of Angkor Wat."

"Angkor Wat?" queried Tessa, puzzled.

"Yes, you chose that place as an unusual location of which you have positive recollections. When you see this image, you must force your mind there immediately, to distract yourself. You can do this by saying 'Angkor Wat' in your head, or even out loud if you like, but then your adversary may realise you are employing other embedded controls to thwart theirs. But I cannot stress enough how important it is that you react quickly in order to force your mind to remain in normality. If you do not react fast enough, you will lose control. Regrettably, I cannot guarantee that my other reprogramming, which should have reasserted your conscience, will prevail if you are under someone else's control.

"However, if you were to be hypnotised against your will, it is likely that at some point you would be released. When this happens, you will see in your mind's eye an image of Beng Mealea. You chose that as a memorable place where your last defining memories were unpleasant ones. In this instance, you should seek help. However, the intervening changes made to your mind may have been substantial and you might again not be able to tell the difference between reality and fantasy, or who is a friend and who is not... I'm afraid that's the best I can do."

Tessa raised her eyebrows, horrified that she had so little with which to defend herself.

"Wonderful," she reflected sarcastically. "Will that always work?"

"Yes. But the problem is the images won't be visible for very long; a bit like seeing a static wall poster from a speeding Shinkansen train. If you're not expecting to see it, you probably won't. That's why you need to practise, and why I have embedded a susceptibility to this gong." She placed a five inch hammered copper gong and mallet on the table. "Don't be alarmed, this trigger can be removed with a simple voice command by either myself or Matsumoto. Now, close your eyes and relax."

For several minutes, the three of them sat in silence.

Suddenly Tessa heard the doleful *clang* of the gong. It seemed to reverberate through every fibre of her body and momentarily an image of the causeway within the main enclosure of Angkor Wat flashed up in her mind. As Tessa struggled to think herself there, another image flashed into her brain; it was Beng Mealea. She opened her eyes to find some chopsticks were now on the table. She had been to get them without realising.

"Hmm! I presume that didn't go too well," she observed disconsolately.

Although Matsumoto looked concerned, the Professor smiled.

"Don't be discouraged. I would have been very surprised if you had managed to defend yourself so soon. You must try and learn to react to the sensation of starting to lose control, rather than the sound of the gong itself. I understand you have very quick reactions. You will need them to defend yourself against these attacks. Now, let's try again."

They carried on practising for several hours. Slowly, Tessa became better at defending herself, but it was far from easy. Eventually, the

Professor seemed satisfied.

"I think you are getting very good. It'll be a strain, staying alert at all times, but there is no alternative until you have found Paul and identified the others involved.

"There is one other thing. I have also embedded another instruction which might help and should remain effective even if you have been hypnotised against your will. Frequently, people do not appreciate the impreciseness of what they have said. They assume others understand exactly what they intended. So, if at some stage you have lost control and an ill-defined command is issued, you will interpret it literally, thereafter resolving any ambiguities as *you* see fit, without asking for clarification. This might not sound particularly powerful, but in my experience it could be most advantageous.

"Right, well, I believe that is all I can do for you now. If ever you find out more about the embedded triggers, I would be happy to remove them for you. I therefore suggest that when you hypnotise me, you also insert a trigger which will allow you to remind me of what we have done during these few days..."

By late afternoon, Tessa was finally satisfied she had managed to hypnotise the Professor correctly and installed the necessary safeguards to ensure she would not knowingly remember her experiences at Matsumoto Castle. That done, she went with the Professor, and her gong, on a long walk round the castle gardens, practising defending herself while Matsumoto prepared a veritable feast.

CHAPTER 24

As they were finishing their breakfast, Tessa turned to the Professor with a generous smile.

"I would like to thank you for helping me," she said, bowing. "Although I wish you had been able to remove all their evil, I at least feel somewhat better able to defend myself."

Matsumoto bowed in agreement.

"Indeed, Kawashima-san, I too would like to express my gratitude," he added warmly.

The Professor bowed graciously, but the past few days had clearly drained her.

"It has been a pleasure to meet you both, and an honour to have been of assistance to the legendary Chrysanthemum League. Not to mention having had an opportunity to see your wonderful home."

Suddenly the sound of a helicopter could be heard approaching and it was not long before the General joined them. For a while they all sat talking and drinking tea. But then he asked the Professor if she would mind going for a walk for a few minutes while he, Matsumoto and Tessa discussed what to do next...

"Well," said Tessa, eventually, "from what Paul said in the container about my killing the Emperor, crushing the League and so on, murder and mayhem is clearly high on their agenda. But I doubt that'll be the end to it."

"Hmm," considered the General. "I suppose if the League had been destroyed, it would facilitate the assassination of the Emperor. But although terrible, it would only be a temporary difficulty."

"Perhaps they intend to do something during the hiatus," pondered Matsumoto.

"Yes, and maybe whatever that is," interjected Tessa, "has something to do with them being so desperate to get their hands on my Amafuji sword?"

"Possibly," mused the General. "But Paul's focus on the League suggests he doesn't understand the importance of the Chrysanthemum Guard. For over a century, the Guard has been primarily responsible for protecting the Emperor. The Chrysanthemum League comprises only two, now small, clans on whom the Emperor can call if assistance is needed. To achieve anything substantial, both the League and the Guard would need to be destroyed... It would certainly help if we knew who, apart from Paul, is orchestrating all this."

"The kidnapping of those high-profile young women," postulated Tessa "was no doubt intended to prime the media and put the Special Forces on edge. However, the friendship between the Emperor and Minister Miyazaki is well known, so the eventual involvement of the Chrysanthemum Guard would have been easy to predict by anyone who knew it existed. If, through that involvement, the League could somehow be implicated or discredited, then that would point directly back to the Emperor. But what role does my Amafuji sword play? And why would anyone want to destroy both the League and the Emperor in such a convoluted manner?"

"I'm not sure, Nariko-san," admitted the General. "But Paul presumably, like me, thought you were a member of the Chrysanthemum Guard, when in fact you had become a member of the League by marriage. Maybe that is significant?"

"We all know," said Matsumoto, "that the Chrysanthemum League has only ever had one serious coherent enemy, and that was the Fujiwara. However, we all thought the last of their line died ten years ago, and the Amafuji stopped making weapons well before that."

"Yes, but supposing a true Fujiwara survives?" probed Tessa. "None of us realised Hachiro was a Fujiwara until the last moment; perhaps he had a child with Bryani. After all, Paul is neither the boss nor a genuine Fujiwara."

"If that was true," acknowledged Matsumoto, "it would mean we need to take the Chrysanthemum Fujiwara decrees into account."

Gyobu shifted uncomfortably while Tessa looked blank; her eyes beckoning Matsumoto to enlighten her.

"Nariko-san, when I told you about the original Matsumoto Castle here being destroyed by the Fujiwara I didn't tell you the end of the story. I didn't think it could ever be important, but maybe I was wrong.

"It all started when the Emperor asked the Matsumoto to purge

Japan of the Fujiwara for ever. Fully intending to do as ordered, we began by destroying their castles in Kyūshū and dismantling their power base. We had all but finished when we were forced to hurry back to Kanazawa to retake our home, and we brought our prisoners with us. By the time the fighting here was over, the Matsumoto had detained the vast majority of the surviving Fujiwara. Although we had been granted the authority to put them to death, we were reluctant to annihilate the entire clan. So we set out for Edo, intending to present our captives to the Emperor and let him adjudicate personally over their fate. But our caravan was ambushed by a substantial force of mercenaries, largely comprising Samurai disenfranchised after the fall of Aizu Wakamatsu in 1867. The Matsumoto forces were outnumbered, however they were also better equipped, better trained and battle-hardened. The conflict which followed was brutal and extensive, but we were victorious.

"The Emperor was furious when he learned what had happened and redoubled his efforts to seek out and exterminate any Fujiwara who remained alive. He was determined to extinguish the line for ever and substantial rewards were offered to anyone who delivered the head of a Fujiwara clan member. Despite this, some did evade capture and they vowed revenge on the Emperor and the Matsumoto for their clan's fall from grace.

"The Matsumoto and Amakuni were so worried by this threat of a timeless feud that they vowed the Chrysanthemum League would no longer participate in attempts to eradicate any Japanese clan. Unfortunately, this did nothing to appease the Fujiwara and simply angered the Emperor who felt it was not for the League to dictate punishments for those who had broken the law. So he issued an edict that in future *only* one of the League's clan members *without* the mark of the chrysanthemum would be permitted to kill a Fujiwara or seize their property. The penalty for breaking this decree was, and still is, the forfeit of everything held by *all* League clans. It has since been suggested that the decree was meant to say *with* the mark rather than *without* it; but who knows?

"Nevertheless, the edict as promulgated meant that only the League's children could rightfully kill a Fujiwara, since adults either bear the mark or are never going to receive it.

"Now, because of the League's unorthodox set up and ancient rights, many Japanese old laws still apply to it. These are laws which were made before or during the Edo period which have not yet been superseded. Anyway, they forbid a person who is not of age to lawfully claim ownership of another clans' property. So, even after the death of a Fujiwara at the hand of an unmarked League member, in all probability everything the deceased owned would simply be inherited by their clan successors.

"Everyone realised the edict was problematic. However, no amendments were ever passed since only a handful of Fujiwara had survived the purge and all their property was transferred to the Emperor soon after the Meiji Restoration. Meanwhile, Japanese law evolved and modern courts may act as they see fit, albeit needing proof of culpability and a perpetrator. But even now it would be legally complicated to implement a death penalty on a Fujiwara. This was a factor in you being asked to deal with Hayato Fujiwara at Kawasaki-ku."

Matsumoto drank some tea.

"So are you saying that only an Amakuni or a Matsumoto, who has come of age but doesn't have a Chrysanthemum tattoo, can kill a Fujiwara and claim their possessions?"

"Technically, yes. But the Amakuni generally don't take up arms against anyone now."

"Wow! That would mean that *if* there are some surviving Fujiwara, other than that bastard Paul, and *if* the Chrysanthemum League could be destroyed, it would be extremely difficult to stop a Fujiwara doing whatever they wanted in Japan, criminal or not. Surely that can't be right?"

"Unfortunately, it is," replied Gyobu. "All those almost-forgotten old laws would have to be declared void and new ones substituted. And in our modern transparent world, that sudden requirement would probably result in an enormous outcry; human rights lawyers would have a field day. Furthermore, the whole process would be hindered by the fact that the laws to be annulled were Imperial decrees, so if the Emperor had been killed that would impose further delays.

"I don't doubt it could be done, eventually, but prior to that the Fujiwara would be virtually untouchable."

257

"Well, that must be it," asserted Tessa, sitting up straight. "At first, apart from wanting to settle some personal grudges, they would have regarded me as the ideal assassin to target the Emperor. Also, since they presumably thought I was a member of the Chrysanthemum Guard, rather than the Chrysanthemum League, and originally had a tattoo, they wouldn't have believed I could be a danger to any existing Fujiwara. I suppose they may have started having doubts when they saw my tattoo was gone, but were simply prompted to redouble their efforts to control or incapacitate me."

"Indeed," added Gyobu, "if they had known you were a member of the League by marriage, without a tattoo, they would almost certainly have killed you. Furthermore, they would have been concerned that Nyunt would qualify as she does not carry the mark. It may yet prove necessary for you to face her in battle, Nariko-san."

Tessa tried to ignore the implications of that, and continued her hypothesis.

"So they probably want my Amafuji sword as some sort of trophy to mark their clan's resurrection and the destruction of the Matsumoto, and they'll do something outrageous during the time it takes to replace the old laws. So be it. I will go back to London, Paul's original hunting ground and see if I can find out where he's hiding…"

After all the farewells had been exchanged, everyone convened by the helicopter. As the Professor was waiting, Tessa suddenly stepped forward and whispered in her ear.

"Understood," chimed the Professor, climbing in and putting her blindfold on.

Tessa and Matsumoto watched the helicopter leave. Alone again, they enjoyed a relaxed lunch and afterwards went for a long walk together. General Gyobu had agreed that his helicopter would collect Tessa after breakfast the next day and take her to Narita Airport from where she would fly on a scheduled flight back to the UK. She felt that a low-profile return would be the safest option, although she had dyed her hair black to help conceal her identity.

"Nariko-san," said Matsumoto as they watched the sun wane, "it is plain to see that your recent experiences have changed you. In addition to your usual determination, I sense a new hardness, perhaps even a degree of recklessness. You must seek justice, not revenge, and for that you must cast aside animosity."

"I know," she replied, placing her hand on his. "I won't let anger blur my vision. I am simply focussed on finishing something evil which I didn't start. And I do not intend to live out the rest of my life knowing that there are people out there who, without warning, could seize control of me."

"I understand, but I counsel you not to let your goals, no matter how laudable, consume you. There is more than altruism driving you at the moment, and we both know that anger compromises technique. Make sure you are in the correct frame of mind and only do what you need to do to obtain closure and inner peace. Above all else, please ensure you remain alive at the end of it."

Tessa smiled and looked him the eye.

"It is going to be a battle, maybe a war, but I have every intention of returning here afterwards. This is truly my home now."

"Then let the fight back begin, *omae*. And in whatever battles that lie ahead, may our actions be righteous and our victory honourable and complete."

CHAPTER 25

By the time Tessa arrived at Estuary Airport, she was pleased to be back in London. And that was despite knowing she could neither return to her house nor contact Nyunt. After all, Paul was likely to be having both watched, especially if he still doubted that she had died on the container ship. She had sent an encrypted SMS to Potter asking whether someone from the UK Special Forces could meet her at the airport. Therefore, it came as no surprise when she heard an announcement over the airport public address system.

"Would Dr Isamu please go to the Meeting Point where her driver is waiting?"

Tessa smiled at the use of the name Matsumoto had given Major General Sinclair, and surveyed the stand from afar. There were several uniformed drivers waiting for their clients. She instantly recognised the man holding a large card with MGS on it.

"Hello," she said, walking up to him confidently, "I think you dlive me Cheltenham?"

"Ah, yes, that's right, Ma'am. Welcome to London. Please come this way."

In the armoured Special Forces black taxi, Tessa could contain her amusement no longer.

"You look terribly dashing in that uniform, Potter. It suits you."

"Hah! You think so? Sometimes I wonder whether being a taxi-driver wouldn't be a better option than having to deal with all the other stuff the world seems to throw at us. It's good to have you back, Nariko; especially looking so well."

"Thanks. But it has all been a bit wearing, hasn't it? And it's not over yet. Anyway, how are things here?"

"Well, the Calver Cats are going from strength to strength and the Peacekeepers, of whom Nyunt is one, are having a devil of a job keeping things under control. Both sides have lost a lot of people. But as we both know, it's nowhere near as difficult to find a brutal thug as it is a good Peacekeeper."

"Hmm. Same old, same old, then?"

Potter nodded

"Have you heard any news of Khin?"

"No. I understand Paul told you he was dead, and by all accounts it was a bloody confrontation at Moulmein. The Burmese Military Police certainly didn't hold back, there were lots of casualties, mostly innocents. But we still haven't received any confirmation that Khin was among them, which I regard as significant. Htet had trained him extremely well. If anyone could have got away amidst the chaos, it would be him."

"I sincerely hope you're right," responded Tessa. "I'm fairly sure that Paul told me all sorts of lies; let's hope that was one of them."

"I've had the secure flat that you used a while back prepared," continued Potter. "It'll help you to keep a low profile, for a while at least. As you asked, Lee has taken your Porsche to Stanhope Gate. He drove it there at three a.m. in full stealth mode. I warned John Brown, and he assured me it'll be ready whenever you need it."

"Great, thanks. I need to see Lee."

"Well, we'd better not go now. But I have an engagement tonight. If you like, I could pick you up at, say, eleven and take you over to SKS?"

"Oh, that would be brilliant. Thank you."

"No problem. We've got one hell of a struggle on our hands here. I just hope we can resolve it quickly without excessive bloodshed."

"I hope so too. You know, it was a very close call for me over there."

"Yes. From what I heard it sounds diabolical, you're lucky to have survived. You shouldn't have come for me."

"You know I had to. However, I'd appreciate it if you wouldn't get yourself taken again."

"I will most certainly do my utmost in that respect," agreed Potter with a wry smile.

"It was also good of you to have people everywhere watching for me," added Tessa. "Although I'd managed to get away, I was in no state to complete my escape unaided."

"Oh, you're welcome. Johnson was pretty chuffed to have been able to help, although I suspect her husband didn't enjoy himself quite so much. OK, we're here. You should find just about everything you'll need is already in the flat, but let me know if you're short of anything. Oh, and by the way, only Flood and I know you're in London."

Meanwhile, in Tokyo, Matsumoto was having another meeting with General Gyobu; the atmosphere was fraught.

"You know I'm right, old friend," implored the General. "Professor Kawashima was not able to remove any of the hypnotic programming, and the defences she installed only have minimal efficacy. We know that Nariko is, or will be, programmed to assassinate the Emperor. We must be able to stop her."

"She won't follow it through. Her conscience will prevent it, I'm sure."

"And if it doesn't, and only you stood between her and the Emperor, could you stop her, even if she weren't your wife? You know how skilled she is. You and I are a good match, but I'm not sure I could beat her. In all honesty, could you?"

"Maybe… I don't know," admitted Matsumoto dismissively. "But I still refuse to sanction anything pre-emptive."

"All right," Gyobu conceded. "Let's just go to Police headquarters and have a word with Yamanouchi. We can do it in confidence and at least make him aware of… the problem. Then, if we do need to respond to a threat, we will at least all be prepared."

After a pause, Matsumoto took a deep breath, and nodded his assent.

They reconvened in Chief Inspector Yamanouchi's office. He was in his late-thirties, young for his position and unusually tall for a Japanese man at slightly over six foot. However, apart from a somewhat unorthodox hairstyle, he looked smart and professional. He listened intently.

"… so there you have it," finished the General. "It's not as though we believe Nariko will attempt to assassinate the Emperor, it's just that, in certain circumstances…" Yamanouchi raised his eyebrows, "…and I don't intend to elaborate, she might."

Matsumoto shifted position, reflecting his uneasiness with the turn of this conversation.

"Hmm. Justifiably or not," noted Yamanouchi, "Peacekeeper Nariko has a worldwide reputation for supreme swordsmanship. She will take a lot of stopping."

"That's why we're here," asserted Gyobu, glancing at Matsumoto.

"So what is your role in this, Mr Matsumoto?" queried Yamanouchi.

"Oh," he replied, as though surprised to be asked to contribute, "I am simply an interested party. If the need arises, I will be working with the General to ensure the Emperor's safety."

"Very well," said Yamanouchi, nodding and sitting back in his chair. "I think I understand the situation. But if you wish my resources to be prepared, I will need to share this information with my senior staff."

"Who's that again?" queried Gyobu, purely for Matsumoto's benefit as he already knew the answer.

"Inspector Maeda and Ms Mizoguchi. She's my Strategic Planner."

Gyobu nodded towards Matsumoto.

"Is that really necessary?" he asked.

"I believe it would be prudent," confirmed Yamanouchi.

"You will only speak with them?" probed Matsumoto. Yamanouchi nodded. "And you are sure they will not share this information with anyone else? This knowledge must reside only with you three."

"Not a problem. I can guarantee their complete discretion."

"Very well," agreed Matsumoto unenthusiastically, flashing a disapproving glance at Gyobu.

"So be it," said the General, standing. "We'll leave you to tell them what they need to know..."

It was 11:20 p.m. when Tessa walked inconspicuously into Barnaby Mews. She felt a strange sense of vulnerability coming to her old Samurai sword school without a weapon. But as soon as she reached the main entrance, one of the doors swung open and Lee's smiling face beckoned her out of the darkness. She felt reassured seeing the glint in his eyes – just as bright as ever.

"Welcome back, Nariko-san, we were worried about you."

"I was rather worried too," admitted Tessa. "It's good to be back. Potter will be outside at twelve-thirty."

"Very well," said Lee, smiling at his wife, who had joined them, "then we have time for some tea. I think we would both like to be brought up to date."

For nearly an hour, the three of them sat in Lee's private rooms behind SKS while Tessa recounted what had happened to her since she had left London. Although she spared them many of the more horrific details, she revelled in being back in these familiar, friendly surroundings. But she was surprised by how difficult it was for her to describe even a little of what had taken place in Insein and the shipping container – it had clearly affected her deeply. As midnight approached, Lee nodded to his wife. She left them for a while, returning with a locked attaché case and a long burgundy-coloured velvet bag. Barely able to contain her joy, Tessa grinned gleefully at the sight of them.

First she opened the case. In it were her Kevlar body suit, her knives, shuriken, and over-the-shoulder sword harness, which she immediately put on. Then she untied the velvet bag and carefully removed the Amafuji sword inside, caressing it with glee.

"They were desperate to get their hands on this," she mused.

"And there is no doubt some terrible significance in that," said Lee, reflecting on the implications. "It makes one wonder whether…"

"Indeed," agreed Tessa, nodding. "I cannot understand how our earlier intelligence could have been so wrong."

"In due course, we would all like to know about that. But first, balance must be restored. Let us only hope we really can end it this time."

"Lee-san, thank you very much for keeping everything safe for me. And, naturally, your brother sends his regards to you both."

Lee smiled and laid a fine mahogany box on the table.

"This is a present from Kono," he added. "It contains exploding shuriken, like the ones you used in Cambodia some time back; there are four, two for each of you perhaps. I have a feeling you will need them all."

"I suspect you're right. You know the castle is vulnerable."

"Yes. But I also know that it and my brother are as well prepared as they can be. We two here are too old to be of significance now, but we are concerned for you both."

"We'll be fine," replied Tessa, "and you will both always be of significance to us."

Suddenly, a completely unexpected idea popped into Tessa's head.

"Do you think Kono would mind if I phoned him now? It's a bit late?"

"I'm sure he will not," replied Lee, placing his mobile phone on the table.

"*Konichiwa*, Kono-san," Tessa began hesitantly. But he was so delighted to hear from her that she had difficulty in getting in another word for some time. Lee listened patiently while his wife went to make some fresh green tea.

"Well," said Tessa eventually, "I was wondering whether you would be able to make something more for me..." She described what she wanted. "I know the weapon is a trifle unconventional, and I'm afraid I'm in a rush... Perhaps a pair?" There was a palpable silence on the other end of the phone and even Lee looked taken-aback. "Yes, I know they're brutal, but I have some big vermin to immobilise..." Tessa heard Lee taking a deep breath. "I understand. Thank you, Kono-san. I will collect them the day after tomorrow."

As Tessa finished the call, Lee's wife returned.

"Nariko-san, those are vicious," chided Lee. "They haven't been used for centuries. What made you think of them?"

"I really don't know. The thought just came to me."

"Are you sure their application is justified; honourable even?"

"There is a lot at stake for us and them, and it's already proved to be a truly brutal struggle. However, if at all possible, I would like to take Paul, and whoever, alive."

They drank some more tea in silence until Tessa looked at her watch.

"I should be going, Potter will be waiting."

"When will we see you again?" asked Lee's wife.

"When you grace our home with a visit," replied Tessa with a warm smile.

She bowed.

"Nariko-san," said Lee, "we shall miss you. Be careful, be righteous, and may you be victorious."

They all stood up and bowed deeply to each other. Then Lee led Tessa back into the practise room. There she slid her Amafuji sword into its harness. They bowed to each other again, but not a word more was said. Tessa picked up her attaché case, together with the wooden box from Kono, and walked back up Barnaby Mews to the waiting taxi.

As they drove away, Potter glanced at her in the mirror.

"You look rather happier now you've got a sword again."

"Indeed, but I still need the right opportunity to use it. However, I have a plan."

"I thought you might. I was simply wondering whether you'd be sharing it with me."

Tessa grinned.

"How could I not, Potter? Can we talk, or do you need to be elsewhere?"

"Sure. I just hope there's something other than green tea in the flat."

Twenty minutes later, he was lounging across one of the sofas. He had taken off his shoes and was enjoying the coffee Tessa had brewed for him. She was sitting opposite him in an armchair, drinking some water. Her attaché case and sword were close by. She felt comforted by their proximity.

Do you know where Nyunt is?" she started.

"Yes. She's at her flat in Chelsea."

"You have her under surveillance?"

"Not really, I expected you to ask. She's still an active Peacekeeper and in that capacity has extensive rights. Although we're suspicious of her trustworthiness, there isn't any concrete evidence which would empower me to take action against her. Needless to say she was able to tell us a convincing tale after her retrieval from Waley and, to the best of my knowledge, hasn't broken any law."

Tessa tried to restrain the powerful emotions which were welling up inside her; a contradictory combination of concern, love and anger.

"Could you continue to keep a discreet eye on her, please? At some point in the not too distant future we might need to act quickly."

"Yes, we can do that, but it won't be full twenty-four seven cover."

"Fine. Thank you. So, do you have intelligence of anything imminent that the Calver Cats are planning?"

"Ah. By chance, I do. Although I still need to check it out. We received a tip-off that the Cats are planning to rob the Kensington High Street Branch of Floyds Bank tomorrow morning. It's apparently due to go down sometime between two and three a.m."

"Hmm, sooner than I'd hoped; there's something else I've got to do; but I suppose that'll have to wait. Were you intending to invite

266

Yoshino to intervene?"

"Yes, she'd be the obvious choice."

"So be it. Does she still dress for Mission actions in a dark purple outfit?"

"Yep."

"Good. So why don't you confirm the intelligence and pop over sometime so we can discuss how to respond."

"OK. I'm not sure what time I'll come, but I don't think you should go out anyway…"

Tessa had nearly given up on Potter for the morning when just before noon the doorbell rang. He was soon relaxing again on the sofa, this time with sandwiches and a coffee he'd brought with him.

"It's confirmed," he said, between mouthfuls. "Tonight, well early tomorrow morning to be precise."

"OK," acknowledged Tessa, keen to put her plan into action. "And Yoshino has accepted the action?"

"Yes."

"Couldn't be better." Tessa took a deep breath. "Potter, I'd like you to make sure she doesn't attend. I will take her place. In fact, I'd like you to lock her up very securely, probably for a couple of weeks. Use an obscure location and, daft as it may sound, make sure its impervious to radio signals."

"Wow! On what grounds? I can't just…"

"Do you accept that Yoshino endangered a Peacekeeper's life?" interrupted Tessa.

"Well, yes, yours. Sort of."

Tessa ignored the *sort of*.

"And do you accept that anyone who does that becomes a legitimate target for the Peacekeeper concerned, and even deadly force may be employed if deemed appropriate?"

"Yes. But to the best of my knowledge no Peacekeeper has ever used it against another Peacekeeper. And don't forget, you walked over that bridge in Waley of your own volition" he replied uneasily. "Not to mention the fact that Yoshino is still your daughter."

"I am aware of that, Potter, which is precisely why I want you to do as I have asked. Technically, I do believe I'm entitled to move against her, but all I want is for you to keep her safe. That way, between us, maybe we'll be able to save both her life and her reputation. However, it's absolutely imperative that you keep her somewhere safe and out of sight, particularly as far as Paul and his cronies are concerned."

Potter looked troubled.

"Nariko, I hear what you say, but she's on active duty and has accepted a Mission against the Calver Cats."

"So have I, and for the time being I will assume her responsibilities in London."

"I'm sorry, but if you really want me to do this, you're going to have to explain why?"

Tessa hesitated.

"You mentioned that the Calver Cats had become increasingly successful here, despite the best efforts of the Peacekeepers."

"Yes."

"And Yoshino has been one of them. So, have there been any instances when she was tasked with stopping something, say a hijack or a robbery, and failed to deliver the results you expected?"

"Yes, but no one's perfect. Not all Peacekeepers are as good as you, if any."

"She's better than she realises," professed Tessa dryly, "and probably much better than you give her credit for."

"Maybe, but surely you're not suggesting that she's in cahoots with the Calver Cats?"

"We know she's been going out with Paul, and probably still is, and we both know he's involved up to his neck in this."

"Yes, we do," admitted Potter. "But only from what you've told us. We don't have much else against him, and there isn't an iota of proof that implicates Nyunt. She gave a very credible story about how she was coerced into doing their bidding in Bangkok. I prefer to think she's simply suffering from youthful inexperience."

"But you must have your doubts, especially after Waley?"

"Yes, of course."

"And how would you react if Paul showed up again?"

"I'd have him brought in for questioning. But..."

"Well, perhaps taking Yoshino off the streets will help smoke him out."

"Nariko, I understand, but I still think holding her incommunicado for an indefinite period would be interpreted as a trifle extreme."

"Potter, please. I'm sure she's not knowingly working with the Calver Cats, she has too strong a sense of what is right and what is wrong for that. But she's not been herself ever since she went to Burma with Paul. Maybe she's being manipulated, brainwashed even."

"Are you sure you're not taking this too personally and maybe over-reacting a little?"

"Well, if I attend actions which she was tasked to resolve and achieve better results, we'll know, won't we? But if we do find that she has somehow been got at, we must know that she is safe."

"But why the Faraday cage?"

"You know what they did to me in Insein?"

"You don't think she's had a pump installed?" exclaimed Potter.

"I certainly don't know she hasn't. When she came back from Burma she said she'd had an emergency appendectomy in Naypyidaw, and went off the deep end when I suggested she have it checked out here. It prompted her to walk out on me," said Tessa bitterly.

"Hmm," said Potter, still doubtful.

"When's her next Peacekeeper medical due?"

"Not for several months. She had one just before she went to Burma with Paul."

"She would, wouldn't she?" muttered Tessa sarcastically. "Didn't you have her examined after Waley?"

"No. I tried, but she refused – quite vociferously, in fact. She wouldn't even present herself for a check-up."

"Figures. And you're still not convinced?"

"No, I'm not. It's all too circumstantial. Currently, there aren't proper grounds to detain her. She could cause one hell of a stink when she gets out."

"I don't think she would. Paul would want her to, but I suspect he'd need to be closer to her to do that, and he won't dare show his face because I doubt he's sure that I'm dead."

"OK," Potter acquiesced. "It's against my better judgement, but I'll do it for you – only for a week, though. And that still means you owe me one."

"Thank you," said Tessa, smiling. "But that sounds as though you already have collection in mind?"

"As a matter of fact, I do. How about if I join you for dinner? But I'll bring my own, if you don't mind…"

Potter returned early evening. He ate a Chinese takeaway while she enjoyed some sashimi and rice.

"Now, about that favour I'd like from you," said Potter. "It's very simple really, and less onerous than you think. You remember that rather special sintered knife Sinclair gave you?"

"Of course," bemoaned Tessa.

"Well, I think it's high time you gave it back."

"That's a big one, Potter. I really like it."

"I know, and I also remember seeing how well you can use it," he replied, eyeing her with a steady gaze.

She took a deep breath and went into the bedroom, returning with the unusual-looking all-grey knife in her hand. Tessa truly adored this knife. It was perfectly balanced, unbelievably sharp and incredibly hard, quite capable of sinking into concrete, if thrown correctly. With considerable reticence, she handed it to Potter.

"Thank you," he said with a smile. He opened his briefcase and placed it carefully inside. "You'll be pleased to hear that the UK continues to maintain its world lead in sintered knives. The newest prototype is even stronger than this old version, and still has no magnetic or X-ray signature; in fact, it outperforms the older versions in just about every respect…" Tessa nodded, still trying to come to terms with having had to give back the knife she had got so used to carrying. "…The latest version even does tricks. It can be programmed to be user-specific, so if one or more strangers grip it cumulatively for more than five seconds, it disintegrates. Furthermore, the self-destruction process is quite violent. It's not exactly an explosion, but will almost certainly strip most of the flesh off the potential miscreant's hand. Alternatively, a programmed user can simply twist the boss at the top of the hilt and the knife will automatically self-destruct after five seconds, unless a programmed user grips it and turns the boss back. It's all designed to ensure we don't lose sight of any more."

"Sounds very impressive," acknowledged Tessa, disconsolately.

"It is," agreed Potter, with a laugh. "Would you like to *borrow* one?"

"Oh! You tease! Yes, please. Very much."

Grinning, Potter produced a black velvet bag from his case and handed it to her. Tessa carefully removed the knife and unsheathed it; its smoother finish even made it look superior to her old knife. Meanwhile, Potter placed a sophisticated box of electronics on the table and started pressing various buttons. Soon the knife had been programmed for him and her to use.

"One thing, Nariko," said Potter, seriously. "If you're going to be captured, twist the boss regardless, please."

"I promise. I won't let anyone take it."

"OK," he replied, nodding as he repacked his briefcase. "I've arranged for Flood to pick you up at one a.m. He'll drop you off and join me. I'll be taking Yoshino into protective custody. Oh, and John Brown says your Porsche is ready to go. He's around himself during the day, but he's made sure Anderson, who's on nights, knows to give you access to it whenever you want."

Tessa nodded.

"One other thing you should perhaps be aware of," added Potter, standing up to go. "The Calver Cats have three teams in the UK now. Top of the pile is their so-called Kick Ass squad – a bit of a misnomer really since all they seem to do is kill people. Anyway, they're the elite; a group of six who are extremely well-trained, a level or two above the others. I doubt you'll be up against them tonight, but you never know. If Paul has somehow got wind of your return, he could send them as back-up in case they're needed."

"Understood. But if I'm right about Yoshino, they won't be expecting much resistance tonight and, with a bit of luck, I'll have a chance to find out where Paul is…"

CHAPTER 26

At twenty past one in the morning, Tessa merged quietly into the shadows under the entrance arch to Adam and Eve Mews, almost opposite Floyds Bank. It was mid-week so Kensington High Street, which would still be busy at the weekend, was almost deserted. This was doubly convenient for Tessa since she wanted as few spectators as possible.

However, she found herself watching Flood drive away with mixed feelings. It wasn't that she was scared. In terms of what she had done in the past as a Peacekeeper, this was unlikely to be anything of consequence. But Paul had put her through hell, and as a result, she didn't feel as self-assured as before. She suspected that Matsumoto and Potter had their doubts about her too. Perhaps they were right; maybe her confidence had been broken. She tried to pull herself together, took a deep breath, and put on her headset.

It was 2:30 a.m. when Tessa noticed a grey van slowing down as it drove past the bank. The street was completely empty now, so it was even more suspicious when the van returned five minutes later to drive past again. On the third occasion, it stopped not far from the bank. Its back doors opened and three men got out. They ran to the bank's substantial double doors and one adjusted what looked like a large water pistol with two cylinders slung beneath it. He kneeled down by the lower right hand corner, pulled the trigger and started tracing around the doors. A thick trail of glutinous blue explosive was deposited from the end of the gun. Another two ruffians got out from the front of the van, leaving the engine running. Although the driver stayed close to the vehicle, the man from the passenger side nonchalantly joined the other men in front of the bank.

The man with the explosive applicator finished and handed the gun to one of his colleagues. As he returned it to the van, the first man stuck a small blue box to the beginning of the explosive, and pressed a button. They all backed well away. Then the entire explosive track started glowing red before sprouting bright white flames as it melted through the reinforced steel. There was little noise during this process, but barely had the flames subsided when both doors fell outwards with a loud *crash!*

Tessa took a deep breath. It wouldn't be long now, back in the control room everyone would have seen the pictures from her headset camera. She decided a direct approach would be best. There were only five of them and soon some would be committed inside the bank.

"Peacekeeper, green light," pronounced an emotionless voice in her headset. For a moment she wondered what back-up Potter had organised, but then she flexed her muscles one last time, switched off her headset and set off towards the men.

"Headset to continuous, please," urged the voice. "We've lost audio and visual signals."

But Tessa didn't hear and simply continued towards the bank.

Barely fifty yards away, in Wrights Lane, Potter and Flood watched and listened with interest. They exchanged disapproving glances as a status message flashed up indicating Tessa's headset had been disabled. Their car was in full stealth mode, silent and invisible to anyone who didn't know it was there.

"I hope she's up to this," Flood remarked, changing the grip on his sword.

"So do I," admitted Potter, checking the aim on their parabolic microphone, keen to listen to what was being said. "How long will it take for the team to get here?"

"Two minutes. I thought it would be a good idea to give her a little space."

Potter nodded.

"Peacekeeper!" announced Tessa, taking care not to stand where the streetlights would illuminate her face. "Discard your weapons and stand facing the wall. You have been warned."

For a moment the thugs stopped what they were doing and turned round to stare at her. All of the men had knives, but Tessa could see only one gun, holstered, on the man from the passenger side of the van. The driver immediately started edging back towards his vehicle.

"Stay where you are!" barked Tessa glaring at him and stepping closer.

"It's all right, lads, I'll handle this," responded the man with the gun, whom Tessa had correctly assessed as the team's leader. He quickly stretched out his left hand, fist clenched, then opened it vertically, pointing at Tessa, clenched it again and opened it palm downwards. Then he yelled "*Bang! Bang!*" For the briefest of moments, Tessa was convinced she was standing in front of Angkor Wat; then she froze, her mind blank.

"Paul orders you to do what I say," commanded the man, walking towards her. "Do you understand?"

Tessa's brain was struggling to digest what he'd said. She couldn't see Paul amongst them. Her indecision clearly annoyed the man.

"Yoshino," he shouted, "do you understand?"

Suddenly it dawned on Tessa that she wasn't Yoshino. The man couldn't have been talking to her. An image of Beng Mealea flashed up in her mind. She was horrified. There was no doubt that she had just been hypnotised. However, events didn't seem to have advanced much, so hopefully he hadn't issued her with any instructions.

"Bloody hell, Yoshino, what's the fucking matter with you?" demanded the man angrily.

Tessa bowed her head, making it more difficult for him to see her face, but nevertheless kept a careful watch on how close he was coming.

"Where is Paul?" she bleated. "I must see him, it's been so long."

"I'm sorry, darlin'. He ain't here," replied the man, relaxing. "What are you guys gawping at? Get on with it! You've only got sixty-three seconds left."

Three of the men disappeared into the bank while the driver moved to the back of the van. The bank echoed to a loud *boom!*

"But where is he?" pleaded Tessa again. "Please, tell me."

"He's a long way away, in Japan."

"But where in Japan?" pressed Tessa. "I need to know. Please."

"Don't ask so many questions, darlin'. You just wait there until we've finished, and then call it in. OK?"

Just as the other three men ran out of the bank weighed down by large holdalls, Tessa raised her head.

"No, you listen to me," she rasped. "If you want to live, you will tell me where I can find Paul."

"Jesus Christ! You're not Yoshino. Who the fuck are you?"

"Where's Paul?" insisted Tessa in a menacing tone, altering position slightly to improve her angle on his colleagues.

"Bloody hell, I know who you are!" screamed the man, reversing towards the van. "Guys! Kill this bitch... Now, you idiots."

The three men by the doors hesitated before reluctantly discarding their bags. Meanwhile, the man with whom Tessa had been talking started reversing away. She didn't move a muscle.

"I think she's frozen!" exclaimed Flood, reaching for the door handle.

"You can't help her from here," stated Potter. "Let it play out. She has to do this on her own."

"Kill her!" urged the leader, reaching for his pistol. As the three who'd dropped the bags unsheathed knives, Tessa sprang into action. She drew two knives and threw them. They sank into the foreheads of two of the men. The third threw his knife at Tessa. It was a good throw, but she simply caught it and threw it straight back – shortly afterwards, he collapsed with his own weapon sticking in his chest. Meanwhile, she'd thrown another of her knives; it hit the leader in the thigh. He yelped in pain, dropped his gun and crumpled to the ground. Finally, as the fifth man attempted to scramble back into the driver's seat, Tessa threw a shuriken. It emitted a shrill whine as it whisked through the air towards him. There was a dull *twang* as it buried itself in his temple. Already dead, his body slid clumsily out of the van and onto the road.

Tessa walked up to the leader as he frantically groped for his gun. She kicked it away.

"Now, let's try that again, shall we? Where's Paul?"

"Japan, that's all I know."

"I don't believe you," retorted Tessa, dismissively. She kneeled down to assess the damage her blade had inflicted. Seriously painful, but not life-threatening – she had aimed well. She gripped the hilt, prompting yelps of pain from the man. She needed information, and fast, but how far was she prepared to go to get it? How much like Paul was she willing to become? She yanked her knife out, causing the man to scream in agony. She toyed with it in her hand, continually changing her grip. He knew what she was thinking.

"Fuck off, bitch!" he screamed, grabbing his leg. "You can't do that, you're a bloody Peacekeeper. I've got rights."

"*You* have *rights*?" exclaimed Tessa in disbelief, raising her voice. "Paul didn't pay any attention to my rights in Burma, why should I bother with yours? Tell me where he is."

"I don't know, I swear. He'll kill me," replied the man, changing position.

Tessa purposefully brought the blade down over the man's genitals. He got the message instantly and lay back flat on the road, abandoning any thoughts he might have had of trying to escape.

"Well, knowing Paul, he'll probably have you killed anyway because you talked to me. But if you tell me where he is, he won't ever be able to get to you. Now, are you right- or left-handed?" she purred. He said nothing so Tessa decided for herself. She drew her last knife and, choosing a spot carefully, rested the tip of the blade on his right shoulder. "My patience is fast running out. Where's Paul?"

"Oh, god! Please, you can't do this," he moaned. "It's illegal."

"I'll forward your complaint to Paul when I see him," replied Tessa, exerting just enough pressure on her knife for it to pass through his leather jacket and pierce his skin; he twitched as he felt the cold steel. "Now, unless you want me to push harder, and if I do the blade will shatter your shoulder joint, I suggest you tell me where I can find him."

Meanwhile, Potter and Flood were shifting uneasily in their car.

"Sir," Flood queried tentatively, "isn't that overstepping the mark?"

"Well, perhaps a little. But if we had that man in custody, what would we be asking him?"

"I understand. But we're going to have to report it."

"I know. But her headset is off, so we'll have the only record. You know what they did to her?"

"Yes, sir. But they act outside the law. We don't."

"I don't believe she's forgotten that or her responsibilities as a Peacekeeper. She's got good reason to be in a hurry. I think we'll give her a few seconds more."

Tessa increased the pressure on the blade. Like a hot skewer passing through butter, it sank deeper into his shoulder, but she held back from the joint. He cried out and raised his left hand in an attempt to strike her. Tessa simply swung her other knife round to block his swing, ending up with half the blade protruding from the back of his hand. He wailed in agony.

"Now, you did that, silly," she scorned, withdrawing her knife and using the flat of the blade to press his head back down. You should have realised by now, nobody's going to come and save you. However, I promise I'll stop as soon as you tell me where I can find Paul."

Tessa returned the knife to the man's genitals and started pushing down, not quite hard enough to pierce his trousers.

"Shit, no! Look, please, I'm begging you."

"Where is he?" she insisted, preparing to increase the pressure on both blades.

"...Karatsu!"

"Karatsu, Japan?"

"Yes, yes! Please, let me go. You promised."

"I did indeed. Thank you. Now, that wasn't so hard, was it? I'll just clear up and get you some help. Don't move a muscle and you'll be fine."

She cleaned and re-sheathed both her knives and walked over to the dead gang members with her knives protruding from their foreheads. With her back to the ruffian she'd just interrogated and listening carefully, she bent down to retrieve the weapons with her legs apart. She heard the man roll onto his side and start drawing his own knife.

"Sir, she's got her back to him!" cried Flood, pulling at the door handle in alarm.

Just as the thug prepared to throw his knife, Tessa threw both hers from between her legs. One crunched into his shoulder, sinking into the wound she'd made earlier; the other pierced his heart. His dead body flopped backwards and his knife clattered uselessly on the road.

"Stupid predictable bugger," scoffed Tessa.

She looked down the road to where she'd heard a car door opening. A vehicle shimmered and became visible as it was switched out of stealth mode. Flood and Potter got out and, after she'd collected all her weapons, Tessa joined them.

"Morning, gentlemen."

"Nariko," started Flood. "You do realise we've..."

"Everything all right?" interrupted Potter.

"Hmm, mostly straightforward," replied Tessa, shifting her gaze to Potter. "But I think I may have switched off my headset at some stage. Sorry about that. Maybe I'm not used to this type."

"Yes, but..." attempted Flood.

"Not to worry, these things happen" continued Potter. "We've got a full audio-visual recording anyway."

"Oh, really?"

"I think you and I need to go and have a look at it before you dictate your report. Flood, could you organise the clean-up here?"

"No problem, sir. But may I know what we're doing with the recording?" he asked as he watched Potter eject the memory card."

Potter looked at Tessa.

"In due course, I will be filing it, Flood. But if anyone asks, tell them it was Peacekeeper Yoshino who attended."

"Very good, sir," he replied, shrugging. He nodded to Tessa and strode out towards the prostrate bodies.

"Come on, Nariko, we need to talk," said Potter, gesturing her to get into the car.

"What, now?"

"Yes."

Not a word was said while they travelled back to the secure flat. It was only when they were sitting there with warm drinks that Tessa broke the uneasy silence.

"Potter, I know it was wrong of me to threaten him like that, but I didn't really hurt him. I only gave him a quarter-inch-deep wound in his shoulder to scare him. It would have healed completely without any permanent damage. Is that going to be regarded as unacceptable by the do-gooders?"

"Of course it is," replied Potter, "especially if they hear that you described them that way. The truth is, you tortured a man while no one nearby was in immediate danger. You must have known we'd be watching and that there would be consequences. I know we all want to see this ended quickly, but... I suppose I could delete the data."

"Thanks for the offer," sighed Tessa, "but you shouldn't do that. The truth is the truth, and I suppose I was out of line. I'll put everything in my Incident Report and await the outcome of their deliberations."

"I'm glad you said that, Nariko. However, I will delay filing the recording. But you know they're likely to revoke your OCL?"

"Hmm. Well, I hope they don't do that. It would be tantamount to imposing the death penalty on me. I would become a target for all low-lifes with a grudge and wouldn't legally be able to defend myself. I would have thought my offering to retire permanently from active service would satisfy their requirement to be seen to have done something."

"Is that what you intended all along?"

"Yes," admitted Tessa quietly, "I've had more than my fill of this. I'd had enough after Rippleside yet here we are more than ten years on and not only is it still happening, it's getting worse. However, I've experienced what those bastards did to the likes of Karen Weissman and Toshie Miyazaki. It may well be the last thing I do, but I will stop them from torturing anyone else in that inhuman way."

Potter nodded his understanding.

"It won't be long before Paul gets wind of this," he added.

"I know. He'll soon connect Yoshino's disappearance with the demise of one of his teams."

"It also seems your suspicions concerning her have been vindicated."

"Indeed," acknowledged Tessa sadly. "I presume you agree now that there are sufficient grounds to keep Nyunt locked up and insist she has a full medical, including a body scan, as soon as possible?"

"Yes, I do. But it'll take me twenty-four hours to obtain the necessary authority. Anyway, let's get your Incident Report written."

It was an hour and a half later when Tessa finished dictating her report. Potter had sat quietly throughout, nodding occasionally. The memory card with the record of the night's events had stayed on the table all the time. However, much to Tessa's surprise, Potter had made no attempt to play it back to her. He simply took the report, scanned it briefly and signed it. Then he looked up at Tessa and smiled.

"I think we both know you've left something out."

"What do you mean?"

"Well, I bet you don't know what my grandfather did for a living?"

"Er, no, Potter. I don't... Should I?"

"He was a professional hypnotist. For a while he had a hell of a stage act, but he was so good at it, he spent most of his life using his skills for medical purposes."

Tessa shifted position uncomfortably.

"Do you know what happened to you in front of the bank?"

She breathed out noisily.

"Yes, I do. It's part of the baggage Paul left me with."

"I suspected as much. Do you have any means of fighting it?"

"Yes, I just need to make a call. You know the command they gave me was meant for Nyunt?"

He nodded.

"Why don't you make your call? I'll stay with you. I'm not particularly skilled, but I do have some knowledge and might be able to help."

Tessa smiled her thanks and phoned Professor Kawashima. It took a while to get through and then Potter had to leave the room for a minute while Tessa had a private chat with her. But the Professor soon freed herself from her other commitments and, with Potter listening and performing the hand gestures, the tape was played and the hypnotic instruction removed from Tessa's mind. It was 5 a.m. when they finished.

"What do you intend to do now?" asked Potter, placing the memory card in his briefcase.

"At some point, I need to tell our friends in Japan about Paul being in Karatsu; it could be important. But there are a few things I need to do before going back."

"OK," said Potter. "So are you going to get some sleep now?"

"Nope. No time. Any chance you could give me a lift to Stanhope Gate? I'd like to pick up my car."

"Sure. Then what?"

"I'm going to drive to Papa Edinsay, it's one of the Orkney Islands…"

Potter had only just sat down behind his desk when there was a knock on his office door. Flood entered.

"Morning, sir. Everything's sorted at Floyds."

"Good. I've got her report here. I'm pleased to say she insisted it contain everything. I'm going to hold on to it for a day or two and then file it in the usual way. Are you OK with that?"

Flood thought for a moment.

"Yes, sir. It's the least we can do after all she's accomplished for us. What's her plan now, sir?"

"She's collected her car and is driving to Orkney of all places; apparently she's got something important to do up there. Then she's coming back to SKS to collect a couple of items Kono is making her, before going to Japan. I have a suspicion she thinks the rest of this will be played out there. Maybe, with a bit of luck, we won't be in the firing line for a change. In the meantime, we'll keep Yoshino locked away."

Flood nodded.

"I still think she'll go ballistic when she realises a tracking transponder was installed without her knowledge."

"I expect so," agreed Potter, "but when she escaped it wasn't clear what state she'd end up in. At least we can keep an eye on her if necessary, although I've confirmed with Japan that we'll only activate it if we have to. I've even had one of those new-fangled ones implanted myself after my Waley adventure…"

CHAPTER 27

As the last daily roll-on-roll-off ferry approached Papa Edinsay, Tessa gazed at the island with feelings of heart-breaking nostalgia. It reminded her that the first property she had owned in Orkney had been a bequest from her friend Penny, while this island had been a legacy from her first true love, David. She desperately hoped it wasn't destined to develop similarly poignant associations.

The sun was setting when the ship moored. She would have preferred to arrive sooner, but she'd wanted to place some flowers at David's family crypt in St Magnus Cathedral on Mainland. That was always a deeply emotional experience for her. She had bought an enormous bouquet of exotic blooms and had handed a substantial donation to the Dean, requesting the flowers were well tended.

She smiled as her car approached a striking man standing on the quayside scrutinising the vehicles off-loading. He was comfortably over six foot tall, fit and strong with shoulder-length jet-black hair and shining grey eyes. In his mid-fifties, Alasdair McClellan was the elected Island Chief. He was a proud and conscientious man, keen to honour his responsibilities to the islanders in every respect. As such, he rarely missed keeping an eye on who was visiting the place. His weather-beaten face was wearing a serious expression, but the moment he saw Tessa's Porsche, that melted into a broad hospitable grin. She brought the car to a standstill by him and opened the window.

"Hello, Alasdair," she said warmly. "How are you?"

"I'm very well, Ma'am," he replied. "Welcome home, it's been a while."

"Indeed it has; far too long. I've been a bit tied up. Anyway, it's good to be here now, although I'm afraid I'll only be staying the one night."

"In which case, Ma'am, you timed it just right. We're celebrating coming top of the Orkney Island School League again. It's the sixth year in a row now. I hope you'll be able to come to the Ceilidh, eight o'clock in the Village Hall? Everyone'll be delighted to see you."

"I wouldn't miss it for the world," Tessa accepted enthusiastically. "I'll see you this evening, Alasdair."

She drove the short distance up to her moated manor house and deactivated the alarms. After she'd parked the car in the secure underground garage, she checked that nothing had been disturbed in the house – it hadn't. As far as she could tell, no one had visited since she was last there, corroborating the alarm system's records.

After gulping down a mug of green tea, she changed into some scruffy clothes and went out to the tool shed, returning with a pickaxe, a large cold chisel, a sledgehammer and shovel. Then she opened the trapdoor into the cellar.

While still on the steep stone stairs, she studied the fine dust she'd sprinkled over the floor. It further substantiated that no one had been here since she had left. She carried on down and studied the ostensibly ancient back wall. Then she started hacking away at it with the pickaxe. It took twenty minutes of hard work before she had cleared a way through to the secret high-security sword safe which Kono had installed before she'd left for Burma. She entered the codes and with a reassuringly heavy *clunk, clunk* the thick steel door unlocked and swung open with a gentle sigh.

"Now there's a very happy sight," she exclaimed, grinning from ear to ear. She removed the burgundy-coloured velvet bag and took out her third sword, her real Kimi Amakuni weapon. Discarding the tools, she went back upstairs and carefully cleaned all her weapons. Finally satisfied, she put them away in her normal sword safe and cleared up the mess from the cellar. After that, all she was fit for was a restful cat-nap.

By the time she walked down to the Village Hall, the Ceilidh was in full flow. Loud music accompanied by the raucous screams of communal merriment greeted her, and it wasn't long before she was joining in with gusto. Truly relaxed for the first time in months, she had forgotten all the challenges which still lay ahead. Tonight she was determined to focus all her energy on having a fun-filled evening.

But at 9:30 p.m., all that changed. While Tessa was in the midst of a competitively fast jig with Alasdair, five burly strangers burst in to the hall; all of them were armed with knives, and two carried heavy staffs. The music faltered and stopped as everyone looked round in surprise.

"OK, folks," announced the newcomers' leader, "do as I say and no one gets 'urt. But if one of you tries anything stupid, you all pay. Got it?"

In response the man encountered a cold seething silence...

"Who...?" started a woman. But she stopped talking when one of the gang waved a knife in front of her face.

"Don't speak unless you're spoken too, woman. You two," the leader continued, gesturing towards some of his men, "collect up anything these country bumpkins could use as weapons."

Cutlery and any other potentially lethal objects were placed in two buckets and unceremoniously tossed out of the building. When he was satisfied, the leader stood on the stage and addressed them all again.

"OK. Now, who lives in the bloody big house up the hill, and where are they?"

"I think you should tell us who you are first," responded Alasdair indignantly.

"None of your bloody business, mate... Oh, are you the fuckin' Island Chief?"

"I am, but I'll ask you to watch your language. We don't talk like that around here."

"I don't fuckin' care how you bloody talk, mate," retorted the man, prompting some of the children to start crying. "I won't ask again. Who lives up there?"

"Do your worst," insisted Alasdair, "we're not saying anything."

The man laughed.

"Do you really want to see me cut this pretty little slut you're with, just to protect some rich fart who don't care nothin' for you?"

"Can I have her first, boss?" interjected one of his men, leering at Tessa. "She's a fit 'un."

Alasdair clenched his fists and was about to hit the man when Tessa put her hand on his arm to hold him back.

"Please, don't hurt him," she said, turning to the thugs' leader. "I'll tell you what you need to know."

"Well, bugger me, if she ain't a clever cunt too."

"Look, you really should mind your language!" added Tessa. "There are children present."

284

"I'll do what I want, when I want – and no pissing poonani ain't going to stop me. So, starters for ten, darlin', who the hell are you?"

"Amongst other things, I keep the house up there. But if you want me say any more, we're going to have to go somewhere private where your foul manners won't offend everyone and your apes won't scare these children. There's a room behind you, how about in there?"

The man shrugged.

"If you want, bitch."

"OK. How about letting everyone else go then?"

"Piss off!" he replied, laughing at her in disbelief.

"Look, you can't even get near the place at the moment, can you? I know how to disarm the security systems. I'm willing to tell you what you need to know, but you've got to let everyone else go."

"No, darlin', they're staying here – as my insurance. Now shut yer mouth and come with me."

"I am not letting you take her in there on her own," interjected Alasdair.

"Oh, fuck me!" retorted the leader, turning to his men. "You two, come with me and bring both the buggers. You two, lock the door from the outside and stand guard. Nobody leaves 'til I come back. Got it?"

They nodded and Tessa led Alasdair and the three ruffians into the small room behind the stage.

"Don't you worry, …er," said Alasdair uncertainly, "I won't let them harm you."

Tessa turned, laid a hand on his shoulder and kissed him gently on the cheek, at the same time whispering in his ear.

"Thank you, Alasdair, but I'll be fine. Just stand well back from me, please."

He looked surprised, but nodded. They entered a bland twenty-foot square room with two tone cream walls. As the door closed behind them, the leader turned to Tessa.

"Well?" he demanded.

"Do you see the road leading up to the manor house," she said, pointing to the window behind him. "And where the trees start?" The man turned and moved closer to the glass so he could get a better view. "By the way, did Paul phone you all the way from Karatsu to send you here," she added, in a surprisingly friendly tone. "I hope he's paying you well."

"Not bloody likely," he grunted; then he spun round. "How the fuck...?"

"You poor sods," hissed Tessa. "He sent you here to die."

"What?" snapped the man. "Who the...?" Then he thought for a moment. "Oh, fuck! Kill her!" he yelled to his colleagues, drawing his knife and throwing it. Tessa caught it neatly but didn't have time to throw it back as the other two men were throwing theirs. So she flicked it at the man to her left, then caught his knife and tossed it at the man to her right, finally catching his knife. Meanwhile, the leader of the gang had dived towards the door leading outside. He had just grabbed the handle when the third knife struck him in the back of the head.

"You'll have to do better than that, boys," muttered Tessa as all three men collapsed dead. She turned round to look at Alasdair. He had a stunned expression on his face.

"Are you all right, Alasdair?" she asked, grinning. "You're looking a bit peaky."

"Yes, Ma'am. I'm just a little surprised, that's all. I thought you needed looking after, but it seems you don't."

"Oh, I do," replied Tessa wistfully, "but not from the likes of these morons. Anyway, I doubt we're done yet. These guys were amateurs, probably only sent to delay us... I'll just go and sort the other two."

Tessa retrieved two knives and went out through the back door. Not long afterwards came the muffled scrunching of bodies falling on gravel, and the sound of something heavy being dragged round the corner of the building. Then she came back, still brandishing the knives.

"OK. The coast is clear. Take everyone up to North Farm, it should be safe there," she insisted, looking him in the eye. "I'm going to get some gear and then I'll go down to the quay. If there are any more of them, they'll either be there or waiting near the manor."

"Are you sure you'll be all right, Ma'am?"

"Absolutely. You just get everyone to safety."

As Tessa started jogging up the road to the manor house she heard the sound of the hall emptying behind her. She knew Alasdair would lead everyone out across the fields. Within a couple of minutes they would all be out of harm's way, lost from view to unfamiliar eyes.

Back at the manor house, Tessa was pleased to find no one waiting. She quickly put on her Kevlar suit, slipped her sword harness over her shoulders and armed herself. Five minutes later, she was walking briskly back towards the quayside. She arrived to find three strangers hovering near a small motor launch from Kirkwall; two were armed with guns, the other had a sword and a knife. He was finishing what appeared to be a stressful conversation on his *cbc*.

"Well, suit yourself... Yes, the guys went up to the Hall about twenty minutes ago... No, not a whisper, but the music has stopped... Well, I haven't seen anyone, but some lights went on in the house... Yeah, OK, fifteen minutes. We'll pull out as soon as you're here..."

He finished the call, put the phone away and looked up. Tessa was standing illuminated by the quay's nightlights, watching him. At first he appeared surprised to see her, then he reached down for his phone.

"Leave it, or you're dead," she ordered. She stepped on to the jetty, barring the men's way.

"Oh, for fuck's sake, this gets worse by the minute. Who in buggery are you?" demanded the man, unsure whether he dared reach for his phone despite Tessa's warning.

"I'm guarding the island," she replied. "Who are you?"

"None of your bloody business – just get out the fucking way."

"I'm afraid I can't do that. You see, I'm a Peacekeeper and you're foul-mouthed ruffians who are trespassing. Now, throw down your weapons and surrender, or face the consequences. You have been warned."

"You bloody Peacekeepers, always making a bleeding nuisance of yourselves. I haven't got time for this. Guys, just blow this bitch away," snarled the man.

The men with guns raised them, but Tessa had thrown two knives before they'd even finished aiming. Both of them collapsed on to the jetty with knives projecting from their forehead; their guns clattered onto the ground.

"Don't move a muscle," ordered Tessa, "or you'll be as dead as them."

She calmly walked past the man. As she reached the first prostrate body, she kicked the man's gun into the water and recovered her knife. Then she went to the second man and did the same. Finally, she walked back to the beginning of the quayside.

"Clever boy," she noted. "I was convinced you'd try something stupid, but you didn't… and that's why you're still alive. Now, throw your weapons in the water." The man did as she said. "I suppose Paul sent you?" He nodded. "Is he still in Karatsu?" Again the man nodded.

"Are you going to kill me?"

"Not if you answer my questions honestly," declared Tessa. "I'll simply bind you and hand you over to the Special Forces. So, why did Paul send you here?"

"To search the big house. I was told it would be unprotected."

"What were you looking for?

"Computers, files, anything of value. We were told to torch the place as we left."

"And who's going to be here in fifteen minutes?"

He hesitated, nervously shifting from foot to foot.

"Look, please, get me away from here. If they see me talking to you, they'll kill me."

"Tell me quickly then," urged Tessa.

"The Kick Ass squad."

"How do they know there's a target here?"

"I don't know," he answered, almost screaming. "Please, let's just go!"

"Last question. How many of them are there?

"Six."

Tessa had heard Alasdair approaching and knew he was watching.

"OK." She shrugged and turned around.

"Alasdair, can you bring some rope, please? There's someone here who needs tying up."

But then Tessa heard an all too familiar clicking noise behind her. Abject fury welled up inside her and she spun round to find the man furiously punching the black button on a small grey box.

"Look, I don't know what it does, I was just told to…" he blurted out desperately.

"You fool," growled Tessa, drawing her sword. There was a brief *ping* as she severed his neck. The blow was so strong that as the man's body crumpled his head flew high in the air, bouncing along the quayside before finally plopping into the water.

"Sorry, Alasdair. We won't be needing that rope after all."

Then Tessa heard the sound of some people jogging down the road. She looked round to find Flood's enormous bulk approaching the quayside, leading four burly men; all were heavily armed and dressed completely in black.

"Hello, Flood. That's a clever trick, how did you get here?"

"Stealth helicopter – it's parked a mile away."

"Impressive. Have you come to join our Ceilidh?"

"Not exactly," he replied, glancing at Alasdair. "I had a feeling you might be having some gate-crashers. But I see you have the situation under control."

"Sort of. We've sent the islanders up to North Farm to keep them safe. Maybe you could go up there and help them come home?..."

As his men set off, Tessa continued.

"So what prompted you to go mobile? And come to think of it, how did you know I was here?"

"Ah," replied Flood, with a guilty expression on his face. "You're bugged. Location beacon."

"Surely not?" challenged Tessa.

"One was implanted in Japan when you were… well, when people weren't sure how things were going to turn out. I had to go through all sorts of channels to get the activation code, only to find it was already on."

"What do you mean?"

"Somebody else had already activated it."

Tessa went quiet for a moment.

"So it wasn't meant to be on?"

"Not as far as we, or the Japanese authorities, were concerned."

"Who exactly has the activation and tracking codes?"

"I'm not sure, but I know Potter had them."

"Can you tell when the thing was activated, and by whom?"

"No," replied Flood. "But that's how I knew where to come."

"Understood. But, hold on, why did you have to jump through hoops if Potter had the codes?"

Lost for words, Alasdair was watching this exchange in amazement. Flood walked up to him and smiled.

"Flood," he said, holding out his hand.

"Good evening. Alasdair McClellan, I'm the…"

"I know. Pleased to meet you, Alasdair," he replied, smiling and turning back to Tessa. "Well, you'll never believe it but Khin has surfaced. He's fine. Apparently a Burmese woman nursed him back to health and helped him over the border…"

"Oh, yes!" exclaimed Tessa, punching the air with joy. "Was the woman called Ohnmar?"

"Indeed, but how?… She gestured for him to go on. "Anyway, he still had those papers from Moulmein Hospital and Curtis faxed them to London. Potter was over the moon, but worried that the Calver Cats might have found out because we received intel. that Paul was in London. So, he went to escort Nyunt into full protective custody. He took two guys with him, both of whom are dead. It seems Potter and Nyunt have been snatched again. They're on their way to Japan."

"How do you know?"

"Well, Potter had two tracking transponders fitted; Nyunt had one too. Both their standard devices stopped transmitting not long after they were taken, but Potter's other one is very difficult to detect and only emits a signal if he activates it. He's been sending us occasional blips. There's no doubt about it, he's bound for Japan, and it seems reasonable to assume Paul and Nyunt are with him."

"Oh, dear!" exclaimed Tessa. She glanced at her watch, and took out her *cbc*. "Excuse me a minute."

"*Anata*… Yes, I'm fine. But I think we may have a problem. Did you know I was bugged… Wonderful! We need to talk about that. Did you also know the transponder had been activated? Flood here doesn't know when or by whom… Yes, but maybe I was being tracked while I was with you and now they've waited until I'd collected my real swords… Well, I know they were suspicious about the one I gave them at Waley. Anyway, it seems they've got Potter and Yoshino, and they're on their way to Japan… I'm not sure yet, but Paul has been hiding in Karatsu; according to my *cbc* it's a town on the northern coast of Kyūshū. Do you know it?" After a while, Tessa moved the phone away from her ear and studied it, checking the connection. "*Anata*, are you still there…? Yes, I think they might be coming after you; maybe you should prepare the castle…? Well, can you close the main gates?… I told you we should have got them fixed... No, that's OK, we'll make sure Lee and Kono are safe." Flood nodded, and took out his own *cbc*. "I'll come back as soon as I can... Absolutely, mobilise the villagers."

"I have a jet standing by for you at Lossiemouth," interjected Flood.

"...Yes, well, when you talk to the General, ask him to check Karatsu, but I think he should do it low-profile. He should only use his people. We can trust no one we don't already know..." Tessa heard a boat approaching. "*Anata*, I need to go. I have some work to do. Yes, I'll be careful... I love you too," she said, finishing in a considerably softer tone.

"Who's this?" inquired Flood as a boat neared the jetty.

"That's Mackie-Brown's boat out of Kirkwall," interrupted Alasdair. "He won't be pleased to have been dragged out at this hour."

"I doubt he had much choice," professed Tessa.

"Nariko, are they who I think they are?" demanded Flood, checking his sword. "Why did you have me send the lads away?"

She smiled and flexed her muscles.

"Flood, this is my island and all I want is it to be peaceful, progressive and prosperous. I've attracted these bozos, so it's my duty to make it clear that we don't tolerate people bent on mischief here."

"I'll help."

"No, thanks. But you can have any that get past me."

Flood had Alasdair move well away while he himself stood at the beginning of the jetty, legs apart and arms crossed.

Meanwhile, Tessa strode forward. She stopped near the centre of the wide quay, in an area not obstructed by the three dead bodies. The ship began its final approach, its searchlight illuminating her on the jetty. As it slowed and moved alongside, six men jumped out, all of them were armed with swords and knives. Tessa moved back slightly. The men followed her, abandoning the boat which, despite considerable swearing from the leader of the ruffians, quickly roared off. The six men studied Tessa and cast a dismissive eye in Flood's direction.

"I'm a Peacekeeper and you're trespassing," announced Tessa. "Drop your weapons and surrender. You have been warned."

"You're as good as dead, whore," rasped the leader. On his signal, the men followed him down the jetty. "Standard triple-twos, boys," he ordered. "This won't take long."

Tessa drew her swords. Both started ringing loudly, until she flicked her wrists to silence them. The thugs responded by drawing their weapons, but neither side made any attempt to attack the other. The six men continued to advance, splitting into two columns of three, one on each edge of the jetty. Apart from the gentle lapping of the water, the only sound was the rhythmic tread of their feet on the concrete quayside.

When they stopped, the closest pair was directly to Tessa's left and right; another was some eight feet in front of her, while the final pair with the leader was the same distance behind her. She took three deep cleansing breaths and raised her weapons. The men also readied themselves and an expectant hush fell.

Suddenly, Tessa darted forward into the middle of four assailants. But with her final steps, she veered towards the man on her left as the other three closed around her, effectively blocking the other two from approaching. She twisted round to her left, lashing out with both her swords at full reach. She caught the man now on her right across the neck, slitting his throat, while the man to her left suffered a fatal wound across his chest. He staggered back and fell off the jetty. Then Tessa quickly pivoted her Amafuji sword round under her arm and thrust backwards. The man creeping up on her suffered a debilitating wound in the abdomen. He dropped his weapon and fell to his knees. She spun round to face the last of the four. The powerful swing of her Amakuni sword forced him to retreat momentarily, but he quickly came back at her. She fended off his vicious stroke and, using her Kimi sword to temporarily obstruct his weapon, stretched forward to thrust her Amafuji blade deep into the man's chest, rupturing his heart.

She turned to face the remaining two fighters, advancing past the thug she'd wounded earlier in the abdomen. He was still on his knees with his sword on the ground beside him. Tessa stopped just in front of the man, but then heard him pick up his weapon. She spun completely round allowing her Kimi sword effortlessly to decapitate him before again facing the final two assailants.

Trying to seize the initiative, they attacked immediately with powerful downwards diagonal strokes from two directions. Tessa raised both her weapons to deflect the blows. Twisting round and moving to her left, she flipped over her Kimi sword and struck that assailant's blade with the back of hers. A tell-tale *chink* confirmed his sword had shattered. Tessa unwound her twist to catch the hapless man with her Amafuji weapon, inflicting a deep wound in his side. Then she brought her sword vertically down on his skull, splitting it completely.

The leader was alone now. He attacked hard, furious and desperate. A quick exchange followed, but as he attempted yet another downwards stroke, she knelt down and raised her Amafuji sword to block his swing. Then she lunged forward with her Kimi sword, piercing his left lung. His energy depleted, she calmly stood up and, with her Amafuji sword, struck his weapon so hard that it flew out of his hand. For a moment she contemplated the deflated ruffian, but then he went for his knife. There was a brief *ping* as her Kimi blade decapitated him. His head rolled along the jetty before finally splashing into the water.

Tessa breathed out nosily. The conflict had taken barely four seconds.

"Welcome back, Nariko," she droned, flicking her swords clean and re-sheathing them.

"Nicely done," observed Flood, wryly.

"I don't believe what my eyes have just seen," Alasdair blurted, joining them.

"But you didn't see anything," responded Tessa seriously. "Nothing at all, Alasdair. And please, don't ever forget that."

"Right... Yes, Ma'am. I understand. But I thought that sort of stuff only happened in films," he gasped.

"I wish. But I regret to admit that it's what I do. I've been doing it for years, and it has cost me dearly. Until now Papa Edinsay has been a sanctuary for me, one of only two places where I felt truly safe. But my cover here has been blown."

"Well," he concluded, "I clearly don't know the half of it, Ma'am, but the people on this island love and respect you. You will always be safe here."

"Thank you, but my presence would only act as an invitation to more thugs like these. I couldn't risk compromising the islanders' safety...

"Anyway, don't worry about the mess, Flood will take care of all that. Just say whatever it was that happened down here, must have taken place while you were back at the Hall. All you know is that it's safe again now. Good-bye, Alasdair."

He peered at her curiously.

"You won't be coming back, will you, Ma'am?"

"No, I'm afraid not. I've already started transferring ownership of Papa Edinsay to a trust for the Island Council to administer. I am leaving in the knowledge that the island is in very capable hands. Hopefully, Nyunt will come back to the house one day. If she does, keep an eye on her for me, will you?"

He nodded.

"Good luck, Alasdair. You'll be fine, and so will Papa Edinsay."

"Ma'am, I understand what you're saying, but if things change, or even if they don't, you'll always be welcome here. Just *haste ye back*, Ma'am."

Tessa walked over to him and gave him a hug. Then she turned to Flood.

"Helicopter to Lossiemouth?" she asked.

He nodded.

An hour later, Tessa was streaking across the sky en route for Japan in an extremely fast, but not terribly comfortable, fighter trainer jet. She was deeply concerned about the security of Matsumoto Castle, and convinced that speed was of the essence. When possible, she called Matsumoto, struggling to make herself heard over the roar of the powerful engines.

"*Anata*, are you all right?" she asked.

"So far, yes. But we have spotted coachloads of ruffians preparing to enter our lands. All the villagers who can fight are ready to honour their obligation, but the castle cannot be secured."

Tessa couldn't think what to say, she was so worried for his safety.

"*Anata*, I'm..."

"Don't worry, *omae*. How long will it be before you get here?"

"Just over six hours to Toyama."

"OK. I will ask Gyobu-san to send a helicopter to meet you and bring you here. He is deploying as many of the Chrysanthemum

Guard as he can spare to help defend the castle."

"That's good. You know we're still reacting?"

"Yes. But now is not the time to attempt to regain the initiative. However, I suspect our opportunity will come soon enough now."

"*Anata*, please be careful."

"Of course. See you soon."

Tessa finished the call and pressed the intercom switch.

"Excuse me, gentlemen, can we go any faster?"

"We'll do our best, madam," replied the pilot.

Feeling powerless, but accepting that there was nothing else she could do now, Tessa tried to rest, not even attempting to phone Japan again. She knew Matsumoto would be busy organising the defences, and possibly already fighting. However, her cramped and noisy conditions conspired to keep her awake and exacerbate her feelings of helplessness…

CHAPTER 28

As the helicopter carrying Tessa neared Matsumoto Castle it was clear that a widespread battle was being fought with numerous fires raging. Efforts to hold back the invaders halfway along the honmaru in line with the torii, seemed to have failed as the defences were breached in several places. However, so far, the Samurai house looked untouched.

"Three minutes," shouted the female co-pilot.

"Drop us behind their lines, near the lower gate," yelled Tessa. "We'll fight our way up from there."

"OK. But we can't land, we'll hover for you to bail," advised the woman, turning back to the controls.

In addition to the helicopter, General Gyobu had sent two Chrysanthemum Guard Ninjas to meet Tessa at Toyama Airport. Their orders were to escort her to the castle and provide support as required. Tessa had immediately taken a liking to them, finding them to be highly trained, intelligent fighters. They were dressed completely in black with a gold chrysanthemum embroidered on the left breast of their tunics. There was a man called Noboru, who was not tall but extremely strong, and a woman called Ayane who was slightly shorter. Both were typically Japanese in terms of looks and attitude. Short black hair, brown eyes and totally focussed on the job in hand. Tessa soon realised that the woman was the senior of the two.

"Do you know how to abseil?" she inquired.

"Not out of a helicopter," admitted Tessa, putting on her gloves. "It seems you have three minutes to teach me."

Ayane nodded, adjusted her two short swords and came over to explain…

"OK?" she queried after some hasty tuition.

Tessa nodded and duly attached herself to one of the three ropes coiled ready for throwing down. The helicopter swooped lower, starting its final approach.

"I will go first," insisted Ayane. "Then you, then Noboru."

"Thirty seconds!" yelled the co-pilot. The door in the side of helicopter glided back and there was a strong gust of rushing wind. Then the helicopter began to hover, seemingly frozen in space.

"When we're down," shouted Tessa to the Ninja. "Keep in formation and follow my lead."

"Go, go, go!" yelled the co-pilot, as the ropes were tossed out of the door.

Ayane stepped calmly out, followed by Tessa who was concentrating so hard on abseiling down correctly she didn't see much else. She landed somewhat ungracefully, but safely nevertheless, and quickly detached herself from the rope. She looked round to find the Ninja waiting patiently to either side of her.

"Cool!" she exclaimed with a big smile. Then she drew both her swords and rushed up the short flight of stairs to the honmaru. A few of the Calver Cats, recognisable by their blue jeans and black leather jackets, had turned back, having been attracted by the downdraft from the helicopter. However, it wasn't long before they were all down as Tessa, Ayane and Noboru bulldozed their way forward.

The battle for the castle had clearly been brutal. There were bodies strewn all around, with people groaning in agony as they attempted to limp or crawl away.

Undaunted, Tessa's elite and fresh team of three fought together extremely effectively. She led them diagonally across the honmaru and up along the perimeter wall towards the Samurai house. They unerringly ploughed a deep furrow through the ranks of the Calver Cats. Frequently defending each other, they moved in synchrony like a scythe cutting tall grass.

At last Tessa caught sight of Matsumoto fighting ferociously. He was wearing his burgundy-coloured fighting tunic with the Matsumoto clan coat-of-arms on its breast. General Gyobu was not far away, also fighting hard. Between them they were holding off a vast force. But then Tessa spotted a small group of Calver Cats creeping up towards the house's courtyard wall. One was carrying what looked like a large black cylinder and had two tanks strapped to his back. Tessa changed direction and headed straight for him, quickly dispatching any Cats that attempted to block her way.

"What the hell do you think you're doing?" she demanded on

reaching the man.

"I'm going to torch the stupid tinderbox!" yelled the man without bothering to turn round to see who had addressed him. "Just watch it burn."

"You moron," hissed Tessa. "That's my home!"

The man spun round with a shocked expression on his face, but barely had time to cower away from Tessa's speeding blade before the *ping* which marked his death. Then there was a gushing sound from the two tubes leading to the tanks which had also been severed. To her dismay, Tessa noticed that there was a flame already alight in the nozzle and that it was about to ignite the fluid gushing down the man's back.

"Run!" she yelled, turning away. There was a bright flash and a loud *whoomph!* She looked back to see a gaping hole in the perimeter wall.

"Oh, bugger!" she groaned, and re-joined the fray.

Together, her team continued to force its way through the enemy lines, cutting down significant numbers of the invading forces. It wasn't long before the tide had turned decidedly in favour of the castle's defenders and Matsumoto and General Gyobu found themselves with no one attacking. They re-sheathed their weapons and sat down philosophically on the steps leading to the courtyard porch, contemplating the extermination of the final attackers. In particular, they watched Tessa and her two colleagues mopping up the flagging resistance.

"Must have had a good teacher," asserted Gyobu, nodding towards her with a smile.

"Nariko was outstanding before she came here," responded Matsumoto, wiping some blood off his tunic. "The three of them make an excellent team."

Gyobu nodded.

Eventually, Tessa joined them.

"There seems to be a very large hole in the wall," remarked Matsumoto in mock surprise.

Tessa laughed, flicking her swords clean and re-sheathing them.

"Well, the castle's needed renovating for years and had you been able to close all the gates…"

"It's good to see you," he purred.

"You too," she replied, sitting next to him. "Are you all right?" He nodded, prompting a smile in response from Tessa. "General," she continued, "thank you for sending Ayane and Noboru. They are both very good, we fought well together."

"I noticed, Nariko-san," acknowledged Gyobu. "But don't think that by winning this battle our work is done. There were never enough of them to seize the castle. I suspect depleting our forces was the only goal of significance here. However, I believe we do now know the purpose of this whole saga."

Just then Ayane arrived. She bowed deeply to the General, who simply nodded in response.

"Take charge, Ayane. Have our people's wounds tended and clean up this mess."

She bowed again and backed away.

General Gyobu took a deep breath.

"A few hours ago the Emperor received a letter purporting to be from the head of the Fujiwara clan, heir to its holdings. Although the document bore no personal signature, it stated a formal claim to Karatsu and the associated surrounding feudal lands as assigned by Shōgun Tokugawa Ieyasu after the Battle of Sekigahara in 1600. This letter not only articulated the legal basis of this claim from that time, it also substantiated the claim's validity past 1870 when it was believed that ownership of all Fujiwara seized lands was transferred to the Emperor. Copies of the original title deeds were enclosed, together with various defective edicts whose drafting, either by accident or design, was at best ambiguous. Naturally, we have investigated the claim and it does appear to be sound. Ownership of all the lands assigned with Karatsu Castle by the Shōgun was indeed never correctly transferred."

"What lands are we talking about?" queried Tessa.

"Well, allowing for hereditary developments since that time, effectively Kyūshū."

"What? All of it? The whole southern island?"

"Essentially, yes. The Emperor and the State did correctly assume legal ownership of some of the Satsuma Domain, to the southwest of Kyūshū, but although it has a coastline, it is otherwise completely surrounded by Fujiwara holdings. Furthermore, since the lands they claim extend all the way to Fukuoka in the north-east, the Fujiwara control the only land route between Honshu and Kyūshū."

Tessa roared with laughter, prompting a scowl of rebuke from Matsumoto.

"How do you think the King of England would feel if somebody proved that he did not own Liverpool, Birmingham and Manchester?" he queried.

"Sorry, I do understand, but it's just... mind-boggling," she answered, having difficulty in stopping laughing. "And I must admit... unexpectedly impressive. So, how important is Kyūshū?"

"Very. It's about fifteen per cent of Japan by area and there are several key industries and ports there, including Nagasaki. A substantial proportion of the trade between South Korea, Taiwan and even America passes through Kyūshū.

"Furthermore, the letter also demands levies for the Emperor's use of these lands since 1870. Suffice to say, the amounts involved are so high that it is debatable whether even Japan can afford to pay, let alone the Emperor."

"Surely the claim can be challenged in the courts?" asked Tessa, finally thinking seriously.

"Possibly; but it would take a long time and we're being told by constitutional lawyers there's a good chance an appeal by us would not be successful."

"But how could something as fantastic as this simply be dropped on the Emperor's desk without anyone knowing it was coming?" she questioned. "The Fujiwara would have needed to confirm that their claim was still legally binding and collect documentary proof."

"Indeed. They recruited people within the land registry, legal section and various other government departments, even on the Emperor's personal staff, as well as..." he hesitated, "within the Chrysanthemum Guard itself. Most of those concerned have fled, presumably to Kyūshū. Anyone who could not leave, for whatever reason, has performed seppuku. I have lost three and the Emperor two. Another two are dead in the land registry and it seems five have gone from within the Special Forces. Actually, not all of the deaths appear to be ritual suicide, so there may have been some targeted cleansing of people who knew too much. Chief Inspector Yamanouchi is investigating."

"Yamanouchi?" asked Tessa.

"Yes. He assumed the role of Chief Inspector of Police some eighteen months ago," added Gyobu. "His second in command is Inspector Maeda, the only son of the deceased Chief Inspector whom you knew."

Tessa pursed her lips. She had acted as Chief Inspector Maeda's Kaishakunin when he'd committed seppuku at Narita Airport. The Inspector had elected to take his own life after it became known that he had been mistaken in trusting the renegade Peacekeeper, Hachiro. He had been exposed as Hachiro Fujiwara, the last surviving member of the Fujiwara clan. Or so it had been thought at the time.

"Have you mentioned me to Maeda?" she asked.

"Yes. I… er… don't think he harbours any bad feeling about what happened. Well, certainly his mother doesn't. I spoke to her several times after her husband…"

Tessa nodded. She wasn't convinced. The young Maeda had good reason to harbour a grudge, even if what happened had not been her fault.

"Anyway," continued the General, "we know from what you were able to tell us, Nariko-san, that delivery of this claim was planned to coincide with an attempt to assassinate the Emperor. However, since you managed to escape, presumably the original plan has had to be adapted…"

Gyobu waited for Tessa to reach the obvious conclusion.

"Oh, no," she murmured.

"Indeed. That is what we believe too. Your daughter, Yoshino, has no doubt just been kidnapped so that she may act as assassin in your place. Remember, Paul did talk of such a possibility. I have already doubled the personal guard on the Emperor and his family. If Yoshino appears anywhere in their vicinity, she will be killed."

Tessa swallowed but tried to remain focussed.

"Hmm. Paul's not signing that letter is probably significant too," she noted. "I've never believed he's bright enough, let alone man enough, to be the leader. And he did use the word 'we', and mention being second in line."

Gyobu grunted in agreement. "It seems highly unlikely that his is the organising mind behind this scheme. The writer of the claim document is certainly adamant that they will have no difficulty whatsoever in authenticating their lineage."

"Everything you've said fits with what I learned and it does explain why Paul is based at Karatsu," Tessa accepted, nodding her thanks to Noboru as he returned all the weapons she had thrown, duly cleaned.

Gyobu nodded.

"Obviously, we are trying to ascertain who his partner might be. But we don't know whether there is one or more of them, or of what genders they are."

"And they've set themselves up in Karatsu Castle?" probed Matsumoto, pensively.

"Yes," confirmed Gyobu, "it was closed to visitors some twelve months ago, purportedly for major historic renovations, though it seems more likely the facility was prepared for occupation. The castle that's there now is a concrete replica built in 1966. The original structure was razed to the ground by the Matsumoto, on the orders of the Emperor Meiji, and the plans destroyed. However, we don't even have the detailed design of the building which was reconstructed any more, since they have either been incinerated or removed as part of the Calver Cats' clean-up. But we do know the renovation budget was substantial, with the entire cost being born by local businesses. It seems this plan has been in the making for a long time."

"So the castle could be very strong and very well defended?" queried Tessa.

"Highly likely, but a full military assault is out of the question anyway; such an action would generate an enormous media outcry. For all we know, Unified Korea and China might well support the Fujiwara demanding to be heard in the UNWP, and don't forget, there are no individual powers of veto any more."

"Yes, but the partitioning of Japan wouldn't exactly be an easy pill for many countries to swallow," argued Tessa. "They might find they have similar problems – China with Tibet for example. But surely, if the lands were granted by Tokugawa Ieyasu, they can simply be removed now by the legal authority entitled to act in the Shōgun's name, presumably the Emperor?"

"It's debatable," confessed the General. "Not only were the laws affecting land forfeiture not correctly applied to Karatsu, but, by a similar omission, the Emperor was not granted clear authority to take them back at a later date. After all, no one thought such powers would ever be required. Either way, it would be absolute chaos while the legal quagmire was being addressed. And even if the lands were deemed to be forfeit now, the usage levies might still endure."

"So," probed Matsumoto, "the Fujiwara claim to ownership originates from the early-1600s?"

"Yes," acknowledged Gyobu. "That's when the Shōgun originally granted the lands, and then after the Meiji Restoration they were not correctly transferred as intended."

"But if current laws don't apply to those lands, does that mean the old laws still do?" ventured Matsumoto, looking up hopefully.

"It would seem so," replied Gyobu with a smile, "or at least those that are still on the statute books. And that does indeed present another possibility, which is maybe what they were worried about all along... Theoretically, we have two courses of action. We could negotiate, or," he paused and took a deep breath, "we could seek a solution permitted under the relevant old laws. If we were to succeed, we could use the new ownership to rescind all the Fujiwara claims."

"Am I missing something here?" asked Tessa, nonplussed.

"The Fujiwara," explained Matsumoto "will have realised that we are unlikely to negotiate. So, they will have concluded that our only other course of action is to try to win control of the lands by the sword, ensuring we do so legally according to the surviving remnants of old law which apply to such takeovers. They attacked here simply to weaken us before we could take such a step. However, they could be planning to return later and use the very same old laws to seize Matsumoto Castle."

"OK. But you said only someone from the League's families who did not bear the mark of the chrysanthemum would be permitted to kill a Fujiwara and claim their lands. If they didn't know we are married, that would exclude me and Yoshino in their minds, which only leaves..."

"Yes, which is why Seiji was brought up in secret by the Hayasaka. Few apart from them, us and the General know he is my son. But maybe it has leaked out. After all, we never thought to consider that while you were hypnotised, you might have been asked if such a

303

person existed."

"Hmm. All right," concluded Tessa. "So we need to make sure Seiji is safe and get him to the right place at the right time," Matsumoto nodded tentatively and exchanged looks with Gyobu. "But that still doesn't really explain why they wanted me so badly."

"Well, they probably weren't sure about you and Nyunt, and maybe that worried them. They'll have known that you're the first non-Japanese person to be awarded membership of the Chrysanthemum Guard, and that Nyunt is not ungifted with the sword and yet does not bear the mark. Also, as we know, they want your Amafuji weapon."

"Yes, but do you really believe they were worried that Yoshino might be qualified to take back their lands?"

"Possibly," continued the General. "They certainly seem to have taken her out of the frame; do you believe she's reliable at the moment?"

Tessa fell silent.

"Assuming, as I think is likely," interjected Matsumoto, "they don't know that we are married, their interest in you was probably only founded on the fact that you've killed a lot of their clan and possess the only Amafuji blade made for a Fujiwara. Remember, you destroyed their original family sword when you fought with Ryuu Fujiwara in Germany, and Hachiro's when you killed him here. But his sword was one of a pair commissioned by Bryani, and you still carry that blade. It would be invaluable to them. Probably the icing on the cake was to have you assassinate the Emperor and help bring down the League, not least since it may represent the only viable means of legally taking Karatsu by force. But what they don't know is that since we are married, and as you no longer bear the chrysanthemum mark, you are also entitled to kill the Fujiwara and claim their lands."

Tessa glanced at Gyobu for confirmation.

"I believe that is correct," he admitted.

"Hmm," countered Tessa. "But if the Fujiwara have been planning this since before the castle was re-built in 1966, they'll be ready and waiting. Their forces could be massive."

"According to the satellite images we have, they have marshalled something sizeable, but it's not massive, and most of it is dispersed throughout the town."

"So how many of the Guard remain available for action?" asked

Matsumoto.

"Perhaps twenty – all well-equipped and highly skilled. It is a good foundation but hardly sufficient to retake Karatsu. We have no choice but to involve Japan's Police and Special Forces."

"And presumably," mused Tessa, "that will also have been considered, as will the fact that this needs to be done before the world wakes up to the media reporting Japan's political and financial disintegration?"

Gyobu nodded.

"Indeed. Effectively we have until dawn."

"In which case," said Matsumoto, standing up, "we have no time to waste. We should contact Yamanouchi and plan our attack."

"Let's find out whether there have been any developments back in the UK first," countered Tessa pensively. She took out her *cbc*. "Flood, it's Nariko... Yes, fine, thanks. Is everything quiet at your end now?... Good, and Potter?... OK. Thanks... Yes, you can get back to sleep now. Sorry...

"Potter is at Karatsu," she reported. "But they've lost track of Nyunt – which all fits." Neither Matsumoto nor Gyobu reacted visibly to this. "OK. But isn't it risky using the Police and Special Forces; we don't know how many of them have been recruited? The Fujiwara cleansing operation is bound to have left some trustworthy spies."

"I accept that, but we don't have any choice. There isn't time to involve another country," said Gyobu, "and it would be difficult anyway, given the delicacy of the situation."

"Fine, I wish you every success then. I'll just wait here."

Gyobu looked at her, dumbfounded.

"But..."

"I'm sorry. I became hemmed in like this in Burma, and everything is still happening according to their plan. They want me there and I cannot be relied upon." Tessa described what had happened in London and how she had been momentarily hypnotised even though Yoshino had been the intended target. "But that's not really a problem for you as Seiji can still do the honours, can't he?"

"Unfortunately not," replied Gyobu as Matsumoto looked uncharacteristically sheepish. "He was assigned elsewhere before all this blew up and we don't expect to be able to get him back in time. I'm afraid it will have to be you, Nariko-san."

"No," reiterated Tessa, becoming agitated. "Everything points to them expecting precisely that, and if I lose control, all your plans could fall apart. Who knows what I might do if their hypnotism overcomes my defences. No, I should just stay here; I can be your back-up plan. Send a fast jet for Seiji. I was able to get here, wasn't I?"

"I'm sorry, Nariko-san," sighed Gyobu, "but that is simply not possible."

Tessa looked at each of them in turn, pursed her lips, but said nothing. Instead she stood up and walked to the hole in the perimeter wall; she noticed Ayane watching as Matsumoto joined her.

"Nariko-san, it is important that you are there. We must try to finish it tonight... And I believe we can."

"They only want you dead," replied Tessa bitterly. "The fate they have planned for me is far worse. We could end up fighting each other."

"I know, but there is Nyunt to consider and the Professor has helped..."

"She's tried, that's all. When are people going to stop asking me to do their dirty work for them?"

Matsumoto didn't reply.

"It's just not fair," moaned Tessa.

"I agree," he commiserated.

"I'm scared, *anata*," she confessed, looking down.

He placed his hands on her shoulders and gently turned her to face him.

"So am I, *omae*. So am I," he admitted. She gazed into his eyes, and found a hardness there she had never encountered before. "Finally, the time has come and the stakes are incredibly high, for all of us... But I will be there too, and I promise I will do everything in my power to ensure no harm comes to you."

Tessa nodded. He smiled sadly and followed her as she re-joined the General.

"So be it," Tessa confirmed. "I suggest you tell Yamanouchi that only a handful of the Chrysanthemum Guard remains; keep the others on close stand-by."

"I agree. Let's go," replied Gyobu, standing and gesturing for Ayane to accompany them.

CHAPTER 29

As far as Tessa was concerned, the journey to Tokyo passed far too quickly. It seemed as though they'd barely taken off when she realised they were zooming over the Emperor's palace and swooping down into the Chrysanthemum Guard compound. As they descended, she noticed an official-looking limousine approaching in the distance. It was followed by an articulated truck carrying an unmarked black container. She felt a creeping sense of menace emanating from it; she doubted she'd ever be able to look at a shipping container again without feeling uneasy.

The helicopter landed and the three of them walked to the main building. Once inside, Gyobu and Matsumoto headed for the stairs with an uncharacteristic air of urgency. Tessa lagged behind, surprised to see in the polished marble walls, the reflection of the limousine gliding to a halt behind them. But Gyobu and Matsumoto were clearly in a hurry, so she had to rush in order to catch up with them.

The General led the way to his suite of rooms on the third floor. It turned out to be completely different from what Tessa had been expecting. True, his office was certainly sumptuous and to an extent traditionally furnished, but it was also modern, functional and bristling with technology. He gestured for them both to sit at his meeting table.

"We will complete our preparations here," he ordered. "Yamanouchi has already been told to expect us at Special Forces Headquarters."

Some green tea arrived, together with various satellite images of Karatsu Castle, the town and surrounding countryside. They had been discussing them for a few minutes when Gyobu's phone rang. He took it at his desk.

"Hmm. Minister Miyazaki is here. He would like me to debrief him concerning our plans. I will be back shortly."

He bowed and left Tessa and Matsumoto to continue studying the maps. Gyobu came back after ten minutes and looked at Tessa.

"The Minister is about to leave, but wondered if it would be convenient for you to speak with him about what you heard concerning his daughter."

"Of course," replied Tessa, and after declining the offer of a guide, preferring to be alone for a while, took directions and went in search of the conference room.

Eventually, she found the door she was after, knocked and went in. A blinding white light met her eyes...

"OK?" queried Matsumoto as she returned, gesturing absentmindedly towards a chair next to him.

"Yes, fine."

She smiled to see fresh tunics for them, lying neatly folded on the table. Matsumoto's was burgundy while Gyobu's was black – both had been folded to display the gold motifs on the left breast. She had already changed into a clean Kevlar tunic back at the castle.

"So, how far have you got?" she inquired, continuing before they responded, "I'd be inclined to try and rescue Potter and Nyunt first. If we don't get them out, they'll only be used as bargaining chips against us."

"Absolutely," affirmed Gyobu. "We'd reached the same conclusion. However, we will need to be prepared for all eventualities. On finding either or both of them, it may not be possible to liberate them safely. And, we shouldn't ignore the possibility that Yoshino might... er... resist."

"In that case the priority must be to save Potter," responded Tessa quickly. "Yoshino will have to be extricated as quickly as possible thereafter."

Gyobu looked as though he was about to say something more, but Matsumoto's glare stopped him in his tracks. He simply shrugged.

"We thought the attack should take place in three phases. First, you should make a stealth approach on the castle along the coast from the north-west – aimed primarily at freeing Potter... and Yoshino, naturally. Secondly, two larger forces will approach simultaneously from the south-west and the east. Their task will be to neutralise any Fujiwara or Calver Cat resistance in the town and, once that has been done, to assist with taking the castle. After our main forces have made contact with the enemy, Matsumoto and I will make a low-profile entry from the west to help provide intelligence on the disposition of any residual hostile forces. Of necessity, your stealth team will have to be small. We thought that it should perhaps comprise just you and Ayane. What do you think?"

Tessa nodded, still wishing that she wasn't even here.

The General, pointed to the map with his index finger. "We can get you both *here* unnoticed by helicopter and then Ayane can drive you, hopefully, to *here*." He indicated a car park not far from the main footpath to the castle. "You will need to pose as locals to pass through the Calver Cats' checkpoints. But once you have been dropped off, you will be able to arm and proceed up to the honmaru. Ayane will then join and take charge of our reserve forces to the south; as agreed, we won't tell anyone of these resources. Noboru will lead the south-western faction, and Inspector Maeda the eastern."

Tessa nodded unenthusiastically. "Sounds reasonable to me."

There was a knock at the door and Ayane entered carrying three microphone headsets.

"Excellent," continued the General. "These headsets can be tuned to different frequencies by twisting this knob on the right. Position two, which is currently selected on all of them, gives access to the Chrysanthemum Guard frequencies. These are encrypted and not available to those who do not have appropriately enabled headsets. Position one gives access to the Special Forces frequencies, and then there's the *off* position. However, these particular headsets are also able to block out external sounds, but only if the switch is set to minus one, if you will, in which case a noise-canceller is activated and nothing will be audible, not even external sounds. OK?"

Tessa and Matsumoto nodded and each took a headset.

"OK," stated Gyobu, authoritatively. "Let's go and tell Yamanouchi what we want his people to do..."

It wasn't far to the Special Forces Headquarters building and their limousine was soon entering the secure underground car park beneath the twenty-three-storey building. It had been a long time since Tessa was last there, but it didn't seem to have changed much.

Gyobu led them into the office which had once belonged to Chief Inspector Maeda. Tessa looked round, full of sad reminiscences. It all seemed so familiar; the only substantive alteration was the addition of numerous vertical cables visible through the windows. They resembled decorative detailing, but Tessa knew they generated a dampening field which would ensure unsanctioned electronic signals could neither enter nor leave the building. The equivalent safeguards had been applied rather more discreetly at the Chrysanthemum Guard compound, but presumably the same budget was not available here.

Tessa couldn't help reliving the last occasion she'd visited this place. She'd met the Peacekeeper Hachiro and had fought side by side with him at Kawasaki-Ku. However, the man she'd seen as a hero then had subsequently betrayed the Chief Inspector Maeda's trust which had resulted in his ritual suicide.

She snapped back to the present as a young man stood up from behind the expensive black metal and beech wood desk. He was taller than Tessa would have expected, but otherwise looked like an archetypal, fit, young Japanese man; except for his hair. It was black but oddly styled; cut very short except for a sausage of much longer hair starting at the crown of his head and extending down to the nape of his neck. That section had been greased and tied into a man bun at the back, giving him an almost Hispanic look. Tessa was surprised that such a peculiar combination of looks could make him appear handsome to her, since he was definitely not what she would have described as her type. His deep brown eyes met her inquisitive gaze, without blinking.

He smiled and bowed deeply.

"It is a shame we are meeting in such strained circumstances," he proffered after greetings had been exchanged. Gyobu accepted this by waving a hand dismissively. Then, as the three of them sat down at the meeting table, Yamanouchi went round closing all the blinds, obscuring both the external windows and the internal glass partitions.

"Yamanouchi-san, I'm afraid we don't have time for niceties, so I will just wade in." The General spread the map he had brought with him across the table. Yamanouchi peered at it with interest, occasionally frowning in surprise. "I think you should have Inspector Maeda join us," suggested Gyobu. "We have work for him tonight too and it will save time if we only have to go through this once."

"That would be better," concurred Yamanouchi. "Perhaps Mizoguchi should join us also?"

Gyobu nodded and Yamanouchi went outside to summon them both. Two minutes later, another young man entered. He was tall and thin, stylishly dressed, with conventional short black hair, sensitive deep brown eyes and a friendly smile. Tessa recognised his facial features immediately, even his walk; they were the spitting image of his father's.

Although she felt hesitant about greeting the son of the man she had aided to his death, she nevertheless smiled warmly at him. He bowed deeply to her, clearly nervous. If Gyobu noticed the awkwardness of this exchange, he didn't intend to let it derail proceedings. Finally, a sinewy, strong-looking woman entered. She had long black hair tied at the back in a long plait, and was dressed in a well-tailored grey trouser suit with a light blue silk blouse. The woman reminded Tessa of someone she'd met once, and it troubled her that she couldn't place her. More greetings were exchanged and additional chairs pulled up to the conference table.

"Ladies and gentlemen," announced Gyobu confidently, "the task we have before us is highly confidential and will need to stay secret indefinitely. If any of you have qualms about participating in an operation with conditions such as these, say so now." He stared round inquisitorially, but nobody said a word. "Good. Tonight we travel to Kyūshū where we will use force to lay siege to and recover Karatsu Castle and town. Both have been seized by the Calver Cats led by at least two surviving members of the Fujiwara clan. I do not intend to go into the reasons why we need to do this tonight, but suffice to say, time is of the essence and this is a matter of utmost importance to the integrity and security of Japan.

"The plan of attack is as follows: Nariko will pursue a stealth approach on the castle from the north-west – aimed primarily at freeing two hostages, the Head of UK Special Forces and… another Peacekeeper. She will be driven in by Ayane, one of my people, but will endeavour to breach the castle's defences on her own in a low-profile surprise attack. At the same time, two larger forces will approach the castle in a pincer action through the town, subduing resistance as it arises. The first force will attack from the south-west. It will be led by Ayane as soon as she can join it. However, Mizoguchi, since you are with us, I suggest you lead this force until Ayane is able to take over." The sinewy woman bowed. "The other force will approach from the east. It will be led by Noboru, another of my people, seconded by Inspector Maeda." Here Maeda bowed, and muttered a guttural affirmation. Gyobu accepted this with a perfunctory nod, quickly returning his attention to the map.

Tessa, meanwhile, was having difficulty repressing her conviction that all this felt very wrong. She was sure something fundamental didn't stack up, but couldn't pinpoint what exactly; which she found extremely frustrating. However, had anyone asked, she would have said she didn't just feel afraid now, she was downright terrified.

"...As I said," continued the General, "these two forces will neutralise the Calver Cats in the town and then proceed to the castle, providing support there as required. Unfortunately, due to an earlier action this evening, there are only a few of the Chrysanthemum Guard available so they will be shared equally between the two main forces. Finally, Matsumoto and I will make another stealth approach from the west as soon as concerted resistance is met by our main forces, providing intelligence concerning the disposition of any other Calver Cats fighters – Yamanouchi-san, you should join us to assist with command and control. According to our intelligence there are not many Cats in the area through which the three of us will be approaching, so it should be possible to make speedy progress to the castle and assist Nariko. Overall, our forces should be virtually equal in terms of number but superior with regards to equipment and training. However, this does not mean the resistance should be underestimated; in fact, quite the opposite. After the main action is complete, we will leave it to the Prefectural Police to round up any strays.

"Yamanouchi-san, I have detailed orders for your people here," added the General, placing a number of sheets of printed text, maps and diagrams on the table.

"That seems clear enough," he acknowledged, taking the documents. "As you know, I have thirty eight people. Would you like them divided equally between the two main forces?"

"Yes, I think so," replied Gyobu, glancing at Matsumoto, who nodded. "Any questions?"

"Not from me," said Yamanouchi. He glanced at Mizoguchi, who simply shook her head.

"Nor me," added Maeda.

"Nariko?" asked Matsumoto, gently. She also shook her head.

"Good, then we're finished here," confirmed the General. "So, Yamanouchi, I would like to come with you to address your men. Matsumoto-san, perhaps you would care to accompany us?"

He nodded and glanced at Tessa.

"I'll just wait here," she mumbled offhandedly.

"My office is at your disposal," offered Yamanouchi graciously.

Everyone else left and Tessa moved to a comfortable armchair, leaned back and relaxed, soon closing her eyes. Sometime afterwards, she felt a draught, suggesting that the door had been opened. She looked up to find Inspector Maeda had come in.

"My apologies," he said, "I did not wish to disturb your meditation, but I was wondering…"

"Of course," replied Tessa, gesturing with her hand. "Please, sit down. We *should* talk."

He nodded and sat opposite her.

"Regrettably, we do not have much time," started the young man, "but maybe I won't get another opportunity to mention this. You see, for many years, my mother has wanted to thank you. Apparently, my father spoke of you often so she knows how well you got on together and how difficult it must have been for you to…"

"Young Maeda-san," replied Tessa, her voice overflowing with emotion, "your father and I were always close friends. From the moment we met to the moment he passed, we liked and respected each other. I have only ever thought of him with the highest esteem. Your mother has nothing to thank me for. I only did my duty, and it was an honour to serve your father in his final request. My only regret is the nature of that request. However, I suppose I should not have been surprised to be asked that by a man as decent and moral as your father… Please return your mother's best wishes with my heartfelt thanks and appreciation. It is a privilege for me to meet the son of my dear friend. I am sure he would be very proud of you."

Maeda bowed and stood up.

"Thank you. I will do that if circumstances permit. However, we both know that every battle is a new one. Whatever we achieved before today is no longer important, it is what we do tonight which counts. It is all too easy for life simply to be snuffed out." He snapped his fingers.

Tessa paused and then smiled; for an instant the sound had unsettled her.

"That is true. But we should never go into battle expecting the worst. A defeated mind beckons the body to join it. That is a foolish and wasteful way in which to allow one's destiny to be determined. Personally, I am delighted to see you are following in your father's footsteps, and wish you every success. However, first let us both focus on returning tomorrow as victors." She stood up and bowed to him. "*Sayonara*, Maeda-san."

"*Domo arigato gozaimasu*, Nariko-san. *Sayonara*."

He bowed deeply three times and reversed out of the office.

Tessa sighed and sat back down. Once more she leaned back and closed her eyes, trying to calm her thoughts and marshal her strength for the fight ahead.

Again she noticed a breeze, followed by a slight rustling noise, reminiscent of papers swishing around. She wearily opened her eyes, and as the mistiness cleared General Gyobu addressed her.

"When you are alone ascending the hill to Karatsu Castle I would like you to discard your headset. That way, no unwanted sounds can be transmitted over them. Do you understand?"

"Yes."

"Good. Let's keep this a secret between us two."

"OK."

"I will join you there as soon as I am able. You may close your eyes again now..."

Tessa wasn't sure how long it was before Matsumoto returned with the General.

"That seemed to go on for much longer than necessary," complained Matsumoto, glancing at Tessa.

"Nariko-san, are you ready?" asked Gyobu.

"Yes," she said, taking a deep breath and getting to her feet.

"Good. Ayane is waiting for you on the rooftop helipad."

As they walked up the stairs, Matsumoto held Tessa back for a moment.

"You will be careful, won't you?"

"I'll certainly try. After all, I only have a castle to..."

"And you haven't had any visions of Angkor Wat or Beng Mealea?"

"No," she replied, concerned that he'd asked.

"Good. Then let battle commence."

The helicopter travelled at high speed and Tessa was soon gazing into Fukuoka as they flew southwest. They were so low that she could even see Shinkansen trains entering and leaving Hikata station.

Soon, they were swooping down in stealth mode to land in a field near Hizenmachi Kirigo, a sleepy little village some ten miles from Karatsu. A small hybrid car was waiting there for them to use. It was several years old and unremarkable; exactly what was required to remain low-profile.

Except for a couple of knives each, Tessa and Ayane wrapped their weapons in blankets and stowed them behind the front seats. They put on some casual clothes over their tunics, and secreted their knives where they could reach them quickly. After exchanging glances to confirm each other's readiness, they set off. Not a word was said during the uneventful twenty-five-minute drive. However, as they pulled off the highway into the suburbs, it was clear that something was wrong. Instead of the bustling activity they had been told to expect in night-time Karatsu, the streets were deserted. All the bars and restaurants they passed appeared to have been closed. Even the Pachinko halls were locked up with none of their usually exuberant lighting on.

"They know we're coming," noted Tessa wearily.

"It looks that way," agreed Ayane. "Roadblock ahead."

They both checked their knives as their car stopped in front of two trucks which had been parked so as nearly to block the road. A number of men who were milling around surrounded their vehicle. Ayane lowered her window.

"Where are you going?" demanded one of the men. "Don't you know there's a curfew?"

"No, we didn't, sir," she replied, obsequiously. "A curfew because of what?"

"I asked where you're going?" he insisted, ignoring her question.

"We're on holiday. We're going to find a Ryokan and stay for a couple of nights. Have you any suggestions as to where we might try?"

"What do you think I am, your personal reservations service?"

"Well, I just thought…"

"Women shouldn't think."

One of his colleagues came round to Tessa's side and stared in at her through the closed window. Then another came over to the man talking to Ayane and whispered something in his ear. He sniffed.

"OK. You can go," he said dismissively, and walked away.

As the car started moving, Tessa looked at Ayane. She shrugged. Words weren't necessary. They both felt they'd been recognised and were simply being drawn further into some sort of a trap.

They didn't stop again until Ayane brought the car to a standstill in the small car park near the coastal path which led up to the castle. They both got out, looking round on high alert. But there was no one to be seen and the only noises were the sounds of waves lapping up against the nearby sea defences and muted music from a distant television. Tessa shed her casual clothes, donned her swords, knives and shuriken, and then put on her headset. Then she carefully clipped to her belt the two pocketed black velvet bag which she had declined to discuss with anyone. Ayane looked questioningly at it – she was intrigued to know what was inside.

"Special weapons," proffered Tessa, not wishing to be drawn. "Be careful, Ayane."

"Always," she replied, grinning. "I will try to get as close as I can to my forces by car. However, if our suspicions prove correct, it will not be long before I am forced to travel on foot. *Sayonara*, Nariko-san."

They bowed to one another and Tessa watched the car start moving; slowly at first, but soon gathering speed. Then she set off along the path into the darkness. To her left she could see white plumes from the breaking sea while to her right stood a row of houses, barely more than large beach huts. None of them had lights on although Tessa was convinced many were occupied. Soon the sight of the castle rampart looming dark in the distance demanded her attention. There were no lights illuminating the donjon; large and foreboding it stood silhouetted ominously against the star-spangled sky.

It took her another five minutes to reach the lower slopes of the hill on which the rampart stood. She stopped to listen and look around. To her left, she could make out the road which skirted the steep promontory as it jutted out into the sea, while to her right it led back into town. Diagonally opposite was one of the three tracks which lead up to the castle. Tessa walked over to it. She suspected she would be able to continue unopposed until at least halfway up, where this smaller path joined the main track. She set off at a brisk pace, keen to end the prelude to what she predicted would be a challenging night.

After a while, she again stood still and listened. She couldn't hear anyone, so she decided that this was as good a place as any to complete her final preparations. She removed her headset, fondling the device in her hand, wondering why the General would have wanted her not to have it. But then she shrugged and placed it on a large rock. Then she threw away her black velvet bag and slid the missiles into her belt. Finally, she checked all her other weapons and set off once more…

Meanwhile, as the second helicopter passed over Fukuoka, Gyobu showed Matsumoto the tablet computer on which he was monitoring all the status reports. Ayane had submitted two. The first simply saying that *the package* had been delivered safely. The second stated that she had been stopped and forced to fight her way through a roadblock, but that she was now making good progress and expected to join her force on schedule.

Matsumoto nodded.

Then Gyobu pointed to a red flashing headset symbol. The same icon by his and Matsumoto's names remained green. Matsumoto frowned and looked at his watch, as if trying to speed up time. Gyobu placed a reassuring hand on his arm.

"My friend, I am sorry." Then he tapped his headset. "Ayane, Noboru, confirm encryption." Both responded affirmatively. "New order. Prepare for Nariko termination. Repeat, Nariko termination – alert. Await final sanction. Confirm…"

CHAPTER 30

Finally, Tessa's path joined the main access route up. It was much wider than she'd expected and was metalled too, making it more of a narrow roadway than a track. As such, it was uncomfortably exposed. Nevertheless, she turned onto it and moved quickly upwards, darting from shadow to shadow.

As she approached the rampart, Tessa peered round a corner to find a solitary guard-post. The three guards there barely slowed her progress; she simply threw two shuriken and a knife to dispatch them. However, she was encouraged to have met someone who had wanted to block her path, and hoped that it meant her visit wasn't anticipated after all.

She next stopped just short of the honmaru, which lay barely thirty feet above her. Still in complete darkness, the castle donjon towered above her. She shook her head despondently and checked her weapons yet again – she sincerely hoped this would be a fair fight. But she couldn't suppress her increasing sense of uneasiness, and the nagging suspicion that she was already lost.

The road turned sharply to the right and then the left, finally cutting back on itself before stopping abruptly by some stone steps leading up. Reaching the top of these, Tessa found the honmaru was much larger than she'd expected, although much smaller than that of Matsumoto Castle. The donjon stood diagonally opposite her on the left, while flat gravelled ground extended out towards the sea to her right. Near the far end, illuminated in the moonlight, she saw Potter and Nyunt standing tied to wooden stakes. She took a deep breath and set off silently towards them. Potter saw her instantly and gave a barely discernible smile. But Nyunt didn't react at all. She seemed oblivious to everything, her eyes unfocused with large dilated pupils.

Tessa was barely five yards away from them when a familiar voice called out.

"One more step and they're dead."

There was a loud *clunk* and powerful floodlights were switched on, illuminating both the donjon and the honmaru with a cold, bright white light. Tessa stopped and smiled at Potter, whose expression had turned into one of furious defiance.

"I was beginning to think you'd chicken out," droned the hateful voice. "I should have had more faith."

"Hello, Paul. I promised I'd come for you."

Tessa turned to face him. He was standing in front of a group of eleven men. Surprisingly few in the circumstances, she thought. As he approached her, Tessa studied his back-up. They were all heavily armed, but she couldn't see any guns. Nevertheless, they were blocking her way back down. However, what annoyed her the most was that Paul was wearing Nyunt's Amakuni sword on his belt.

"Well, look who we have here," he mocked, addressing his men. "The arrogant, self-centred Nariko, greatest Peacekeeper of modern times. Hah! Now she's delivering herself to us precisely as scheduled and, with her Amafuji sword too... Remember that whore's movie, boys? Is it just me, or does she look less feminine with her clothes on?"

Tessa smiled grimly, waiting for the cackles of appreciative laughter to die down.

"You should learn to keep your mouth shut, Paul. I was thinking how much more manly you look with your clothes on."

Another ripple of laughter went round. He seemed irritated by it.

"We both know you've never seen me without my clothes on."

"Is that really what you want them to believe? How's the nose, by the way? It doesn't look quite straight to me."

"I've wiped that cocky grin off your face before," he hissed. "I'm looking forward to doing it again. Hasn't anyone told you yet that your conditioning is complete? Perhaps you'd care to give us an impromptu exhibition of your voracious sexual appetite."

As the men jeered and made obscene gestures, Tessa wondered what Paul had meant. Surely that couldn't be possible? After all, the pump had been delivering lower doses than intended and she had interrupted the programme by escaping.

"Paul, let me tell you what's really going to happen here tonight," insisted Tessa, trying to calm her own fears. "First, I'm going to take back that sword of mine which I lent you at Waley; and, while I'm at it, Nyunt's too. Then I'm going to free my daughter and my friend, and after that I will turn my attention to you and any of your friends who don't have sufficient common-sense to surrender themselves to the police in town."

"You think? Well, I tell you what, before I demonstrate how wrong you are, I *will* let you have a crack at getting your sword back… provided you don't use the Amafuji weapon to do it. Agreed?"

"You always want to start me off at a disadvantage, don't you, Paul? Ever wondered why? Anyway, on the off-chance it might reduce the amount of drivel I have to listen to from you, I accept. But you're too much of a coward to do your own fighting, aren't you? So who'll I be up against?"

"I have no problem admitting I am not such a good swordsman as you. But Tony is, and that's why he's your opponent. However, not only is he our best swordsman, he's already pissed off with you for killing his brother Jack. So don't expect him just to give it to you."

A burly man stepped forward.

"My," exclaimed Tessa, grinning, "you even look like Jack. He died with a surprised expression on his face and a blade through his heart. Is that a family tradition?"

"Bitch!" he yelled, drawing the sword which she recognised only too well as the one she'd taken with her to Waley.

He advanced to within six feet of her, fondling the weapon confidently in both hands.

"Are you ready?" asked Tessa with a sweet smile.

He nodded, clearly puzzled that she hadn't even bothered to draw her own weapon.

"Well, go for it then," she urged.

He tensed, raised the weapon and began his attacking stroke. Tessa responded by moving her right arm up like lightning – her sword sheath shot down and the hilt was catapulted into her waiting hand. As she swung the weapon quickly over her shoulder, the blade started ringing enthusiastically. Mid-flight, she flipped it over. With a brief *whoosh*, she brought it down in a diagonal stroke. The blade struck Tony's sword some nine inches from the tip and passed completely through, making only a brief *chink* sound. Then she swished her sword backwards and forwards, *chink, chink, chink*, every time closer to the hilt of Tony's weapon. In a fraction of a second, she had cut through her opponent's blade four times, leaving barely six inches. Dumbfounded, he stood rooted to the spot. Tessa winked at him and calmly thrust her sword deep into his chest, straight through the heart. As he keeled over backwards, Tessa histrionically leaned forward to study his face.

"Yep, that's the same expression, all right. They must have been brothers... Sorry, about the sword, Kono-san."

Potter roared with laughter.

"Hah! I should have known. You gave them that copy sword I examined once, and they didn't even know!"

"You killed him," admitted Paul, clearly surprised.

"Er... Yes, Paul," replied Tessa. "That's what happens to someone who takes on a Peacekeeper."

"But you weren't meant to kill him."

Tessa shrugged. It seemed that, for whatever reason, the night's proceedings had just shifted in her favour. Encouraged, she raised her voice and addressed the group of ruffians.

"If you guys want to live, you should leave now. There are Police in town, where your colleagues have already either surrendered or died. This is your chance to choose. However, if you stay here, I promise you will not live to see another dawn. You have been warned."

She turned and started walking back to Potter.

"Thanks for delivering both your real swords now," sneered Paul in a completely different tone. Then he clapped his hands twice and muttered, "Shōgunate restored."

Tessa stopped moving and looked down. She had in fact hoped turning her back on him would prompt Paul to try and hypnotise her and had been preparing by repeatedly saying *Angkor Wat, Angkor Wat* in her mind. For a moment his words seemed to echo in her right ear, but she found it surprisingly easy to resist his attack.

"Now, that's what I like to see... obedient at last," boasted Paul. "Nariko, I command you to kill Potter and Nyunt. They've served their purpose now that we have you again."

Tessa looked up. Potter, defenceless, with his hands tied behind his back, was staring at her with a very worried expression on his face.

She started towards him, purposefully drawing the sintered knife he had given her.

"Nariko! You mustn't do this," he implored. "Paul's hypnotised you. I am your friend, Nyunt is your daughter. Please…"

However, when she was only three feet away, and sure no one else could see, Tessa winked at him.

"Er… Don't do this, Nariko, please. You should not do what he says!"

Brandishing her knife, Tessa stepped behind him, and, making sure that Paul could not see her face, whispered urgently.

"When I say, collect Nyunt and carry her over the fence behind you. It's a steep grass slope down to the road, but at the bottom you'll find help waiting."

Tessa couldn't believe what she'd just said. How did she know that?

"Please, don't!" pleaded Potter; then continuing more quietly. "But I have a pump now. They can use it to kill me."

"…Not a problem, they have a van with a Faraday cage." Again Tessa was bemused. She had no idea where any of this stuff was coming from; she was simply hearing the words in her head. "Now, die convincingly."

"Tessa…," he started, but finished with a blood-curdling cry, prompted by her digging the hilt of the knife hard into his back. She fully intended to hurt him a little since she thought it would enable him to be more persuasive, certainly the noise he made sounded convincing to her. His eyes opened wide with a shocked expression, and then his head drooped. Tessa cut his bonds, allowing his body to collapse limply to the ground.

"Well done, Nariko. Now the other one."

Acting like an automaton, she walked over to Nyunt. She stopped in front of her daughter and gazed into her eyes. Tessa could imagine all too well why the girl wore that vacant dazed expression. She brandished the knife in her right hand, as though seeking the ideal place on Nyunt's torso in which to plunge it.

"Don't worry, darling," said Tessa softly. "I will take care of you." As a glimmer of recognition crossed Nyunt's face, Tessa stretched out her left hand between them. First clenched, then opened vertically, then she clenched it again and quickly opened it with the palm downwards.

Finally, she uttered. "*Bang! Bang!* Yoshino, Paul orders you to do only what I or Potter tell you. Do you understand?"

"Yes, I understand," replied Nyunt.

Tessa reached up with her left hand and pressed her fingers to Nyunt's neck, temporarily interrupting the blood supply to her brain. With a brief moan, she went limp and Tessa cut her bonds, allowing Nyunt's body to bump against hers to break the fall.

"Well done, whore," congratulated Paul, "you passed the test with flying colours. Now re-sheathe your knife and come back here."

Keeping her head bowed, so he couldn't see her face, she walked back to him.

"Now, Nariko, here's a syringe for you. Inject yourself with it."

A scruffy-looking man approached her, flicked open a case and held it out to her. Tessa obediently removed the already-filled syringe. She used her mouth to detach the plastic cover and spat it away before re-gripping the syringe in her right hand and expelling the air bubble. But then she appeared to hesitate. The man moved closer, wanting to make sure there wasn't a problem. But she yanked him still nearer and thrust the syringe in his shoulder, quickly injecting its contents. His eyes rolled upwards and he collapsed clumsily to the ground. She looked up at Paul and smiled. He was staring back in amazement. She dropped the syringe and trod on it.

"I was tempted to inject you with it, Paul, but I was worried that then you might not appreciate the rest of this evening's proceedings."

"But…" he stuttered.

She calmly removed one of the special weapons attached to her belt and held it up so everyone could see what she was doing. It certainly didn't look particularly threatening and Paul clearly had no idea what it was. It appeared to be simply a pointed stainless steel rod about half an inch in diameter.

Then she discarded a ring from the back and threw the clamp with all her might. It made a outlandish whirring sound as it spiralled through the air, transforming from a plain rod into a sleek shiny pointed dart with two sets of six sharpened metal prongs extending forwards from the rear and backwards from the front. There was an abrupt *crunch* as the clamp hit Paul's kneecap and tore its way through. The point soon appeared through the back of his leg, followed by the first set of prongs which immediately fanned out backwards. Despite the clamp having come to rest, the rear set of prongs carried on spinning, screwing their way up the threaded shaft of the dart until they pierced his flesh.

Paul screamed in agony and reached down to his knee, only to discover that, not only could he not release the clamp but his leg was seized in position; any attempt to move it simply made both sets of metal prongs dig in more.

"Get this bloody thing off me, you bitch!" he yelled. "How the fuck…"

"Now that seems to have wiped the cocky grin off *your* face," scoffed Tessa. She looked past him towards his thugs. "Listen to me. Paul is finished, just like this pathetic little rebellion. The town has already been taken by the Chrysanthemum Guard and this castle is about to follow. If you throw down your weapons and leave now, you will live. Anyone who stays will die. You have ten seconds to decide. Potter, you should leave now."

She listened to him getting up and heard him walking over to Nyunt. But then Paul reached into a pocket and produced a black box with a red button on it.

"Watch them die, bitch!" he screamed, beads of perspiration running down his forehead. However, as he fumbled the box in his bloody hand, Potter saw Tessa twist the boss at the end of the sintered knife's hilt and throw it. Like a hot wire cutting through butter, the blade cut the box in two, severing three of Paul's fingers as it cartwheeled through the air. Again he cried out in pain. The knife flew on until it struck a man in the thigh, effortlessly sinking in up to the hilt. Although it was not a fatal wound, the man sank to the ground clutching his leg in excruciating anguish. One of his colleagues grabbed the knife and yanked it out, causing the injured man to pass out. But as the man toyed with the knife, it started emitting a high pitched humming which quickly increased in volume. Before he could let go, the knife appeared to blur, finally disintegrating in a cloud of incredibly hard shards. The man's hand took the full force. All the flesh and several of his finger joints were simply blown away. He flopped down on his knees, shrieking as he grasped the bony remnants of his hand.

"Hmm. That worked well, Potter," observed Tessa without turning. "You really should go now.

"As I was saying," she continued, addressing the throng once more, "this nonsense is over. Surrender or die, and that applies to whoever's hiding in the castle too," she added after seeing a shadow move past one of the open windows."

Carefully watching the remaining thugs in front of her, Tessa heard Potter grunt as he strained to clamber over the fence at the end of honmaru while carrying Nyunt. Then there was some muffled swearing and the sound of bodies tumbling down the slope. Meanwhile, three of Paul's people left; the two injured by the sintered knife and one person helping them. That left six opponents.

"I should perhaps warn you guys," added Tessa calmly, "I singlehandedly defeated the Cats' UK Kick Ass Squad before coming here. All six of them are dead. Not to mention the two other teams I came across."

This prompted another man to discard his weapons and walk away; two even left from the castle, but Tessa still wasn't convinced it was empty yet. She walked up to Paul. His face was damp and pallid. He let go of his injured hand and used the other to wipe his eyes so he could watch her, it left a clumsy red smear.

"You had your chance, Paul. You poisoned me, insulted me and had others abuse me. But despite all that, only justice awaits you... well, and this." She punched him on the nose once more, hard enough to break the bones again. Momentarily stunned and unable to bend his leg, he pivoted over like a plank.

"Time's up, guys," she announced, and before Paul had even hit the ground, she had drawn and thrown both her exploding shuriken. Each entered the donjon through a different window, prompting bright flashes and bangs shortly afterwards. A myriad bright white fireflies appeared to be darting around inside, casting a surreal gyrating light over the honmaru. A rifle, two composite bows and a crossbow clattered to the ground from upper windows. But Tessa wasn't watching. She had already thrown two knives. Then she drew her swords and started hacking her way with merciless finality through the remaining Calver Cats. It was all over in seconds. The only sound was Paul's moaning.

Tessa flicked the blood off her weapons and returned them to their sheaths.

"Well, that didn't take long," she mocked, walking back to him. "You're not looking so confident now, Paul? Maybe I should have made a film of this?"

"Why the fucking nose again? I'd have thought you'd just kill me?"

"I'm still too angry with you to trust my judgement alone, so I'm going to leave others to preside over your miserable demise. Besides, you of all people should know there are worse things than death."

She kneeled down and removed Nyunt's sword. Paul wanted to resist, but he knew any such attempt would be futile. With Nyunt's sword in her hands she gazed back down at him. Even now, she couldn't find one iota of compassion for him.

"How did you do it? I should have been able to hypnotise you."

"I consulted an expert, the commands were removed."

"What? In the last three hours?"

Tessa's satisfied smile evaporated. She felt stunned as the gravity of what he'd just said sank in; three hours ago she'd been in Tokyo. With a horrible sinking feeling she doubted there had been any operational justification for her discarding the headset. In fact, had it really been the General whom she received the instruction from? She tossed Nyunt's sword away and, yelling "No!" continuously at the top of her voice, started sprinting for the fence over which Potter had disappeared a few minutes earlier.

"Stop it! Stop it! I can't hear!" she heard a voice pleading in her head. But Tessa was determined to do her best to drown out any other noises and jump over the fence. Then a rustling sound bored deep into her mind. After a fleeting flash of colour before her eyes, she froze. It seemed as though her feet had become glued to the ground...

Meanwhile, at the start of the main track leading up to the castle, Matsumoto and Gyobu were in the midst of a ferocious skirmish. They'd been ambushed remarkably soon on their way through Karatsu and had long since lost touch with Yamanouchi. Both of them were still wearing headsets, though.

"Reports?" demanded Gyobu, not pausing as he exchanged blows with a Calver Cat.

"Ayane, sir. Cats to south and west virtually defeated by our reserves. Mopping up. Over."

"Noboru, sir. Facing persistent resistance east of town... Forces split

– significant defections. But Maeda fighting like a tiger. Over."

"Understood," acknowledged Gyobu, dispatching some assailants before continuing to speak. "We have been ambushed on the main castle approach. Lost contact with Yamanouchi. Advance to honmaru when possible, over and… Oh, hold for Tokyo update… Hmm. So be it. Nariko, termination order – final sanction, effective immediate. Repeat, Nariko T.O. immediate sanction. Forces confirm. Over."

There was a short delay.

"Ayane, sir. Nariko termination order, immediate. Confirmed. Ayane out."

"Noboru sir. Nariko termination, immediate. Noboru out."

"Gyobu, out."

Matsumoto glared at him.

"My friend, I have no choice," called the General. For a moment the two of them concentrated on fighting. There were a lot of attackers, but they were all vastly outclassed by the two master swordsmen. "I will hold them," he added. "Go and see what you can do."

Matsumoto grunted his approval; hastily dispatching several more Calver Cats before turning and running up towards the castle…

Tessa was desperately willing herself to get over the fence, when she heard a voice.

"Nariko, turn round."

With every muscle in her body straining to defy what her mind was instructing them to do, she obeyed. Across the honmaru, she saw Yamanouchi smirking confidently at her, backed by three heavily armed fighters.

"Now come here," he instructed, pointing to the ground in front of him.

"You guys, go back to the sentry post and wait for Matsumoto; he's bound to be coming soon. Disarm him and bring him here."

Tessa stopped where Yamanouchi was pointing.

"Kneel down," he ordered. She watched the fighters walk away, leering. "You really have been one hell of a nuisance, Nariko. But all's well that ends well… You may talk now."

"Why?" asked Tessa, surprised that her tongue suddenly seemed able to function once more.

"Haven't you worked it out yet? I'm simply finishing what my father started. In a few hours, Japan's loss of Kyūshū will become public knowledge. Japan will be destabilised and then the Emperor will be assassinated by a discredited rogue Peacekeeper having an improper relationship with a member of the Chrysanthemum League. That's you and Matsumoto by the way. He won't be saying much in his defence because he'll already be dead. Japan will be leaderless and thrown into confusion. But in this moment of chaos, the Fujiwara will rise once more: to calm, to lead, to unify. I will establish myself as the new Shōgun, the first since the end of the Edo period. I will present an alternative form of government and the Fujiwara dynasty will be restored to its rightful position at last."

"You're mad. But how are you a Fujiwara?"

"Hachiro was my father and Bryani my mother. You killed them both, didn't you? Now do you understand why I have planned your miserable future so comprehensively?"

"I wish you guys would get it through your thick skulls that I did *not* kill Bryani. It was one of Caprice's men who shot her, I don't use guns."

"Yeah, yeah. Don't speak again until I permit it."

Yamanouchi walked over to Paul, looking down at him with disdain.

"Wow! You really fucked up this time, didn't you?"

"Shut up and help me get this fucking thing out," hissed Paul.

"I don't think so, dude. Look at you. You're a mess, an absolute bloody mess."

"I thought you instructed her not to kill anyone up here?"

"Really? Don't know what gave you that idea," boasted Yamanouchi. "I thought you'd rumble me when your Kick Ass team got pasted... Anyway, you must admit, the knee clamp was a very considerate touch. Mind you, I did expect the whore to top you straight away."

"You bastard! You planned all this. What's the matter with you? I'm your cousin..."

"Sorry to be pedantic, but I think it's you that's the bastard. Anyway, you're no longer of any use to me."

He picked up Nyunt's sword.

"What do you mean?" demanded Paul, watching in horror. "I'll be fine once this thing has been removed... What are you doing?"

"Sorry, *cos*, but this is where our ways part. There isn't any space for you at the top."

"Don't be ridiculous, I got us here. We have an agreement…"

"Rescinded," replied Yamanouchi. Then he plunged Nyunt's sword into Paul's stomach and cut from left to right. For a few seconds Paul screamed in agony, then fell silent as his body relaxed. Yamanouchi cleaned the sword, returned it to its sheath and walked back to Tessa. She was smiling.

"Oh, liked that, did you? Try this." He put down Nyunt's sword and reached over to draw Tessa's Amafuji weapon." Her smile was transformed immediately into a furious scowl. Yamanouchi caressed the blade, "At last, I have our family sword in my hands…"

When Matsumoto reached the sentry post, he found three bodies; but then three more men appeared.

"If you want to see Nariko alive, give me all your weapons and come with us," one of them ordered.

Matsumoto took a deep breath and withdrew his hand from his sword hilt…

Hearing his men returning, Yamanouchi turned to Tessa.

"Nariko, draw one of your knives and place the point lightly on the left hand side of your stomach. Then grip the hilt tightly with both hands."

With her hands trembling, and desperately wishing she could resist, she did as ordered.

"Good. Now, don't move."

It wasn't long before Tessa saw Matsumoto appear on the bailey, flanked by three Calver Cats.

"*Konichiwa*, Yamanouchi," greeted Matsumoto. "I had a feeling you were involved."

"You may address me by my real name, now. Kurou Fujiwara – soon to be Shōgun."

"Really?" replied Matsumoto with open scorn. He glanced at Tessa with a concerned expression, while the man with his weapons held them up like trophies.

"Nariko-san…" he began.

"Oh, it's no use talking to this whore. She's completely under my control."

"So what happens now?" asked Matsumoto. "You're not going to let her kill herself, are you? Surely she's far too valuable for that?"

"No, I just wanted to make sure you were appropriately compliant. Nariko's got a busy day in front of her. She's going to assassinate the Emperor soon. Assuming she gets away after that, and I do anticipate she will, I'll lend her to the Sheikh for a while. After all, he did pay a deposit. But eventually I'll bring her back to train my personal guard and be a play thing for whoever else pays me enough."

"And me?"

"Oh, you're going to die. How else can I ensure the final destruction of the Chrysanthemum League? The Amakuni will be given the opportunity to choose; either they make weapons for the new Shōgunate, or they too will be killed."

Suddenly Tessa smiled at Matsumoto. She had a remarkably relaxed, resigned expression on her face. Then she took a deep breath, and tensed her arm muscles, and with all her strength she started pulling the knife towards her. The point dug into her suit, quickly passing through and piercing her flesh. A droplet of blood oozed out around the blade tip.

"No, Nariko-san. Don't do that, please," pleaded Matsumoto.

Yamanouchi spun round.

"Nariko!" he shouted. "I order you to stop. Let go of the knife."

She didn't. With her hands trembling and beads of perspiration rolling down her forehead, she tried pulling the knife harder, but the resistance she was encountering was monumental; the knife barely moved.

Yamanouchi clicked his fingers twice and shouted, "Shōgunate restored."

Suddenly Tessa's mind was filled only with an image of Angkor Wat, then it was gone.

"Nariko, put the knife on the ground."

This time Tessa could not resist.

"Very impressive," observed Yamanouchi. "You have much more residual willpower than I would have expected. But we'll soon fix that. You two," he said pointing at his men, "hold Matsumoto. You," he continued, gesturing towards the third, "draw your sword and kill him when I say. I want him to watch this first." He produced a small black case, removed a syringe from it, took off the cover and primed it. "Nariko, take this syringe." Tessa reached up for it, studying it forlornly.

"Nariko," said Matsumoto earnestly, "look at me." With Yamanouchi laughing, she gazed at him. "I am so sorry. I really did want to see Angkor Wat and especially Beng Mealea…"

"Oh, puke! Do you two really have something going together? Well, I hope you didn't have plans," mocked Yamanouchi. "Nariko, place the needle on your left thigh, push it in all the way and the press the plunger down completely."

Tessa's hands started trembling, but she couldn't stop them from moving the syringe over to her leg. The needle hovered over her flesh. With considerable effort she managed to force her leg out of the way.

"Bloody hell! Do it," shouted Yamanouchi. "Do it now!"

Tessa grunted and somehow managed to grab her left thigh with her left hand. She pinched the flesh together as hard as she could and thrust the needle in, right up to the hilt and carried on pressing as hard as she could, then she pushed the plunger down.

She moaned quietly as she watched the light blue fluid empty from the phial. Then her head bowed down and the empty syringed toppled from her grip. Matsumoto's shoulders drooped in defeat.

"Well, that's that," boasted Yamanouchi. "Come to think of it, maybe I should kill him myself." He picked up Tessa's knife. "Look at him, the last steward of Matsumoto Castle, beaten, dejected, and ready to die. But I'm not going to make it that easy."

He threw the weapon and re-gripped the Amafuji sword in his right hand. The knife struck Matsumoto in the thigh and blood started trickling down his leg. But he didn't move a muscle; he simply smiled.

"You lose," he boasted.

"What?" queried Yamanouchi.

"That's *my* sword," hissed Tessa. She was swaying slightly, but nevertheless standing not far away from him.

Yamanouchi gazed in astonishment as Tessa's Kimi sword sped through the air towards him. A moment later the blade passed through his arm, severing it near the wrist with such force that his hand and the sword spun separately high in the air.

Staggering back in shock, Yamanouchi grabbed the stump of his arm.

"Kill him!" he screamed at colleagues.

But Tessa had already brought her sword back. She flicked it over and struck her Amafuji sword mid-air, just under the tsuba, rocketing it hilt-first towards Matsumoto. Then, as the third man raised his sword to strike, Tessa launched her weapon at him. He had barely completed half his swing when the blade disappeared into his skull. Meanwhile, Matsumoto had pivoted his fists strongly upwards, punching both the thugs holding him in the face. He shoved them aside and caught the Amafuji sword. Spinning round he slashed the man to his right across the chest fatally, and then decapitated the other.

With disaster suddenly staring him in the face, Yamanouchi started to run.

"Like hell," sneered Tessa. She drew her remaining knee clamp and threw it. Again the outlandish whirring sound filled the air. Although the clamp missed his knee, it nevertheless made an abrupt *crunch* as it entered his thigh, shattering the bone as it passed through. Then it locked shut.

"Bitch!" shrieked Yamanouchi, as he stumbled and fell. Then he rolled on his back and clicked his fingers twice, uttering, "Shōgunate restored. Nariko, kill Matsumoto."

Tessa stopped in her tracks, momentarily confused as an image of Angkor Wat flashed into her mind. She kneeled down and picked up Nyunt's sword, standing up purposefully and turning towards Matsumoto.

Then she heard another sound, like a whispering in her right ear. "*Click, click, Shōgunate restored* – you are no longer hypnotised."

An image of Beng Mealea appeared in her mind.

"What the…" she muttered.

Then Yamanouchi clicked his fingers again. Matsumoto immediately raised the Amafuji sword and adopted a defensive stance. But then there was another whispering in Tessa's ear and again she saw an image of Beng Mealea.

"Stop him from clicking his fingers," urged the whisper.

"Good idea," agreed Tessa, striding over to Yamanouchi. He was just about to click his fingers again when she trod on his hand with such force that his fingers splayed out. As he feverishly attempted to raise his thumb and forefinger, Tessa brought the point of Nyunt's sword to rest at the base of his thumb.

"I don't think it's possible for someone to click their fingers without a thumb" she growled. "Let's see, shall we?"

She pressed down, prompting the thumb to fly off Yamanouchi's hand. He gasped and Tessa removed her foot. She calmly watched him clicking his remaining fingers together in various combinations, but none had any effect on her.

"That's better," she confirmed, and looked at Matsumoto. "Amazing what a difference a few seconds can make, isn't it?"

He smiled and lowered his sword.

"Indeed it is, Nariko-san. Welcome back." He sat down awkwardly and started removing a selection of medicinal herbs and mosses from his waist-bag. He studied the knife hilt still protruding from his leg and decided in his own mind how he intended to treat himself. Tessa went to help him, collecting her swords on the way.

It wasn't long before the knife was out and the wound cleaned. Tessa was completing the final sutures when Gyobu hobbled onto the honmaru with a pronounced limp.

"Hello, Gyobu-san," said Tessa. "You missed all the fun."

"Trust me, I didn't," he replied, apparently in some discomfort.

CHAPTER 31

Gyobu switched his headset to speaker mode and gestured Matsumoto to discard his.

"Reports," he snapped.

"Ayane, sir. Cats subdued, no further resistance, Police handling arrests. Awaiting instructions by main castle access. Over."

"Noboru, sir. Cats restrained, no further resistance. Maeda commanding police clean-up. Moving to rendezvous at main castle access. Over."

"Most satisfactory," noted Gyobu. He looked round the honmaru, pausing briefly as his eyes fell on Paul's body and Yamanouchi's writhing torso. Then he studied Tessa for several seconds; clearly he was thinking and she soon found his searching gaze objectionable. He tapped his headset.

"Tokyo, report current status... Excellent... Confirmed. Ayane, Noboru, cancel Nariko T.O. Repeat, Nariko T.O. – immediate cancellation. Confirm. Over"

"Ayane, sir. Nariko T.O., pleased to confirm stand down. Over."

"Noboru, sir. Nariko T.O., stand down confirmed. Over."

Tessa glared at him.

"Nariko," said Matsumoto, desperately trying to derail her train of thought. "I watched you inject that syringe, how is it that you are not drugged?"

She slowly turned to face him.

"The injection was intra-muscular, so the syringe had a long needle on it. He only told me to push the needle in hard and press the plunger – I interpreted his instruction literally. I pinched my thigh so tightly I was able to push the needle in at one side, and out the other. I injected the drugs on to the ground."

"Very clever!" laughed Matsumoto.

"...Ayane," commanded Gyobu, "secure all access routes to the castle. No one comes up until I give the all-clear. We have some unfinished business here. Over and out."

Tessa stood up and glanced at Matsumoto with a wry smile.

"Savour the moment," he urged, beaming.

Tessa went back to Yamanouchi.

"You're going to love this," she mocked. "Kurou Fujiwara, as unchallenged victor in this battle for Karatsu, I claim this castle, its lands and all its perpetual rights as granted in various edicts dating from the early-1600s until the present time."

"Meaningless drivel, Caucasian whore!" he scoffed. "You're no Matsumoto."

"Really? No chrysanthemum, right?" she stated, holding up her arm. He shrugged. "Now meet my husband." Matsumoto limped into his field of vision.

"No! That's not possible. I would have been told…"

"Congratulations, Nariko-san," said Matsumoto, "it would appear you're a wealthy landowner in Japan. Enjoy it, for a while at least."

"Ah, yes," interjected Gyobu, "and on that note, I need to tell you about how the land should be transferred. There is a protocol, you'll need to meet with the Emperor."

"No!" yelled Yamanouchi. "Gyobu, you…"

"Oh do shut up!" insisted Tessa. "By the way, did you really rape me in Hpa An?"

"I certainly did. Not that it was particularly memorable. I've no idea why everyone was raving about your sexual prowess. You were shit as far as I was concerned."

"Really," said Tessa, drawing her sword and letting it hover over his genitals.

"You just try, slut!" hissed Yamanouchi. "Your conscience couldn't live with it anyway."

"Oh, my conscience wouldn't be troubled in the slightest, especially since you're such a foul-mouthed piece of evil. But I didn't kill Paul because I had no intention of stooping to your level, so I won't be violent now either. It will be far more enjoyable seeing you crippled in court. To watch you being condemned to death and forced to wait in prison until somebody ends your sad existence… Besides, I think you're lying."

As she walked away, Matsumoto approached Yamanouchi.

"Why were you and Paul so cruel to her?" he asked.

"It wasn't about her! She is nothing. She was just a commodity for which people were willing to pay good money. I only wanted the Amafuji sword; then we realised we could be of use to us too. But she's of no value; she's only a fucking hermaphrodite freak, for God's sake."

Matsumoto looked at him curiously, and roared with laughter.

"Kurou, you are a murderer, a kidnapper and a thief, together with many other even crueller things. You are typical of the dross which holds society back. I have no doubt that you will soon be judged worthy only of extermination. Furthermore, it is not for you to criticise the birth defects of others. What she and Penny were is no business of yours, or anyone else's. You would be wise to consider the severity of your own *abnormalities* before demonstrating naive prejudices by sneering at what you perceive as others'. Anyway, I agree with her, I don't think you raped her either. However," continued Matsumoto, adopting a more determined tone, "when a man rapes a woman it is cowardly and disgusting, and an insult to all men." He was almost shouting now. "…But when a man rapes a woman using drugs to facilitate his actions, it is much worse; the lowest form of cowardice and depravity." He appeared to calm down. "Fortunately for you, as honourable Peacekeepers, Nariko and I are willing to let the courts judge you for your crimes." Yamanouchi heaved a sigh of relief. "But when a man attempts to destroy my wife, and then insults me as her husband, if I stand by and do nothing, I have accepted those heinous injustices. My conscience could not tolerate that…"

Tessa turned to Gyobu. "I think he's angry."

"Oh, I would say, absolutely livid."

"So," bellowed Matsumoto, menacingly, "as Nariko's husband, I feel it my duty to protect her. Whatever she and Penny were it was a damned sight better than being a eunuch."

In one swift fluid movement, Matsumoto drew his sword…

"No!" yelled Yamanouchi in horror. "Gyobu!"

"*Anata*," urged Tessa, "I think he's got the message and I suspect it is only the timing of his demise which is in question now. Why bother?"

Matsumoto sighed, re-sheathed his weapon and kicked the knee-clamp.

Yamanouchi screamed in pain.

"Ouch," observed Tessa, laughing.

"Sir," came a voice over his headset, "Ayane, over."

"Proceed."

"Our forces have re-grouped at the base of the castle rampart; all access routes are secured. The town is calm and Inspector Maeda has taken control of the Police and Special Forces. The survivors are being taken into custody and will be transported to Tokyo. The wounded are being transferred to Fukuoka Hospital. Over."

"Good. Hold your position. Prepare my helicopter... Oh, what about Mizoguchi? Over."

"By the time I arrived with our reserves, she was leading the other forces I had been allocated, against us. However, we overran them. She is dead, I fought her myself. Over."

Yamanouchi wailed in dismay.

"You bastards! You killed my wife."

"Hmm, Ayane."

"Yes, sir."

"Make sure Mizoguchi's body receives a comprehensive post-mortem. I want it checked for childbirth. If there are any offspring, I want them traced. We need to ensure they are brought up with a more balanced view of society."

"Copy that, sir."

"Await further instructions. Out."

Gyobu smiled at Tessa.

"I think we're nearly ready. I'll just report in."

Tessa raised her eyebrows.

"We all have bosses, Nariko-san," he said, switching off his headset and raising his *cbc*.

Tessa went to collect her other weapons while Matsumoto sat down to rest his leg. As she passed Paul's body, an idea germinated. She kneeled down and rummaged through his pockets to remove his *cbc*. It was another few minutes before the three of them reconvened.

"We're not quite finished yet," declared the General. "Will you come with me, please? Both of you."

Tessa exchanged glances with Matsumoto, and they both followed Gyobu back to Yamanouchi. He gazed up at them with a defiant grimace.

337

"Gyobu-san…," he started to say. But the General gestured him to be silent.

"Kurou Fujiwara," he pronounced in an official tone, "you were born on the twenty-third of July 1990 in Kōchi, Shikoku, and have retained your Japanese nationality despite having been brought up in America. It is there we believe you met Adam Caille, also known as Paul, whom you recently murdered. Together you hatched this plan to destabilise Japan and assassinate the Emperor. These crimes constitute treason and murder. You are hereby sentenced to death by the Emperor of Japan for crimes against the state and the Japanese people. It has been decreed that this sentence should be implemented immediately by the Emperor's chosen representative… which is me."

"You can't do that," yelled Yamanouchi, desperately trying to marshal his thoughts given the intense pain he was suffering. "You…"

"Just be quiet and listen," replied Gyobu with a smile. Yamanouchi appeared to be appeased, prompting Tessa to frown at Matsumoto. "You forfeited your rights to be judged by the Courts of Japan when you attempted to seize Kyūshū in compliance with old laws. Accordingly, the Emperor, to whom I was just speaking, has judged you under those very same laws." Gyobu turned to Tessa and Matsumoto. "Although technically no endorsement is required, the Emperor has asked that I confirm his judgement with you both.

"So, Matsumoto, as head of the Matsumoto clan and a member of the Chrysanthemum League, do you concur with this ruling."

"I do," he replied without hesitation.

"Nariko, as a member of the Chrysanthemum League and one who has suffered as a direct result of the actions and orders of this man, do you concur with this ruling?"

"I do," replied Tessa, her voice steady and devoid of emotion.

Slowly and purposefully, Gyobu drew his Amakuni sword. Amazingly, the only response this prompted from Yamanouchi was a smile. He seemed to be relaxed, almost gloating victoriously.

"Should we offer him a Kaishakunin," volunteered Tessa, keen to be seen to do the right thing.

Gyobu peered down at Yamanouchi.

"You won't be needing one, will you?"

Yamanouchi shook his head and started to laugh, but then Gyobu thrust the sword into his stomach and cut from left to right. Eyes wide in shock, Yamanouchi let out a shrill cry which was soon transformed into guttural moan. Then there was silence as his body fell limp.

"Good riddance!" exclaimed Gyobu dismissively, not bothering to clean or re-sheathe his weapon. "Now, Nariko-san, we need to visit the Emperor's Palace in Tokyo to complete your work, and we need to do it fast, before any media reports are issued concerning the events of tonight."

Tessa looked at him and smiled, but as soon as he had eye contact, he simply clicked his fingers. "Nariko, go to sleep." Tessa immediately closed her eyes and collapsed while Gyobu swung round, aiming his sword at Matsumoto. However, he was already moving back, and so the blade only slashed a cut across his tunic at chest height.

"Gyobu-san, what are you doing?" demanded Matsumoto, drawing his own weapon.

"She owns Kyūshū, I own her and you're excess to requirements, Sorry, old friend, but you will die now." Gyobu was standing straight, unencumbered by the wound he'd feigned.

Matsumoto reversed away, playing for time. Normally they would be evenly matched, but with his wounded leg and Gyobu almost fresh, it was far from an equal fight.

"But how…"

"How did I get the hypnotic instruction installed?" Matsumoto nodded. "Oh, that was easy. I'd uncovered Yamanouchi's true lineage some time ago. Once I'd agreed to help and installed him as Chief Inspector, it was easy to persuade him to give me a recording of his instruction. While Nariko was in the Neuroscience Unit in Tokyo, I placed my own version of his command in her mind. I knew Professor Kawashima wouldn't be able to distinguish between the two, or remove any of them. So I just waited for the competition to be eliminated and for Nariko to assume ownership of Kyūshū. As soon as you're gone, I'll take her to meet the Emperor, he'll be killed and my pension will be somewhat enhanced."

"So, why the termination order?"

"Because lifting it would put everyone at ease with regards her access to the Emperor; failing that, there would be no loose ends."

"You allowed Kurou to double-cross Paul, and then you double-crossed Kurou?"

"Yes. That became an attractive prospect once I'd learnt that Nariko was a member of the Chrysanthemum League, rather than just the Chrysanthemum Guard. I simply neglected to mention it to Kurou. Now, shall we?"

"Oh, Gyobu-san," bemoaned Matsumoto. "You fool, you have betrayed and disappointed so many."

He raised his sword and the two closed. They clashed repeatedly and Gyobu realised that, even wounded, Matsumoto was no easy kill. Desperate for a quick result, he backed away and re-sheathed his sword. Then he drew a small handgun.

The sound of a helicopter approaching interrupted the moment. Gyobu tapped his headset impatiently.

"Ayane, go back. You're not needed up here."

"It's not us, sir."

He looked up to see an official government helicopter swooping down.

Then his headset crackled.

"General Gyobu, this is Minister Miyazaki. I will be with you shortly. I have heard everything and am relieving you of command. Discard your weapons."

Gyobu breathed out as his shoulders sagged.

"I have a microphone transmitter, old friend," revealed Matsumoto, touching his collar. "Everything you said was broadcast. Our suspicions were aroused because the Fujiwara claim had progressed so far before we learned of it. But I did not wish to believe that you were party to such dishonourable actions."

Suddenly Tessa sat up.

"What happened?" she exclaimed. Then she saw Matsumoto's sword and stance and, drawing a knife, immediately adopted a similarly aggressive pose; only then realising he was facing General Gyobu.

"...and Nariko has an earwig," added Matsumoto, "Tokyo is constantly monitoring her..."

As soon as the helicopter had landed, Minister Miyazaki got out and started walking toward them. His expression was stern and determined.

"One more thing, Gyobu-san," quizzed Matsumoto. "How did you ensure you maintained Yamanouchi's trust? Did you feed him useful information, like where he could find Toshie Miyazaki?"

The General looked down and sighed.

"I regret that, but it was necessary."

The Minister stopped in his tracks and groaned mournfully.

Tessa's mouth fell open as she finally understood.

"I don't believe it," she blurted. "Gyobu-san, how could you? I suppose you told them when I originally planned to enter Burma too? Did you know what they would do to me?" He looked at her with a melancholy expression. "...Aren't you ashamed?" demanded Tessa in disgust.

"I have no children, and my wife died three years ago. I simply wanted purpose back in my life. This seemed, well... but perhaps not." He took a deep breath and put his feet together. Then he bowed deeply to them all and spoke in a clear voice. "Minister Miyazaki, Matsumoto-san, Nariko-san, I apologise for my actions most sincerely."

Then he raised the gun, put it below his chin pointing upwards, and pulled the trigger.

"Hmm. I'll take that as a yes," purred Tessa dismissively. "Now, will somebody please tell me what's been going on here?"

"Well done," whispered a woman's voice in her ear.

"...And why do I keep hearing a voice in my ear?" she added.

"That'll be Professor Kawashima," replied Matsumoto, visibly surprised by her question. "She's talking to you via the earwig you had fitted."

"I don't remember that," protested Tessa, looking blank. "When was that done?"

"Er... In the Chrysanthemum Guard headquarters, when you met Minister Miyazaki."

"Was that my idea?"

"That's all in the past now," replied Matsumoto evasively. "Let me take it out for you."

He took a step towards her. But she responded by taking two quick steps back and drawing her sword.

"Get away from me!"

"Wow!" exclaimed Matsumoto, recoiling, "I didn't expect that."

"Er, sorry," continued Tessa. "Actually, it's not me that's apologising,

341

it's the voice inside my head. It says… Oh! It says I was hypnotised to forget that the device was installed and to resist any attempt to remove it. The voice recommends we go and see her before we do anything else, not least because she's heard too much already. But apparently I can fix that and all the other hypnotic commands can be removed now because there's a recording of the triggers."

"Sounds like a very sensible suggestion to me," professed Matsumoto, whole-heartedly.

"Quite," confirmed Miyazaki, "so, Tokyo headquarters, then the Palace."

"Not until I've been told everything else that's been going on,"

Miyazaki and Matsumoto exchanged glances.

"Well, it seems General Gyobu strayed from the path he had followed loyally for many years. He discovered the Calver Cats' intentions and pretended to befriend Yamanouchi and Paul, while in fact plotting their demise so that he could take over from them. It's all very sad, and a terrible waste. I think we should leave now."

"Hmm. Just a couple more things. First, I need a favour," requested Tessa.

"Ask it," responded Miyazaki.

"While I was a prisoner, I swore that all those involved in trying to ruin my life would be prevented from doing the same to anyone else – no one should suffer what I had to go through. Do you think it would be possible to delay the announcement of Paul's death? Also, I would like his body to… er… disappear, say, for a few weeks. Finally, I was wondering whether announcements could be put in the media that one of the gang's leaders managed to escape, and that a Peacekeeper is also missing."

"I see no problem there," replied Miyazaki, quietly pleased she'd asked.

"*Omae*," pleaded Matsumoto, moving closer to her. "Haven't we done enough already?"

"Possibly." She looked round and her glance lingered on the bodies of Paul and Yamanouchi. "And perhaps even *I* might be able to achieve closure with this. But what about the other women's families? Don't they deserve closure too? Then there are all the other people who might still be abused by those who we haven't dealt with here. Isn't it our duty to protect them?"

Matsumoto paused for a moment, took a deep breath and looked at Miyazaki, nodding in unenthusiastic acquiescence.

"Very well, it will be done," acknowledged the Minister. "Shall we go?

"Then there's just one more thing. The pair of you need to explain why I was bugged and fitted with an earwig without my consent, and then set up as bait without being consulted. Not to mention why you permitted a termination order to be issued against me!" Tessa's voice was charged with emotion. "How could you, *anata*?"

"*Omae...*" pleaded Matsumoto, reaching out to her; but she shied away.

"He had no choice in the matter," interrupted Miyazaki, totally unashamedly. "It was my plan and I insisted he carry out my orders, no more and no less. If you feel there is a need to blame anyone, then blame me, not him."

"Minister, I wish that it were that simple, but it isn't, is it? You both betrayed me..." They looked at each other, unsure what to say. "However, you will no doubt be relieved to hear that I do not intend to let that come between us finishing what Kurou and Paul started. Nevertheless, I will leave as soon as possible."

"No, *omae*, please," pleaded Matsumoto. "Come back to Matsumoto Castle with me, we need to talk this through first."

Tessa pursed her lips and breathed in noisily.

"So, I will leave tomorrow."

The Minister nodded and switched his headset back on.

"Ayane," he barked. "This is Minister Miyazaki."

"Yes, Minister," she replied, respectfully.

"I have taken over from General Gyobu; I'll elaborate in due course. We're ready up here. Leave Maeda in charge. No one else should be allowed up for a few hours. Come up by foot with Noboru, and bring a combustible body bag. Over."

"Yes, sir. Shall I have Seiji return to..."

"Yes," he interrupted quickly, but the damage had been done. Tessa was glowering at Matsumoto again, having realised that Seiji had been on stand-by to intervene if she had proved to be expendable.

"Very good, sir. We'll be with you in five minutes. Out..."

In Tokyo, Professor Kawashima removed all Tessa's hypnotic instructions, and, during a brief and remarkably informal audience with the Emperor, Kyūshū was returned to the Japanese State, without anyone knowing it had been in danger of being lost.

Back in Gyobu's old office a number of newscasts were drafted, describing how the Calver Cats had suffered a serious setback during a major confrontation in Karatsu. They also revealed that although many of the gang had been killed or arrested, one of the leaders had escaped and a non-Japanese Peacekeeper was also missing. It was further stated that several senior Special Forces operatives had perished, including Chief Inspector Yamanouchi, whose position had been assumed by the newly promoted Chief Inspector Maeda. Then Matsumoto and Tessa were taken back to the castle.

They spent a very frosty interlude together. He endeavoured to convince her that Dr Miyazaki had had no choice, and so neither had he. But Tessa remained deeply hurt that he had acquiesced to a plan which allowed a Termination Order to be issued against her.

Soon after a furiously competitive training session, Matsumoto and Tessa convened for breakfast in stony silence. While he cleared away the table, she finished packing her bag. When the pair of them met in the audience hall, they could already hear the sound of a helicopter approaching.

"*Omae*, I do not wish you to leave like this."

Tessa looked into his eyes, taking in the forlorn expression.

"Would you do it again?" she asked, quietly.

Matsumoto breathed out noisily.

"You are asking whether I feel you are less able now to complete a task you believe to be right. Nariko-san, I realised from the day we first met that there is a determination within you which drives you relentlessly to overcome any obstacle in order to attain your goals. So, if I were truly convinced that your goals had been set by an evil third party and that it was no longer your own conscience which guided you, then yes, I would do it again. I am sorry if that is not what you wish to hear, but I will not lie to you."

Tessa sighed, thinking carefully before she answered.

"I need some time, some space."

Matsumoto nodded.

"I will start the castle renovations as we discussed. Take as much time as you need, but I will always be waiting here for your return."

Tessa forced a little smile, then turned and walked down the rampart to meet the helicopter. There was no one in it apart from the pilots. So it came as no surprise when she was summoned to a private meeting room in Haneda Airport. Dr Miyazaki was waiting there.

"Minister," she said, bowing.

"Nariko-san," he replied, bowing deeply and gesturing for her to join him at the table. "I am sorry to delay you, but we have always been somewhat preoccupied with other matters during our recent meetings. I was wondering whether you would mind telling me precisely what it was that you overheard concerning my daughter?" He spoke with only a slight tremor in his voice but he was clearly immensely emotional. "Toshie is, was, our only child. My wife and I are not able to... would you mind?"

"Of course," replied Tessa, her initial hardness quickly melting away. "Although I didn't hear much, my understanding from what Paul said was that your daughter repeatedly rejected the life which had been planned for her. She attempted to escape on many occasions, but when that finally failed she refused to allow herself to be taken back into captivity. She exerted her right to self-determination one last time and contrived to ensure she was shot dead... Having been subjected to the same treatment as she was, at least in part, I understand her thinking completely and am convinced she died a brave and honourable death."

He looked down at the table and breathed out heavily.

"Thank you, Nariko-san. It is kind of you to tell me what you know, and especially to express it so sensitively and generously."

"Dr Miyazaki, it is the truth. You should be very proud of her."

"We are, and always will be," he replied, struggling to maintain his composure. "So, what do you intend to do now?"

Tessa breathed out noisily, angered by her own bitter memories.

"I was tortured, auctioned as a slave and subjected to a heinous drug therapy. I am determined to make sure that no one else suffers a similar fate at the hands of those who forced it on me."

"I suppose it would not be possible for me to persuade you to let other Peacekeepers carry out this dangerous work, instead of you?"

Tessa shook her head.

"I accepted a Peacekeeper Mission in London to stop the new Calver Cats gang, and this is an integral part of their activities which still needs to be addressed."

"I understand," continued Miyazaki. "However, I hear one of the parties resides within a country which is not yet a signatory to the International Peacekeeper Treaty?"

"I have a plan which will hopefully enable me to honour my Mission objectives without breaking the law."

"Also, Nariko-san, you no doubt know that a hearing has been convened in London to decide if you tortured a member of the Calver Cats, and whether your OCL should in consequence be revoked."

Tessa shrugged.

"None of us should be above the law, Minister," she replied with an edge to her voice. "Was it really necessary to subject me to so much of their disgusting plan before exposing the perpetrators?"

"Perhaps not, "he admitted resignedly. "But it was the only foolproof strategy I could come up with. I had my suspicions about Yamanouchi, and Mizoguchi, but I wasn't at all sure about Gyobu... I respect your abilities so highly that I felt the only way I could protect the Emperor in the long term would be to allow them all to expose themselves. Do not for a moment think it was a decision I took lightly. As for Matsumoto, he voiced his opposition extremely forcibly. Furthermore, I'm sure I don't need to remind you that he risked his life in order to save yours..." Tessa looked down to avoid his steady gaze. "...You should also understand that Professor Kawashima had diagnosed your hypnotic programming as extremely deep and indicated that she could not remove it without learning the triggers. Who would win that night in Karatsu was balanced on a knife edge, Nariko-san. But we *had* to win... Could you have come up with a better plan in the circumstances?"

"I'd better go..." she responded evasively.

The Minister looked at her and smiled.

"Then it only remains for me to wish you a speedy and successful conclusion to your endeavours. Regrettably, since you will be active outside our country, there is not much Japan can do to assist you...

officially. However, as I have now assumed temporary stewardship over the Chrysanthemum Guard, I have been able to consider other possibilities. I thought unlimited use of the Guard's private jet together with the support of two Chrysanthemum Ninja, might come in handy. Naturally, they are not permitted to become directly involved, but they are well equipped to support you in, say, preparing the groundwork."

Tessa was stunned into silence. Just not needing to travel on scheduled flights would be a considerable boost in her efforts to remain incognito.

"That is most kind, Dr Miyazaki. I gratefully accept your generous offer."

"Excellent. That's it for now then," concluded Miyazaki, standing up. "Your plane is outside, fuelled and ready to go wherever you want and your team is already on board. Good luck, Nariko-san. Be victorious and return safely."

They bowed to each other and Tessa was just about to open the door when Miyazaki spoke again.

"Oh, and by the way, Nariko-san. Nyunt and Potter have both had their pumps successfully removed and Professor Kawashima is going to ensure that any hypnotic commands are removed."

Tessa nodded. In fact she had already spoken to Flood and even knew when they were due to return to the UK.

CHAPTER 32

Tessa sauntered towards the smart triple-engined executive jet soon realising it was the plane which had collected her from Tunisia. But now she was properly conscious, she began to appreciate what a truly magnificent machine it was. Apart from looking sleek and purposeful, its three engines would make it extremely fast; while, its gleaming black livery, broken only by a single gold chrysanthemum motif, projected an air of subdued determination.

The door opened and some steps unfurled. As soon as Tessa was inside, they were raised again and the door closed. Five people greeted her, bowing deeply. She put her bag down, smiled and bowed back.

"*Konichiwa*, Ayane, Noboru, lady and gentlemen. I am pleased and honoured to be leading our mission. Some difficult challenges lie ahead and we don't have much time. Nevertheless, I think it is important that we get to know each other first. Then I will describe the task in hand…"

The six of them spoke for nearly an hour. The flight crew comprised two men and a woman, two pilots and an engineer, although all of them could swap roles if required. Ayane and Noboru, of course, were well known to Tessa who was delighted to have them with her. She already liked and respected them for their fighting abilities, but it turned out that they were also well versed in espionage and electronics. Noboru quickly demonstrated his prowess by hacking into Paul's *cbc*. Furthermore, Ayane had authority to draw assistance from any Japanese embassy worldwide. Tessa was greatly encouraged that her team seemed to bond quickly, making her feel increasingly confident.

"OK," she said eventually. "I think it's time we made a start. I would like to fly to Berlin where I shall have a meeting with Oberst Müller; he's one of my Peacekeeper Guardians and Head of Special Forces Germany…"

It had been five days since the Karatsu confrontation when Potter and Nyunt arrived in London's Estuary Airport. Flood met them at the top of the jet-way.

"Morning, sir," he said cheerily, grinning to see Potter's arm in a sling. "Hello, Yoshino, good to have you back."

Nyunt nodded, without looking at him. The usual confident sparkle was absent from her eyes; she looked pale and drawn, still haunted by her entrapment and what had followed.

"Hello, Flood," replied Potter, casting a sideways glance at Nyunt. "Thanks for collecting us. We'll take Yoshino home and then go straight to the office…"

Flood's *cbc* rang as they passed through Immigration. He answered it and looked at Potter.

"Sorry, sir. You have an urgent video call from Oberst Müller – a private room has been made available for Yoshino."

This turned out to be somewhat sparsely furnished, but it was pleasant enough.

"We'll be back as soon as we can," Potter assured her. "Do you want a coffee or something?"

Nyunt shook her head dejectedly and flopped down on the sofa.

As soon as they had gone, she sat back and unwrapped the picture she was carrying. A collage she'd made comprising her original birth certificate, the two restored pictures of her parents which Tessa had been given in Burma and, most prominent of all, two pictures of her with Tessa. She studied them lovingly and closed her eyes. The removal of the pump had left her abdomen aching, but nowhere near as much as the psychological and emotional wounds she had suffered. Not long afterwards, she heard the door open and felt someone sit down on the sofa with her. Then a hand brushed the hair away from her eyes.

"Why are you looking so sad, darling?"

Nyunt sighed, not even opening her eyes to see who had addressed her.

"I don't have anything to be happy about."

"Now that is most definitely not the case, young lady. You need to put things in perspective. Besides, I didn't come all this way just to listen to you feeling sorry for yourself… Look at me, darling."

"Mum!" she exclaimed, hugging Tessa. "How…?"

"Shh! That's not important. What is important is that you have lots of reasons to be happy, not least because you're all right and so am I."

Nyunt burst into tears.

"But I'm not all right!" she sobbed. "I'm to blame for all those terrible things that happened. You could have been killed! I… I'm so sorry. How can you ever forgive me?"

"Darling, there's nothing to forgive. It's been a lesson to us all and demonstrated that there are still many evil people in the world. But there are an awful lot of very good ones too. Now, I don't have long…"

"What do you mean? Aren't we going home now?"

"You are, but I need to tie up some loose ends first."

Nyunt looked puzzled.

"Please, come home with me," she implored. "I want to be with you… I need you."

Tessa smiled.

"Darling, for the first part of my life, I was busy finding myself. For the second, I was blessed with finding you. I have enjoyed and been enriched by both. Now it's time for you to find your own way, as shall I. Here's my new email address and *cbc* number. Potter will have them soon. Keep in touch; let me know how you're getting on. And as far as men are concerned, don't forget that they're not all bad. One simply needs to be selective and remember the five Ts which make a successful relationship: talk, tact, touch, trust and time."

"But…"

Tessa put her finger to Nyunt's lips.

"Don't worry, darling. Take your time over things, don't rush. Do you remember Coyle, my solicitor? Good. I've given him instructions to transfer some money to you; more than enough to keep you going. I've also asked him to assign you full ownership of the manor at Papa Edinsay and the South Kensington house."

"What! Won't you be living there?"

"No, but don't worry, I'll be fine. Now, you still look a bit peaky, so make sure you rest and recover properly. But don't forget to train with Lee, that'll help. Then do what you feel you need to do to make your life a good one."

Nyunt was stunned; she didn't know what to say.

"Please stay, Mum. I don't think I can manage without you."

"Of course you can, and it's high time you did... Look, darling, you have just suffered a major set-back. But now you have to decide whether you're going to carry it as a burden for the rest of your life, or use it to strengthen yourself for the future."

"But I lost my sword."

"Ah, yes. That was a trifle clumsy. But Amakuni swords have a habit of finding their way back to their rightful owners. When you draw it again, wield it well and wield it wisely. I must go now. Whatever you do, make Htet and Thuza as proud of you as I am. And don't forget, darling, I love you, a lot, and always will."

"I love you a lot, too," replied Nyunt as tears streamed down her cheeks.

"I know, darling," said Tessa, kissing her on her forehead, her own eyes damp. "Give Potter my best regards. Now, close your eyes and rest for a while."

Tessa looked at the picture, smiled, and left.

It was another ten minutes before Potter returned. He looked at Nyunt who, once again, was sobbing.

"Are you OK?"

"Mum was here."

"What? Nariko?" he exclaimed, looking round in disbelief.

"Yes, she asked me to give you her best regards. She's going to tie up some loose ends."

Potter looked nonplussed, but then something caught his eye.

"I suppose that would explain how your sword case has miraculously reappeared. Mind you, I pity the loose ends."

Nyunt spun round in surprise. She grabbed the case and rushed to open the catches. In it was her Amakuni sword. Tied round the hilt, were Tessa's house keys and the security lock for her Porsche.

That evening, Tessa was sitting with Ayane, Noboru and Oberst Müller in the back of an unmarked grey van crammed with electronics. A meeting had been in progress for some time. Potter was participating via a secure satellite link.

"...The house has four storeys," continued Ayane, "but since it's on a hill, only the top two are visible from the road; the lowest floor is beneath ground level." She nodded to Noboru and a picture of a nondescript flat-roofed white building was added to the display they were all peering at. "We have the original construction plans for the house, and no layout changes have been filed, but it has been fifteen years since the house was erected so it is likely to have been altered. The property is equipped with a highly sophisticated, essentially external alarm system comprising a variety of sensor networks and cameras. We have managed to obtain the plans for that too. Herr Doktor Krollheim arrives home about six every weekday evening; Frau Doktor Krollheim usually returns some thirty minutes after him. They do not have any children, and we do not know of anyone else we would expect to find in the house."

"Has either of them any form?" queried Potter. Adding, "committed crimes in the past?"

"Both, sort of," responded Ayane knowledgeably. "He originally qualified as a surgical support nurse, then as a psychologist. It is in this capacity that he eventually became Head of the Stuttgart Clinic for the Mentally Challenged. The Institute was investigated some six years ago following three mysterious deaths. In all these cases post-mortems indicated that the victims had suffered serious brain damage, notably to their amygdala and hippocampus. It was claimed that this was as a result of incorrect medicines or dosages having been administered. The only action taken was an instruction that the facility tighten up its drugs control procedures. Furthermore, ten years ago, he was arrested concerning the disappearance of two prostitutes. However, there was insufficient evidence to support a prosecution and he was released without charge. It was during this investigation that he met his wife-to-be, who had been retained by the police to support their investigation. They married three months later. She trained as a brain surgeon, but now works in the gynaecology department of Stuttgart General Hospital. She has also appeared in court, first for malpractice, although the case was dropped following the unexpected death of a key witness, apparently from natural causes, a brain haemorrhage. I could go on, but neither of them has ever been far from controversy. Also, there have been an unusually high number of unexplained abductions of young females in Baden Wurttemberg since the Krollheims have been living here.

"They are extremely well off, but it is not clear how they accumulated their wealth. The house alone cost in excess of twenty-five what they earn annually, and they paid for it in cash. They both drive top-of-the-range luxury vehicles, a large Mercedes saloon for him, while she has an Audi sports car. Both of them were out of the country for the first few days when Nariko was held captive in Burma… Everything is contained in the detailed files which were sent to you earlier."

"Understood," acknowledged Potter. "Thank you, Ayane. That was both comprehensive and informative. Personally, I have heard enough. Although circumstantial, this all fits the profile we would expect and, in my opinion, constitutes sufficient grounds for a direct investigation. I am willing to support Nariko's proposal to go in and search the premises."

"I'm not so sure," returned Müller. "I agree the report is persuasive, and would support a detailed examination of the Krollheims' background. But immediate Peacekeeper intervention sounds a little heavy-handed to me, especially when one or more of the Krollheims are expected to be in residence. We have no substantive proof that either of them has done anything wrong, especially Frau Doktor Krollheim, let alone that they are involved with the Calver Cats. I think my department should do more exploratory work first."

"That won't be enough," protested Tessa, exasperated. "They'll get wind of the investigation, destroy the evidence and run – we'd lose track of them. I would like to go in tomorrow."

"We know that, and I am truly sympathetic," insisted Müller. "…By way of a compromise, how about if you and I go in together, tomorrow if we must?"

"The two of us?" retorted Tessa, aghast. "How would that work?"

"I have no idea. I thought I'd let you and your team formulate a plan. But I want to be there when they're confronted, so that if I think they're not our culprits, we can make a prompt and polite exit."

"That could be… complicated," advised Tessa unenthusiastically.

"I agree," noted Potter. "Nevertheless, Nariko, in the circumstances, perhaps it is a workable way forward. Why don't you give the proposal some thought?"

Tessa cast a sideways glance at Ayane; she nodded.

"No need. We'll make it work. But that is definitely the man who injected me in Waley. So don't blame me if you get caught in the cross-fire."

"I won't... get caught or blame you," replied Müller with a smile.

At 4.45 p.m. the following afternoon, Tessa let herself in to the secure car park beneath the Stuttgart mental clinic. She strode straight to a black Mercedes and pressed one of the buttons on the remote-control unit Noboru had given her. The car's indicators flashed as the alarm was disabled. Another press brought the boot lid up. Tessa reached in and placed a large grey cylinder on the floor of the compartment. There was a dull *thud* as an air hole was punched. Satisfied with her work, she climbed in, reached up and closed the lid. Then she re-set the car alarm and waited.

Far above, in the clinic's security office, a camera screen which had been malfunctioning burst back into life. The car park looked fine, just as it had before, so the operative sat back in his chair, relieved he didn't need to do anything after all.

After twenty minutes, the car moved off. The doctor was listening to classical music, and, with several of the loudspeakers mounted through the boot space, so was Tessa. She was treated to several operatic extracts from Wagner Operas.

Eventually, the car paused, drove down a short steep hill and stopped. It was just after 6 p.m. Tessa heard the garage door closing, then the car alarm was activated, a substantial metal door clanged shut, and the garage fell silent.

After two minutes had passed, Tessa checked her knives and deactivated the car alarm. She pulled the boot release and carefully peered out. The garage was in darkness. She pushed the boot lid up and sprang out, quickly adopting an offensive position, but she was alone. She shut the boot. Now she had to let Müller in before Frau Dr Krollheim returned.

She went over to the metal door which led into the house. It was not locked. She eased it open and peered into the brightly lit corridor which ran in both directions. She reconfirmed her mental image of the house plan and quietly moved off to her left. As she approached an outside door, she readied another of Noboru's electronic boxes. She attached it near the door's alarm sensor and pressed the third button on the remote control. The door clicked open. Tessa tapped her headset.

"Side entrance clear."

"Cameras down, sensors disabled," announced Noboru. "Go now, sir. You have five seconds."

Shortly afterwards Müller appeared out of the darkness, panting. He had been forced to sprint down the drive and round the house. As soon as he had entered, Tessa shut the door and removed Noboru's box. Another click confirmed the door had re-locked.

"We're in," she rasped.

"Copy that," responded Noboru. "We still don't have access to their main computer systems, but we are receiving good audio and visual from both your headsets."

"Copy that. Proceeding. Out," said Tessa under her breath. She nodded to Müller. "I still wish you'd brought a weapon."

"I believe you have sufficient for both of us," he retorted, following Tessa's lead back along the corridor.

She carefully led the way up the ultra-modern dark hardwood stairs to the third floor. This corridor, leading along the centre of the house, was also brightly lit but not far away they could see light streaming out from the doorway to the study. The whirring sound of a computer being switched on broke the silence. Tessa padded to the open door. On the other side of the room, with his back to her, sat the doctor she'd met in Burma. Even though she could only see him from behind, there was no doubt in her mind, this was the man who'd thrust a hypodermic needle up her nose. Anger surged inside her. But her thoughts were interrupted by Ayane's voice speaking quietly in her ear.

"Can you get closer so we can watch him logging on to their cloud server?"

Tessa turned to Müller; he nodded and indicated he would stay where he was. Tessa drew a knife and moved silently into the room.

"Perfect," acknowledged Ayane.

Tessa stood stock-still, breathing very lightly.

Completely unaware of her, the doctor continued tapping the keyboard. The computer screen burst into life and a large entry field appeared for his username, then another for his password. He entered both, slowly and purposefully.

"Intercepted," affirmed Ayane. Tessa couldn't stop herself from smiling. "We need that terminal to be logged off now."

"Good evening, Dieter," greeted the computer. "You are logged on to the Krollheim cloud. Full access to all systems and data is available."

Tessa walked forward, only stopping when she was directly behind the doctor.

"*Guten abend, Liebling*," she whispered menacingly.

The doctor pressed two keys and turned round. As Tessa grabbed him by the scruff of the neck, the computer screen went blank and then displayed the message *X-Log off complete*. Tessa yanked him up and away from the keyboard.

"I promised I'd find you," she hissed.

"*Gott im Himmel!*" he exclaimed, trembling. "Who are you? What are you doing in my house? Do you want money? I will give it to you... please, don't hurt me." Then he raised his left hand, fist clenched, opened it vertically, quickly clenched it again and opened it palm downwards. Then he muttered "*Bang! Bang!*"

"Nasty twitch you've got there," mocked Tessa. "Hypnotic commands will not save you now."

"What do you mean? I..."

"Stop babbling, you know who I am. This is Oberst Müller, Head of German Special Forces. We're going to ask you some questions, and you'd better answer them truthfully – your life depends on it. Understand?" Tessa hurled him across the room, where he landed roughly in an armchair. "I told you to be scared, Doktor, and you should be. Very, very scared," she sneered, brandishing her knife.

"Nariko!" interrupted Müller.

"There is no doubt," she assured him, "this is the quack who drugged me."

"Quite possibly, you were certainly right about the hand gestures. But we're still going to do this by the book."

Tessa shrugged and waved her knife to indicate he should watch the doctor; she went over to the computer terminal, sat down and tapped her headset. There was no response. Müller was standing over Herr Dr Krollheim who had adjusted his position to sit upright with his right arm dangling over the side of the chair.

"Herr Oberst," said Tessa, "I think our headsets have..."

But then she heard a faint shuffling noise behind her. She sprang up, spinning round – knife in hand. Framed in the doorway stood Frau Doktor Krollheim; an air pistol in her right hand and a knife in her left. Oberst Müller yelped in pain and there was an abrupt *phut* as the air pistol fired. Tessa just had time to bring her knife up. The dart hit the blade with a loud *ping* and ricocheted off harmlessly into the wall. She quickly glanced at Müller, collapsing to the floor with a knife wound in his shoulder. His right hand was bleeding too. The Doktor had already yanked himself up on one arm of the chair and was preparing to stab Müller again. Tessa immediately flicked her weapon at him – the blade sank into the centre of his forehead. As he crumpled back in the chair, dead, Müller sank to the floor moaning. By now Krollheim's wife had discarded the pistol and was holding the knife in her right hand. She started forward screaming and shouting like one possessed. Tessa chuckled enthusiastically and stepped out to meet her.

As the woman raised her right arm to strike, Tessa reached up with her left hand and grabbed it, then punching the woman hard on the forehead. She was momentarily stunned, and Tessa pushed her back so she could slam her right forearm across the edge of the open door. There was a dull *crack* as the bones snapped. The woman screamed in agony and dropped the knife. Tessa jerked her round pushing her up against the doorframe; the back of her head made a dull *clonk* as it hit the metal. Tessa glanced at Müller. He was propped awkwardly against the armchair babbling incomprehensibly, clearly in considerable discomfort, but didn't appear to be seriously injured. However, his eyes were wide open with hugely dilated pupils.

"What was on the knife?" demanded Tessa, turning back to Frau Doktor Krollheim.

"Whore! Murderer! Why should I tell you?"

Tessa gripped her hard by the neck and drew a knife, positioning it on the woman's thigh.

"You wouldn't dare!" she taunted.

"I'm a Peacekeeper, you have threatened my life and are endangering my colleague's. I can do whatever I like. Now, tell me."

Frau Krollheim reacted by spitting in Tessa's face.

Tessa's response was quick and considered; the blade passed through the woman's trousers and deep into her leg. She screamed in pain, but Tessa knew the blade had not severed any major blood vessels.

"Tell me," demanded Tessa, "or it'll get a lot worse."

The woman clenched her jaw shut, determined not to say anything. So Tessa began to twist the knife, prompting a loud groan in response.

"I said, tell me."

"It's a sedative hallucinogen, it will wear off – twenty minutes!" yelled the woman.

"Are you sure?" pressed Tessa, forcing the knife just a little further into the woman's thigh.

"Yes, yes," she shrieked. "Please, no more."

"Thank you," said Tessa, removing her knife and cleaning it on the woman's white blouse.

"*Oh, scheiße*, Nariko," blathered Müller, clearly struggling to speak coherently. "Don't... er... kill..."

"Aren't you the lucky one?" scorned Tessa at the Doktor.

"Hah! When I tell people of our achievements, they will congratulate me. I have advanced science and the understanding of the brain."

"Rubbish!" they'll be disgusted," replied Tessa, feeling in her waist-bag for some tie wraps. "Evil such as yours retards the human race. Anyway, your procedures are flawed. Why else would I be here?"

"Perhaps I underestimated the hardening resulting from your earlier treatments," replied the woman thoughtfully. "It would be interesting to investigate that further."

"You're sick," retorted Tessa.

"I am a scientist. I am not ashamed. Maybe I'll be awarded the Nobel Prize..."

"Oh, do shut up," asserted Tessa, and punched her in the jaw. As her body crumpled to the floor, Tessa tightened long tie wraps round her feet and rolled her on to her front. Then she strapped the Doktor's elbows and wrists behind her back and pulled her feet up so she could bind the two tie wraps together. Finally, she cut off the sleeves of the woman's blouse. She used one to bandage the gashed thigh and the other to wipe the spittle off her own face before making a gag for the Doktor's mouth.

"Silence is golden," professed Tessa, and went over to Müller. She quickly tended his wound with bandages from her waist bag and moved him to an armchair. He smiled at her weakly: but was only vaguely aware of what was happening. Tessa went to the computer terminal. She sat looking at the keyboard for a moment, trying to decide what to do. Then she shrugged and pressed the Enter key and was greeted with the login screen.

"Phew!" she muttered, grinning as she heard a gentle *click* in her headphones.

"Is everything all right?" asked Ayane urgently.

"It is now," replied Tessa, turning so that her headset camera panned round the room. "We certainly had the right targets. Switch to secure one-on-one comms."

"Copy that."

"OK. Can you get full access to their cloud systems now?"

Noboru grunted in the background.

"Yes. We've just logged in."

"OK, delete all the existing usernames and passwords and replace them with one of our own. Something obscure so we're guaranteed sole access while we implement the rest of our plan."

"Understood."

"Müller's OK for now, I'm pretty sure I recognise his symptoms. Call for support in fifteen minutes. I'll go and explore before he comes round."

"Copy that. Ayane out."

Tessa removed a large bunch of keys from the Doktor's belt and went downstairs. She thought it likely that whatever unpleasant things were kept in the house would probably be secreted in the two lower storeys.

But she didn't find much of interest on the first of these, the garage level. It simply comprised a bathroom, an exercise room, a kitchen, sitting room and bedroom with en-suite bedroom; all large but only functionally furnished. However, there was a sophisticated multi-screen CCTV system, albeit currently inactive. At the bottom of the stairs leading to the basement storey, Tessa was confronted by a substantial locked metal door. She eventually found the correct key, but a few feet on had to go through the same process with a similar door. Past this was yet another door, but made from vertical metal bars this time, as one would expect to find in a prison. Clearly, whatever was on this floor was kept very secure.

Along the corridor, Tessa found five more locked doors. The two on the left, each with a reinforced one-way inspection window, were sizeable self-contained prison cells comprising a large room with a bed, and a bathroom. Beside the door to each cell was an alcove containing a gas cylinder; it seemed the occupant could be gassed whenever required from outside. Furthermore, the beds bore a harrowing resemblance to the gurney she had been restrained on during her captivity in Insein. Tessa could feel the hackles rising on the back of her neck. There was no doubt that she was in a place where untold evils had been inflicted on numerous people.

The next door she opened confirmed her worst suspicions: it revealed a fully equipped operating theatre. The array of equipment was extremely impressive; modern and comprehensive, it even included an X-ray machine and a small MRI scanner. However, it seemed that nearly all the apparatus was oriented towards working on the brain, although she did find several pumps similar to the one which had been implanted in her.

"Ayane, are you getting all this?"

"Yes," she replied, clearly shocked by what she was seeing. "We've started looking at the data files on their cloud systems. They're awful. There's even one on you."

Tessa took a deep breath and went to the penultimate door. Inside she found a pharmacy stacked high with all sorts of drugs in boxes and bottles. One cupboard caught her eye in particular. It had a glass door through which she could see names she recognised, including her own and those of Toshie Miyazaki and Karen Weissman.

"Those are the mind-control drugs they were developing," interjected Ayane. "I have the chemical constituents here in the files, even the testing procedures and usage regimes."

Tessa opened the cabinet and looked inside an unmarked cardboard box on one of the middle shelves. It contained an air pistol and a box of hypodermic darts.

"Hmm. See if you can work out what I'd need to knock out a ninety-kilo man."

"Copy that."

Tessa went back into the corridor and opened the final door. At first, she didn't understand what she was looking at. The lights were very bright and the walls, floor and ceiling were all painted brilliant white. Then she realised she was in the records room. She walked over to the first of several wide horizontal filing cabinets. She opened the top drawer and took out one of the blue files. It began with a large picture of the subject, a fifteen-year-old boy... what they'd done to him was horrific. She replaced that file and took out another, a pink file this time, that of a thirteen-year-old girl...

The cabinets were positioned in chronological order, so Tessa went to the last. In it she found her own file and those of Toshie Miyazaki and Karen Weissman. She removed all three and placed them on top of the cabinet.

On the other side of the room was a row of four white cabinets. These all boasted green LEDs, which, together with the gentle humming of pumps, suggesting to Tessa that they were refrigerated. The nameplate on one of them caught her eye, Toshie Miyazaki. She pulled down the large chromium handle and eased the door open.

She took a step back in shock. Facing her was the head of a young Japanese woman, eyes misted over but wide open, staring ahead. Tessa recognised her instantly from the pictures she had seen in the media.

"Oh, no," she groaned.

On the same shelf were glass jars and Petri dishes with what appeared to be samples of brain tissue. On the bottom shelf was a used drugs pump, and a tin marked *Asche*. Tessa stood staring into the fridge for several seconds, before clearing her voice.

"Don't worry, Toshie," she breathed finally. "It's over now. We've come to take you home."

"Ayane." There was no reply. "Ayane," repeated Tessa, slightly more urgently.

"Yes, sorry, I..."

"Me too. We need a refrigerator. I want Toshie to come with us." She could hear Ayane conferring with Noboru.

"No problem, we can do that. I saw some freezer boxes down there."

"Yes, good. Have Noboru come down. I want to remove everything which references me or Toshie Miyazaki. I'll take the Weissman file to show Müller. Oh, and tell Noboru to take that air pistol and whatever else we need to be able to use it."

361

"Copy that. He's on his way. I'll call for the ambulance now."

Tessa lingered a while inside the dungeons, but then, with a heavy heart, made her way back upstairs.

When she reached the ground floor she passed Noboru on his way down. He was carrying a large attaché case. Back in the study, Tessa went to Müller.

"Herr Oberst?" she said, gently lifting his head.

He looked her in the eye, the old sparkle slowly returning.

"What the hell did they give me?"

"Apparently a hallucinogen of some description, nothing dangerous, there shouldn't be any after-effects."

"After the dreams I've been having, I don't need any."

"Been there, done that," replied Tessa, grinning.

"I know," he mumbled, "and I don't blame you."

"Oh, good. An ambulance is on its way, but we need to talk first. Are you up to it?"

"I think so. What have you found?"

"Well, it's pretty bad down there."

"How bad?"

"Disgusting beyond belief, actually. I've seen some terrible things in my life, but what's down there has shocked me to the core. It's been going on for years."

Müller breathed out heavily and shook his head, awkwardly taking out his *cbc* and calling for back up.

"Help me up, please," he said weakly, nodding to the computer.

Tessa guided him on to the chair in front of the terminal.

"What's up with this?" asked Müller.

"He logged off and jammed our headsets," answered Tessa.

Müller grunted.

"I don't suppose you happen to have the username and password?"

"They seem to have changed, but you can always ask her," replied Tessa, nodding towards the trussed up woman.

Noboru appeared at the door, struggling with the polystyrene freezer box firmly strapped shut and the now-heavy attaché case. He nodded at Tessa.

"I'll join you in the van in a few minutes. Stay out of sight."

"What exactly is he removing?" asked Müller, concerned.

"Only my file, and both the file and the remains of Toshie Miyazaki; there are a few other odds and ends, but nothing of fundamental importance to your case. You're welcome to have a full list if you need one. Here's Karen Weissman's file to give you an indication of what I mean; there are lots more like it down there."

Müller flicked through the papers.

"*Oh, mein Gott!*" he exclaimed. "Already I am not looking forward to interrogating her."

It was another two hours before Tessa, Ayane and Noboru were able to drive away from the house in Stuttgart. Thanks to the remoteness of the exclusive property, Müller felt it would be relatively straightforward to ensure a media blackout concerning the events of the night. But Tessa knew she needed to act even more quickly now.

However, first she wanted to visit a private crematorium in Stuttgart. She had decided that Toshie's head and other remains should be cremated and added to the ashes that had already been collected. She was sure it would be less stressful for Minister Miyazaki and his wife if their daughter's remains were at least returned in just one container. So, an expensive Fukagawa Seiji funeral urn had been rushed from Düsseldorf.

When they reached the crematorium, Müller joined them. He looked pale and his arm was in a sling.

They started by incinerating Tessa and Toshie's files. Then they held a short and sombre service in Japanese for Toshie. It was as near Buddhist as time and geographic constraints could make it. Tessa couldn't hold back the tears. It brought home to her how many of her own friends' funerals she'd witnessed, and how close she had come to being another of the Krollheims' victims…

CHAPTER 33

Ten hours later, the Chrysanthemum jet was over India speeding towards Mae Sai in northern Thailand. The journey had been a very quiet one. The three of them had been deeply affected by the horrors witnessed in Stuttgart, and had barely slept. Tessa constantly found herself looking at the carefully stowed funeral urn, willing it messages of comfort.

However, as the plane started its final approach, Tessa forced herself to concentrate on the job in hand. She had already arranged a meeting, primarily to implement the next part of her plan, though she was also looking forward to it immensely for entirely different reasons. A beautifully wrapped box stood on the seat opposite her.

As soon as the plane had landed and the steps lowered, Tessa hurried down. Three people came forward to meet her.

"Morning, Curtis," said Tessa. "It's good to see you again."

"You too," he replied, grinning.

"Khin," greeted Tessa, embracing him warmly, "I cannot tell you how delighted I am to see you, and to meet your wife too. What a good idea it was to go to Kyaiktiyo. *Mingalabah*, Ohnmar..."

Ayane and Noboru joined them with the gift box which Tessa promptly presented to Khin and Ohnmar. Then all five of them went to a secure meeting room while the plane was refuelled.

For nearly two hours, they exchanged stories. While Ayane and Noboru dozed, the others recounted horrific experiences, near-misses and eventual escapes. Finally, the conversation found its own way back to what still remained unresolved.

Tessa updated Curtis on what had happened in Stuttgart. Then Noboru explained that he had managed to track numerous communications between the Krollheims, Paul and the Sheikh; sufficient to suggest new messages could be issued authentically. Furthermore, that Paul's *cbc* could be used as one of the sources as no one had tried to access it since Tessa had removed it from Karatsu.

"...So, Khin, as I mentioned to Curtis, I was wondering whether you and Ohnmar could do something for me. I don't think it will be in the slightest bit dangerous, and, it is all expenses paid."

"We'd love to," he grinned, taking up Ohnmar's hand, "how can we help?"

"Well, I would like you to cross into Laos and travel down to Pakse." She placed Paul's *cbc* on the table. "Take this with you and book yourselves into a good hotel – not the best, I'm afraid. Sorry, but it would be unwise to attract too much attention. I'll call you on your *cbc* when I need you to switch on Paul's; we'll be using it to route messages. We'll send some text to it which you'll then need to cut and paste, and resend as a new message to the address we specify. Would that be all right?"

Khin looked at Ohnmar, who nodded and smiled, and then at Curtis.

"Not a problem," he said. "How long would you like them to stay there, Nariko?"

"At least a week, possibly two... Oh, and Khin, I recommend you wile away a day by going downriver to Wat Phu. The Khmer ruins there are marvellous..."

After the lengthy farewells were over, the Chrysanthemum jet headed back to Germany. Meanwhile, Khin and Ohnmar set off for Vientiane, from where they would catch a Lao Air flight south to Pakse.

Totally exhausted, Tessa, Ayane and Noboru found they were able to get some sleep, at last. They didn't convene again until the plane was nearing Stuttgart. Khin had just sent an encrypted text to say he and Ohnmar were installed in the Pakse Grand Central Hotel.

"...Well," stated Tessa, "until we get a response we won't really know how best to proceed. However, assuming we can lure him out of Irabya, it will be one of the two options I just outlined. Otherwise, we might have to go in and get him."

"With respect, I have reservations about that," confessed Ayane hesitantly, not wishing to overstep her authority.

"I understand, Ayane. I'm not exactly enthusiastic about it either. Thank you for being candid," acknowledged Tessa, encouragingly. "But I propose that, apart from accepting we might have to consider all possibilities at some point in the future, we leave worrying about the details until then."

"OK," continued Ayane, deciding to throw caution to the wind. "Just for the record, I think the first two options sound rather risky too, particularly for you."

Tessa shrugged her acknowledgement and offered her some more fruit. She smiled and took another piece of papaya.

Forty minutes later, the three of them were huddled round a computer screen.

"I think it's good to go," said Tessa, reading the text one more time before sitting back.

Dear Sheikh Simitar,

I hope this communication finds you well.

As you may have heard, our plans in Japan did not develop as anticipated. Indeed, I cannot deny we suffered a setback there. However, the Calver Cats organisation remains strong elsewhere and, following Kurou's death, I have assumed full control.

It is in this capacity that I am pleased to inform you that, as I made my escape, I was able to bring your package with me. Keen to ensure it received the best possible attention, I left it with our German friends for completion of the refinishing process. I am reliably informed that the goods will be available for dispatch in three days.

I accept it is a while since we discussed this transaction and that you were understandably disappointed by Kurou's refusal to refund your deposit following the problems at Tunis. However, I am now in a position to complete our agreement, and, as a gesture of goodwill, am willing to deliver the package as before for a fee of only 50% of the outstanding balance.

I trust this will be acceptable and, as always, look forward to hearing from you.

May your God bring you good fortune,
Paul

Tessa glanced at Ayane and Noboru.

"Well? Any comments, suggestions or reservations?" Both shook their heads. "OK, Noboru, please send it to Khin for forwarding."

He nodded and, shortly afterwards, Khin confirmed successful receipt and onward transmission.

"Good," noted Tessa. "Now we wait."

After a while, the three of them relocated to a suite in a Stuttgart airport hotel; two of the pilots were in the neighbouring room, while the third remained on the plane. Noboru was monitoring all the relevant email accounts, including those on the Krollheims' cloud system. Although nothing had been said, they were all beginning to wonder when, if ever, the Sheikh would respond...

Suddenly one of the computers beeped, then another. They quickly huddled round the displays. There were two messages, both from the Sheikh; the first was to Paul, the second to Herr Dr Krollheim.

Paul,
I am pleased to hear you, at least, were able to escape. With regards to the package, I will consider your proposal and respond shortly.
Simitar

Sehr geehrte Herr Doktor Krollheim,
I understand that you have been working on my package. What is its current condition?
Simitar

Barely able to contain her excitement, a broad grin spread across Tessa's face.

"We're in business," she observed. "Looks like it'll be either option one or two, Ayane. Let's issue Paul's reply from Pakse first, then the Krollheims'. But there's no rush, we'll keep him dangling for a bit first."

Dear Sheikh Simitar,
Your reply is much appreciated. However, it would be most helpful if you could let me know whether or not you intend to proceed at your earliest convenience since otherwise I need to contact other potential purchasers. Thank you.
May your God bring you good fortune,
Paul

Dear Sheikh Simitar,

I can confirm your package is in excellent condition. We have both inspected it carefully and can assure you that our adjustments have produced an outstanding result, as predicted.

Furthermore, we have been able to dispense with the pump, a slow-release pellet now maintains the background levels required. We will need access to replace it every six months, a simple ten minute procedure.

So, the package is fully ready and we are sure you will not be disappointed. Should you require any further information, please do not hesitate to contact either of us.

Mit freundlichen Grüßen
Herr & Frau Dr Dieter Krollheim
Stuttgart

It was midday and they had just finished lunch when the Sheikh's response arrived.

Paul,

I am willing to accept late delivery of the package. However, as so much time has passed since our agreement was originally sealed, I propose to pay only 25% of the outstanding balance.

Assuming this meets with your approval, I will collect the package in Tunis as before.

Simitar

Tessa read the message with raised eyebrows.

"I'm not sure there's much love lost between those two. Maybe I did get through to him at Insein," she laughed and pressed the carriage return key to send her reply from the Krollheims' cloud system.

Dear Sheikh Simitar,

Thank you for responding so soon. I have now been able to inspect the package in its final condition personally and can assure you it is even better than I expected. I am therefore hesitant to accept such a low sum for what is clearly a truly unique opportunity. However, I do acknowledge you suffered considerable inconvenience and am keen to demonstrate that we can establish a good trading relationship for the future. Therefore, I would like to suggest a compromise. Let us agree on 37.5% of the outstanding balance with handover in three days (i.e. Thursday) in Tunis, essentially as before.

I hope this meets with your approval and look forward to hearing from you again soon.

May your God bring you good fortune,
Paul

The response arrived after only ten minutes.

Dear Paul,

That is acceptable.

I will be travelling by yacht to La Goulette and will bring the negotiable bonds with me. These will be handed over once I have inspected the package for myself.

Simitar

Tessa smiled at Ayane and Noboru with a glint of accomplishment in her eyes.

"Option two it is," she declared. "Yes, I know it's dangerous, Ayane, but I don't see we have much choice. Neither Tunisia nor Irabya has signed the International Peacekeeper Treaty yet, even if Tunisia is likely to sign soon. So, I cannot undertake Peacekeeper actions in either country without being hauled before the tribunal, again. Even in international waters I can only act as a private individual protecting my rights; unless I have special permissions, which I don't. However, if this works according to plan we'll get his yacht into British Territorial waters and then I'll be able to respond as a Peacekeeper under attack."

"Assuming we reach British Territorial waters," retorted Ayane, quietly, as if she hardly dared speak the words.

"True. But that will depend on you two as much as me. However, whatever happens neither of you should get yourself into trouble. We're a good team, and we've done well to get this far, but if anyone is going to go down for overstepping their authority, it's only going to be me. Understood?" They both nodded. "OK. Now, Noboru, what do we know about his yacht?"

"Well, he has two. Both are large, sophisticated, ocean-going vessels. *Simitar 2* is a converted military ship, purchased from France six years ago. It has eight decks, a crew of one-hundred-and-fifty and two helicopters. There's a landing pad on the back…"

"Wow!" exclaimed Tessa.

"Indeed. However, he's used *Simitar 1* for all his previous sea trips to Tunis. It is a faster, much smaller vessel, less than half the size of *Simitar 2*. But it still has five decks and a crew of thirty-five. I have the deck plans of both."

Tessa nodded and sent a quick acceptance email to the Sheikh and told him full details of the handover would follow. But she took her time with these. It was only on Tuesday morning when she sent what she hoped would be the last potentially controversial communication.

Dear Sheikh Simitar,

I am pleased to confirm that your package is in transit. Regrettably, however, I will not be able to attend the handover myself on Thursday. Although I was able to escape from Japan with the package, that was not before it inflicted some damage on me. The doctors are tending my wounds and assure me I will make a full recovery, but are adamant that I should rest now and not travel.

Accordingly, I have delegated the handover to a team led by my two most trusted associates. It is they who will meet you in the hotel lobby with the room key. They will also provide you with an air pistol loaded with a sedative dart. Of course, you will not need it as any instructions you give in the agreed manner will be followed to the letter. Nevertheless, I wasn't sure how you were intending to transport the package to your yacht, and thought this might give you peace of mind. Furthermore, in the room with the package will be an appropriately sized trunk in which the package is used to travelling.

My sincere apologies for not being able to be present at the handover. But perhaps, if convenient, I could visit your country soon in order to hear how you are enjoying the goods?

May your God bring you good fortune,
Paul

They had to wait barely five minutes for the Sheikh's reply:

Dear Paul,

I am sorry to hear you have been injured. You had not mentioned that before. But I am willing to allow your associates to complete our transaction on your behalf. My guard will also comprise two people.

Rest assured, you will be made most welcome in Irabya, as will the package.

I await the final details and wish you a full and speedy recovery.

Simitar

It was soon confirmed that the handover would take place in the Hotel Grand Tunis at 4 p.m., a time the Sheikh had selected in order to clash with afternoon prayers and so help guarantee privacy. Just the room number needed to be advised. It would only be made known once the negotiable bonds had been inspected.

CHAPTER 34

The jet was airborne an hour later, heading for the same secluded aerodrome south of Tunis from which Tessa had been collected some months before. A Japanese Embassy car had been dispatched to drive the three of them back to Tunis.

Ayane and Noboru checked in to the hotel on Wednesday evening, taking separate, neighbouring rooms, numbers 521 and 523. Their baggage included a large, heavy trunk. As soon as the hotel staff had left, Tessa used the secret release to let herself out of it.

Having got accustomed to the layout of the rooms, they settled down together in room 521. Noboru used his laptop to hack into the harbour security cameras and with alarming alacrity soon had live views of the ships moored in, entering and leaving La Goulette.

They ate dinner together early and tried to get a good night's sleep. None of them was particularly successful in this respect and they soon gathered again for a subdued breakfast. Afterwards, with a palpable atmosphere of tension in the room, they carried on with their preparations. Finally, Ayane carefully filled the tranquilliser dart and, after double-checking her handiwork, and turned to Tessa.

"Nariko, I don't wish to speak out of turn," she started hesitantly, prompting Tessa to chuckle since clearly that was precisely what she intended to do, "but I think allowing them to sedate you is… er… tempting fate. Who knows what they will do to you while you're unconscious?"

"I agree it is dangerous, but it might be even more so if I just pretend to do what he says. When he asks you, tell him the dart will knock me out for three hours. That will give him more than enough time to get me back to the ship and into international waters. We both know I'll be coming round in just over an hour."

"But suppose he ties you up?"

"Well, either I'll cut my way out with the knife hidden in the trunk or you'll have to release me."

"But suppose we're not able to get on the boat?"

"I have every confidence in you. If our friends at our respective embassies do their jobs properly, you'll have more than sufficient time to beat me to the ship and stowaway aboard. Failing that, follow me in the stealth RHIB that's on stand-by. We know it's faster than his yacht and they won't be able to see it on their radar so you should be able to approach unobserved in the dark. Failing that, you'll have to get the helicopter to bring you." Ayane looked doubtful. "I know. But none of us could think of anything better when we discussed it in Stuttgart. Has that situation changed?" Ayane shook her head. "OK, then we'll go with this. Noboru, you're sure you can handle the yacht?"

"Absolutely, I was brought up in a fishing village – I'm used to boats."

"Oh, excellent. Then as soon as you're aboard, your job will be to take control of the bridge and get the ship to British Territorial waters as quickly as possible. Once we're there, put out a ship-wide announcement. Ayane, you come and find me. I should be in one of the four suites we suspect he uses as prison cells. Now, not wishing to repeat the obvious, don't forget to wear your gloves, and only use the weapons I've left fingerprints on."

"All right," conceded Ayane, sighing unhappily. "But isn't your Peacekeeper Tribunal set for the same time you're meeting the Sheikh? I thought attendance was mandatory; supposing your license is revoked?"

"Ah, yes. I must admit the timing of that is a rather unfortunate coincidence. However, this is too important to let my peacekeeping future get in the way. Besides, if something goes wrong with our plan, I won't have a future. I sent an extremely apologetic email to the tribunal explaining why I will not be able to attend in person. Hopefully that will lead to a postponement or something."

Ayane looked unconvinced.

"Please, Ayane, you're starting to make me worry too."

Late that afternoon, Ayane opened the adjoining door to room 523. Tessa took a deep breath, went in and handed back her bathrobe. She stood in the green nightie she'd worn when escaping from the container; although this time she was wearing a pair of knickers too.

"See you in couple of hours then," said Tessa, trying to appear calm...

Ayane and Noboru were seated in the hotel foyer when the Sheikh and two burly armed guards entered. They both stood and bowed, and Noboru gestured towards the three armchairs opposite. But not a word was said. The Sheikh placed a chromium briefcase on the table between them. He flipped open the locks, opened the lid and spun the case round so the contents were clearly visible. Ayane made a random selection of bonds and validitated them using her netbook. She nodded acceptance to Noboru and he pushed a small mother of pearl box towards the Sheikh; in it was the air pistol and the key card to room 523.

The Sheikh removed the room key, but left the air pistol. Noboru looked up at him quizzically. He simply smiled and indicated that Noboru and Ayane were not to move. Then he raised his right hand and clicked his fingers. Another two men entered the hotel pushing a baggage trolley with a large trunk on it. The Sheikh joined the men with the trunk as they entered the lift...

Tessa was standing near the window feeling vulnerable when she heard the door open. She turned round and smiled at the Sheikh.

"*Habibi*. I'm so pleased to see you. I've been terribly lonely here all on my own."

"Oh, you needn't be lonely any more. But first we must travel home." As Tessa braced herself for the impact of the sedative dart, two men wheeled another trunk into the room and opened the lid. The Sheikh clapped twice and drew a gold-plated handgun, a real weapon not the expected air pistol, and he aimed it at her. "Nariko, I'd like you to get in the trunk now."

"If that's what you want, I'd love to," chimed Tessa, thinking it had taken less than ten seconds for her plan to go horribly wrong.

She sauntered over to the trunk and climbed in. She could see there were air holes, but the last thing she remembered was the lid being closed and hearing a hissing sound.

Not long afterwards, the trunk was wheeled back out of the lift. Ayane tried desperately hard not to look concerned, but was already worried that her worst case scenario was unfolding before them; they were about to lose track of Tessa.

374

The Sheikh nodded to one of the men pushing the trolley.

"Send our regards to Paul. We look forward to doing business with him again soon. My colleagues will stay with you for thirty minutes..."

After thirty-one nerve-racking minutes, Ayane went into overdrive. She called the plane and told them to locate the yacht before it got too dark. Then she and Noboru were driven away from the hotel at breakneck speed.

The video from room 523 showed that Tessa had been gassed in the Sheikh's trunk. Meanwhile Japanese embassy observers confirmed that the trunk had been transferred straight from the hotel to the yacht. They soon received a response from the plane; *Simitar 1* was cruising at a leisurely fourteen knots along the international shipping lane towards Irabya. As they stopped by the RHIB, Noboru finished his calculations.

"We can just catch it," he shouted. As their gear was quickly stowed in the boat, they hurriedly donned wetsuits and cast off. Ignoring harbour regulations, Noboru yanked the throttle lever over to maximum.

It was an hour before they finally caught sight of *Simitar 1*. It had been a very rough journey, but the timing was good. It was nearly dark...

Consciousness announced its return to Tessa with an echoic buzzing in her ears. She fought hard against the urge to open her eyes and simply lay still, marshalling her strength and senses. Then she surreptitiously checked that her legs and right hand were not restrained. She didn't attempt to move her left hand as she could feel a strange tingling sensation moving across it. Eventually, as she was facing that way, she eased her eyes open to find a smartly dressed woman wearing a black hijab with her burqa, both with gold embroidered decoration, painting an intricate henna design on her hand.

"I didn't give my permission," murmured Tessa, slurring her words to make it sound as though she felt groggy.

The woman looked at her, apparently surprised she was awake.

"The Sheikh wants you to have this. You must always do as the master says; we all must."

Tessa raised herself unsteadily to look at the woman's handiwork; it was an extremely beautiful design. She also saw two guards watching her, seated either side of the door. One was toying with an air pistol, but neither of them was really concentrating.

"It's lovely," noted Tessa, smiling at the woman.

She nodded, put down the henna applicator and reached for a hypodermic syringe on a finely patterned brass saucer. But as she used her teeth to remove the plastic cover from the needle, Tessa hit her sharply on the jaw, simultaneously rolling off the bed clutching a pillow. The guard to the left of the door aimed the air pistol and fired, but the dart simply buried itself in the pillow. A moment later, she punched him hard on his Adam's apple; gasping for air, he collapsed to the floor on all fours. Tessa didn't stop moving. The second guard had stood up and was drawing a knife. She spun round on her left foot and kicked the man hard in the stomach. He doubled up, winded. Tessa approached, cupped both hands together and hit him abruptly on the back of the neck. There was a hollow *crunch* as it snapped, and the man fell forward, dead. By now, the other man was reaching for his knife. But Tessa calmly drew the other man's and threw it. Then there was silence.

Tessa gathered both knives and injected the woman with the contents of the syringe. Then she cut sufficient strands of bedding to comprehensively silence and restrain her.

She quickly searched the room and found some more tranquilliser darts. She reloaded the air pistol and put one of the men's belt on so she could slip the knives through it. She looked at her hand, now with its tattoo smudged.

"Shame," she muttered, wiping as much of the henna off as she could. "Not sure it suited me though."

Suddenly there was a commotion outside the cabin. Tessa smiled as she recognised the fighting cries of one of the protagonists. She flung open the door to find a man with his right hand already swinging down to stab Ayane in the back. Tessa grabbed his forearm with both hands and quickly thrust it upwards and round. He had no choice but to turn and face her. But she simply kneed him in the groin, drew a knife and stabbed through his back straight into his heart. She had already concluded that this was no time to stand on ceremony; these opponents had to be silenced quickly and permanently.

Meanwhile, Ayane was confronting another man in front of her while one more was approaching from behind him; both were armed with long knives. Tessa threw one of her knives at the second man. It struck him in the eye and he fell, dead. Ayane soon dispatched the other.

"*Konichiwa*, Ayane," greeted Tessa, grinning. "It is very good to see you,"

"*Konichiwa*, Nariko," replied Ayane, clearly relieved. "It is very good to see you too."

Suddenly the PA system crackled.

"Bridge secured," gasped Noboru, trying unsuccessfully to stifle a groan. Clearly he had been injured. "British Territorial waters in twelve minutes – prepare for full speed."

Tessa jammed herself in the doorframe while, further down the corridor, Ayane twisted a door handle on the other side of the corridor. It wouldn't budge so she hurriedly backed off and kicked it open, bracing herself against the corridor wall. Then, as Noboru selected full speed, the yacht lurched violently as it rose up and started ploughing through the rising sea.

"Sports armoury," rasped Ayane, moving towards the open door.

Tessa was about to join her when a shot rang out. Blood spurted from Ayane's left thigh as a bullet grazed her. She didn't make a sound, simply lunging into the armoury and disappearing from view.

Tessa was just about to ask her whether she was all right, when the answer came in the form of a harpoon gun being slid across the floor towards Tessa, a second one followed. It hit the first, which Tessa was then able to use to hook over the other so she could pull that one in too. Some more shots ricocheted down the corridor as guards tried to keep them pinned down. But this didn't stop Ayane. A stream of high quality knives followed the harpoon guns.

"OK," said Tessa, wondering what she was going to do with the vast array of weapons she had accumulated. "I think that should do."

"There are quite a lot of them," responded Ayane.

She moved nearer the armoury door.

"Have you been hurt badly?" asked Tessa.

"I can defend, but not attack," gasped Ayane.

"OK," acknowledged Tessa, grabbing the harpoon guns. "It's my turn now anyway. I'll be back."

There was another door in her room leading to the neighbouring suite, the only one remaining between her and the ship's atrium and central stairwell, from where she thought the guards were firing.

She moved to the door but, just as she was about to open it, the handle started turning. As she heard the lock unlatch, she brusquely shoved it partly open. Through the gap, she found herself facing a somewhat surprised man. She simply jabbed the harpoon gun deep into his chest. It was a fatal wound and he staggered back moaning, allowing the door to swing further open. Tessa found two other men in the adjoining suite, both armed with guns. She quickly shot one with her harpoon gun. The spear passed straight through his chest and propelled him backwards, pinning him to the wall behind. The second man fired at where Tessa had been, but she was already safe behind the metal wall.

On a nearby cupboard, she saw a mirror on a stand. She grabbed it and, pushing it with the empty harpoon gun, slid it into the doorway to locate the other guard. A hail of bullets came her way; one smashed the mirror while another knocked the harpoon gun out of her hand. As it slid across the floor, Tessa felt sure it had been damaged by the impact. However, as soon as the firing stopped, Tessa reached round and shot the other harpoon gun. She missed her attacker, but was close enough to force him to dodge out of the way. That gave her ample time to throw a knife. It struck him in the shoulder, the next caught him in the back of the head.

It was quiet in both rooms now so Tessa went back to the door opening out into the corridor.

"Ayane, are there any more harpoons?" she asked.

"Just a minute."

More bullets whistled down the corridor. Ignoring them, Ayane tossed several harpoons towards Tessa. She was able to reach all but one of them.

"Nine minutes," interjected Noboru on the PA system, though a loud hammering in the background suggested someone was trying to break into the bridge.

"I think Noboru might need some help," ventured Ayane.

"On my way," replied Tessa. "Stay safe, don't be brave."

She reloaded her harpoon gun and went back into the adjoining room. It was then that she noticed a young girl on the bed. About sixteen years old, she was extremely beautiful with long black hair and sparkling brown eyes. Her hands and feet were bound and her mouth was gagged. As soon as she saw Tessa, she grunted and started thrashing around. Tessa went over to her and smiled.

"Don't be afraid," she said reassuringly, "I've come to rescue you." She put a finger over her own mouth to signify the girl should remain silent, and cut her bonds. Then she removed the gag, and gestured for the girl to crouch down in the corner of the room behind the bed. She sat up and rubbed her wrists and ankles, before taking cover as suggested.

Tessa smiled and wondered how many more captives there were in the other suites. She moved to the door which led into the atrium and cautiously opened it a little to peer though. She could see a lot of the central hallway, but not where the guards were shooting from. Then she noticed a pair of large vases on a sideboard opposite the bed. She took one over to the door and checked her harpoon gun was ready. Then she drew the tranquilliser pistol and put it on the floor within easy reach. She was just about to open the door when the young girl said something in Arabic. Tessa had no idea what it meant, and shrugged with a puzzled expression on her face. So the girl smiled, got up, collected the second vase and joined Tessa by the door. Then she put her vase down and took the first from Tessa grip, gesturing that she would throw it through the doorway as a decoy. Tessa showed she understood this by picking up the harpoon gun, but also made sure the girl knew to stay well out of harm's way. She nodded, took a deep breath and opened the door. She yelled something vehemently in Arabic and flung the vase out.

Bullets rained down on the place where the vase landed and Tessa used the distraction to reach round the door. She saw two men, both with machine pistols. She shot one with the harpoon gun and discarded it, quickly picking up the air pistol. But the other man's gun was already pointing at her. However, he didn't pull the trigger because he saw the second vase which the Arabic girl had hurled, heading directly for him. It was an excellent shot, thrown from a position which put the girl at considerable risk. However, the man was forced to put up an arm to deflect it, which gave Tessa more than enough time to shoot him with a tranquilliser dart. She turned to the young girl and bowed, gesturing her to hurry back to safety. Then she reloaded the harpoon gun.

Tessa peered into the atrium again. She knew that whoever controlled this space controlled the ship, since all access routes passed through it. However, she wasn't sure how many guards were left. Ayane and Noboru would certainly have taken out a few, but there was a lot of banging coming from above; some at least were still trying to gain access to the bridge.

Suddenly, a red dot dancing on one of the walls suggested that a gun with a laser sight was being used. Tessa spotted another two men peering in her direction from a corridor two decks above. However, they were across the stairwell from her and she wasn't convinced the air pistol would be accurate enough over that distance, so she drew a knife and readied herself. She toyed with it momentarily, getting to know its balance and weight. In her mind, she thanked the Sheikh for his desire to have only the best, even when it came to hand weapons.

Then she spotted a big red fire extinguisher secured in a recess opposite where the men were standing. She slid the knife back her belt and picked up the harpoon gun. Quickly checking the extinguisher's location, and waiting until the red dot had moved away, Tessa leaned round and shot the harpoon. It hit the middle of the extinguisher which promptly exploded, engulfing the men in a cloud of acrid white gas. They withdrew, allowing Tessa to advance into a new position with two knives drawn. As the gas dissipated, she caught a glimpse of one man and threw her first knife. She knew it had found its mark when the laser red dot gyrated around the walls as he dropped the weapon. The second man foolishly kneeled down to pick up the rifle. In almost full view he was an easy target, and her next knife found its mark.

She drew two more knives and began skirting the atrium balcony, scanning the doors and entrances to corridors. From where she was standing, she could see into one storey below her and two above. There were no visible signs of movement. But then a waiter appeared below, urgently tugging a waitress behind him; they scurried fearfully out of sight. As Tessa looked round again, she saw a number of people rushing past the elliptical portholes. The whirring of hydraulics suggested they were busy launching the lifeboats.

"So the rats are deserting the sinking ship," she jeered with a wry smile. "Well, it just goes to show, when the chips are down, you can't buy loyalty."

With weapons ready, she climbed the stairs. On the top landing, she checked the corridors leading off the atrium. She found one more guard, but he wasn't even looking in the right direction and hadn't heard her approach. He quickly fell. As she neared the bridge, the PA system crackled again.

"British Territorial waters," broadcast Noboru, his voice tinged with a mixture of relief, exhaustion and pain. "*UAR* issued and acknowledged from Gibraltar."

"Yes!" exclaimed Tessa as she finally reached the short corridor leading to the bridge.

She found four men in front of the armoured access to the bridge. But the reinforced anti-terrorist door was staying firmly shut, and Tessa was sure Noboru would have closed the external shutters. He was in a secure citadel. Then she saw one of the men clip a blue box to a glutinous explosive track which traced the perimeter of the door.

"I am Nariko," yelled Tessa, "licensed International Peacekeeper whose life you have threatened. Drop your weapons and surrender, you have been warned."

The response came in a rapid stream of guttural Irabyan.

"What the hell did that mean?" she shouted.

"Go fuck yourself," came the abrupt response.

"Lovely," she purred. "I rather hoped you'd say that."

Suddenly there was a bright flash and a loud *boom* as the charge detonated. The large door fell off its hinges onto the passageway floor and the corridor filled with dense smoke. There was a momentary pause as everyone seemed to be taken-aback by the force of the explosion in such a confined space. Then two weapons started firing. But even as a bullet grazed Tessa's left arm, she threw two knives in the direction of her opponents. She knew they'd struck home from the groans. So she moved to a better position and hurled a torrent of knives after them. The sound of falling bodies preceded an eerie silence. With two more knives ready, Tessa walked into the dense swirling cloud.

"Noboru?" she asked quietly. "Are you all right?"

"Just about," he moaned. "Wow! Did we really do it?"

"Oh, yes," confirmed Tessa, checking all the guards outside the bridge were dead.

She found her associate slouched on the floor near the control panel, and looked at his wounds. A stab wound to his thigh, a nasty gash in his side, a bullet graze on his right shoulder and some shrapnel wounds; nothing which wouldn't heal given time.

"You'll live," Tessa assured him, prompting a broad grin. "I think I'd better check the ship is truly ours," she added, passing him a couple of knives. "Will you be all right for a few minutes?"

He nodded, and with her help, hauled himself onto the captain's chair. Then he opened the security shutters and throttled back. The lights marking the entrance to Gibraltar harbour were visible in the distance.

"We scuttled our RHIB," he remarked, offhandedly. "But I think some of the crew escaped in the lifeboats."

"Yes, I saw them," endorsed Tessa, nevertheless concerned that there might be stragglers.

She made her way back to Ayane, passing the young girl on the way, still huddled in the corner of the suite. She gestured for her to stay there.

"Ayane-san," said Tessa as she approached the armoury door.

"*Konichiwa*, Nariko-san," came the cheery but weak response.

Tessa went in and inspected her wounds, assuring her that Noboru was fine. In addition to her injured thigh, another bullet had grazed Ayane's shoulder and she also had a defensive cut on her forearm. She had bled quite a lot, but was not severely injured and in remarkably high spirits. Tessa bound her wounds and helped her to the same room as the young girl. She was clearly overjoyed to be alive and free, and gladly helped Ayane make her way to the bridge.

Tessa continued her search of the ship. Satisfied the crew were all gone or incapacitated, she opened the other prison suites. She found two young boys and three more girls; all were drugged, with vacant expressions on their faces. Disgusted, she informed Noboru and headed for the master suite. A substantial locked anti-terrorist door greeted her. She picked up the extension phone on the wall nearby and selected the bridge.

"Noboru-san?"

"Yes," he replied cheerily. Clearly he was already feeling better.

"Is Ayane with you now?"

"Yes, she is."

"Good. I'm pretty sure the ship is ours, but keep your eyes open and advise Gibraltar of our ETA. Also, can you put me through to the master suite or do I need to use the main PA system?"

"Either."

"OK. Main PA, please."

"Go ahead."

"Sheikh Simitar. This is UK Peacekeeper Nariko," announced Tessa authoritatively. "We have entered British Territorial waters and your guards have either abandoned ship or been subdued. I am in control of this vessel which will dock in Gibraltar shortly. Open the door. You have been warned."

A brief pause followed, ending with the whirring sound of substantial bolts sliding aside. The door swung open to reveal a cavernous area spanning the full width of the ship. It was sumptuously furnished and had a thick off-white shag-pile carpet, brocade-covered walls and a domed ceiling, from the centre of which hung an enormous crystal chandelier. Even Tessa was surprised by the suite's opulence. However, opposite her, on a large circular bed, the Sheikh was kneeling and holding a knife to the neck of a little girl, whom he swung round to shield himself from Tessa. The hostage was sobbing miserably.

"Don't come any closer," he screamed, "I'll kill her."

"No you will not, you pervert," insisted Tessa. "Do you really want to add the witnessed murder of this innocent child to your other crimes? In a few minutes, I'm taking you into custody; it's entirely up to you what state you'll be in when I do it. But letting that child go can only improve your position."

Tessa allowed the Mexican stand-off to continue for a few seconds, but then started forward.

"No closer," he insisted, "I will kill her!"

"Don't be stupid. You know she's far too pretty for that, and an innocent. Let her go," demanded Tessa, raising a knife. "Now!"

He released his grip and the girl jumped off the bed and ran behind Tessa. Terrified, she clung to Tessa's flimsy nightdress.

"Nariko," started the Sheikh obsequiously. "I'm a very rich man, maybe…"

"I warned you in Insein. Now you will face justice for your crimes. You *have* brought disgrace upon both your family and your country."

Then she re-sheathed her knife and shot him with the tranquilliser pistol. With the dart projecting from his thigh, he keeled over backwards and lay on the bed like a beached whale.

Tessa bent down, picked up the little girl and returned to the bridge. The yacht was just entering Gibraltar harbour.

"Potter will be waiting," said Ayane, as the young Arabic girl took charge of the newest arrival.

"Hmm," replied Tessa, grinning. "This is going to take a bit of explaining, isn't it?"

"Do we need to tell him the truth?" asked Ayane, making no secret of the fact that she expected to be in horrendous trouble.

"Not exactly. Potter's a clever man; he'll work it all out for himself in a couple of minutes. Is the plane waiting?"

"Yes," confirmed Noboru. "It landed thirty minutes ago."

"Good. Any weapons with your fingerprints on?"

"No," assured Ayane, checking with Noboru.

"Excellent."

"Are *you* all right?" queried Ayane.

Tessa looked down. Her arms and legs were covered in scratches and there were spots of blood on her nightdress, which now had a couple of large tears in it. There were also a couple of splinters protruding from her thigh. She plucked them out, noting as she did that her knickers were missing.

"Nothing too severe," she observed, inspecting the shallow bullet graze on her arm. "When we dock, your main task is to get back to the plane; I'll join you as soon as I can… Ayane, Noboru, that was an outstandingly good job you just did, thank you."

"You're welcome," replied Ayane, looking pale but smiling. "He needed to be stopped, that was clear."

CHAPTER 35

As Noboru expertly drew the yacht alongside, some UK Special Forces agents jumped aboard, to complete the mooring. Tessa could see Potter standing on the quayside, his arm in a sling; Flood and Gwen Johnson were with him. It wasn't long before Tessa joined them. Ayane and Noboru stood a discrete distance away.

"Morning, Potter, Flood, Johnson" Tessa greeted them cheerily.

"Morning, Nariko," replied Potter. "I see you dressed for the occasion."

"Yes, well, I was abducted, in Tunis of all places. But I'm pleased to say I've brought you a present. Sheikh Simitar, as he likes to be called. He's on his bed, tranquillised – he'll be out for a couple of hours. I understand he's wanted for all sorts of nasty crimes back home. You'll also find a number of children on board. I suspect they're all minors he has also had abducted."

"Flood, check it out, will you?" ordered Potter. Flood nodded, grinned at Tessa, and went aboard.

"Big boat," noted Potter.

"Very big boat," acknowledged Tessa.

"Lots of guards?"

"Surprisingly few actually. It seems most took to the lifeboats when they realised the game was up. I'm afraid there were a few fatalities, but I was being kidnapped and things didn't heat up until the yacht entered British Territorial waters."

"Hah! Of course they didn't. And how do you intend to explain those two?" demanded Potter, nodding towards Ayane and Noboru.

"Oh, they're just a couple of friends who happened to see me being taken. Unfortunately, they're not terribly good at this Peacekeeper stuff and, despite my best efforts, managed to get in the way once or twice. Nothing serious though."

"Almost totally unbelievable," he retorted.

"Hmm. Potter, how did you break your arm?" ventured Tessa.

"Skiing accident?"

"Hah! *I* didn't break my arm," he exclaimed indignantly. "*You* broke it! That gentle slope you assured me I had to roll down in Karatsu was as near as dammit, a bloody cliff! I was lucky it was only my arm that broke."

"Ah, sorry about that. But at least I saved your life. Again."

Potter grunted and turned to Gwen Johnson.

"Find her some clothes, will you? Oberst Müller sends his regards to you, and your *friends*. I had a long discussion with him. He'd like you to call when we're done."

"OK."

"So, Nariko, I presume you're going to assure me that you took control of the ship all on your own?"

"Yes, that's right."

He sighed, shaking his head.

"And what about the fact that you failed to attend your Peacekeeper tribunal."

"I am truly sorry about that," she replied, apologetically. "But I was anaesthetised and being shipped out of Tunis in a crate at the time."

"I suppose that might appease them... slightly."

Potter paused while they all watched the children being led ashore by a couple of policewomen. The Sheikh followed on a stretcher, still unconscious.

"Quite frankly, Nariko, the tribunal members were incensed by your absence, and with some justification too." Tessa gulped. "Personally, I can hardly believe they were even willing to consider listening to my plea for clemency, not to mention that of Oberst Müller..." Tessa's eyebrows went up "...but what really swung it was the impassioned audio-visual submission on your behalf from Minister Miyazaki." He paused for effect. "After due consideration, they decided that since the felon in London had already ordered his co-conspirators to kill you and had threatened your life himself, you were in fact within your rights to employ lethal force. Furthermore, they were willing to accept that you would have spared his life had he not attempted to kill you a second time. So, given that the amount of torture you employed was small, they decided, on this occasion, to let you off with a suspended sentence. If there are no other *incidents* within the next six months concerning your conduct as a Peacekeeper, the matter will be deemed closed."

"Wow," exclaimed Tessa, relieved. "Thank you."

"You're welcome."

Johnson returned with a black tracksuit and some trainers, as Tessa was still barefoot. She appeared to be having difficulty stopping herself from laughing.

"Johnson," chided Potter, "please, this is serious."

"Sorry, sir."

"Nariko, I'll need an Incident Report from you and your friends."

Tessa looked round.

"What friends would that be, Potter?"

He looked over to where Ayane and Noboru had been standing. There was no one there.

"Oh, for goodness sake, I'm retiring in six months."

"Well, depending on how quick we can sort the report out, I'm retiring in six minutes."

"Wonderful!" he continued, shaking his head. "Johnson, this is the sort of stuff you're going to have to contend with when you take over."

Tessa spun round.

"Agent Johnson, that's fantastic news. Congratulations!"

"Thank you. I'll be the UK's first female Head of Special Forces. Curtis is going to be my number two. Flood's keen to stay where he is, i.e. acting as the glue which holds everything together, but he'll be assuming wider UK responsibilities..."

"All right, that's the warm and cuddly stuff over," interrupted Potter, "we need to get on with the admin. And let's have a comprehensive Incident Report, please, Nariko; preferably a credible one too."

"Yes, sir," smiled Tessa.

Two hours later, the three of them were sitting in a sparsely furnished office. Potter had just finished reviewing the lengthy document. Tessa was sipping some water.

"Looks almost plausible," he admitted in amazement. "I suppose some things never change. It was a nice touch only using weapons you found on board... God, I hope everyone else believes it."

"Well, you do have the Sheikh," replied Tessa, grinning. "That'll be a substantial feather in your retirement cap."

He chuckled.

"OK, we're done here. I want to have a word with Flood, now." He stood up, looking Tessa straight in the eye. "You'd better come with me, Johnson."

Tessa stood too.

"Goodbye, Potter," she said, smiling and shaking his hand. "Thanks for everything. I hope you enjoy your retirement."

"Likewise…"

It wasn't long before Tessa was climbing into a black limousine waiting outside the terminal building. She boarded the Chrysanthemum jet fifteen minutes later…

"She's gone, sir," advised Johnson studying her *cbc*.

"By plane, I presume," mused Potter.

"Yes, sir, a Japanese executive jet; black with a gold chrysanthemum motif. Sounds like the one which collected her from Tunis – it's bound for Tokyo."

CHAPTER 36

On the plane Tessa, Ayane and Noboru attended to their wounds and settled down to a feast of Japanese food, even treating themselves to several glasses of sake. They exchanged stories and Tessa listened in awe to how the two of them had chased the Sheikh's yacht in the RHIB for some time before finally being able to board. But eventually the conversation petered out and Ayane and Noboru went to sleep, so Tessa phoned Germany.

"*Guten morgen*, Herr Oberst."

"*Morgen*, Nariko. How's it going?"

"Very well. The Sheikh and his yacht are secure in Gibraltar and a number of kidnapped children have been freed. Potter has all the details."

"Excellent. We will start extradition proceedings, but I suspect the Sheikh will be serving many years in a British prison before we are able to welcome him to one of ours."

"I'm sure in both countries he'll receive better treatment than he deserves," replied Tessa. "Anyway, I wanted to thank you for appealing on my behalf to the Peacekeeper Tribunal."

"It was nothing. I only told the truth."

"Well, I'm very grateful. Also, Potter mentioned you wanted to talk to me... I don't need the media blackout any more, if that's what you needed to know."

"Oh, fine. But are you bothered how we treat the rest? You know, their research and so on?"

"Not really."

"Good. You see, both our governments have deep misgivings about the morality of what the doctors were doing. Even though we weren't able to gain access to their cloud systems, there was more than enough evidence in the file room to convict them both of multiple crimes attracting the death penalty several times over. So it has been decided that all the records, and the house, should be destroyed. We've already repatriated the remains of virtually all the victims concerned. The Weissman family send their thanks, by the way."

"That's kind of them. Er.., Herr Oberst," proffered Tessa tentatively, "I might be able to get you access to those remote systems, if you still wanted it."

"Hmm. Well, to be quite frank, I don't think that's relevant any more. Perhaps if you get the opportunity, you could simply delete it all?"

"Are you sure?"

"Absolutely."

"OK."

"In the meantime," added Müller, "we have planted a number of incendiary devices within the Krollheim's property, we intend to burn it down completely. As the Peacekeeper responsible, would you care to issue the initiation code?"

"If you like."

"Good. I'll call you in an hour or so when I know everything's prepared..."

Müller stopped his car outside the Krollheims' house and got out with a resolute look on his face. He took a deep breath and discharged the remaining guards. Then he went down to the basement floor and unlocked the door to the first cell.

"*Guten morgen*, Frau Doktor."

"Why was I drugged and brought here like this?" she demanded, glaring up at him form the gurney.

"We thought you might like to experience how those you tortured felt."

"Release these restraints immediately."

"No." He proceeded to read out the long list of crimes it had been proved that she and her husband had committed.

"I will put all that in context when I am in court," she sneered.

"Frau Doktor, you will not be going to court. Nariko is going to finish what she started."

"But you ordered that whore not to kill me!"

"That was then, this is now," replied Müller offhandedly, struggling to hide his revulsion. "We were determined that first everything possible should be done to ease the burden of the people related to those unfortunate enough to be the subjects of your cruel and twisted experiments. Furthermore, all those who have *ever* been in contact with you or your husband are being investigated. *Aufwiedersehn*, Frau Doktor."

She watched him leave and heard him locking the door to the cell.

"Good riddance," she hissed.

Müller left the house and crossed the road to his car from where he made a couple of confirmatory calls before telephoning Tessa.

"*Hallo*, Nariko. The house is ready. All you need do is send the text *OCL625* to this number in Germany..."

"OK. So the house is empty?"

"I checked it myself and I'm still parked outside. Everything is *ready*."

Tessa paused, guessing what he was hinting at.

"Is that truly what you want you want, Herr Oberst?"

"Yes, Nariko. I can assure you the matter has been discussed at great length, and everyone involved is in full agreement. Furthermore, I can confirm that this act will be taken as formal completion of your Mission against the new Calver Cats. Your daughter and another Peacekeeper are leading a joint action against the remnants of the Cats. Their Mission will close once the clean-up is complete."

"Is the second Peacekeeper called Seiji?"

"Yes, he is."

Tessa smiled; maybe there was hope for those two yet. Then she typed the message, pausing to gaze sadly at the Japanese funeral urn.

"This is for you, Toshie," she whispered, and pressed the *send* key.

"Herr Oberst, it is done."

"Thank you, Nariko, always a pleasure. Have a good flight, and... well done."

Inside the house, Frau Doktor Krollheim first suspected something was happening when she heard the air conditioning system speeding up. Then she was amazed to see a small section of the ceiling start glowing, then another, and another. The spots grew larger, turning white as a mixture of molten steel and concrete started dripping on the floor around her. She realised the house was on fire, but for some reason, the sprinkler system hadn't switched on. Then she understood.

Momentarily stunned, she simply stared at the ceiling in disbelief. Then she screamed with all her might. However, the house had been comprehensively sound-proofed, so nobody heard.

Müller was still outside. He was listening to the final Act of *The Damnation of Faust* by Berlioz. Occasionally, he cast a vaguely curious eye at the shimmering white halo of intense heat rising from the scene of the Krollheims' crimes.

CHAPTER 37

It was early evening when the Chrysanthemum jet landed at Haneda Airport. Once more, Tessa, this time together with Ayane and Noboru, were ushered into a meeting room.

Tessa had expected Minister Miyazaki to be there, but there was a woman too. She had considerable poise and was dressed in a beautifully decorated silk kimono with her hair tied up in the back with a wide black ribbon. However, her eyes were slightly red and she looked sad. Tessa correctly guessed that this was Toshie's mother.

First, greetings were exchanged. Then Dr Miyazaki studied Ayane and Noboru, both bearing the scars of the conflict on the yacht; he looked at Tessa with raised eyebrows.

"Nariko, I trust there will be no repercussions from the non-involvement of Ayane and Noboru in the actions you initiated?"

"None whatsoever, Minister," replied Tessa confidently. "However, I would like to express my sincere gratitude for the assistance that they were *not* able to provide. Without *not* having it, I doubt the Mission would have been completed so quickly and effectively. It has been an honour and a pleasure *not* to have worked with your colleagues."

"Just as well," noted Miyazaki wryly. It would be most embarrassing if the new Chief of the Chrysanthemum Guard were to be embroiled in a scandal so early after assuming the role, Ayane."

"Sir?" she stammered.

"Congratulations on your well-earned promotion, Ayane. You too, Noboru, you will be her second-in-command."

They both bowed deeply muttering their thanks.

"We'll attend to the formalities later. In the meantime, I suggest that you both take a couple of days' vacation… to recover from your vacation. There's a car waiting."

After numerous congratulatory farewells had been exchanged and only the three of them were left alone, Miyazaki turned to Tessa.

"So, have you forgiven me yet?"

She looked at him and breathed out noisily.

"I'm working on it, Minister."

"Oh, good, that's a relief."

"Thank you for supporting me at my tribunal," she added.

"Credit where credit is due, Nariko-san," he said, looking at his watch. "Anyway, would it be possible for you to share with me and my wife whatever else you were able to find out about our daughter?"

Tessa wasn't sure how to begin and cleared her throat uncertainly. They looked at her yearning, expectant.

"I have led two successful actions which together will ensure none of the original perpetrators will ever be able again to subject anyone to the treatment that I, Karen Weissman and your daughter were forced to endure. During one of these, I managed to establish more of the details surrounding Toshie's death." A pause followed while Tessa selected her words. "In particular, I confirmed that your daughter died instantly from a single gunshot wound inflicted after she had been cornered while trying to escape – the last of many such attempts. There is no doubt that Toshie was an extremely resolute, brave young woman. Although completely alone, she continued to strive single-mindedly to retain her honour and right to self-determination, irrespective of the personal consequences. You should be very proud of her. Furthermore, I am pleased to inform you that I was also able to recover…" There was sharp intake of breath as Tessa reverently removed the funeral urn from the black rucksack that Ayane had placed on the table. "…Toshie's remains. I sincerely regret that the news I bring of your daughter is not better, but I hope you will at least be able to draw solace from knowing she has come home to you now."

Tessa walked over to Dr Miyazaki and, bowing deeply, presented the urn to him with outstretched arms. He breathed out, his shoulders sagging, and took it from her. Tessa backed away and gave him another long deep bow.

Choked with emotion, he stood motionless, hugging the urn tightly. Finally, he turned and handed it with veneration to his wife. Tears were already streaming down her face and she clasped the urn to her bosom in a desperate attempt to comfort her baby.

"Thank you, Nariko-san," he stammered. "I would say more, but…" he turned to his wife who was whimpering softly and seemed close to breaking down completely "...perhaps some other time. Thank you again, we... Please, excuse us... Oh, you have another meeting, there's a limousine outside."

"Couldn't it wait? I was rather..."

But he and his wife had already gone. Tessa shook her head and went to find the car...

It was just before dawn when Tessa finally neared Matsumoto Castle. The helicopter had dropped her off outside Kenrouken Park in Kanazawa. She had continued on foot, deep in thought.

When she had a clear view of the castle, she stopped and sat down on a rock, filled with awe and admiration. She had only been gone a short while, but already the white perimeter wall round the honmaru had been repaired and repainted, and reconstruction of the six watchtowers was also underway. Even the work to remove the weeds from the rampart sides and restore the original polished surface to the dark stones was well advanced. Then the sound of exquisite shamisen music drifted down to her; doleful pleading tones, tinged with hope.

On reaching the honmaru, she found Matsumoto sitting on a stone bench with a tray, a teapot and two cups. He put his shamisen down and gestured her to join him.

"*Ohayou gozaimasu, omae.*"

"*Ohayou,*" she mumbled, offhandedly.

"I am truly pleased to see you, Nariko-san, and I hear congratulations are in order." She looked at him with a mixture of sheer joy at being back, tainted with concern that he had been expecting her. "The Minister's aide called me after you left Tokyo," added Matsumoto, sensing her unease.

She sat down in silence, slightly apart from him, and, much to his disappointment, without kissing him first.

"There's still something wrong, isn't there?"

"Yes. I've been wondering how to verify that this is all real." Without thinking, she poured two cups of tea, moving one over to him. "How can I be certain that Paul, Kurou and the German doctors have not succeeded in altering my mind? How do I prove that all this, which I think I see and feel, is genuine and not simply a figment of my imagination generated to mask my actual circumstances and actions?"

"Hmm," replied Matsumoto pensively, beginning to doubt whether his wife would ever be completely free from the effects of the horrific tortures she had endured. "I would have thought that the probability of this just being a dream is very low. Not only is there the treatment you have had from many experts including Professor Kawashima, there is also the not insignificant matter of Kurou killing Paul, of General Gyobu killing Kurou and then committing suicide himself; and of you rescuing Potter and Yoshino. Not to mention you sorting out all those 'loose ends.'"

"It still might only be in my mind."

"I suppose it's a possibility," replied Matsumoto. "But surely then Kurou, Paul or General Gyobu would still be alive and instructing you to do their dastardly deeds, and I would be dead; maybe the Emperor too. He is most definitely alive, as am I, and you have had more than ample opportunity to dispatch us all." He picked up his cup and sipped the tea. "You don't look convinced."

"Not completely, but I do accept your arguments are persuasive. However, what else could I expect you to say?"

"Well, maybe you never will be convinced. Maybe this is a dream. Maybe it is a dream in my mind too and we are both sharing the same nightmare. Is anyone ever truly able to differentiate between what is in their minds and what is real…? Personally, I do believe that this is as real as real can be. I accept that our adversaries attacked us with every weapon in their evil arsenal; but we fought against them honourably, and won. We are here, together, while they are no longer in this world. Furthermore, for the first time in many years, no one is trying to kill either of us. So, all I can say is that if I am dreaming this," he gestured round at the castle, ending with his hand outstretched towards Tessa, "it seems a very generous dream to me."

She paused to drink some tea.

"I've been damaged by what happened," she confessed.

"I know, *omae*. We have both been damaged. This has been an unimaginably brutal and far-reaching affair. But we mustn't allow ourselves to be embittered by it. Our hurts will only become permanent if we allow them to. Ensuring that it doesn't is our main challenge now, and we should confront it together, one day at a time…

"However, if you need longer, I understand; do what you feel is necessary. But when you are ready, please come back. I will still be here waiting for you."

She took another sip of her tea. Then she turned to him and smiled.

"On reflection, *anata*," she said, with a glint in her eye, "I think I am willing to accept what you said."

"Oh, good... Why?" he asked, surprised by her apparent sudden change in position.

"Well, if I were dreaming all this, I suspect I would be feeling happier about having killed yet more people. Also, I think that if you'd been lying, you would have sounded rather more convincing. Furthermore, I doubt my programming would ever have permitted me the luxury of questioning whether this was real or not. And finally, I think it highly unlikely my wrist would hurt so much."

Matsumoto raised his eyebrows and Tessa turned her wrist towards him. On it was the most splendid chrysanthemum design. He grinned, stood up and gently lifted her arm so he could study the new tattoo.

"Nariko-san, this is the finest chrysanthemum I have ever seen. But your wrist looks very sore. I think the design has not only been applied with considerable skill, but also quite deeply."

"I suspect the tattoo artist had been instructed to make it difficult to remove."

"Indeed. Nevertheless, I am delighted, if not surprised, to see it has been replaced. How about if we now concentrate on *our* future, and finish renovating the castle? The rest will take care of itself."

"I hope that applies to our children too," mused Tessa dryly.

"Well, it's about time it did," responded Matsumoto.

"So how did the villagers react to your suggestion they help with the reconstruction?"

"Oh, very well indeed. The Calver Cats had caused considerable damage to many of their crops. So our offer to compensate them for their losses, while also paying for their work here, was most welcome; the promise of electricity from our wind turbines sealed the deal."

"Excellent. When will they be starting today?"

"Oh, in a few hours. But don't worry about that. You've been working, you should rest."

"You're probably right. I would welcome some time in my own bed," mused Tessa, adding with a smile, "Are you going to come too?"

CHAPTER 38

Two years later, the last of the artisans finally left. For the first time since Tessa had returned from Gibraltar, she and Matsumoto were alone in the castle.

Smiling contentedly, she walked across the drawbridge over the inner moat and stood just past the newly built torii. Not only was that an excellent vantage point from which to savour the stupendous end result of all their efforts, but the drawbridge was also the renovation of which Tessa was most proud. She had personally managed its reconstruction, and the carpentry alone was magnificent. In many ways the bridge epitomised her agreement with Matsumoto concerning the amount of modern technology which would be incorporated in the refurbished castle, and, more importantly, the amount which would be visible. As such the castle was now a repository for many of the most advanced and sophisticated mechanical and electronic systems available, albeit discreetly. So, ostensibly restored precisely as it had originally been built many centuries earlier, the drawbridge was now operated silently by electric motors powered by electricity from the three wind turbines gracefully rotating on the ridge many miles away. When the bridge deck moved, up or down, the only noise was the clanking of the chains which had always operated it.

Eventually, Tessa whispered, "Drawbridge up," and prepared to watch the sun set. Slowly, the distant villages transformed from being a plethora of grey rectangles to twinkling pinpricks of light. Then the plasma lamps positioned around the honmaru perimeter wall ignited. Although worlds apart in technological terms, the torches mimicked perfectly the light from the hundreds of ancient oil-fired torches they had replaced. The flames from their modern counterparts were whipped into careening multi-coloured beacons by rotating filaments containing strontium, copper and sodium.

As the sun finally relinquished its grip on the day and darkness once more asserted its hold, the castle rampart seemed positively to glow with pride. The massive, previously grey, lichen-covered rocks were now pitch black and foreboding. Already glistening with early-evening dew, they radiated a sense of timelessness which warmed Tessa's soul.

While she looked round with satisfaction, the drawbridge chains enthusiastically rattled into action once more. Matsumoto was revealed standing looking at her. His expression, like hers, was one of unabashed fulfilment with their joint achievement. As he walked towards her a narrow vertical beam of green light from the top of the torii glanced across his face.

"*Sayonara*, Matsumoto," bid the recognition system politely.

He smiled and walked up to her, kissing her gently on the lips.

"*Omae*, I have to admit, this bridge is indeed a very fine and sensitive piece of work. Without doubt it will outlast us both."

"*Anata*, I'm so pleased you like it. I absolutely adore it."

"And with good reason. Now, I have something to show you."

Arm in arm, they went back up to the Samurai house courtyard. There, illuminated by the light of the welcoming glow from the audience hall and the six stone courtyard lanterns, Matsumoto led her to a small burgundy-coloured curtain secured to the porch wall. Tessa frowned, she was not aware of any work having been required here. He pulled the curtain away to reveal a newly engraved stele. On it was an inscription detailing their joint reconstruction of the castle. This new stone matched the two not far away, which had been placed there by Matsumoto's relatives hundreds of years before.

Tessa read it several times, grinned and caressed it.

"*Anata*, this is a great honour. It makes me very proud."

"It is nothing if not well-deserved, *omae*. We have both striven long and hard for all this. Why shouldn't our efforts be recognised for as long as this stone endures? I am sure that what we have accomplished here, and elsewhere, will be an important part of our legacy for many generations to come."

"Thank you, *anata*," said Tessa, kissing him on the cheek. "Perhaps time for dinner? Maybe we should celebrate?"

"Good idea, *omae*. After all, there is much to celebrate. We've just received a message from Seiji and Nyunt. They're engaged to be married…"

THE END

GLOSSARY

Please note: Throughout the Samurai Revival Trilogy, references to people, places or road names are used entirely fictitiously, while any references to brand names are intended to be complimentary. Furthermore, uses of non-English languages and historical references have been simplified, with apologies to purists. Finally, the author would like to thank the various public domain databases used for research, in particular, Wikipedia.

Aizu Wakamatsu	a town (and impressive castle) in the western part of Fukushima Prefecture which was a loyal and powerful supporter of the *Tokugawa Shogunate*.
Amafuji	See *Amakuni*.
Amakuni	(pronounced 'Arm-a-koon-ei') a legendary Japanese sword-maker of around 700 AD who it is said to have made the first reliable Samurai sword (i.e. not shattering on impact). Amafuji followed about 50 years later as another sword-maker. A sword made by either would be worth a fortune today.
Anata	a Japanese term of endearment, loosely translated as 'darling husband'.
Barnaby Mews	a fictitious Mews leading off Old Brompton Road near *South Kensington* underground.
Beauchamp	('Bee-cham') is a boy's name with French origins. Literally it means beautiful field.
Bokken	a Japanese wooden sword used for training in place of a real sword; it too can be lethal when used by an expert. In these books, bokken is interpreted more broadly to include long martial arts staffs more correctly called 'jo'.
Bryani	a girl's name with English and Greek origins referring to a flowering vine used in folk medicine.

Burqa

an enveloping outer garment worn by some Islamic women to cover their bodies when in public. In some styles, the *niqab* of its veil is attached by one side, and covers the face only below the eyes, allowing the eyes to be seen. (Also see *hijab*).

Calver (Cats)

a fictitious violent criminal gang. The name is derived from 'calvered' as applied to salmon that is cut up alive.

Caprice

a girl's name (pronounced 'Ka-preese'), of English, French and Italian origins meaning whimsical, playful or fanciful.

Caroline Charles

one of London's most respected womenswear designers with an international business which she founded in the 1960s and remains active in 2013.

cbc

a fictitious invention (cloud based communicator) intended as a highly sophisticated successor to 2013's smart mobile phone/pda (personal digital assistant).

c'est la vie

French for 'that's life'.

Chäus, Liebling

an informal German phrase meaning 'Good-bye, sweetheart'.

Chelsea

an area or district of West London bounded to the south by the River Thames.

DKBA

the Democratic Karen Buddhist Army (now Democratic Karen Benevolent Army) is a breakaway group of Buddhist former soldiers and officers of the predominantly Karen Christian led Karen National Liberation Army (KNLA), one of the larger insurgent armies in Burma. In Dec. 1994, the DKBA signed a ceasefire with the military Junta to obtain military and financial assistance in exchange for supporting the Junta's offensives against the Karen.

(Domo) arigato	Japanese for 'thank you (very much).' If 'gozaimasu' is appended, the thank you is even more generous and polite.
Edo	during the Edo period (1603-1868) Japanese society was under the rule of the *Tokugawa Shōgunate*. This era (the heyday of the Samurai) enjoyed economic growth, strict social order, isolationist foreign policies, environmental protection policies, and widespread enjoyment of arts and culture. The Shōgunate was officially established in Edo city (now Tokyo) on March 24, 1603, by *Tokugawa Ieyasu*. The period came to an end with the *Meiji Restoration* on May 3, 1868, after Edo city fell.
Emperor of Japan	the symbol of the Japanese state and the only remaining monarch in the world reigning under the title of Emperor. He is a ceremonial figurehead under a form of constitutional monarchy and is head of the Japanese Imperial Family whose lineage is the oldest in the world with the Empire having been founded in 660BC.
Escrow	a legal arrangement or account formed contractually between parties, whereby an independent third party receives/disburses money or documents for the transacting parties at a time dependent on the fulfilment of certain agreed conditions.
Fukagawa Seiji	a pottery near Arita. The items made are renowned for their high quality, almost transparent white porcelain and beautiful deep blue designs.
Geta	a form of traditional Japanese footwear (resembling clogs and flip-flops) with a wooden base (held onto the foot with a fabric thong) elevated by two wooden blocks.

Gott im Himmel!	German exclamation meaning 'Good heavens!' (lit. God in heaven).
GP	A general practitioner (GP) is a medical practitioner/doctor who treats acute and chronic illnesses, providing preventive care and health education within the community.
Guten morgen	German for 'Good morning'.
Guts Nächtle	Swabian (see *Schwäbisch*) German for 'Good night'.
Habibi	an Arabic greeting (lit. 'my beloved') used to address a male object of affection (the feminine form is *habibati*), also used for less formal relationships or as a term of endearment at peer levels (*e.g.*, *friend* or *darling*).
Hachiro	a Japanese boy's name meaning eighth son (see *-san*).
Hamon	a visual band created on a sword blade by the hardening process (from the Japanese meaning 'blade pattern'). The hamon is the transition between the region of harder martensitic steel and the softer pearlitic steel of the blade. This wavy line is a result of the hardening process but, due to its aesthetics, can also push up the value of the sword a lot.
Haneda	or more correctly Tokyo International Airport, is one of the two main airports serving Tokyo (see *Narita*). It is located in Ota, some 10 miles south of Central Tokyo.
Hayasaka-san	the informal form of the Japanese surname Hayasaka. A key (fictitious) character throughout the Samurai Revival Trilogy.
Heroin	(diacetylmorphine) is an opium-based drug with sedative and euphoric properties. Dependence can develop as can withdrawal symptoms on discontinuation.

Higashi Chaya district	one of three well-preserved *chaya* districts in Kanazawa: Higashi Chayagai (Eastern Chaya District), Nishi Chayagai (Western Chaya District) and Kazuemachi. A *chaya* (teahouse) is an exclusive type of restaurant where guests are entertained by geisha who perform song and dance. During the Edo Period, *chaya* were found in designated entertainment districts, usually just outside the city limits.
Hijab	a veil that covers the head and chest, which is particularly worn by a Muslim female beyond the age of puberty. (See *burqa* and *niqab*).
Honmaru	*Maru* (baileys) are the enclosed area round the donjon (main keep). Japanese castles can have several maru, but usually they have three, called respectively the *honmaru* (main bailey), *ninomaru* (second bailey) and *sannomaru* (third bailey).
Hookah	a device for vapourising and smoking flavoured tobacco called shisha. Before inhalation, the vapour/smoke is passed through a water basin, often of coloured glass.
Irabya	a fictitious Middle Eastern/North African country.
Kanazawa	(lit. 'marsh of gold') the capital of Ishikawa Prefecture on the northwest coast of the Sea of Japan, flanked by the Japan Alps. With a prestigious history, Kanazawa is renowned amongst other things for its beautiful Kenrouken Park, the (restored) castle, its Samurai quarter and geisha districts.
Karen	a group of people (some 7 percent of the 50 million Burmese) speaking a Sino-Tibetan language mainly living in Kayin State in southern/south-eastern Burma.
Kaishakunin	a trusted Second acting for a person committing seppuku. Performing kaishaku

(decapitation) should leave a slight band of flesh attaching the head to the body, so that the head may be hung in front as if embraced. Due to the precision required for such a manoeuvre, the Second would be a highly skilled swordsperson.

Keffiyeh

a traditional Middle Eastern headdress often made from a square of cotton, maybe with a distinctive woven check pattern. Typically worn by Arab men to protect against the sun.

Kenrouken Park

established during 1676-1850 by Maeda Tsunanori and several other people. It is one of the most picturesque walk-around style gardens in Japan (see *Kanazawa*).

Kimi

('Kee-mee') a Japanese girl's name meaning 'righteous' (see *-san*).

Kimono

a Japanese traditional garment, often elaborate, worn usually by women and children. It is a T-shaped, straight-lined robe with hems to the ankle, attached collars and long, wide sleeves. It is wrapped around the body (left side over the right except when dressing the dead for burial) and secured by an *obi* (kimono belt).

KNLA

the Karen National Liberation Army is the military wing of the Karen National Union (KNU) operating in eastern Burma along the Thai border. The KNU is a political organisation representing the Karen people in Burma. (See *DKBA*).

Konichiwa

the Japanese for 'hello', but can mean 'good afternoon'.

Kono-san

the informal form of the Japanese surname Kono (see *-san*).

Kurou

a Japanese boy's name meaning ninth son (see *-san*).

Kyay zu tin bar de   the Burmese for 'thank you very much.'

Longyi   a sheet of cloth (c. 6½ ft. by 2½ ft.) worn around the waist (male or female), held in place by folding fabric over without a knot.

Mahouq-pa   Burmese for 'no way!' (adding '-bù' is politer).

Manga   popular Japanese comics conforming to a style developed in the late 19th century. They have a long/complex pre-history in earlier Japanese art.

Matsumoto Castle   the current (magnificent) structure was built around 1600. Located on flat land beside a swamp, rather than on a mountain or between rivers it has triple moats and high, strong stone walls to aid defence. It is also known as Crow Castle because its black walls and roofs look like spreading wings.

Matsumoto   a Japanese surname and key character in this trilogy. Also a city in Nagano Prefecture, c.100 miles northwest of Tokyo. (See -*san* and *Matsumoto Castle*).

Meiji Restoration   a chain of often bloody events that ultimately restored imperial rule to Japan in 1868 under Emperor Meiji which prompted major political and social restructuring.

Mingalaba(h)   'Hello' in Burmese.

Mit freundlichen Grüßen   a respectful sign-off to formal letters in German (loosely 'with kind regards').

Moshi-moshi   a Japanese telephone greeting, generally equivalent to 'hello', derived from the verb 'to say'.

Mon   the Mon ethnic group lives mostly in Mon State, around Bago and the Irrawaddy Delta along the south Thai-Burma border. One of the earliest peoples in southeast Asia they spread Theravada Buddhism widely and founded much of Burmese culture.

Nariko   a Japanese girl's name (see -*san*) generally agreed to mean thunder (pronounced 'Nah-ree-koh').

Narita   a city located in Chiba Prefecture, Japan. It is perhaps best known for being the site of Narita International Airport, the main international airport serving Tokyo. Narita handles the majority of international passenger traffic to and from Japan. It is located some 50 miles east of Tokyo city.

Ninja   were mercenary covert agents and assassins in feudal Japan. They varied in competence but clans from the Iga region were renowned for their training in espionage and sabotage. Mainly active during the 12th – 15th centuries, they were skilled in clandestine warfare, a stark contrast to the Samurai.

Niqab   a cloth, for example with either eye-slits or dense gauze, which covers the face as a part of a *hijab*. It is worn by some Muslim women in public areas. (See *burqa* and *hijab*).

NLD   The National League for Democracy party was formed in Burma in 1988 after the brutally supressed, so-called, 8888, uprisings seeking democracy which ended when the Junta seized control. During the democratic election of 1990, the NLD, led by Aung San Suu Kyi, took 59% of the vote winning 392 out of 492 seats. The governing National Unity Party won 10.

Oberst   formerly **Herr** (Mr) **Oberst**, is a military rank in many German-speaking and Scandinavian countries, broadly equivalent to Colonel.

OCL   Open Carrying Licence. A fictitious construction to indicate a licence to carry an uncased Samurai sword in public (see *RCL*).

Oh mein Gott!   German exclamation meaning 'Oh my God!'

Ohayou gozaimasu	the Japanese for 'good morning'. The abbreviated form, 'ohayou', is less formal.
Omae	a Japanese term of endearment, loosely translated as 'darling wife'
Orkney (Islands)	comprise some 70 islands, 10 miles northeast of mainland Scotland. Kirkwall is the capital.
Pagan	(also Bagan) the (9th-13th century) Burmese capital some 430 miles north of Rangoon, famous for its c. 2000 temple remains.
Pagoda	a generic term for a tiered tower, mostly East Asian, mainly built for religious purposes, typically Buddhist. In Sanskrit pagoda (or stupa – lit. 'heap') meant tomb.
Papa Edinsay	a fictitious Orkney island. (See *Orkney*).
Parabolic microphone	uses a parabolic reflector to collect and focus sound waves onto a receiver allowing sounds to be picked up from many metres away.
Poonani	(lit. 'vagina') is used as a slang/degrading term for a woman.
RCL	Restricted Carrying Licence. A fictitious construction to indicate a licence to carry a cased Samurai sword in public (see *OCL*).
Reason and hope – tools of dignity	the translation of the Kanji characters, pronounced as 'Rheagan Greene', comprising the author's Hanko (Japanese signature stamp).
RHIB	Rigid-Hulled Inflatable Boat, a light-weight, high-performance boat constructed with a solid, shaped hull on which a tough inflatable collar is mounted. Very stable and highly seaworthy, frequently used by the military, rescue services and pirates.
Rohypnol	(also Flunitrazepam, 'date rape drug') is an intermediate acting psychoactive drug used as an hypnotic, sedative, anticonvulsant, antianxiety and muscle relaxant drug.

Sake	an old Japanese alcoholic drink made from fermented rice. More like beer than wine, sake is produced by brewing and often has a higher proof than wine or beer.
Samurai	the military nobility of pre-industrial Japan ('those who serve'). Some 10% of pop. by the 12th century, they followed the bushido rules (still popular) of conduct. (See *Bitter Truths*).
Sashimi	a Japanese delicacy of thinly sliced pieces of very fresh raw fish (occasionally meat).
Satsuma-Chōshū Alliance	an uneasy military alliance between the feudal domains of Satsuma and Chōshū, in southern Japan, formed to overthrow the *Tokugawa Shōgunate*.
-san	the most common Japanese honorific, technically used to denote respect and formality (similar to 'Mr', 'Mrs' or 'Miss' – and usually masculine). It denotes familiarity when used with a first name. However, since correctly used Japanese honorifics are quite complex, they have been simplified in this Trilogy to just '-san'. Apologies to purists.
Sawadee ka/krup	Thai for 'hello' ('-krup' is the male form).
Săwngthăew	(lit. 'two rows') a Thai share taxi usually adapted from a pick-up truck.
Sayonara	('Si-o-na-ra') Japanese for 'Good-bye'
Scheiße!	a crude German expletive, equivalent to 'Shit!' in English.
Schwäbisch	(Swabian) is a strong German dialect spoken in Swabia in Germany's southwest, i.e. Baden-Württemberg and its regional capital, Stuttgart.
Sekigahara	a small town in central Japan (Gifu Prefecture). The Battle of Sekigahara (21st October 1600) cleared the path to the Shōgunate for *Tokugawa Ieyasu* although it

took three more years for him to consolidate power over the outgoing Toyotomi clan. It marked the start of Edo Period (see *Edo*).

Sehr geehrte a formal, respectful greeting often used to start letters in German (loosely 'Dear').

Seppuku a form of Japanese ritual suicide by (left to right) disembowelment (lit. 'stomach-cutting'). Originally only for Samurai, it was part of the bushido code of honour and often used voluntarily to die honourably rather than fall into the hands of an enemy.

Shamisen (lit. 'three strings') a three-stringed, long-necked, Japanese (post c.1500) musical instrument (somewhat like a banjo/guitar) played with a large plectrum (bachi).

Shanky urban slang term used to describe a person, generally accepted to mean 'messed up'.

Shinkansen a high-speed railway network (c.1,500 miles) operated by Japan Rail, also called 'Bullet Train'. Fast (200 mph), efficient and popular.

Shōgun (lit. 'military commander') was military governor and de facto ruler of Japan, essentially hereditary despite ostensibly being appointed by the emperor.

Shuriken (lit. 'sword hidden in the hand') a traditional Japanese concealed weapon generally used for throwing. Commonly known in the West as throwing stars or ninja stars, they took many forms during the time they were used.

Sintered a method for forming objects with specific properties from powders, e.g. metals and ceramics. It is based on atomic diffusion which occurs very quickly at high temperatures (below the components' melting points) and pressures.

Skyliner Express see *Ueno*.

Sensei	(lit. 'person born before another') used in Japan after a person's name as a title (meaning 'teacher'). It shows respect to one who has achieved a high level of mastery in a discipline such as writing, music, law or the martial arts.
South Kensington	a district of London in the Royal Borough of Kensington and Chelsea in London, loosely around the underground station.
SPDC	The State Peace and Development Council, the military regime (Junta) which control in Burma during a military coup (1988) to put down a popular uprising. (See *NLD*).
Stele	usually a stone commemorative slab erected to record significant events, e.g. important historical events, funerals, territorial markers.
T&T	Tanqueray gin and tonic.
Tatami	a traditional Japanese floor mat made of rice straw with a covering of woven soft rush. Mats are made in standard sizes, with the length exactly twice the width. The long edge is often finished with brocade or plain cloth.
Thanaka	a yellowish-white, predominantly Burmese, cosmetic paste made from ground bark from the Murraya (thanaka) tree. It has a fragrance like sandalwood and is commonly applied to the face and/or arms, of women and girls.
Thawb	an ankle-length garment, usually with long sleeves, often worn in Arab countries.
Tokugawa Ieyasu	(1543-1616) founder and first Shōgun of the Tokugawa Shōgunate which ruled Japan after the Battle of *Sekigahara* in 1600, until the *Meiji Restoration* (see *Edo*).
Tokugawa Shōgunate	a feudal regime in Japan established by Tokugawa Ieyasu following the pivotal battle of *Sekigahara* in 1600 (see *Edo*).

Torii	a traditional Japanese arch typically comprising two pillars and one or two lintels (possibly joined midway), the topmost of which may be curved, most commonly at Shinto/religious shrine entrances marking the transition from profane to sacred.
Tsuba	a round, or rounded-square, disk/finger guard between the hilt and the blade on Japanese weapons, such as a Samurai sword.
UAR	a fictitious construction standing for 'Urgent Assistance Required'.
Ueno	a district in northeast Tokyo, well known for its large Japan Rail station which is a major commuter hub and the terminus for many long-distance trains from northern Japan. Nearby is Keisei-Ueno Station which is the terminus of the Keisei Main Line and the Keisei Skyliner which serves Narita Airport.
UNWP	(United Nations for World Peace) a revamped, credible and fully effective United Nations organisation – regrettably fictitious.
Vauxhall	an inner city district of central London within the London Borough of Lambeth on the south of the River Thames.
Yoshino	a Japanese girl's name meaning respectful or good (pronounced 'Yo-shi-no').
Yukata	a Japanese cotton or silk garment worn by both men and women with straight seams and wide sleeves. Men's yukata have shorter sleeves than women's.
Zabuton	a Japanese cushion, often highly decorated, generally used when sitting on the floor (see *tatami*).

MAPS

MAP 1: JAPAN

N

JAPAN

100 miles

Hokkaido

Honshu
J6
J2
J3
J1
J5
J4
J7
J8
Shikoku
Kyushu

J1. Tokyo
J2. Kanazawa
J3. Matsumoto
J4. Iga Ueno
J5. Kyoto
J6. Toyama
J7. Karatsu
J8. Kochi

MAP 2: SOUTHEAST ASIA

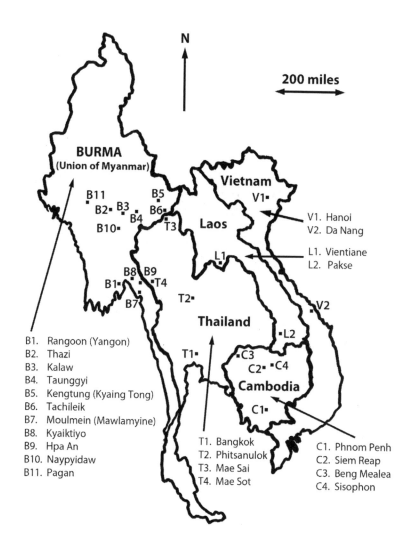

N

200 miles

BURMA
(Union of Myanmar)

Vietnam

V1∎

Laos

V1. Hanoi
V2. Da Nang

B11∎
B2∎ B3∎
B10∎   B4∎

B5∎
B6∎
T3∎

L1∎

L1. Vientiane
L2. Pakse

B8∎ B9∎
B1∎ ∎T4
B7∎

T2∎

∎V2

Thailand

∎L2

T1∎

∎C3
C2∎ ∎C4

Cambodia

C1∎

B1. Rangoon (Yangon)
B2. Thazi
B3. Kalaw
B4. Taunggyi
B5. Kengtung (Kyaing Tong)
B6. Tachileik
B7. Moulmein (Mawlamyine)
B8. Kyaiktiyo
B9. Hpa An
B10. Naypyidaw
B11. Pagan

T1. Bangkok
T2. Phitsanulok
T3. Mae Sai
T4. Mae Sot

C1. Phnom Penh
C2. Siem Reap
C3. Beng Mealea
C4. Sisophon

We sincerely hope you enjoyed reading:
The Samurai Revival Trilogy by Rheagan Greene

In particular, if you liked this novel please recommend it to others, and perhaps leave a positive review on Amazon, which many use as a reference.

In any event, we are delighted that you have chosen to read one of our books.

THANK YOU

Hamon Publishing